AN EYE FOR AN EYE

AN EYE FOR AN EYE

Jeffrey Archer is one of the world's bestselling authors, with sales of over 300 million copies in 115 countries and 48 languages.

Famous for his discipline as a writer who works on up to fourteen drafts of each book, Jeffrey also brings a vast amount of insider knowledge to his books. Whether it's his own career in politics, his passionate interest in art, or the wealth of fascinating background detail – inspired by the extraordinary network of friends he has built over a lifetime at the heart of Britain's establishment – his novels provide a fascinating glimpse into a range of closed worlds.

A member of the House of Lords, the author is married to Dame Mary Archer, Chair of The Royal Parks, and they have two sons, two granddaughters and three grandsons. He splits his time between London, Grantchester near Cambridge, and Mallorca, where he writes the first draft of each new novel.

www.jeffreyarcher.com

Also by Jeffrey Archer

THE WILLIAM WARWICK
NOVELS
Nothing Ventured
Hidden in Plain Sight
Turn a Blind Eye
Over My Dead Body
Next In Line
Traitors Gate

THE CLIFTON
CHRONICLES
Only Time Will Tell
The Sins of the Father
Best Kept Secret
Be Careful What You Wish For
Mightier than the Sword
Cometh the Hour
This Was a Man

NOVELS
*Not a Penny More, Not a
Penny Less*
Shall We Tell the President?
Kane and Abel
The Prodigal Daughter
First Amongst Equals
A Matter of Honour
As the Crow Flies
Honour Amongst Thieves
The Fourth Estate
The Eleventh Commandment
Sons of Fortune
False Impression
The Gospel According to Judas
*(with the assistance of
Professor Francis J. Moloney)*
A Prisoner of Birth
Paths of Glory
Heads You Win

SHORT STORIES
A Quiver Full of Arrows
A Twist in the Tale
Twelve Red Herrings
The Collected Short Stories
To Cut a Long Story Short
Cat O'Nine Tales
And Thereby Hangs a Tale
Tell Tale
*The Short, the Long and the
Tall*

PLAYS
Beyond Reasonable Doubt
Exclusive
The Accused
Confession
Who Killed the Mayor?

PRISON DIARIES
Volume One – Belmarsh: Hell
*Volume Two – Wayland:
Purgatory*
*Volume Three – North Sea
Camp: Heaven*

SCREENPLAYS
Mallory: Walking Off the Map
False Impression

AN EYE FOR AN EYE

JEFFREY ARCHER

HarperCollins*Publishers*

HarperCollins*Publishers* Ltd
1 London Bridge Street,
London SE1 9GF
www.harpercollins.co.uk

HarperCollins*Publishers*
Macken House,
39/40 Mayor Street Upper,
Dublin 1
D01 C9W8

First published by HarperCollins*Publishers* 2024
24 25 26 27 28 LBC 5 4 3 2 1

Copyright © Jeffrey Archer 2024

Image page 375. David Hartley the Younger. Credit: Granger
Historical Picture Archive/Alamy Stock Photo

Jeffrey Archer asserts the moral right to
be identified as the author of this work

A catalogue record for this book is available from the British Library

ISBN: 978-0-00-864011-8 (HB)
ISBN: 978-0-00-864018-7 (US-only HB)
ISBN: 978-0-00-872923-3 (Special sale-only)
ISBN: 978-0-00-864012-5 (TPB)
ISBN: 978-0-00-864017-0 (IN)

Typeset in New Caledonia LT Std by Palimpsest Book
Production Ltd, Falkirk, Stirlingshire

Printed and bound in the United States of America

Alison Prince
1963–2023

PROLOGUE

Simon Winchcombe Henry Howard Hartley saw the Prime Minister for the first time that morning, and his father for the last time that night.

It happened thus:

For the past two hundred years, the Hartley family had either taken holy orders, ending their days as bishops, or entered the House of Commons, before joining the Cabinet as a minister of the Crown.

Simon's father, the Rt Hon. John Hartley PC KBE MC, was no exception and ended a distinguished career as Home Secretary before being elevated to the upper house as Lord Hartley of Bucklebury. His wife Sybil was first and foremost a housewife and a mother, who occasionally involved herself in good works, which was no more than was expected of a Hartley spouse. So, when Sybil delivered a son, Simon – all Hartley children were named after disciples – they both assumed he would follow in the family tradition and either become a bishop or a Cabinet minister. Had he done so, this tale would never have been written.

Their only child, Simon Hartley, showed from an early age that he had no interest in the family tradition, when at the age of eleven he won a scholarship to the North London Grammar School, despite having been offered a place at Harrow, the family alma mater. And on leaving school, he progressed to King's College London to study law, rather than going up to King's College Cambridge to read divinity or politics.

When Simon graduated three years later, he bucked another Hartley trend by becoming the first member of the family to be awarded a first-class honours degree, rather than the usual second or even the occasional third. And, if that wasn't enough, after leaving university Simon migrated to Boston to join a bunch of colonials at somewhere called the Harvard Business School, an establishment his father wasn't sure he approved of.

Two years later, as a graduate of the other Cambridge, Simon returned to his native soil to be offered a dozen jobs in the City of London, ending up as a trainee at Kestrals Bank with a starting salary well in excess of anything his father had earned as a minister of the Crown.

During the next decade, he rarely left the square mile, other than to travel to distant lands, where he would negotiate deals that left his colleagues in awe, while making a fortune for his bank.

By the age of forty, Simon had married a beautiful and talented woman, Hannah, who had borne him two sons, Robert and Christopher – neither disciples – and had joined the board of Kestrals as the company's youngest director. It was assumed it could only be a matter of time before he would become chairman of the bank.

And, indeed, he might have done, had he not received a call from Number 10 Downing Street asking if he would be kind enough to join the Prime Minister to discuss a matter of national importance.

By the time Simon left the Prime Minister's residence, he'd promised Mr Blair he would consider his proposal and let him know his decision by the end of the week.

Once Simon was back on Whitehall, he hailed a cab that took him to Paddington, well in time to catch a train to his family home in Berkshire.

During the journey to Bucklebury, he reflected on the Prime Minister's offer and how his family might react to the news. His father would tell him he had no choice, repeating words such as 'honour', 'duty' and 'self-sacrifice'. He couldn't be sure how Hannah would respond, although he was in no doubt his two teenage sons would express their firmly held opinions on human rights – or the lack of them – in Saudi Arabia, especially when it came to women.

Hannah was waiting for Simon outside the station, a sad and forlorn look on her face.

He kissed her on the cheek before climbing into the passenger seat of their car and immediately asking, 'How's Father?'

'No better, I'm afraid,' she replied, as she switched on the engine and eased the Mini out of the car park and onto the main road. 'Your mother spoke to the doctor this morning, and he's saying it can only be a matter of weeks, possibly days before . . .'

Both of them fell silent as Hannah drove onto a quiet country lane surrounded by acres of green fields with little groups of sheep huddled in corners, suggesting rain.

'I know he's looking forward to seeing you,' said Hannah, breaking the silence. 'He was saying earlier that there are a couple of family matters he needs to discuss with you.'

Simon knew exactly what his father had in mind, painfully aware one of them couldn't be avoided any longer.

After a couple more miles, Hannah turned off the main road, lowered her speed and proceeded slowly down the long drive that led to Hartley Hall, a home the family had lived in since 1562.

As Hannah brought the car to a halt, the front door opened and Lady Hartley appeared on the doorstep. She came down the steps to greet them, giving her only son a warm hug, while whispering in his ear, 'I know your father wants to see you, so why don't you go up and join him while I give the rest of the family some tea?'

Simon walked into the house and proceeded slowly up the stairs. When he reached the landing, he stopped to admire an oil painting of his distinguished ancestor, the Rt Hon. David Hartley MP, before knocking quietly on the bedroom door.

It had only been a few days since his last visit, but his father had visibly worsened. Simon hardly recognized the frail figure with thinning hair and a sallow complexion, who was propped up in bed, his head resting against two pillows. Breathing heavily, he held out a bony hand, which Simon held onto, as he sat down on the bed next to him.

'So why did the Prime Minister want to see you?' were his father's opening words, before he'd even said hello to his son.

'He's invited me to lead a British delegation to Saudi Arabia in order to negotiate a major arms deal.'

His father couldn't hide his surprise. 'That won't be greeted with overwhelming acclamation,' he suggested, 'not least by the Prime Minister's colleagues on the left of his party, who keep reminding us that the Saudis continue to outlaw trade unions.'

'Possibly,' said Simon. 'However, if we could land the

4

contract, those same trade unions would welcome the thousands of jobs that would suddenly become available up and down the country.'

'Not to mention the millions that would start flowing into the Treasury.'

'Billions,' said Simon, 'and Blair didn't stop reminding me that if we don't get the contract, the French will.'

'Reason enough for you to accept this assignment, my boy,' said his father, 'and as you are bound to be away for several weeks, possibly months, there are one or two matters we need to discuss before you go.

The old order changeth, yielding place to new,' the old man continued, quoting his favourite poet, 'so I can only hope that in time you will come and live in Hartley Hall and take care of your mother. 'Tis the natural order of things.'

'You have my word on it,' promised Simon.

'And I don't want your mother worrying about financial matters. She still tips waiters a shilling and considers it extravagant.'

'Fear not, Father,' said Simon. 'I've already set up a trust fund in her name, which I'll personally administer on her behalf, so she won't have to fuss about any temporary financial difficulties.'

'And then there's the important issue,' said his father, 'of what you should do with Jefferson's Declaration of Independence which, as you know, has been in our family for over two hundred years. We should have carried out the President's wishes long before now. With that in mind, I made an appointment to see the American Ambassador in order to hand over the Fair Copy along with the letter that shows the great man had always intended it to be bequeathed to the American people.'

'"In the fullness of time",' Simon reminded him.

'To be fair,' said the old man, 'it hadn't occurred to me that it was of any value other than as an historic memento, until I read recently that one of Benjamin Franklin's printed copies of the Declaration sold for over a million dollars, which is when I felt concerned for the first time.'

'No need to feel concern, Father. Once the negotiations for the arms deal have been completed, the first thing I'll do when I get home is visit the American Embassy and hand the Declaration over to the Ambassador in your name.'

'Along with the letter expressing Jefferson's wish that it should be given to Congress, which will remind people that our family played their part in a footnote of history. However, the other five letters should remain in the family archives and must be passed on to your firstborn, who I do believe I can hear heading towards us – either that or it's a pack of wolfhounds that are about to appear.'

Simon smiled, glad to see that his father hadn't lost his sense of humour. He climbed off the bed and opened the door to allow the rest of the family to join them.

Robert was the first to greet his grandfather, but even before he reached his bedside, the old man said, 'Robert, I need to be sure you can repeat the words Thomas Jefferson wrote to your great ancestor over two hundred years ago.'

Robert grinned, looking rather pleased with himself. He stood up straight and began, 'Dear Mr Hartley.'

'Date and address,' demanded the old man.

'Hôtel de Langeac, Paris, August 11th, 1787.'

'Carry on,' said his grandfather.

I hope you will grant me your permission to impose upon your time by allowing me to send you my Fair Copy of the Declaration of Independence, which I earlier delivered to

Congress for their consideration. You will see that it includes the two clauses you and I discussed in London, namely the abolition of slavery and our future relationship with King George III once we become an independent nation. Copies were made by my friend and colleague Benjamin Franklin and distributed among interested parties. Much to my dismay, when members of Congress divided, both clauses were rejected. However, I would not want you to think I had not taken to heart your wise and sound counsel and tried to convince my fellow congressmen of the merit of your judgement.

'Once you have had a proper chance to peruse the Fair Copy at your leisure, perhaps you would be kind enough, in the fullness of time, to return it to me. I thought you would want to know that it is my intention to bequeath this memento to the Nation in order that future generations of Americans might fully appreciate what the founding fathers were trying to achieve, and not least the role you played. I look forward to hearing from you at some time in the future, and be assured of my sincere esteem and respect.

'I remain, your most obedient and humble servant,

'Thomas Jefferson.'

Simon placed an arm around his mother while his son completed the letter, which like his father and grandfather before him, he had learnt by heart.

'And will you promise me to teach your firstborn those same words and make sure he can also repeat them by his twelfth birthday?' Lord Hartley demanded.

'I give you my word,' said Robert.

Simon could not hold back the tears when he saw the smile of satisfaction on the old man's face, although he feared he was seeing his father for the last time.

BOOK 1

'I think this is the most extraordinary collection of talent, of human knowledge, that has ever been gathered at the White House, with the possible exception of when Thomas Jefferson dined alone.'

President John F. Kennedy addressing a dinner honouring Nobel Prize winners.

29 April 1962

CHAPTER 1

WHEN THE CAR DREW UP outside the club, a guard glanced in the back and nodded before the barrier was raised so the chauffeur could continue on up a long drive, finally coming to a halt outside a palatial villa that could have been plucked out of Monte Carlo. The Saudis can duplicate anything money can buy, thought Simon, as he climbed out of the car and made his way into the club.

Simon had been in Riyadh for a week, after a crash course of 'familiarisation training' at the Ministry of Defence. He had been briefed by a small team of experts, who covered everything from submarine pistons to Sharia customs and beliefs, and how to correctly address a prince of the royal blood. A Mr Trevelyan from the Foreign Office had been on hand to assist him, but tonight Simon was on his own.

He was about to meet Hani Khalil, the local agent recommended by the Ambassador. Although Kestrals Bank disapproved of go-betweens when conducting business in a foreign field, the British government were far less squeamish, not least because their rivals for the arms deal, the French, the Italians and the Americans, all lived in the real world.

Simon already knew that the going rate for an official agent was ten per cent, and if they were willing to do the job for any less, it was because they didn't have the ear of the Minister. If they demanded even more, they were greedy and 'skimming off' from both sides. Simon had wanted neither the former nor the latter, and was well aware that selecting the right person to represent the British for such an important contract would be the most important decision he would make, if they were to have any chance of closing the deal ahead of the French. In the end, he had reluctantly settled on a Lebanese agent called Hani Khalil, who, he had been assured, could bend the ear of Prince Majid bin Talal Al Saud, the Minister of Defence.

It was Khalil whom Simon had been invited to meet tonight, at his club a few miles outside Riyadh – technically called the Overseas Club but known, the Ambassador had warned him, as 'the compromise club'.

• • •

As he approached the front door, Simon had only to murmur the hallowed name of Hani Khalil and he was immediately invited to enter by the manager who accompanied him down a long corridor into a large palatial room. He was ushered towards a man sitting at one end of the bar, an empty seat by his side.

The man wore a smart fashionable suit that had probably been tailored in Savile Row and a smile that suggested they were old friends, despite the fact they had never met before.

'My name is Hani Khalil,' he announced, thrusting out his hand. 'Thank you for joining me. The Defence Minister has asked me to welcome you to Riyadh and say how much he's looking forward to meeting you.' The same warm smile followed. 'What can I get you?'

'Just an orange juice,' said Simon, recalling the Ambassador's warning. Over the years, Simon had often dealt with sharks who swam in the same water as Khalil, some of whom had ended up in jail, while others got knighthoods. He had learned to live with both of them.

Once he'd taken his seat, Simon's eyes slowly circled the room, which was decorated with expensive paintings, stylish furniture, and available women.

'A man of your reputation,' Khalil was saying, 'will be well aware there are only two serious candidates being considered for the arms contract: the French and the British.'

'What about the Americans?' asked Simon, well aware why they had recently made a tactical withdrawal.

'They are no longer in the running while Gore is still hoping to be president,' said Khalil. 'He's clearly not interested in being involved in a deal that might prevent his Jewish supporters back home from bankrolling him.'

'And the Italians?' asked Simon.

'Want too large a slice of the cake,' said Khalil, 'and in any case, everyone knows they can't supply the necessary equipment, so they were never really in the game.'

Although Simon had learnt nothing he didn't already know, he was beginning to get a feel for the man who was sitting beside him. He delivered his next well-prepared line, 'But that doesn't apply to the French.'

'You're right my friend, and in truth, they are your only real rivals. However, with me as your representative, I can promise you they will be returning to Paris empty-handed,' Khalil said, as if the contract had already been signed.

'And what do you expect in return for your services?' asked Simon.

'I feel sure you are well aware, Simon, that ten per cent is the going rate for such deals.'

'Ten per cent of three billion pounds is a very large sum of money, Mr Khalil.'

'And ten per cent of nothing is nothing,' countered Khalil. 'And you have to remember that the Minister has a large family to support, and one in particular who will be expecting to get a big slice of the cake, while, let me assure you, I will have to satisfy myself with a few well-earned crumbs.'

'One in particular?' repeated Simon.

'Prince Ahmed bin Majid, the Defence Minister's second son, who has been a personal friend of mine for many years. Indeed, we have closed several deals together in the past.'

The Foreign Office had already supplied Simon with a thick file on Prince Ahmed bin Majid, and it wasn't flattering, referring to him as the Black Prince.

'I've already arranged for you to have an audience with Prince Majid at ten o'clock tomorrow morning,' Khalil went on, 'which is why I needed to see you this evening.'

Simon listened as Khalil tried to reassure his guest, a little bit too enthusiastically, that the deal was already in the bag. This made Simon even more convinced that Khalil and the Black Prince would eventually walk away with several million more pounds deposited in a Swiss bank account, while he was left to explain to the Prime Minister that the deal had been closed even before he got off the plane.

Simon sipped his orange juice, while Khalil showed no such inhibitions, allowing the barman to pour him a brown liquid from an unmarked bottle, from which the label of a contented grouse had been removed. He tried to concentrate on what the Defence Minister's representative on earth was saying.

'I see that your Italian rival, Paolo Conti, is with us tonight.'

Simon glanced across the room to see a man who had an arm draped around an attractive young blonde, while the other hand rested on her thigh. The Italian looked slightly inebriated, but then he didn't have an appointment with the Minister in the morning. According to the Foreign Office brief, Mr Conti was famed for his Italian good looks and Mafia connections, and although the Italians were on the shortlist, it was no more than what diplomats described as 'a face-saving exercise'.

Khalil took another sip of whisky before remarking, 'And that's another contract he won't be closing.'

Simon took a closer look at the woman seated next to Conti, who was sipping a glass of champagne. She looked to be in her late twenties, possibly early thirties, and there wasn't any doubt how she earned her living; the black leather mini skirt and sheer silk blouse would not have been acceptable on the streets of Riyadh, or even in one of the five-star hotels that littered the city. But inside this private enclave such rules didn't apply, as the scantily clad women and shelves of un-labelled bottles testified.

'Conti still believes he's in with a chance,' said Khalil, as an attentive barman refilled his glass with another shot of the forbidden nectar.

'With the girl or the contract?' quipped Simon.

'Both,' replied Khalil. 'But what Conti doesn't realize is that Avril is one of Prince Ahmed's favourites, and if he turns up and sees her with another man, believe me, sparks will fly. The Minister's son has a short fuse, and I have a feeling Conti's about to light it.'

'Should I assume Avril is aware of the consequences, should the Prince turn up?'

'You catch on fast, Simon, so my advice is to go back to your hotel before Prince Ahmed arrives. Meanwhile, I'll remove the Italian from the shortlist – unless you want Avril after the Prince has left?'

'No, thank you,' said Simon. 'I think I'll take your advice and have an early night.' He didn't give Avril a second look as he thought about Hannah, who would probably be preparing supper for the boys while they did their homework. He'd done his homework; all he needed now was a good night's sleep.

'By the way,' said Khalil, as Simon drained his glass, 'Avril's not French. Her name is Jenny Prescott, and she comes from somewhere called Cleethorpes.'

Simon laughed as a door on the far side of the room was flung open and half a dozen men, dressed in long white thawbs and keffiyehs, marched in as if they owned the place – and they probably did. There wasn't any doubt which one was Prince Ahmed bin Majid Al Saud, or the role his courtiers were expected to play if they hoped to remain on the payroll.

The moment Avril saw the Prince, she moved back, despite Conti leaving his hand on her thigh. The result was exactly what Khalil had predicted, because the Prince walked quickly across the room and, without warning, pushed the Italian to one side before sitting down between them.

'You can fuck off, Eyetie,' said the Prince, a sentiment that didn't need to be translated into any language.

Conti rose unsteadily to his feet, a fist half raised. Although the Prince ducked, the Italian landed a glancing blow that knocked off his keffiyeh, revealing a bald head, which clearly didn't please the Prince.

Simon couldn't believe what was happening in front of his eyes, and it quickly became clear several of the other guests were equally surprised. Only Khalil remained unmoved, almost as if he'd scripted it.

As the Prince adjusted his headgear, Conti began to raise his fist a second time, but not before two of Ahmed's bodyguards came charging towards the Italian, grabbed him by the arms and held him down. They were about to escort him off the premises when Conti defiantly leant forward and spat in the Prince's face. Ahmed immediately leapt on him and Conti tried to defend himself by grabbing the Prince around the throat, which only caused Ahmed to become even more angry.

Before his minders could drag Conti off, the Prince pulled a short, curved dagger from inside his thawb and, without a second thought, thrust it into his assailant's chest. Avril let out a piercing scream, while Ahmed pushed him away and laughed.

The bodyguards let go of their prey, and could only watch as Conti collapsed on the ground, clutching his chest while gasping for breath.

Simon was horrified, and even though the Ambassador had warned him about the Black Prince, he hadn't been prepared for this. He turned to the barman and shouted, 'For God's sake, call an ambulance,' but the man didn't move.

'Best not to get involved,' Khalil said, 'especially remembering he's the Defence Minister's son, and without his backing it won't be your name on the bottom of the contract.'

Simon hesitated while Avril's screams had turned to tears. The Prince ignored her as he bent down and slowly extracted the dagger from Conti's chest, causing him to let out a long, whimpering groan which brought a smile of satisfaction to Ahmed's face.

Simon watched in horror as several other foreigners in the room began to slip quietly away, not wanting to be involved in the unfolding drama. Simon would have followed them, but couldn't come to terms with what was happening in front of him.

An older man who Simon hadn't noticed walked calmly across the room and whispered in the Prince's ear. Ahmed hesitated for a moment before wiping the blade of his dagger clean on Conti's trouser leg. He then adjusted his keffiyeh and walked slowly towards a door that was being held open by one of his followers. He looked back, not at his victim, but at Avril.

'If you're still hoping to keep your good looks,' said Ahmed, crossing his throat with the dagger, 'make sure you keep your mouth shut.' He placed the dagger back in its sheath and left without another word, followed by all but one of his entourage.

Simon couldn't take his eyes off Conti, who was still trying to stem the flow of blood now oozing from the wound like water from a running tap. Khalil seemed to be the only person in the room who remained calm, as if he were watching a scene from a horror movie and had already seen the last reel.

Simon decided to ignore Khalil's advice and go to Conti's aid, hoping he still had time – then he heard the sound of a siren in the distance.

'There's nothing you can do for him now,' said Khalil, placing a hand firmly on Simon's arm, 'so I suggest you leave before the police arrive; and when you see the Minister of Defence in the morning, just remember you were never here.'

Simon still didn't move while the sound of a police siren became louder and louder.

'I'll pick you up from your hotel at nine thirty, so we'll be well in time for your meeting with the Minister.'

Simon stared down at the Italian, who was no longer moving, and reluctantly accepted there was little he could do to help him. After taking one last look at the prostrate body, he made his way out of the club. Once he was on the street, he climbed into the back of his waiting car.

'Back to the hotel,' he said, when he heard the sound of the siren coming closer and closer. 'Get moving!' he added even more firmly, as a police car swung around the corner and moments later screeched to a halt outside the entrance to the club.

That's when he heard the second siren and once again felt guilty he hadn't gone to the Italian's aid.

Simon prayed it was an ambulance and would get there in time.

• • •

Back in the club, the Prince's right-hand man approached Khalil and, without a word passing between them, handed the Lebanese agent a thick wad of cash. He, too, disappeared without even glancing at the victim.

Khalil peeled off some notes from the bundle and handed the first payment to the barman, who pocketed the cash. He then offered Avril a bonus, but she threw the money back in his face. Khalil shrugged and gathered up the notes, before handing out smaller amounts to some of the girls who'd remained behind. They would claim they hadn't seen a thing – not for the first time.

Just as he was handing out the last payment to a waiter, the police came charging into the room. Khalil was still holding on to half the cash, which he immediately handed over to the officer in charge, who pocketed the money before turning his attention to the body lying in a pool of blood on the floor.

Having disposed of the entire baksheesh, Khalil made his own exit, not bothering with his ten per cent on this occasion.

But then he had his eyes on a far bigger prize.

• • •

Once Simon's driver had dropped him back at his hotel, he took the lift to his suite on the top floor, got undressed and had a long cold shower before collapsing onto the bed.

He couldn't sleep as the nightmare relentlessly repeated itself without him having to press the playback button. He tried to concentrate on the carefully worded questions he would need to ask the Defence Minister if he had any chance of finding out if he was aware what his son and Khalil were up to. If he did, he would be catching a plane back to London later that afternoon as murder wasn't part of any contract Simon would be willing to sign.

But his thoughts kept returning to Conti, who had ended up with a contract he hadn't bargained for. Once again, he prayed that the ambulance had got there in time.

Simon woke just after five, his body covered in a sticky sweat. He took another long, cold shower, but nothing was going to wash away the memory of the previous night.

He put on a dressing gown, sat down on the end of the bed and began to pen a series of questions that he hoped would lull the Minister into a false sense of security. He finally gave up and got dressed: a navy blue suit his father would have approved of, a white shirt he would be wearing for the first time, and a green silk tie chosen by his wife. He began to pace around the suite, checking his watch every few minutes as he waited for Khalil to join him.

Simon made an even greater effort to put his questions in the correct order, aware of how much was at stake, when the long-term consequences of the three-billion-pound contract would guarantee a flow of income and jobs for his countrymen for over a decade, or more.

If the Saudis backed the British, a billion pounds would be transferred to the government coffers, one hundred million of which would be deposited in a numbered account in Geneva, with no questions asked as to how it would be disposed of, or to whom.

A second payment of a further billion would be made once the equipment had been despatched to Riyadh.

And the final payment of another billion would be handed over once the equipment had arrived safely in Riyadh, along with six hundred highly trained operatives, who would spend the next six months instructing the local mariners, pilots, engineers and foot soldiers on how to operate their newly acquired equipment.

Simon checked his watch once again, aware that while ministers could keep you waiting for an hour, sometimes two, he still needed to be on time for the meeting that morning.

When the door finally opened, Simon assumed it would be Hani Khalil who would be joining him before they left for the ministry, but to his surprise three men dressed in police uniforms marched in unannounced.

'Are you Simon Hartley?' demanded an officer with three silver pips on his shoulder, before Simon could respond.

'Yes,' said Simon without hesitation, assuming they had been sent to accompany him to the Defence Minister's office.

But without another word, the two younger officers stepped forward, grabbed Simon by the arms, thrust them behind his back and handcuffed him.

Simon was about to protest when Khalil entered the room, no suggestion of surprise on his face. He was confident the handcuffs would be removed within moments and he'd be set free, but his agent remained silent, his expression unmoved, when the senior officer said authoritatively, 'You are under arrest, Mr Hartley.'

It was some time before Simon recovered enough to ask, 'On what charge?'

'Murder,' said the Chief of Police, as the two officers escorted him out of the room.

CHAPTER 2

ARTEMISIA WARWICK STOOD ON HER toes and removed an atlas from the top of the bookshelf. She placed it on the kitchen table and turned to the index at the back. Her eye ran down a long list of countries, coming to a halt when she reached S. She leafed backwards until she came to page 126, when she studied a vast area of land described as the Middle East.

She glanced across at her brother, who was munching his cornflakes, and wondered if he knew the answer.

'Why are we so dependent on oil?' she asked, wondering who would be the first to respond.

'Think about it,' replied her father. 'We need oil for our power stations, not to mention everything from cars to planes.'

'And as we don't have enough of our own,' added her mother, 'we have to rely on other countries to supply us.'

'Including Saudi Arabia, it would seem,' said Artemisia, unable to hide the contempt in her voice.

'And what has Saudi Arabia done to annoy you this morning?' asked her father, as he put his paper down.

'It's not the country that has annoyed me,' said Artemisia, 'so much as the Labour government, who are trying to close an arms deal with the Saudis in exchange for oil.'

'That's what's known as bartering,' her father tried to assure her. 'We supply the Saudis with arms and in return they give us oil. Nothing new in that.'

'But you've always taught us,' said Peter, siding with his sister, 'that two wrongs don't make a right.'

'What makes you think they've done anything wrong?' asked Beth, who agreed with her daughter but wanted her to argue her case.

'If I had been born in that country,' said Artemisia, looking directly at her mother, 'I wouldn't have been treated as an equal.'

'Examples?' said Beth. 'You can't get away with generalizations. Facts win an argument.'

'Women still don't get the vote in Saudi, despite the fact we're in the twenty-first century.'

'If Arte had been born in Riyadh, not London,' chipped in Peter, putting down his spoon, 'she wouldn't have been allowed to go to a school with boys.'

'And if you're gay,' said Artemisia, taking both her parents by surprise, 'you could end up being stoned to death in the market square.'

'I think you'll find that barbaric custom ceased some time ago,' said William. 'In fact, everyone accepts the new Saudi leader is more enlightened and is instigating far-reaching reforms.'

'Not far-reaching enough for those women sitting at home, while their less competent brothers go to work and are overpaid.'

'So what are you up to today, Beth?' William asked his wife, as he suspected he was in a minority of one when it came to the Saudis and the supply of oil.

'Dealing with a lack of funds,' said Beth. 'Not an unusual situation for the director of a gallery like the Fitzmolean,' she added, with a wry smile, 'but this time I need to raise an extra half a million.'

'Is it a new roof or a new boiler you need this time?' enquired William.

'A new picture,' said Beth, 'or to be more accurate, an old picture. The Fitzmolean has been offered a rare preparatory Rembrandt drawing of an angel for a million pounds, and the government has agreed to match us pound for pound if we can raise the first half million and quickly.'

'How long have you got?' asked William.

'Only until the end of the month,' replied Beth, 'and if we haven't raised our half by the deadline, the drawing will come on the open market and probably end up going abroad, never to be seen again. We're past the two hundred thousand pound mark, but I just don't know if we'll get the full amount in time.'

'If someone from Saudi Arabia were to offer you the half million,' asked Artemisia, not willing to let go, 'would you take it?'

William looked across at Beth, glad he hadn't been asked the same question.

'It wouldn't be my decision,' said Beth. 'But if the board were to seek my opinion, I would recommend accepting it, so that millions of women would be able to see Rembrandt's masterpiece.'

'None of them from Saudi Arabia,' Artemisia reminded her mother.

'Perhaps we don't have the right to disapprove of the laws and customs of another country,' suggested William, testing his daughter's resolve.

'Possibly,' said Artemisia, 'but we do have the right not to make deals with a country who refuses to grant women equal rights.'

'But it was no less a figure than Winston Churchill,' said William, 'who told us he preferred Jaw Jaw to War War, even when dealing with his enemies.'

'Does that include Miles Faulkner?' asked Peter, silencing his father. 'Because I have a feeling he doesn't do Jaw Jaw when dealing with his enemies, and I heard Mum saying that he'll be coming out of prison in a few weeks' time.'

'Well, I ought to get moving,' said William, 'if I'm not going to be late for work.'

The rest of the family burst out laughing.

'Was it something I said?' asked William as he got up from the table.

'No,' said Beth. 'I think you'll find it was something you didn't say.'

Artemisia closed her atlas with a bang and returned it to the top shelf of the bookcase, while Peter held the door open for his father.

●　●　●

Prisoner number 4602 held a cup of steaming black coffee in one hand and a digestive biscuit in the other. He stared out of the window onto a patch of green grass; had it not been for the sixteen-foot wall topped with razor wire on the far side of the square, he might well have been at his home in Cadogan Place, rather than in the library of a category B prison.

Miles Faulkner placed his coffee cup on the counter before glancing at the calendar on the wall. Eighteen more days of his sentence to complete before he would finally be released, having served three years at Her Majesty's pleasure for attempting to steal the Crown Jewels, and finally bring William Warwick down. Although the theft had ended in failure, and it was he who had been brought down, Faulkner hadn't wasted the last three years, and already had plans to continue disrupting the lives of Chief Superintendent William Warwick and his perfect wife. If they imagined, even for one moment, that Miles had learnt his lesson and was a reformed character, they could think again. In his case time wasn't a healer.

There was a tap on the library door. Miles walked slowly across and opened it, to find Prison Officer Simpson standing out in the cold.

'Good morning, Mr Faulkner,' he said, handing over a copy of the *Financial Times* to the chief librarian.

'Good morning, Bill,' responded Miles.

'Is there anything else you need?' asked the duty officer, whose income was increased whenever he visited the local newsagent on the prisoner's behalf.

'Not at the moment, but if anything should arise, Tulip will be in touch,' said Faulkner as he closed the door.

Faulkner returned to his chair by the window, settled down and began to read the morning paper, while his trusted deputy, Tulip, made him another cup of coffee – black, steaming hot, with one spoonful of sugar.

He turned to the Footsie 100 and checked his shares. During his incarceration they had risen year on year by nine per cent, and his stockbroker had continued trading on his behalf as if he was still calling from his home in Chelsea.

Every prison officer was aware that Miles had a mobile

phone hidden somewhere in the library. However, only Tolstoy knew where it was secreted: in a copy of *War and Peace*, on the top shelf of the classics section. Not a book that was regularly taken out.

Miles turned the page, satisfied his fortune remained intact, even though he still had to pay his ex-wife Christina a monthly alimony payment that a judge had decided would allow her to continue living in the style to which she had become accustomed.

He continued to turn the pages of his paper until a headline in the arts section caught his eye. FITZMOLEAN ATTEMPTING TO RAISE A MILLION TO SAVE REMBRANDT DRAWING. Miles read the article slowly, but then he had the time on his hands.

A third reading of an interview with the museum's director, Dr Beth Warwick, confirmed that Rembrandt's *Jacob Wrestling with the Angel*, a rare preparatory drawing by the Dutch master, could be acquired by the gallery, if they could raise one million pounds under the government's new inheritance tax incentive scheme – but only then if the full amount was raised by the end of June. Dr Warwick told the *Financial Times* arts editor that they had so far only managed to raise £241,000, and she was no longer confident they could get the full amount before the deadline. Should they fail to do so, Dr Warwick was in no doubt the masterpiece would sell for a far larger sum when it came on the open market.

An idea began to form in Miles's mind. He leant back and closed his eyes, not because he was tired, but because he needed to concentrate on how he might be able to take advantage of Dr Warwick's situation.

Tulip topped up his coffee but wouldn't have considered interrupting his thoughts. He didn't want to annoy Mr

Faulkner while he was still in with a chance of taking his place as chief librarian in eighteen days' time. He placed the pot of coffee back on its little gas ring and continued to put recently returned books in their correct places on the shelves. Once the job was completed, he would begin his morning rounds and collect overdue books from prisoners who were either very slow readers or couldn't be bothered to return them.

The morning rounds were nothing more than an excuse for Tulip to visit his fellow inmates and pick up any inside information he could then pass on to Mr Faulkner, so that he remained one step ahead of everyone in the prison, including the Governor.

Tulip pushed his little trolley silently towards the door, making sure he didn't disturb Mr Faulkner.

Miles opened one eye as Tulip touched the door handle. 'I need to see Billy the Forger,' he announced. 'Tell him to come to the library after breakfast tomorrow morning.'

·   ·   ·

Mrs Christina Faulkner is delighted to accept Lord and Lady Mulberry's kind invitation to join them at Royal Ascot for British Champions' Day.

Christina placed the invitation card on her mantelpiece, and was already thinking about the new outfit she would need and, of course, a hat that mustn't go unnoticed. She had thought about little else all morning. Once a taxi had dropped her off in Mayfair, she set about her task with a shopaholic's conviction.

She spent the first hour walking slowly up one side of Bond Street, and even more slowly back down the other, before ending up at Armani – an Italian who understood that forty was just a number. Elegance and style knew no age.

She tried on several outfits, and one in particular that caught her attention. Although it was a little more expensive – Giorgio Armani rather than Emporio Armani – one had to remember this was Royal Ascot. Christina asked the sales assistant to wrap it before handing over her credit card. While she waited, she began to consider which establishments she would grace to complete the ensemble with a hat and a pair of shoes when an assistant interrupted her thoughts.

'I do apologize, madam,' he said, 'but I'm afraid your card has been declined.' A Bond Street word for 'rejected'.

'Declined?' she repeated. 'That's just not possible. Try again.'

'Of course, madam,' he said, and hurried away, only to return moments later with the same embarrassed look on his face.

'I'll deal with the problem immediately,' said Christina, taking out her phone and checking her contact list.

'Craig Trotman,' said a voice after she'd dialled the number.

'Mr Trotman, it's Christina Faulkner,' she announced as if addressing a bank clerk rather than the deputy manager. 'You've just caused me some considerable embarrassment.'

'I'm sorry to hear that, Mrs Faulkner,' said Trotman. 'Is there anything I can do to assist you?'

'You most certainly can,' said Christina. 'I have just purchased an exquisite outfit from Armani,' she paused before adding, 'for Royal Ascot, where I'll be a guest of the Mulberrys, and when I presented my credit card, it was declined. No doubt you have a simple explanation?'

'Could you hold on for a moment, Mrs Faulkner, while I look into it.'

'A technical glitch,' said Christina, causing the sales assistant to smile.

Christina began to pace up and down the shop, pretending

to consider other items while she waited for Trotman to come back on the line.

In far less salubrious surroundings, Tulip heard the phone ringing and quickly locked the library door, while Faulkner walked across to the classics section and removed Tolstoy from the top shelf. He took out the mobile, pressed the green button, and listened.

'Good morning, Mr Faulkner, it's Craig Trotman,' he whispered, addressing one of his most valued customers. 'You asked me to let you know if your ex-wife needed any,' he hesitated, 'temporary assistance.'

'And does she?' asked Miles.

'I'm afraid she does, sir. It's only a small amount, but she has already gone well over her credit limit. However, if you felt able to cover the cost?'

'How much?' demanded Miles, sensing Christina was waiting on the other end of the line.

'Fourteen hundred pounds, sir, for an Armani outfit that she wishes to purchase for Royal Ascot.'

'Tell her to get lost,' said Miles. 'But thank you for keeping me informed.' He touched the red button and put the mobile back between pages 320 and 572 of *War and Peace*, before returning Tolstoy to his place on the top shelf next to *Resurrection*. Tulip unlocked the library door.

'Are you still there, Mrs Faulkner?' asked Trotman, switching phones.

'I most certainly am.'

'I'm sorry to have to tell you you've exceeded your credit limit.' He avoided adding, 'by some considerable amount'.

'And I'm sorry to have to tell you, Mr Trotman, that if you don't clear this paltry sum immediately, I will have to consider moving my account to another bank.'

'As you wish, madam.'

Christina switched off her mobile and marched out of the shop back onto Bond Street, leaving behind a bemused sales assistant and an Armani suit. She walked by Ferragamo, Prada and Cartier without even glancing into their windows. When Christina passed the Ritz, the doorman saluted. She didn't go in, but continued on her way, hoping the fridge wasn't empty.

• • •

Once Miles's monthly alimony cheque had been cleared, Christina decided to treat herself after suffering three weeks of champagne famine. She weighed up the alternatives – Bond Street or Tramp – and decided an evening at her favourite nightclub would cheer her up, even if she could no longer afford the company of a younger man and would have to satisfy herself with a Caesar salad and perhaps one glass of champagne, possibly two.

Christina arrived at the club fashionably late and fashion-ably dressed that evening, even if her skirt might have been considered by an uncharitable observer as a little too short for someone of her age.

Tony Guido, the maître d', guided his customer to her usual table and moments later a glass of champagne appeared by her side.

'We've missed you, Mrs Faulkner,' said Tony, 'but no doubt you've spent the spring in the Mediterranean.'

'St Paul de Vence followed by Lake Como,' said Christina, although she hadn't strayed far beyond her flat in Chelsea for several weeks. Christina knew she could just about cover the bill, but nonetheless, she sipped her drink while her eyes scanned a dimly lit room, full of gorgeous men, too many of them accompanied by beautiful young women.

She had just reluctantly decided against a second glass of champagne when the maître d' reappeared, bent down and whispered in her ear, 'There's a gentleman seated on the far side of the room who wonders if you would care to join him.'

Christina looked across the crowded dance floor to see a handsome, middle-aged man sitting alone, toying with a drink. She was about to give him a warm smile when a stunning young woman joined him. Christina's eyes moved on to the occupant of the next table.

'But he looks as if it won't be too long before he's collecting his bus pass!' she exclaimed.

'Possibly,' said the maître d', 'but if the *Sunday Times* Rich List is to be believed, Mr W. T. Hackensack III is the nineteenth richest man in America.'

'Is he indeed?' said Christina, returning his smile. She waited for a few moments before she stood up and slowly made her way across the crowded dance floor. The gentleman rose from his place while she was still a few paces away and waited for her to be seated before he sat back down.

'Hi, I'm Wilbur,' he said with an accent that wouldn't have left anyone in any doubt which continent he hailed from.

'Christina Faulkner,' she replied, offering her hand.

'Can I get you a drink, Christina?' he asked, but the maître d' had already anticipated that.

'Do you live in London, Wilbur, or are you just visiting our shores?' she asked, setting out on a fishing expedition.

'Visiting,' he said, as their two glasses touched. 'I'm about to go on what your countrymen used to call the European tour.'

'All alone?' she said hopefully.

'I'm afraid so. My wife and I planned this trip to coincide with my retirement, but sadly Irene died of cancer a few months back but, as everything had been booked, I decided to go ahead with the trip.'

'How sad,' said Christina. 'No children to join you?' she asked, still fishing.

'Two sons who now run the business but couldn't get away. In fact, I was beginning to think I might as well return to Columbus earlier than planned.'

'I've never been to Ohio,' she said, hoping to impress.

'You should – it's full of magnificent parks, theatres, and galleries.'

'I sit on the board of a gallery,' said Christina, waiting for him to ask.

'Which one?'

'The Fitzmolean,' said Christina.

'Packed with Dutch masterpieces, I'm told. It's on my must do list.'

'I'd be delighted to show you around, Wilbur, if you're in town for a few more days.'

'I'm here until the end of the week.'

'And staying nearby?'

'Just up the road at the Ritz.'

'My favourite hostelry,' she assured him. At least this time she was telling the truth.

'Then perhaps you'd care to join me for lunch later in the week? That is if you're not too—'

'I've just got back from the south of France in time for the season,' said Christina. 'I do so enjoy Royal Ascot. But of course, you have a famous racetrack in Columbus,' she said, hoping they did.

'Beulah Park,' said Wilbur, 'where I've spent many happy hours watching my horses fail to be led into the winners' enclosure.'

Christina laughed and raised her glass. 'So, are you in the horse-breeding business, Wilbur?' she asked, casting another fly.

'Nothing so glamorous, I'm afraid. I'm in refuse.'

'Refuse?' she repeated, as if it was a word she was unacquainted with.

'My company collects waste, burns and recycles everything people no longer want, and thanks to my great-grandpa,' he raised his glass once again, 'who founded the company over a hundred years ago, we've led a comfortable existence ever since, and will continue to do so for as long as there are politicians needing to raise funds to fight the next election.'

'Where do the politicians come in?' Christina asked, genuinely puzzled.

'They regularly want to be re-elected, and if you're in business and hope to survive in Ohio, you have to learn to live with them.'

'Which party do you support?' asked Christina, trying to keep up.

'Both the Democrats and the Republicans,' admitted Wilbur. 'We're a swing state, so I can never be sure whether the Grand Old Party or the Donkeys will be in power the next time around. But that doesn't stop them both from knocking on my door looking for a contribution, and if there's the slightest chance of them being elected, they get one. That way I can't lose.'

'That can't come cheap,' suggested Christina.

'It doesn't. And with nineteen mayors, thirty-one state legislators, countless chiefs of police, not to mention a governor and two state senators, it costs me several million a year. But our system is so corrupt I'm allowed to claim any political contributions against tax, even when I support both sides.'

'But who do you vote for on election day?' teased Christina.

'Neither and both, according to who I'm talking to at the time. Whenever they ask, I swear blind I'll be backing them on election day, whereas in truth, I never vote. A piece of advice my grandfather passed on to me and I've passed on to both my boys.'

Christina burst out laughing – a genuine laugh. She was surprised how much she was enjoying Wilbur's company.

'But enough about me,' said Wilbur. 'Why don't you tell me what a beautiful woman like you is doing all alone?'

• • •

Eleven o'clock. Miles had chosen the time carefully, an hour before the library opened, so he was confident they would not be disturbed. Tulip had already left to fetch Billy Mumford from the arts and crafts room, on the flimsy excuse that he needed to collect a catalogue on Rembrandt from the library before he could continue his work. That much was true, as Prison Officer Simpson had collected the appeal brochure from the Fitzmolean the night before and delivered it to Miles's cell earlier that morning.

When Tulip reappeared with Mumford in tow, Miles ushered his guest towards the only other chair in the room. He waited for him to settle while Tulip made them both a cup of coffee along with a plate of digestive biscuits supplied by the Governor – the equivalent to lunch at the Savoy when you're in prison.

'How can I help you, Mr Faulkner?' asked Billy, well aware

no one was invited to join the chief librarian for coffee and biscuits unless he wanted something.

Seven precious minutes had already evaporated before the library would open at twelve, so Miles didn't waste any more time.

'First, Billy, I'd like to check if the rumours on the prison grapevine can be relied on?'

'Which ones?' asked Billy.

'That you once forged a Murillo that ended up in the Prado.'

'Which is how I ended up in the Scrubs,' admitted Billy, as two cups of steaming black coffee were placed on the table between them.

'But you managed to fool several experts along the way.'

'For just over a year,' said Billy, 'and it wasn't the picture that gave me away, but some bastard who shopped me in exchange for a lighter sentence.'

Miles was well aware of inmate 6071's past record, so moved quickly on to his next question. 'Are you aware of a preparatory drawing by Rembrandt known as *Jacob Wrestling with the Angel*?'

'Of course I am, Mr Faulkner. But then the master only did eleven preparatory drawings that are catalogued, and I doubt if that particular sketch took him more than a few minutes to complete, which is why he's considered a genius, while I am nothing more than a painter and decorator.' Billy stared at the chief librarian for some time, before he said, 'But didn't I read somewhere that the Fitzmolean are trying to buy the original for a million they haven't got?'

'In one,' said Miles, before moving on to his next question. 'So tell me Billy, would you be capable of reproducing a copy of the *Angel* that would fool an expert?'

'I *could*,' said Billy. 'But not while I'm locked up in this place.'

'Why not?' demanded Miles, as Billy tentatively took a biscuit off the plate.

'Because I'd need the correct materials, wouldn't I? And you won't find them in the art department of Wormwood Scrubs.'

'Such as?' asked Miles.

'The correct paper, circa 1650 – not easy to come across. As well as the kind of pen and ink Rembrandt would have used at the time.'

'Anything else?' asked Faulkner, who had begun making a list.

Billy still couldn't believe he was serious, but played along. 'Well . . . the catalogue raisonné, because that will have a full-page photo of the original work.'

Miles made a note. 'You'll have everything else you need by the end of the day,' which caused Billy to spill his coffee. 'But how long would it take you to produce a convincing copy?'

'Two weeks, three at the most,' said Billy, 'unless you also want a convincing signature, in which case it will take considerably longer.'

'A signature won't be necessary,' said Miles, 'but I will need to have the drawing before I'm released on the twenty-third.'

Billy hesitated. 'As long as you can guarantee this isn't going to land me with an even longer sentence, because I don't want to do anything that will harm my chances of getting parole.'

'If your copy is good enough, Billy, the only thing you'll end up getting is a grand in your bank account.'

Billy smiled for the first time. He drained his coffee, rose from his place and shook hands with Mr Faulkner – the only way of closing a deal in prison. He grabbed another biscuit and left the library with the smile still on his face.

'I'll need to see PO Simpson,' said Miles.

'I'm on my way,' said Tulip, who quickly left the library.

Miles leant back and closed his eyes once again as he thought about part two of his plan.

• • •

Alice looked at the man seated on the other side of the table, and wondered how they could have possibly ended up in Sicily together. Inspector Ross Hogan had come into her life because she taught his daughter, Jojo, and she would never have thought it possible she could fall in love with a man who was so unreliable, yet so irresistible.

He was known in the force to be a maverick, eccentric and dangerous. But at the same time brave beyond common sense, loyal to a fault when it came to his friends, and ruthless when it came to his enemies. William Warwick was his closest friend and Miles Faulkner his sworn enemy. On both counts the feeling was mutual.

Alice looked across at Jojo, who was drawing a pepper pot on her paper napkin.

'What's wrong with the drawing pad I bought for you last month?' Ross asked his daughter, as he dabbed some honey on his croissants.

'Filled up every page,' said Jojo, as she continued to draw an outline of the sugar bowl.

'Both sides?' enquired Alice.

'Yes, miss.'

'I do wish you'd call me Alice. After all, we are on holiday.'

'I don't think so,' said Jojo, not looking up.

'Why not?' asked her father, gently probing.

'When I get back to school, I don't want my friends to know I've been on holiday with one of our teachers.'

'Why not?' repeated Ross. 'After all, we've been living together for over a year.'

'Don't remind me,' said Jojo. 'It's so embarrassing!'

Alice and Ross both laughed as Jojo turned the menu over and began to draw a teapot, but wasn't pleased with the result, so tore it in half.

'Can I go back to my room and get my pencil sharpener?'

'Of course,' said Ross, as he selected another croissant.

Jojo got up and quickly left the dining room.

A waitress placed a fresh basket of warm croissants on the table before asking in pidgin English if they needed anything else.

'Do you have any paper?' asked Alice.

'Paper?' said the waitress, pointing to her copy of yesterday's *Guardian*.

'No, paper,' said Alice, holding up a napkin.

'Yes, I go.'

'I have a feeling you're about to get several more napkins,' said Ross, 'which should be more than enough to keep Mary Cassatt occupied until I get her another sketch pad.'

'Two at least,' said Alice, 'before she moves on to table-cloths!'

Ross looked more carefully at his daughter's drawing of a teapot and smiled.

'Inspector,' said Alice, 'you may pose as the scourge of the criminal classes, but Jojo only has to bat an eyelid and you come running.'

'Guilty as charged,' said Ross. 'But what do you expect me to do?'

'Not a lot,' said Alice, taking his hand. 'In truth, you're no different from the vast majority of fathers whose daughters I teach.'

'How good do you think she is?' Ross asked, looking more closely at his pepper pot, as the waitress placed a mound of paper napkins on the table.

'Very good. So keep on encouraging her.'

Ross smiled, abandoned his croissant, leaned across and kissed Alice, just as Jojo came bustling back into the dining room clutching a pencil sharpener.

'So embarrassing,' she repeated, as she sat down and began to sharpen her pencil. She unfolded one of the new napkins and began to draw Ross's hands, but only remained silent for a moment. 'Are you both sending Beth some money for the cause?' asked Jojo, not looking up.

'What cause in particular do you have in mind?' asked Ross.

'Artemisia says Beth's trying to save a rare Rembrandt drawing of an angel for the Fitzmolean, but she has to raise half a million.'

'And how much are you giving towards it?' asked Alice.

'Four weeks of my pocket money,' came back the immediate reply.

'If everyone is as generous as you,' said Ross, 'I feel sure Beth will make it, and I'll send a contribution as soon as we get back.'

'So will I,' said Alice.

'Will that come to a half million?' asked Jojo.

'Not quite. So, what have we planned for today?' said Ross, wanting to change the subject.

'Caravaggio,' said Jojo, before Alice could reply. 'There are two of his most famous paintings in the local museum in Messina that I just have to see.'

'And one of them,' said Alice, consulting her guidebook, '*The Raising of Lazarus*, is considered to be among his finest works.'

'Did he live in Messina?' asked Jojo as she continued to draw.

'No,' replied Alice, turning a page of the guidebook, 'he was on the run at the time, having committed murder in a tavern in Rome, and it was before the Pope pardoned him, making it possible for him to return to the capital, without fear of being arrested.'

'Why would the Pope of all people pardon a murderer?' demanded Ross.

'He wanted Caravaggio to paint his portrait before he died,' said Jojo.

Alice smiled, revelling in that wonderful moment when a child teaches you something and the pupil becomes the master.

'Dad, would you have arrested Caravaggio?'

'Yes. Unlike the Pope, I consider breaking the sixth commandment a mortal sin.'

'So, you would have hanged him?' asked Alice.

Ross paused for a moment. 'I would certainly have locked him up for the rest of his life.'

'I only ask because during Caravaggio's lifetime,' continued Alice, once again consulting her guidebook, 'he painted sixty-seven masterpieces, twenty-four of them while he was on the run. An interesting moral dilemma, don't you think?'

'He could have painted them while he was in prison,' said Ross.

'I agree with the Pope,' said Jojo, still not looking up.

'Me too,' said Alice as she now opened the paper instead.

Ross remained silent as he glanced across at the headline: BRITAIN'S CHIEF ARMS NEGOTIATOR CHARGED WITH MURDER IN SAUDI. He leaned across and tried to read the small print while Jojo continued drawing.

CHAPTER 3

AT ONE MINUTE TO EIGHT, Chief Superintendent William Warwick knocked on the Commander's door. He waited for the usual cry of 'Come' before he entered his office.

It wouldn't have taken an astute detective more than a few minutes to work out what the man seated behind the desk had been up to for the past thirty years. A photograph of Commander Hawksby playing scrum half for the Metropolitan Police at Hendon in his youth hung on the wall behind him, alongside one of him being awarded the Queen's Police Medal by Her Majesty the Queen. A framed photo of his wife, two sons and five grandchildren took pride of place on his desk.

William sat down on the other side of the desk and stared at the thick files piled up in front of him.

The Commander tapped them almost affectionately, before he said, 'One day, my boy, all these will be yours, and possibly sooner than you think, as it won't be too long before I retire.'

Although William had been taken by surprise, he didn't comment.

'I'll be sixty next year,' said the Hawk, 'the statutory age for retirement.'

'No longer, sir,' William reminded him. 'The government's latest directive will allow you to continue to the age of sixty-five.'

'Only if I'm promoted,' said the Hawk, 'and that seems damned unlikely.'

'The Assistant Commissioner in charge of Special Operations has just announced his retirement, so you'd be . . .'

'Along with four other commanders who will be applying for the same job.'

'I'll put Ross on to removing them one by one,' said William, a large grin appearing on his face.

'Chief Inspector Hogan will be fully occupied for the next few weeks,' said the Hawk, removing a file from the top of the pile and placing it on the desk in front of him.

William didn't bother to ask why.

The Commander flicked open the cover of one particular file and said, 'MI6 have been in touch to warn us that Prince Majid bin Talal Al Saud, the Saudi Arabian Minister of Defence, will be making an official visit to England next month. The trip involves a major arms contract, so the Minister will be attending the Farnborough Air Show to find out what we have on offer. Your team will be in charge of their security. Not an easy task, as there's bound to be protests concerning some of the regime's less attractive policies, not least their attitude to women's rights. However, as a three billion price tag is involved, it won't come as a surprise that the Prime Minister wants Prince Majid to be made to feel welcome.'

'Any additional problems we might have to consider?' asked William.

'Yes,' said the Hawk, turning a few pages of the file. 'It seems that Prince Ahmed bin Majid, the Defence Minister's second son, will be accompanying him. According to MI6, he's an unsavoury character – diplomatic parlance for we should keep a close eye on him, particularly when it comes to women, and it's certainly not their rights he's interested in.

'However, the Foreign Office were quick to remind us that while he's a guest on our shores, he'll enjoy diplomatic immunity. And there's an added complication,' continued the Hawk.

'Simon Hartley?' interrupted William. '*The Guardian* are hinting that Ahmed was the unnamed Prince in the Overseas Club the night Hartley was arrested.'

'That's all we need,' said the Hawk.

'Then may I suggest, sir,' said William, 'Inspector Hogan should be delegated as his protection officer for the duration of the stay. That should be more than enough to keep him out of harm's way.'

'For the time being. But you're not the only person who reads *The Guardian*, so we'll have to be prepared for protests. What's Detective Sergeant Pankhurst up to at the moment?'

'Rebecca is overseeing the security for the Queen Mother's one hundredth birthday celebrations, which should keep her fully occupied for the next few weeks.'

'And Detective Sergeant Roycroft and Detective Inspector Adaja?'

'Both have in-trays almost as large as yours.'

'Do you think the crooks have any idea just how under-staffed we are?'

'If they don't,' said William, 'they can't be reading the *Daily Mail*.'

The Commander managed a sigh. 'Be sure to let Inspector

45

Hogan know what he's up against,' said the Hawk, tapping the file once again, 'because the Commissioner has made it clear the Saudi visit is our top priority.'

'Ross is somewhere in Sicily at the moment,' said William, 'but he'll be back by the end of next week.'

'Gawd help them,' said the Hawk. 'He'll try and round up the Mafia single-handed, and then we'll have an international incident on our hands.'

'Not much fear of that while Alice and Jojo are around to keep an eye on him.'

'Let me know the moment he's back,' said the Hawk. 'So, what's our next problem, Chief Superintendent?'

'Miles Faulkner is due to be released from the Scrubs in just over a fortnight's time.'

'He's already done four years?'

'Three. The Home Office, in their wisdom, allowed him a year off for good behaviour.'

The Hawk raised his eyes to the sky. 'God is not a policeman.'

• • •

Simon didn't need to be told it was solitary. He didn't know how long he'd been in the cell. They had taken away his watch, and there was no window to suggest night or day. Whenever the hatch opened, which wasn't that often, he demanded to see his Ambassador. A request that didn't even receive a grunt.

His mother had once told him that he should never get ill or break the law when abroad. For the first time, he really understood what she'd meant. If either of those happens, his father had added, the first person you need to contact is the

British Ambassador. Simon had met Sir Bernard Anscombe on arrival in Riyadh, but had not seen his excellency since. The moment he had been arrested by the Chief of Police he had assumed that alarm bells would have gone off over at the embassy and that Sir Bernard would be pulling out every stop to have him released. That was assuming there were any stops to pull out.

He was beginning to wonder if it had always been Khalil's intention to dispose of the British bid before he met the Minister of Defence, which would confirm the rumours that the French *had* offered Prince Ahmed an extra five per cent to close the deal. Had Conti also been removed so that there was no one left in the field other than the French? People had been killed for far less than fifty million.

Simon knew there were enough witnesses in that room to confirm he hadn't been involved in Conti's stabbing, so felt confident it would not be long before he was released.

Now, he was beginning to have second thoughts.

Perhaps, when you've got a spare fifty million at your disposal, there's enough left over for everyone to have a percentage of a percentage.

• • •

'Never seen him before in my life,' insisted Khalil, when the Chief of Police began to question him in his office later that morning. 'All I can tell you, Chief, is that the Englishman had been drinking a little too much when he was at the club and lost his temper when the girl he wanted seemed more interested in another customer. But I didn't even know his name until you told me.'

The Chief of Police knew only too well from past experience

that Khalil wasn't a reliable witness, and always assumed anyone could be bribed. The only question concerned the amount involved. However, he was also aware Mr Khalil was unofficially the Defence Minister's representative and, therefore, unaffected by the usual rules.

'I can only tell you what I saw,' continued Khalil. 'My close friend, a distinguished and well-respected businessman from Italy, was sitting on a sofa, chatting to one of the girls, when suddenly Hartley jumps off his stool, marches across and begins to threaten him. Mr Conti tried to defend himself but, before I could come to his aid, Hartley took out a knife and stabbed him. But by then there was nothing I could do to help, which is why I called you immediately.'

The Chief of Police didn't bother to remind Khalil that it wasn't him who had called him, but one of Prince Ahmed's followers, who also named Hartley as the guilty party. He looked down at a pile of witness statements he had collected during the past two days. 'Several others who were present have confirmed that's what happened,' said the Chief, 'including the barman, but . . .' He hesitated, before saying, 'Not *every* one of the girls.'

'What about Avril,' enquired Khalil, nervously, 'who was the girl sitting next to Mr Conti at the time?'

The Chief wasn't surprised that Khalil knew which girl was refusing to fall in line, without having to be told.

'Jenny Prescott,' said the Chief, looking down at the list of witnesses, 'or at least that's the name on her passport.'

Khalil nodded.

'When I questioned Ms Prescott, she refused to confirm your story, which might prove a problem if the case ever goes to court.'

Khalil remained silent.

'And I must inform you,' continued the Chief of Police, 'that Hartley has already claimed you were the United Kingdom's agent for the arms deal and you were about to take him to a meeting with the Defence Minister just before he was arrested. Is that true?'

'I'd never seen the man before,' repeated Khalil a little too quickly. 'I've always represented the French for this most important government contract.'

'Not the Italians?'

'No, I couldn't understand how they even got on the short-list. Although I liked Conti, I never represented him, or Hartley, for that matter.'

The Chief made a mental note that Khalil never referred to his friend Conti by his first name Paolo. 'I thought the British were the favourites to be awarded the contract?' was his next question.

'They were in with a chance, but sadly I had to let the Minister of Defence know what happened at the club on Sunday night. He was appalled, and I think you'll find the British have now been removed from the shortlist.'

The Chief of Police knew they hadn't, but kept that information to himself. 'But what would Hartley's motive be for killing Conti,' he pressed, 'if the Italians were never in with a chance?'

'I think you'll find it was personal,' said Khalil. 'Perhaps you should have another word with the girl who won't talk.'

'It isn't that she won't talk,' said the Chief. 'It's that she won't confirm your story.'

'I feel sure she will in time,' said Khalil, without further explanation.

'And then there's the problem of the murder weapon.'

'The knife?'

'That we conveniently found under Hartley's bed.'

Khalil looked embarrassed.

'You may also be interested to know,' said the Chief, 'that Hartley has demanded to see the British Ambassador, and as he's a tier one expat, that's something I can't put off indefinitely.'

'I only need a few more days,' said Khalil, 'by which time I feel sure Avril will have confirmed my story.' He placed a hand in an inside pocket and produced a large wad of notes, which he left on the table. 'You'll receive the same amount every week Hartley remains in jail,' Khalil promised him.

'I'll see what I can do,' said the Chief, as he placed the cash in a top drawer and closed the file.

• • •

Just after 9.40 a.m., a taxi pulled up outside Wormwood Scrubs and a portly man dressed in a dark grey, double-breasted suit and carrying a Gladstone bag, stepped out onto the pavement. He paid the cabbie and waited for a receipt before making his way slowly towards the front gate.

'I have a legal conference with my client, Mr Miles Faulkner, at ten,' he told the prison officer standing behind the counter in reception. He produced a booking form and an embossed card.

The officer checked his appointment schedule and placed a tick next to the name of Mr Booth Watson QC.

'Please follow me, sir,' he said as he stepped out from behind the counter.

Booth Watson began a routine he'd carried out several times in the past. First, the long walk across a barren, weed-covered yard which was surrounded by a towering wall topped with razor wire. When they reached the prison entrance, the officer unlocked the first door – three keys were needed – and once they'd stepped inside, the door was triple-locked again. This was followed by a body search, only reminding Booth Watson how much weight he'd put on since he'd last visited his client.

He then placed his Gladstone bag, jacket, belt, wallet, watch and phone in a plastic tray and watched as it moved slowly along a conveyor belt and through an X-ray machine to be checked for guns, knives, drugs or cash. When his bag and jacket reappeared on the other side of the X-ray machine, a senior officer stepped forward and retained his wallet and phone, a routine Booth Watson was all too familiar with.

'You can collect them on your way out, Mr Booth Watson,' said the prison officer.

Booth Watson nodded, while he waited for another iron door to be unlocked before he could progress – the second of six he would have to pass through before he reached the interview room.

After the final door had been unlocked and then relocked, Booth Watson checked his watch. He was five minutes early for the appointment with his client, but was confident Miles would be on time waiting for him. His journey would have been far shorter, with only his cell door to unlock.

The senior prison officer on duty managed, 'Good morning, sir,' as he escorted the prisoner's silk to the glass interview room. He opened the door before standing aside to allow Booth Watson to enter. He then closed it but remained on watch in the corridor, just a glance away.

Miles rose and shook hands with his brief before the two men sat down in uncomfortable plastic chairs. They were on opposite sides of a large glass table that kept them more than an arm's length apart, ensuring nothing illegal could pass between them.

'Good morning, Miles,' said Booth Watson, as he opened his Gladstone bag. He took out the inevitable file. 'As you only have a fortnight to serve before you're released, I thought it might be wise for us to meet so that when you come out you can hit the ground running, so to speak. But remember for now, we only have an hour, and must make the most of it.'

Miles nodded.

'I've already dealt with all the necessary paperwork, so that when you're released you'll find Collins parked outside the front gate waiting to drive you back home to Chelsea. But I need to know if you have any further instructions for me before then.'

'Three wasted years,' came back Miles's bitter response to his counsel's question, 'which no one can give me back. But that won't stop me making those responsible pay for their actions.'

'Don't you think it might be time to put the past behind you, Miles, and move on?' suggested Booth Watson, with an exaggerated sigh. 'The last thing you need is another spell in prison.'

'I haven't been idle for the past three years,' said Miles, as if he hadn't heard the proffered advice. 'One thing they can't lock up is your mind, and this time I have a foolproof scheme to ensure Mr and Mrs Warwick won't be enjoying conjugal bliss for much longer.'

'I don't have to remind you, Miles, that Chief Superintendent Warwick is now head of the Royalty and Diplomatic Protection Unit, and Dr Warwick has proved such a success as director of the Fitzmolean that I'm reliably informed her name is on the shortlist as the next director of Tate.'

'She won't even get an interview for the job,' snapped Miles. 'Not after what I have planned for her. And this is just for starters. Once I get going, early retirement will be the least of the Chief Superintendent's worries. They need to know I'm back – and that I'm going to make their lives hell for as long as it suits me. So, all I need to know before I make my first move is what Christina has been up to in my absence.'

'Your ex-wife is once again living well beyond her means,' said Booth Watson.

'Despite the fact I'm still paying her a monthly allowance that would impress a footballer's wife.'

'Which only makes a small dent in her overdraft. In fact, the bank has recently put a block on her account which has rather cut down on any extra-curricular activities. However, she's just been appointed chair of the Fitzmolean's fundraising committee, but only because . . .'

'Mrs Warwick needs to raise half a million in double-quick time, and it might surprise you to know I intend to help her.'

'You intend to do what?' said Booth Watson, unable to believe his client's words.

'It's all part of my plan to bring all three of them down at the same time.'

Booth Watson would have pleaded with his client once again to let bygones be exactly that, but he knew he'd be wasting his time, so decided to change tack. 'Can I be of any assistance with those plans?' he asked, anticipating that a large retainer could be involved.

'I need you to transfer one thousand pounds to a Billy Mumford who has an account at Barclays Bank in Little Hampton, Yorkshire.'

Booth Watson made a note.

'I also need you to take ten thousand pounds out of my private account, because if my plan is going to work, I may well need some spare cash at a moment's notice.'

'For any particular reason?' asked Booth Watson casually.

Miles, like a practised politician, answered his question with a question. 'How is Mrs Warwick getting on with raising the amount needed to rescue Rembrandt's *Angel* for the nation?'

'The government art fund has pledged a half a million to the cause, but won't release their contribution until she's raised the first five hundred thousand. So far she's only managed to raise about two hundred, possibly two hundred and twenty thousand, depending on which paper you read—'

'£223,500,' interrupted Miles, 'so she's still £276,500 short of her target, and if she fails to raise the full amount by the end of the month, the drawing will come up for auction and probably fetch well in excess of a million.'

Booth Watson sat silently awaiting his instructions.

'I want you to send a cheque to the Fitzmolean's Rembrandt appeal fund for two hundred and fifty thousand. Make sure it appears to come from an anonymous donor and can't be traced back to either you or me. I don't think we'll have to wait too long before the Fitzmolean announces they've raised the full amount, and the masterpiece will go on show to the public in the near future.'

'So where does Billy Mumford fit into your plan?' asked Booth Watson, still fishing.

'He's already playing his part,' said Miles, once again not answering his question, 'but I also need to know if Lamont is still on your payroll.'

'I've kept the ex-Superintendent on a monthly retainer,' said Booth Watson, 'but he hasn't done a lot to earn his stipend recently.'

'Well, he's about to do so,' said Miles. 'Without his particular skills, my plan will have no chance of working.'

'Which particular skills do you have in mind?' asked Booth Watson.

'If I'm to pull off the switch unnoticed, I'll need the ex-Superintendent to—'

The glass door opened. 'Time's up gentlemen,' said the senior prison officer.

• • •

In the taxi on the way back to his chambers, Booth Watson read through his notes and wondered if Miles would ever give up. The only compensation was that if he didn't, he wouldn't need another client. He put the notes back in his briefcase and took out *The Times*. Some readers read the front page first, others turned to the sports pages. Booth Watson always began with the obituaries.

He didn't waste a lot of time on a major who had won the DSO in Burma, or an academic who had ended her days as head of the natural sciences department at Bristol University. However, the death of the Rt Hon. Lord Hartley PC KBE MC did bring a smile to his face.

The former Home Secretary lived at Hartley Hall, near Bucklebury, which the paper assured him housed the family's renowned art collection, including Constable's *The Old Mill at Bucklebury*. The only other thing he'd left of any interest to Booth Watson was a wife of fifty-three years' standing and an only son, Simon. Booth Watson tried to recall where he'd come across the name of Simon Hartley before, but he was none the wiser by the time the train pulled into Waterloo.

On arriving at chambers, he instructed his secretary to make – not for the first time – discreet enquiries concerning the day of a funeral, which he would attend even though he had never once come across the deceased.

• • •

'You've arrived just in time to join the celebration,' said Beth, as William strolled into the kitchen.

'What are we celebrating?' he asked as she handed him a glass of champagne.

'The Fitz has succeeded in raising the million needed to secure the Rembrandt drawing, only weeks before it would have been put up for auction on the open market, and that would have been the last we'd have seen of it.'

'But I thought you needed another quarter of a million, and had almost given up hope of raising the full amount?'

'I did, and I had,' admitted Beth. 'Then, out of the blue, we received a cheque for quarter of a million from an anonymous donor. He's evidently been an admirer of the Fitz for many years and had already bequeathed that amount to the museum in his will. But given the circumstances, he decided there wasn't any point in waiting.'

'Any idea who it might be?' asked William, as he sipped his champagne.

'No, but I don't consider it a coincidence that there's a new man in Christina's life.'

William didn't look convinced. 'Then you'd better cash the cheque fairly quickly, as Christina's affairs don't usually last too long.'

'I think you could be wrong for a change, Chief Superintendent, because this time he's older than she is.'

'Then let's hope he knows what he's taking on,' said William, raising a glass, having accepted it wasn't a coincidence.

'The board will be making an official announcement in the next few days,' said Beth, 'and they have invited our patron, the Countess of Wessex, to unveil the drawing in July, so that will be one date you can't afford to miss.'

William raised his glass a second time.

'And if that wasn't enough,' continued Beth, unable to contain her excitement, 'the chairman of Tate phoned me this afternoon to ask if I'd be interested in applying for the position as their next director.'

'And when they learn about your triumph with the Rembrandt, it won't do your prospects any harm.'

'Possibly, but don't forget I'd be up against a strong field and I'm not altogether sure I want the job. I love the Fitz, and I mustn't forget how good they've been to me over the years.'

'Understood, but you can be sure they'll all be proud of you were you to end up as director of Tate . . . Where are the twins?' he added, suddenly aware the house was unusually quiet.

'Upstairs, plotting something they don't want us to know about,' she whispered conspiratorially.

'Who's in the firing line this time?' asked William.

'No idea, but the name Hartley keeps coming up. Mean anything to you?'

'What are we having for supper?' he asked, as the twins burst into the room.

CHAPTER 4

SOME UNSCRUPULOUS LAWYERS GAIN A reputation for being ambulance chasers, but not Mr Booth Watson QC. He was of a higher calling, and fell into a category of a 'funeral-attending QC'.

The taxi driver picked up his customer when he emerged from Thatcham station, and drove him to St Mary's parish church.

Booth Watson joined the family, friends and colleagues as they made their way into the Norman church. He slipped into a pew near the back, as he wasn't any of the above. But then funerals are like weddings: at least half the congregation doesn't know the other half, so no one questions who you are or why you're there.

The service was well-attended, and Booth Watson recognized several leading politicians, including a former Prime Minister, who sat bolt upright in the third row.

The last mourners to make an appearance were the family. They were led by an old lady who walked behind the coffin with a younger woman, accompanied by two teenage boys. Booth Watson assumed they had to be her daughter-in-law and her two sons. Everyone was painfully aware who, like Banquo's ghost, wasn't there to accompany his mother. Booth Watson hoped to take advantage of Simon Hartley's absence.

The uninvited guest sat through another funeral service, the only difference being who was resting in the coffin. When the blessing was finally delivered, Booth Watson was ready for the second part of his deception. The organ struck up the funeral march and the widow and her family made their way slowly back down the centre aisle, towards the west door, where they stopped and turned and waited to greet the assembled gathering.

The widow shook hands with all those who had come to honour the former Home Secretary, several of whom had been asked to join the family for a reception at Hartley Hall. Booth Watson was not among them, although he had plans to receive a last-minute invitation. Gatecrashing a funeral is one thing, but gatecrashing a private wake is quite another. However, he had a well-prepared line, which almost always elicited the same response.

He stood dutifully in line, and when he reached the front of the queue, was greeted with a puzzled look that rather suggested the widow was unsure who he was. He bowed low and whispered in the old lady's ear, 'Booth Watson. I had the honour of working with your husband when he was at the Home Office. One of the finest ministers I've ever served. Of course, like the rest of my countrymen, I have protested about the disgraceful treatment of your son and will continue to do so.'

'How kind of you to say so, Mr Booth Watson,' said the old lady, 'and if you can spare the time, perhaps you could join us at Hartley Hall, where I feel sure you'll come across several old friends and acquaintances.'

Booth Watson felt sure he wouldn't, but then his main purpose was to be an eavesdropper, gathering information from any idle, unguarded snippets of conversation that might add to his knowledge.

When he left St Mary's, he followed a group of mourners who were clearly making their way to Hartley Hall. While other guests chatted among themselves during the reception, Booth Watson took a tour of the drawing room, and was quickly able to confirm the Hartleys' large collection of English watercolours was worthy of its trumpeted reputation. However, when he first saw the Constable of *The Old Mill at Bucklebury* that hung above the mantelpiece, even he was moved.

'Quite magnificent, isn't it?' said a voice from behind him.

'It most certainly is,' said Booth Watson, who turned to find the vicar standing by his side.

'And been in the family for generations,' he lowered his voice conspiratorially, 'But it's not the pride of the collection, in my opinion.'

Booth Watson didn't have to ask.

'The Declaration of Independence, handwritten by Thomas Jefferson – which hangs in the great man's study – is, by any standards, unique.'

'How interesting,' said Booth Watson, who'd already decided the trip to Bucklebury had been worthwhile.

'Vicar, what a beautiful service,' said a lady who joined them, allowing Booth Watson to slip quietly away. He glanced around the room to see several mourners deep in conversation, which allowed the chance to leave the room and go in search of the Jefferson.

He walked slowly down the corridor and when he reached a closed door, he looked up and down to check that no one was watching. He tentatively opened the door, peered inside, and immediately spotted what he'd come in search of: The Declaration of Independence. He remembered from his research that one of Lord Hartley's ancestors had been a friend of both Franklin and Jefferson. Which would explain how the document had ended up in Hartley Hall.

He was about to leave when the door suddenly swung open and a young man, whom Booth Watson immediately recognized, stepped in, unable to hide his surprise when he saw the stranger.

'The vicar,' said Booth Watson, without missing a beat, 'mentioned that there was this copy of the Declaration of Independence in your late grandfather's study. I couldn't resist taking a look. I hope you'll forgive me.'

'It's not a copy,' said the young man with the certainty of the young. 'It was written by Thomas Jefferson himself. He sent it to David Hartley MP in 1787, and it's been in the family ever since.'

'How interesting,' said Booth Watson, not giving it a second look. 'But if you'll excuse me, I ought to go and pay my respects to your grandmother before I leave.'

Booth Watson left the young man without another word, and quickly returned to the drawing room, where he sought out the widow.

'Thank you for allowing me to join you for the reception, Lady Hartley,' he said, offering the same low bow, only to receive the same uncertain look as to who the stranger could possibly be.

'Booth Watson,' he reminded her, which caused a flicker of recognition to return.

'If I can ever be of any assistance in the future, dear lady, please don't hesitate to call on me,' Booth Watson said, handing her his card.

'How kind of you,' she said, checking the card, 'Mr Booth Watson.' She placed it in her bag.

'And be assured, as a mark of my respect for your late husband, I would be only too happy to waive my fee.' Another bow followed before the uninvited guest made a discreet exit.

Booth Watson headed back to the station feeling he had cast a fly on the water, and he would now have to wait and see if the salmon would bite.

• • •

When the cell door opened, Simon had no idea if it was the middle of the day or the middle of the night.

They yanked him off the thin, urine-stained mattress, and dragged him out into a dimly lit corridor. He assumed his life was about to end.

The cramped, spiral staircase was the next obstacle to surmount, one guard in front of him, another behind. He didn't know why they bothered. After nine days in solitary, he wouldn't have been a match for a couple of girl guides.

When he reached the top step, he was shoved along a narrow corridor lined with cells on either side, filled with protesting prisoners who were locked up for crimes they *had* committed. The guards only paused when they reached the first of several heavy locked doors, each one requiring three keys to unlock. Once they were through, the doors were locked again, before they could progress to the next one. Finally, he saw an open door, from which a light shone as if it was beckoning him.

After Simon had been shoved into the room, the door was slammed behind him. Once he'd regained his balance, his eyes settled on a man he hadn't met, but assumed could only be the Governor. He sat alone, notebook open, pen poised. As there wasn't another chair, Simon had no choice but to remain standing.

'Name,' said the Governor, looking directly at him.

A slightly farcical question as he clearly knew the answer was Simon's first thought.

'Simon Winchcombe Henry Howard Hartley,' he responded, suddenly alert, adrenalin shooting through his exhausted body. But then he'd spent days preparing for this encounter.

The Governor bent down, picked up a briefcase and placed it on the table. He opened it, extracted a single sheet of paper and pushed it across the table.

Simon took some time reading the confession, only wanting to correct the English.

'Mr Hartley, if you feel able to sign that document, we will send you home later today as an illegal alien.' He smiled, leaned forward, and offered Simon his pen.

Simon would have returned his smile, but the Governor had played his get-out-of-jail card far too early. He wouldn't have lasted a week at Harvard Business School.

'Yes, I can see that would be a convenient solution for all concerned,' said Simon, 'but as I didn't kill Mr Conti, I think I'll decline your generous offer.'

'But if you didn't kill him,' asked the Governor, 'who did?'

Simon didn't fall into his trap, aware that if he named Prince Ahmed, he might not be going home for a very long time, if ever. 'I think you're only too aware of the answer to that question,' he responded.

'Do you know a man called Hani Khalil?' asked the

Governor, moving on down a list of prepared questions he had hoped not to have to ask.

'Yes, I do,' said Simon. 'He wanted to represent the British bid for the important arms deal, which is why I was a guest at his club on the night of the murder.'

'But Mr Khalil claims,' said the Governor, looking at a separate piece of paper, 'that the first time he saw you was when he was seated at the other end of the bar and you were having a heated argument with a Mr Paolo Conti, a rival for the arms contract.'

'Interesting,' said Simon, 'because Mr Khalil was also seated at that end of the bar, when he pointed out Mr Conti and told me that the Italians have no chance of getting the arms contract, but then I suspect you already knew that.'

The Governor didn't comment, but leaned forward and once again lifted the top of his briefcase, this time producing a small, serrated dagger. He placed it on the centre of the table.

'And where do you think the police found this, Mr Hartley?' said the Governor, pointing at the knife.

This was the first question Simon had failed to anticipate as he had assumed the murder weapon would have been disposed of.

'On the table by the door of my hotel room, with an arrow pointing towards it,' suggested Simon, not attempting to disguise any sarcasm.

'Hidden under your bed,' said the Governor, not sounding quite so confident.

'Then DNA will show you that someone else must have put it there,' said Simon. 'And no doubt you've checked the clothes I was wearing on the night of the murder, because if I had killed him, they would have been covered in his blood, not to mention his DNA.'

'You could have disposed of them before the police arrived,' said the Governor.

'Funny that,' said Simon. 'Why would I get rid of my suit, shirt, tie, socks and shoes, but leave the murder weapon under my bed?'

'Criminals always make mistakes,' snapped the Governor.

'As do the police, when they are attempting to frame an innocent person,' said Simon, confident he had his opponent on the back foot. Simon had his next question well prepared. 'Why don't you have a word with the driver who took me back to the hotel that night and ask him if it looked as if I'd been involved in a fight, or if I was carrying a knife, or if my clothes were covered in blood?'

'Your driver has already been interviewed,' said the Governor. 'He says that you came running out of the club in an agitated state, leapt into your car and ordered him to get moving.'

'Another simple mistake, Governor – it was not my car but Mr Khalil's, and the jury might find that piece of evidence quite compelling.'

'We don't bother with juries in Saudi,' snarled the Governor.

'Then you'll have to find a judge who's happy to see his photograph on the front page of every newspaper in the Western world, when he has to explain how everyone except him had worked out I was innocent and that he was the man responsible for the British having to withdraw from the arms deal. I suspect you'll get the odd mention as well.'

The Governor hesitated for a moment before he said, 'I don't suppose the French will worry too much about that.'

'But your new enlightened ruler might,' came back Simon, 'when he reads *The Times* and discovers that you were responsible for charging me, which I note you still haven't done.'

The Governor picked up his pace stick.

'Not advisable, Governor,' said Simon, 'as I suspect you're well aware I'm meeting the British Ambassador tomorrow, and it might not be wise for me to look as if I've just been beaten up.'

'You think you're very clever, don't you, Hartley?'

'No, but I have a feeling you've already worked out that this is going to end in one of two ways, so all you have to decide is which horse to back, because I suspect Mr Hani Khalil is not the odds-on favourite any longer.'

The Governor banged his pace stick on the table, but Simon didn't flinch. 'We will continue this conversation after you've seen your Ambassador.'

'Which should give you more than enough time to make up your mind, Governor,' said Simon.

'Are you threatening me, Hartley?' shouted the Governor.

This time, Simon did allow himself a thin smile and for a moment couldn't help wondering if this would become a case study at Harvard Business School. Funny what crosses your mind when you're possibly facing death, thought Simon. But he knew he wouldn't hear the other side of the story until he saw the Ambassador.

After being dragged back to his cell, he spent another sleepless night.

• • •

The following day, the same routine was carried out, but this time he was greeted by a friendly smile from the person sitting on the other side of the table.

'I'm only sorry, Simon, that we should have to meet again in such unfortunate circumstances,' said the British Ambassador, as the two men shook hands. Sir Bernard looked across at Simon, who had sprouted an unkempt beard and had grown so thin that he hardly recognized him. 'I would have come sooner,' he said, 'but the authorities couldn't have made it more difficult for me to arrange a meeting.'

'That's because the murderer is one of them,' said Simon. 'Prince Ahmed bin Majid.'

The Ambassador didn't react as Simon continued. 'Don't forget, I witnessed the murder,' he reminded him, 'which is why I'm a pawn that can be sacrificed to ensure the French get the contract, and Prince Ahmed ends up with an even larger percentage.'

'Not necessarily,' said Sir Bernard, this time taking Simon by surprise.

'You mean we're still in with a chance of landing the contract?' said Simon, unable to hide his disbelief.

'All I can tell you,' replied the Ambassador, 'is that the Minister of Defence still plans to visit London and Paris next month before he makes a final decision. However, I'm reliably informed that the French have offered Prince Ahmed another five per cent if they get the deal.'

'That's fifty million a year for the next three years,' said Simon, 'of which, no doubt, ten per cent will end up in Khalil's back pocket, so he can retire and live in the lap of luxury.'

'I'm rather hoping he'll end his days in this place', said Sir Bernard, 'sharing a cell with his friend Prince Ahmed.'

'I wouldn't bet on that,' said Simon.

'But what I can't work out,' said the Ambassador, 'is why Prince Ahmed had to kill Conti when the Italians were never serious contenders for the contract.'

'You don't have to look further than Avril Dubois,' said Simon. 'I think you'll find the Prince simply lost his temper when he saw her with another man, and when they needed a scapegoat, I was conveniently on hand. But I still don't know if it was all part of Khalil's plan, or whether I was just in the wrong place at the wrong time.'

'I suspect the latter,' said the Ambassador, 'but it doesn't make my job any easier, because Miss Dubois is a British citizen, and her life is now in danger.'

'Another pawn,' said Simon, 'who can so easily be removed from the board, while they have the King.'

Sir Bernard smiled for the first time, and without explanation said, 'But don't forget we have the Queen.'

CHAPTER 5

COMMANDER HAWKSBY AND CHIEF SUPERINTENDENT William Warwick left Old Scotland Yard at 8.30 a.m. and walked briskly across to King Charles Street. Their only topic of conversation was the latest score in the first Test match against the West Indies.

'Walls may not have ears,' said the Hawk, 'but passing strangers certainly do.'

Although they arrived at the Foreign Office long before the appointed hour, a young man was already waiting for them in reception.

'Please follow me, gentlemen,' he said, before accompanying his visitors up a wide, thick, red-carpeted staircase. William glanced from side to side at the colourful ceramic tiles that graced the walls.

When they reached the first-floor landing, they were greeted by a bust of Charles James Fox along with portraits of former foreign secretaries – Palmerston, Pitt the Elder, Castlereagh, Bevin, Alec Douglas-Home and James Callaghan – before coming to a halt outside the door of the present holder of that high office.

The young man paused at a set of floor-to-ceiling oak doors with the royal coat of arms displayed above them. He knocked and waited for a moment before opening one of the doors and standing aside. The two visitors entered a room the size of a tennis court and made their way towards a diminutive figure with an unmistakable shock of red hair, who was seated behind a large oak desk at the far end of the room. A portrait of the monarch hung on the wall behind him with a bust of Churchill to his right, alongside an Enigma machine displayed in a glass cabinet. Two smartly dressed mandarins were perched like vultures on either side of their master, looking as if they were ready to swoop given the slightest opportunity.

The Foreign Secretary had risen from behind his desk long before his two guests had reached him. Robin Cook shook hands with them both before introducing a Mr Trevelyan, his private secretary, and Sir Geoffrey Cruickshank, the Permanent Secretary. It seemed to William that everyone in the Foreign Office was a secretary.

'It was good of you both to come at such short notice,' Cook said, without any suggestion of irony.

William could only wonder how the Foreign Secretary would have reacted had the Commander told him, 'My diary is a little crowded at the moment, but I feel sure I could fit you in towards the end of next week'.

'There are two reasons I needed to see you so urgently,' said Cook, not wasting any time. 'As you will know, the British government are currently involved in advanced negotiations with Saudi Arabia for an arms deal worth several billions, and to that end we are hosting a delegation from the Saudi Arabian Ministry of Defence next month. Until quite recently, we were considered the front runners for the contract. However, this has received a setback, to say the least, following the arrest of our chief negotiator, Mr Simon Hartley.'

'Who's been charged with the murder of one of his rivals,' said the Hawk, one step ahead of him. 'But it doesn't look to me like a case that would stand up in court.'

'Depends which court you're standing up in,' countered the Foreign Secretary. 'However, Sir Bernard Anscombe, our man in Riyadh, agrees with you. He finally managed to meet with Hartley in prison yesterday. He is certain not only that Hartley's innocent, but also who the guilty party is, which has only added to our problems.'

William wanted to ask who and why, but before he could speak, both questions were answered.

'The guilty party is Prince Ahmed bin Majid,' said the Foreign Secretary. 'He's the second son of Prince Majid, the Minister of Defence, who will be responsible for signing the arms agreement on behalf of his government.'

'The King's cousin, no less,' said William.

'No less,' repeated Cook. 'And it's necessary, Chief Superintendent, to remember that – with the Saudis – "face" is all-important when they are dealing with a foreign country, particularly the British.

'Sir Geoffrey,' he continued, looking to his right, 'has already been in touch with the Saudi Ambassador in London – not an easy man – who is well aware of how much time and money the government has invested in the arms deal to ensure we remain ahead of the French, and so feels he has the whip hand. We suspect he knows only too well that Hartley is innocent and, more importantly, who the guilty party is. So, I'm faced with the double dilemma of trying to hold on to the contract, while remaining on good terms with the Saudi government, and at the same time getting Hartley out of jail without the press finding out what I'm up to. The fact that Hartley has been arrested and charged with murdering his Italian rival has already been well covered by the media, and rumours are already circulating in the press about who the real culprit might be.'

William recalled reading a recent article by Cook written in *The Guardian*, where he didn't leave the reader in any doubt about his strong views on presiding over an 'ethical' foreign policy.

'The French aren't helping,' said Sir Geoffrey, speaking for the first time, 'but I can't pretend we would have behaved any differently had our roles been reversed.'

'However,' continued the Foreign Secretary, 'to our surprise, the Saudi Defence Minister has not cancelled his planned trip to the Farnborough Air Show next month to check on the state-of-the-art equipment we have on offer. However, we should anticipate more protests once the public find out the truth, and the situation isn't being helped by the fact that the Minister's son, Prince Ahmed, despite the Foreign Office's advice to the contrary, intends to accompany him on the trip. So, this is, in political terms, a somewhat' – he paused – 'delicate situation.'

Only the Foreign Office could describe it thus, thought William.

'Hartley told our man that the key witness in the Hartley defence is a Ms Jenny Prescott,' said Sir Geoffrey, 'or at least that's the name on her passport, which the Saudis confiscated when she recently tried to leave the country.'

'Ms Prescott's working name,' said Trevelyan, 'and I use the word advisedly, is Avril Dubois, and she was at the night-club on the evening Paolo Conti was murdered.'

'And more important,' came back Sir Geoffrey, 'she is inconveniently refusing to confirm the Saudi police's version of events, which rather suggests not only that Hartley is innocent, but also that everyone knows he is.'

'If she's the only witness who might be willing to testify to the fact it was Prince Ahmed and not Hartley who committed the murder,' said William, 'her life must be in danger.'

'Our Ambassador and Hartley have already made that point,' said Cook.

'So what role do you expect us to play?' asked the Hawk, cutting to the chase.

'We need someone to go to Saudi,' said Sir Geoffrey, 'track down Ms Prescott, check if she can prove Hartley is innocent, and see if she still wants to leave the country and come home, because if she does we can use her as a pawn in our negotiations with the Saudis.'

'I used to think politics was a dubious profession,' said Cook, 'but that was before I joined the Foreign Office, and I can assure you, Commander, they make the Mafia look like a bunch of Sunday school teachers.'

Both the Hawk and William laughed, while the two mandarins didn't even blink.

'If such a person exists,' said Sir Geoffrey, as if he hadn't heard the Foreign Secretary, 'we might still be in with a chance of defeating the French, or at least of finding out if we're just wasting our time,' he paused. 'And money.'

The Hawk nodded. 'When do you need this man?'

'Yesterday,' said Sir Geoffrey.

'He was on holiday in Italy yesterday,' said William, well aware who the Hawk had in mind. 'But I know he's flying back to London later today, so I could be at the airport and meet him off the plane.'

The other mandarin came in on cue. 'Then bring him straight to my office, Chief Superintendent,' Trevelyan said, handing William his card. 'Because I'll need to brief him before the day is out.'

'Understood,' said the Hawk. 'By the way, his name is—'

'I don't want to know his name,' said the Foreign Secretary, who rose from his place and shook hands with both of them to indicate the meeting was over. The Hawk and William left without another word.

Once the door had closed behind them, they walked briskly back along the corridor, jogged down the wide staircase and out onto King Charles Street to find Danny, seated behind the wheel of the Commander's car, waiting for them.

'You take the car,' said the Hawk, 'and go directly to Heathrow. As soon as I'm back at the Yard, I'll make sure his flight gets priority landing and that he isn't held up by customs.'

William was opening the back door of the car when the Hawk added, 'And bring him straight to my office. I want to see Hogan before the Foreign Office get their hands on him.'

• • •

'Are you Inspector Ross Hogan?' whispered the senior cabin steward as he leant down to address a passenger seated in economy.

Ross looked up from the novel he was reading and nodded.

'Once we've landed, sir, would you be kind enough to join me at the front of the aircraft. There will be a car waiting for you at the bottom of the steps.'

'Crew prepare for landing,' announced a voice over the

intercom. 'Will all passengers please return to their seats and fasten your seat belts.'

'Are you about to be arrested?' asked Jojo, as the steward left them.

'Seems unlikely,' said Ross, as he helped his daughter on with her seat belt. 'The police don't usually give you prior notice if they're going to arrest you.'

'Then who have you annoyed this time?' asked Alice, smiling.

'I'll know the moment I see who's standing at the bottom of the steps,' said Ross as the plane made its descent through a bank of fluffy white clouds, causing it to bump.

Jojo held onto her father's hand.

'But you're not due back at work until Monday,' Alice reminded him. 'So . . .'

'It has to be an emergency. But to be honest, I don't know any more than you do.'

'Does that mean I won't be seeing you for a long time?' asked Jojo, still clutching onto her father's hand.

'I'll phone you every day,' promised Ross, 'wherever I am.'

'Even convicted criminals are allowed the occasional phone call,' quipped Alice as the wheels of the plane touched down on the runway and the engines were thrust into reverse.

Ross accepted that any speculation was pointless, and he'd have to wait and see who was waiting for him when they landed. He couldn't help recalling the last time this had happened, he'd had to fly on to Paris and assist the Prince of Wales in bringing Princess Diana's coffin back to England.

The plane taxied to a halt at the stand.

'Whoever it is waiting for you,' said Alice as she unbuckled her seat belt, 'thank you for a memorable holiday. And if I never see you again, Inspector, it's been nice knowing you.'

'You won't get rid of me quite that easily,' said Ross. He leant across and kissed her, and Jojo pretended not to notice.

Ross leapt up the moment the fasten seat belts sign was turned off, grabbed his carry-on bag from the overhead locker and joined the steward at the front of the plane almost before anyone else had stirred. He waited impatiently for the door to be opened; when he stepped out of the aircraft, the first person he saw was Danny, holding open the door of an unmarked car. But he couldn't make out who was sitting on the back seat.

He jogged down the steps and peered inside to see William waiting for him. The expression on his face gave nothing away.

Even before he'd pulled the door closed, the car sped off. He glanced back out of the rear window to see the second passenger standing on the top step of the aircraft was waving. It was Jojo. He returned her wave.

Before he said a word, William touched a button and a glass partition was raised, alerting Ross that what he was about to be told couldn't even be shared with Danny.

'Have you heard of a Simon Hartley?' were William's first words. No 'did you have a good holiday, Ross,' or 'how's Jojo?'

'Only what I've read in the press,' admitted Ross. 'The guy who's been arrested in Saudi Arabia for a murder he didn't commit.'

'What makes you say that?'

'Motive, motive and motive, Chief Superintendent,' came back Ross's immediate response. 'According to *The Guardian* – Alice's paper of choice – he hardly knew the man he's been accused of murdering. He has no past criminal record, and I'm bound to ask, why would a man on the verge of securing a huge arms deal murder a man in full view of several witnesses, when in truth he wasn't even a rival?'

William couldn't disagree.

Ross looked his friend in the eye and said, 'Perhaps it's time to stop playing games, William, and tell me where I fit in to all of this.'

William took him slowly through the meeting he and the Hawk had just had with the Foreign Secretary earlier that morning, concluding with the words, 'They need someone to fly to Riyadh immediately, track down Jenny Prescott, aka Avril Dubois, and find out why she won't talk. As we're now certain she witnessed the murder, we have to somehow get her back to England, as her evidence could prove vital if we hope to get Hartley released. And there are no prizes for guessing who the Hawk thought was the ideal person for the job.'

Ross felt a familiar rush of adrenalin that always came when his particular skills were required.

'Where are we heading now?' was all he asked.

'Back to the Yard. The Hawk wants to see you before you go on to the Foreign Office, where you'll be briefed by a Mr Trevelyan.'

'Who's he?'

'The Foreign Secretary's private secretary.'

'Typical of the Hawk,' said Ross, 'to want to stay one step ahead of the FCO. And then what?'

'I've already booked you onto an evening flight to Riyadh,' said William as he touched a button and the screen slid back down. 'So how was your holiday, Ross?'

'I thought you'd never ask.'

• • •

Seven hours later, Ross took his seat in business class. The first thing he did was to study the menu, as he hadn't eaten since breakfast that morning on another plane. His mind hadn't stopped whirling after he'd left a three-hour briefing with Mr Trevelyan, along with two experts from the Middle Eastern desk. Later, they were joined by two officers from MI6, who supplied him with his cover story and explained in great detail why he was officially visiting the Middle East and how they had taken advantage of his background, even his mother.

He had to admit the idea the young whizz kid from MI6 – who looked as if he should still be in short trousers – had come up with was nothing short of brilliant. Where did they find these people, Ross wondered. Once they were convinced he knew what was expected of him, Ross was driven back to the airport just in time to catch the evening flight to Riyadh. He was the last passenger to board the plane.

It had quickly become clear to Ross that the first thing he needed to do was somehow make contact – without it being too obvious – with Avril Dubois/Jenny Prescott, and if, as the Foreign Office had suggested, her passport had been confiscated when she tried to leave the country soon after the murder of Paolo Conti, he'd already come up with a way of getting around that problem. Trevelyan had immediately accepted his suggestion, and even managed a slight bow of recognition.

Ross had agreed only to call the embassy in an emergency, and under no circumstances was he to attempt to visit Hartley in prison, as others were handling that particular problem. Ross had also been told about one of the Foreign Office's secret weapons, a Mr Jim Fellows MBE. A hotel concierge by day, a spy by night. Fellows had already been fully briefed about the arrival of Declan O'Reilly from Dublin, who was hoping to close an oil deal on behalf of the Irish government.

Once he'd given the flight attendant his dinner order, Ross set about reading the thick file that Trevelyan had supplied, aware he needed to have completed his prep by the time he landed, as he'd been instructed to hand the file over to the courier who would be meeting him at the airport, in exchange for the two passports he'd requested. 'If you're not familiar with the contents by then, you won't be given a second chance,' were Trevelyan's uncompromising words just before he left for the airport.

As the flight was over eight hours, and Trevelyan had made sure no one was seated next to him, Ross was confident he would have become his new persona long before they landed in Riyadh. Hani Khalil looked like his biggest problem, because if he became suspicious, even for one moment, that Ross was working for the British, it would not only put Avril's life in danger, but possibly Hartley's as well, not to mention that it would most assuredly mean the loss of a three-billion-pound contract.

'No pressure,' said Ross out loud.

'I beg your pardon, sir?' said an attentive flight attendant.

'Just a black coffee, please,' said Ross, before returning to the file.

The Hawk had insisted he must always call him before he spoke to Trevelyan, while the Foreign Office mandarin had made him sign a document confirming he wouldn't contact anyone in England until he returned.

He had lied to one of them.

Ross ate the four-course meal slowly, and only drank water – despite being reminded several times that once they arrived in Riyadh, he'd only be able to get a soft drink until he stepped back on board – with or without Ms Dubois. While others slept or watched a film, he continued to devour the contents of the Foreign Office directive, making only slight adjustments to his back story.

By the time his meal tray had been removed, Ross knew exactly what was expected of him once they landed in Riyadh. He dozed off for a couple of hours, but woke in time for breakfast and one final reading of the file.

Ross recalled the names that would decide if the long weekend would be a success or failure:

Declan O'Reilly

Sir Bernard Anscombe

Jim Fellows

Hani Khalil

And, most important of all, Avril Dubois, née Jenny Prescott.

Pawns on a chessboard, but would the Queen have to be brought into play?

By the time the plane landed in Riyadh, Ross should have been exhausted but had never felt more alert. He'd once done a training course with a dozen other operatives to see how long they could stay awake under pressure. After forty-nine hours, he'd collapsed, but he had been the last man standing.

When Ross entered the terminal, he was met by a young man who could only have worked for the Foreign Office. The Harris tweed jacket, old school tie and highly polished leather shoes wouldn't have fooled a rookie detective. The young man handed over the file in exchange for two passports: one Ross pocketed, the other he presented to passport control.

After a short inspection, Mr Declan O'Reilly, the Irish government's Minister for Marine and Natural Resources, was waved through without being questioned.

A Jaguar and driver were parked outside Arrivals and

whisked Ross off to the Palace Hotel, where he had been booked into the presidential suite.

'A car and driver will be outside the hotel waiting for you whenever you need them,' were the parting words of the man from the FCO before he took a taxi back to the embassy. It had quickly become clear that the young man had no idea who he was, or even why he was in Riyadh, and Ross had no intention of enlightening him.

When he walked into the hotel, he went straight to the check-in desk.

'Good evening Mr O'Reilly,' said the concierge, 'welcome to the Palace Hotel.'

Ross looked at the label on his jacket and said, 'Good evening Mr Fellows.'

CHAPTER 6

ROSS TRIED TO RECALL THE relevant words from the Foreign Office brief. *In the Middle East you can't hope to close a major deal without being represented by an established agent. There are several who have the ear of the Minister, but there is only one you should be interested in, as he's the one person who can lead you to Avril Dubois. However, tread carefully, as they may no longer be on speaking terms, and if they are, it will have been a wasted journey and you could well be on the next flight home.*

Not part of Ross's plan.

By the time Mr O'Reilly reported to the concierge of the Palace Hotel, Jim Fellows already had everything in place. The gentleman in question – if gentleman was an accurate description – had already been briefed and told that a Mr O'Reilly had booked into the Presidential Suite ($1,000 a night) and was hoping to arrange a meeting with Prince Sharif bin Nayef Al Saud, the Saudi Minister of Petroleum and Mineral Resources. Jim had also informed his contact that

Mr O'Reilly seemed 'fairly green' when it came to how business was conducted in the Middle East. 'But then he is Irish,' Jim had explained.

In the short conversation that followed, Jim told Mr O'Reilly he would be surprised if Khalil hadn't contacted him before the end of the day.

'The sooner the better,' was Ross's only comment, because if Khalil were to call Dublin, he would quickly discover why the Minister for Marine and Natural Resources wasn't at his desk. According to the FCO brief, Declan O'Reilly would be spending a quiet weekend in Cork with his mistress (unnamed), but was expected to be back at his desk first thing on Monday morning – midday in Riyadh. Ross accepted that at best he only had a couple of days to carry out his mission (another Foreign Office word). But as they reminded him, in Saudi, Saturday and Sunday are working days.

'Thank you,' said Ross. 'I'll report back if Khalil contacts me.'

'Not if,' said Jim, 'but when. By the way, the Irish accent is good,' he added with a nod of respect.

'It ought to be,' replied Ross. 'It's the only thing about me that's genuine.'

'The dining room is on the far side of the lobby, sir. Breakfast is served between seven and ten,' said the concierge when another guest joined them at the desk.

'Thank you,' said Ross, before heading off to the dining room.

How right Jim turned out to be, because Ross hadn't even ordered his second coffee before a man he recognized from photographs supplied by the FCO was standing in front of him. Ross put down his copy of the *Wall Street Journal*, left open at the page listing the latest oil prices, and looked up.

The man gave him a slight bow before speaking. 'It's Declan O'Reilly, if I remember correctly.'

'Yes,' said Ross, looking puzzled.

'My name is Hani Khalil. We met at a government reception in Dublin a couple of years ago, but you may not remember me.'

Ross could only admire how Khalil could lie so effortlessly and with such conviction. He suspected he was one of those people who didn't even know when he was lying. Something Ross intended to take advantage of.

'How nice to see you again, Mr Khalil,' said Ross, gesturing him to a seat on the other side of the table. 'Won't you join me for breakfast?'

'Thank you,' said Khalil, sitting down opposite him, 'but I can't stay long as I have a meeting with the Minister at ten.'

'The Minister?'

'Prince Sharif, the Minister of Petroleum and Mineral Resources,' said Khalil, without missing a beat.

'How fortuitous,' said Ross, 'as I was rather hoping to meet the Minister myself before I return to Dublin on Monday. But I fear he may consider Ireland fairly low down on his list of priorities.'

'If you were able to tell me the reason you need to see him,' said Khalil, 'I might be able to assist.'

'My government have instructed me to try and open negotiations with the Saudi authorities with a view to signing a long-term oil contract.'

'It would help if I knew the details.'

Ross hesitated for a moment, hoping to leave the impression of being cautious about breaking a confidence with a stranger.

'You can rely on my discretion,' said Khalil, who slid his card across the table.

Ross studied it.

لیلیلخ ع۱ر۱ش م

Khalil Enterprises

Hani Khalil
President

Suite 1206 Habib Towers
+ 966 11 305 6679   Riyadh

'My government would like to purchase fifty thousand barrels of crude a week at spot price for the next five years.' Although he delivered the Foreign Office's exact words with confidence, he only wished he knew what he was talking about.

'I feel sure that can be arranged,' said Khalil, 'but of course, one would have to add a small percentage for services rendered, to ensure the contract lands on the Minister's desk.'

'How small?' demanded Ross, hoping he sounded hard-nosed.

'Ten per cent on top of the agreed price, which is no more than the going rate,' something else the FCO accepted without question.

'I'll have to call the Taoiseach and get his clearance,' said Ross, 'and then perhaps we could meet later?'

'Why don't you join me for dinner at the Fairmont this evening?' suggested Khalil. 'I can assure you they have the best chef in town.'

Ross nodded. 'Seven o'clock?'

'Seven o'clock it is, Declan,' said his uninvited guest as he rose from the table. 'I look forward to seeing you then.'

Ross called for the bill as he watched Khalil leave the dining room. He'd forgotten just how easy it was to con a con man. He signed the bill using his new name for the first time.

Ross strolled across to the concierge desk. 'Thank you, Jim. Hook, line and sinker,' was all he said before making his way across to the bank of elevators on the far side of the lobby, well aware that the embassy would be informed of his progress within minutes.

Once back in his suite, Ross made two phone calls. The first to Commander Hawksby at home – he was already up. The second to Mr Trevelyan on his mobile, who didn't sound wide awake. Both seemed satisfied with his progress so far, although Trevelyan reminded him, 'Your cover will be blown once the Minister returns to Dublin at twelve noon on Monday your time, so make sure you and Cinderella are both on your way back to London before then, with or without her slippers.'

• • •

Ross arrived at the Fairmont a few minutes late, assuming that Khalil wouldn't be on time. He was wrong. Mr Ten Per Cent was already sitting in the lounge looking like an overfed cat waiting for his next helping of cream.

'Good evening,' said Ross as he joined him, taking a seat in one of the gold chairs that were scattered around the room. 'The Taoiseach has given me the go-ahead in principle, but asked me to call him after I've seen the Minister.'

'I've already seen Prince Sharif,' said Khalil, 'and he'll be free to see you at eleven o'clock on Monday morning. Why don't I join you for breakfast on Monday and then I can take you to his office?'

The way you took Simon Hartley to the Minister's office,

thought Ross, while Declan O'Reilly said, 'How did he react to my proposal?'

'As long as you accept that the cost per barrel will always be based on the daily spot price in the *Wall Street Journal* that morning, plus ten per cent, he can't see any problems,' said Khalil, as a glass of sparkling water was placed by Ross's side.

'When you next come to Ireland, Hani, I'll have to introduce you to an old friend of mine, Mr Jameson, who sadly couldn't get a visa.'

'Fear not,' said Khalil, 'he has several relations over here who can be found in a club I only take special friends to, but not before the sun has set. After dinner, perhaps . . .'

'You're a man after my own heart,' said Ross, raising his glass – another bonus point for the whizz kid at the Foreign Office. 'Are you currently involved in any other deals?' Ross asked casually.

'You've probably heard about a major arms deal that's due to be signed fairly shortly.'

'Who hasn't?' said Ross, tapping the newspaper in front of him. 'Three billion is involved, if you're to believe the *Wall Street Journal.*'

'Not to mention an agent's fee of fifteen per cent,' said Khalil. 'So you got off lightly.'

A piece of information Mr Trevelyan would be interested to hear about.

'But the *Journal* suggests the deal hasn't yet been signed.'

'All but,' said Khalil, clearly enjoying himself.

'Congratulations,' said Ross.

Both men raised their glasses of water.

• • •

Following a lengthy dinner and several glasses of sparkling water, they left the hotel to find a silver-grey Phantom awaiting them, driver in full livery. In Riyadh, only foreigners give a Rolls-Royce a second look.

'I'm parched,' said Ross as they climbed in the back.

'Fear not,' said Khalil, 'your friend Jameson is nearby.'

'How is that possible?' asked Ross innocently as the car moved off, 'remembering how strictly Sharia customs are observed and, indeed, that breaking the laws on alcohol is a punishable offence, that would end you up in jail.'

'A gated compound has been built on the outskirts of the city to cater for foreigners' needs. It's treated like an embassy, so you wouldn't even know you were in Saudi.'

'So, none of the locals will be joining us tonight?'

'Several of them – not that you'd notice, because they will be wearing suits tailored in Savile Row with shirts from Jermyn Street, to make sure no one can identify which country they come from.'

'It's good of you to take pity on me,' said Ross.

'It's all part of the service, my friend,' said Khalil as the car came to a halt in front of a barrier, which was immediately raised after one look in the back.

Khalil accompanied his guest into the mansion, and it quickly became clear he was a favoured customer, as every member of staff bowed low as he passed and greeted him with 'Good evening, sir.'

Ross followed Khalil into a spacious lounge where he headed straight for the bar and two empty stools that were clearly reserved for him. He didn't have to order a drink, as the barman began to pour a dark liquid from an unlabelled bottle that, from its shape, could only have been Vat 69.

Khalil slipped the barman a hundred-dollar bill as Ross took his place on the vacant stool. He only took a sip of his drink, as he needed to remain sober, even if later he would appear to be the clichéd drunken Irishman; a role he'd performed so many times in the past that he wouldn't need to rehearse.

Ross began to scan the room, which was decorated with European paintings, stylish furniture and beautiful women. While Khalil continued to boast about his latest enterprises, Ross gave the impression of listening intently, while his eyes slowly circled the room for a second time. He first checked every one of the girls: all foreign, stylish and stunning. Several of them were entertaining potential customers, while the others smiled at every man who entered the room. But the one person Ross was looking for was nowhere to be seen.

Ross's eyes settled on a man seated at the far end of the bar and noticed he was the only person drinking water. When they'd first entered the club, he'd acknowledged Khalil with a slight nod, confirming he was on the payroll.

During the next hour, Ross didn't interrupt Khalil's monologue, when he learnt about a new luxury five-star hotel, a state-of-the-art shopping mall, and the latest six-lane highway that had all been given the green light; for all of which the Lebanese fixer claimed he was representing the relevant 'Minister'.

Although the whisky bottle was now half-empty, Ross was only on his second glass, and beginning to fear it was going to be a wasted evening.

He continued to sip his whisky as different girls disappeared upstairs, accompanied by different men, only to reappear an hour later in search of new punters.

Ross kept up a running commentary about the under-the-table deals he was involved in back home and what his new friend Hani could expect in return should he ever visit Dublin.

He could see Hani was warming to the idea. Fifteen per cent was regularly mentioned.

After another hour of listening to Khalil's opinion on everything from Bill Clinton's Oval Office antics to why gold prices were so high, Ross was more than ready to return to his hotel and come back again tomorrow evening in the hope Avril would be working. What made it more difficult was he couldn't mention her name, or even touch on the subject of Hartley, for fear his cover would be blown.

'I think I'll call it a day,' said Ross, yawning.

'Wouldn't you like to spend an hour or two with one of the girls before you leave?'

'No, thank you,' said Ross, not even bothering to look around the room.

'Just one for the road, perhaps,' suggested Khalil as a door on the far side of the room opened and in walked the woman he'd crossed a continent to meet.

Ross recognized Avril immediately from her photographs in the confidential Foreign Office file. Her most recent customer gave her a warm embrace before departing.

'That one could make me change my mind,' said Ross, as he continued to look at Avril. He turned back to see Khalil staring at him quizzically. Ross immediately realized he'd reacted too hastily, and quickly tried to recover. 'But on the other hand . . .' he said, looking at another girl on the other side of the room, and giving her a warm smile.

She returned his smile.

'I think you'll find your first choice could prove more profitable for both of us,' said Khalil, taking Ross by surprise. 'However, be warned, if Avril thinks you're a friend of mine, she might not be willing to go with you. But if she does, you could do me a favour.'

'What kind of favour?' asked Ross, taking advantage of a retreating enemy.

'Let's just say you would be doing me a great service that would not only guarantee you getting the contract, but I'd also be willing to split my commission with you.'

Ross suddenly realized just how desperate Khalil was to get Avril singing from the same hymn sheet before Hartley appeared in court.

'I'll do anything I can to help, my friend,' said Ross, playing the con man at his own game.

'You won't regret it,' said Khalil, sounding genuine for the first time. 'But first, you'll have to find out if she'll agree to go back to your hotel.'

'I'll do my best,' said Ross, equally genuinely. He slipped off his stool and made his way slowly across the room, to be greeted with a frosty welcome when he sat down on the cramped sofa next to Avril.

'I won't have anything to do with anyone who's a friend of that man,' were Avril's opening words, not even looking at Ross.

'Understandably,' he said, 'and I can promise you I feel exactly the same way about Khalil as you do. So just smile and treat me like a normal customer, because I need to ask some questions.' Avril produced a false smile but didn't look convinced, as Ross continued, his lips hardly moving. 'I'm aware you recently tried to leave the country, but the authorities confiscated your passport. If that's correct, just nod or shake your head.'

Avril nodded as a waiter appeared carrying a bottle of champagne with two long-stemmed crystal flutes on a silver tray. Ross waited for him to pour them both a glass and leave, but just as he was about to speak again, she took him by surprise. 'But if you're with Hani Khalil, why should I believe a word you say?' she asked, the smile no longer in place.

'He thinks I'm trying to close an oil deal on behalf of the Irish government and is hoping to represent me, whereas in fact I'm only here to help you get back to England.'

'I don't have a passport,' she reminded him.

'I've already sorted that problem,' said Ross. She still didn't look convinced, but this time didn't interrupt. 'First, I need to know if you still *want* to go back to England?'

'That won't be possible until the arms deal has been settled one way or the other. Just look around and you'll see how carefully we're being watched. Ahmed has eyes and ears everywhere, so you can't afford to make the slightest mistake.'

Ross was beginning to realize why Avril had become such an intractable problem for Khalil.

'I can make it happen,' said Ross, 'but not unless you're able to pretend I'm a punter and are willing to come back to my hotel.'

'If I agree,' said Avril with an exaggerated smile, 'be warned, that goon at the end of the bar will never be more than a few paces behind.' She paused. 'It's a long story.'

'I know the story,' said Ross, 'and we can take advantage of it, but only if you'll trust me.'

'If I do,' said Avril, 'you'll have to pay the barman five hundred dollars. The only thing that talks in this place is cash.'

'Par for the course,' said Ross, returning her smile.

'And it will help speed things up if you add an extra hundred – that's assuming the Foreign Office can afford me.' The smile turned into a grin.

'Then let's give it a try, shall we?' said Ross. He got up

and made his way slowly back to the bar, aware that several eyes were following him.

'Did she turn you down?' said Khalil, looking disappointed.

'No. She's agreed to come back to my hotel and spend the night, but she doesn't come cheap!'

'Did she say anything about me?' asked Khalil, still sounding anxious.

'She doesn't like you, but I said I didn't either.' Khalil grinned. 'Though it's still going to cost me five hundred dollars.'

'You'll have to pay,' said Khalil, 'otherwise she'll become suspicious.'

Ross took out his wallet, extracted six hundred-dollar bills and handed them to the barman. He looked forward to explaining the entry on his expenses sheet. The Hawk wouldn't question it, but he suspected Mr Trevelyan would want a detailed breakdown.

The barman placed five hundred dollars in the till, and pocketed the other hundred.

'Once you get back to your suite,' said Khalil, 'fuck her once if you want to, but then lock her in the bathroom, come down to the lobby and leave the rest to us.'

Did Khalil think the Irish were that green? Perhaps he really did believe money could buy anything, so he continued to play along. 'And what exactly can I expect in return?' asked Ross, using the only language Khalil understood.

'Not only will you get your contract, my friend, but I'll give you two per cent of my commission, which will make you a very rich man.'

Ross glanced at the goon on the other end of the bar who'd never taken his eyes off them, well aware exactly what Khalil had planned for Avril. 'Five per cent,' he said, once again calling the tune.

Khalil immediately nodded, which only confirmed just how desperate he was.

'Take my car,' said Khalil. 'Tell the driver to come back once he's dropped you off.'

Ross turned and nodded to Avril, who drained her glass of champagne before she got up and strolled across to join him. She didn't once look at Khalil.

'Shall we go?' was all she said, linking her arm in his while accompanying Ross towards the door.

Ross glanced back to see Khalil talking to the man who had been seated at the other end of the bar.

As they left the club, he said, 'Don't say anything while we're in the car, because you can be sure Khalil's driver will be listening to every word and will be reporting back to his master.'

'Do I look that stupid?' said Avril as she climbed into the back of the Rolls.

'The Palace Hotel,' slurred Ross, 'and your boss wants you to go back and pick him up once you've dropped us off.'

'Yes, sir.'

On the journey back to the hotel, Ross gave a convincing performance whenever the driver glanced in his rear-view mirror and observed the two of them embracing each other.

When they were dropped off outside the Palace Hotel, Ross parted with another hundred-dollar bill for which he received a salute and 'Have a good night, sir.'

As soon as they entered the hotel, Ross went straight across to the concierge desk and quickly briefed Jim on what he needed. Jim nodded from time to time, until he spotted one of Khalil's men coming through the swing doors. It was the same man who had been sitting at the other end of the bar in the Overseas Club.

'A car will be waiting for you,' whispered Jim, as Khalil's man walked past, adding, 'Have a good night, sir.'

'Thank you,' said Ross, before walking across to join Avril, who was standing by the lifts with her back to the henchman.

'Don't look back,' she warned him. 'Salim – Khalil's thug – is hanging around in the lobby and he hasn't taken his eyes off you.'

'I'm well aware of that,' said Ross as they stepped into an empty lift. Neither of them spoke again until the doors had closed.

'I don't usually ask for my client's name,' said Avril as the lift began to move, 'but in your case . . .'

'Declan O'Reilly,' said Ross, 'and you're my wife.'

'Forgive me for mentioning this, Mr O'Reilly, but I don't remember you proposing to me.'

'That's possibly because I'm already accounted for.'

'Most of my best clients are married men,' said Avril as the lift reached the top floor and the doors slid open. 'So, what are you hoping to get for your five hundred dollars?'

'Just follow my instructions to the letter, Mrs O'Reilly, and don't waste time asking any questions.'

Ross got out of the lift and headed straight for the Presidential Suite with Avril a pace behind. He opened the door and was switching on all the lights when the phone began to ring. He picked it up, well aware who would be on the other end of the line.

• • •

Salim stood in the lobby and watched the numbers rise on the display panel as O'Reilly's lift progressed to the top floor without stopping. He then walked across and waited for the next available lift. When it arrived, he joined several other guests. While one man swiped his pass card, Salim quickly pressed the button for the Executive Suites. The lift stopped on the seventh, ninth, fourteenth and twenty-first floors as it continued its slow progress to the summit. Salim began to curse out loud.

• • •

'Khalil's man has just got into a packed lift,' said Jim, 'so you've got about a minute, a minute and a half at the most.'

'Understood,' said Ross, quickly replacing the receiver. 'We have to move and move quickly,' he said, grabbing Avril by the arm before heading back towards the door. He left all the lights on and switched the card on the doorknob to Do Not Disturb.

Once they were in the corridor, he began to run towards the lifts. He jabbed the Down button several times, aware that most of his ninety seconds were already up.

• • •

Salim waited as the lift progressed, opening on twenty-one, twenty-three, twenty-five . . . When he reached the twenty-seventh floor, one door opened, and another closed.

Salim stepped out of the lift and walked cautiously across to the Presidential Suite. The first thing he saw was a narrow strip of light shining from under the door and the Do Not Disturb sign hanging from the knob. He retreated to the far end of the corridor, took out his mobile phone and began to dial.

• • •

When the lift reached the ground floor, Mr and Mrs O'Reilly stepped out and headed straight for the main entrance. They found Jim standing outside on the pavement looking as if he was hailing a taxi. When a car drew up, they both slipped into the back without a word passing between them. Ross handed Jim a tip to make it look as if he was a normal customer.

'Thank you, sir,' said Jim as he closed the car door, and the driver shot off, not needing to be told where his passengers wanted to go. Once the car was out of sight, Jim returned to the front desk and made a call. He woke the Ambassador.

• • •

Khalil picked up the phone in his car.

'They're both in the Presidential Suite,' said Salim, unaware that Mr and Mrs O'Reilly were heading towards the airport. 'I'll call you the moment O'Reilly comes back out.'

'That's when you move in. Once you've dealt with the girl, go straight back to the club, but make sure the "Do Not Disturb" sign remains on the door, so they won't find her body until a maid comes in the morning.'

'What do I say if anyone asks when I last saw her?'

'No one's going to ask you anything, because you never left the club. And in any case, the police and hotel management won't want to advertise the fact they found a hooker with her throat slit in the Presidential Suite, especially that particular hooker.'

'And O'Reilly?'

'We've agreed to meet in the lobby, and I won't leave him in any doubt why he needs to be on the first plane back to Dublin.'

'And if they come back out together?' asked Salim.

'Then my next call will be to the Chief of Police.'

• • •

As the car sped along the King Salman Highway, Ross didn't need to look across at Avril to know her usual self-composed front had been replaced by a mask of apprehension. He reached across and squeezed her hand, and she gave him a smile never afforded to a customer.

As they approached King Khalid Airport, they were greeted by a swarm of passengers heading into the concourse, and although the sun had not yet risen, from the size of the crowd one might have thought it was the middle of the day.

The driver came to a halt outside International Departures and handed his passenger two tickets.

Mr Declan O'Reilly stepped out onto the pavement and waited for his wife to join him.

• • •

When Khalil's driver dropped him off at the Palace Hotel a few minutes later, he walked straight into the hotel and began to look for O'Reilly, who had agreed to meet him in the lobby, but there was no sign of the Irishman. He assumed he was getting his money's worth.

On the other side of the lobby, Jim made his second call to the embassy. After briefing the Ambassador, never raising his voice, he put down the phone while keeping a close eye on Khalil, who was speaking animatedly on his mobile along with accompanying hand movements resembling an out-of-control conductor.

'Where the hell is he?' he demanded. 'Because he isn't in the lobby and it can't have taken him that long.'

'He hasn't come back out of his suite yet,' said Salim. 'Do you want me to break in and find out what's going on?'

'Not yet. Don't move until I call you.' Khalil turned off his phone and headed for reception.

'How can I help you, sir?' asked the girl behind the counter.

'Put me through to Mr Declan O'Reilly in the Presidential Suite.'

'You do realize it's two o'clock in the morning, sir,' said the receptionist.

'I do,' said Khalil, 'but it's an emergency. Mr O'Reilly's mother has been taken to hospital and he needs to catch the first plane back to Dublin.'

'I'll put you straight through, sir.'

Khalil waited as the phone continued to ring and ring, until finally the receptionist said, 'I'm sorry, sir, but no one seems to be answering. But if you leave me a message, along with your name, I'll get one of the porters to slip a note under his door immediately.'

Khalil turned his back on her and began dialling.

'Who's waking me at this ungodly hour?' demanded the Chief of Police.

• • •

Mr and Mrs O'Reilly ran into the concourse and headed straight for the British Airways desk.

'How may I help you, sir?' asked the booking clerk.

'I'd like two business-class tickets for your flight to Heathrow,' said Ross, looking up at the departure board.

The booking clerk began tapping away. 'I'm afraid business

---

class is sold out, sir, but I do have a couple of vacant seats in first class.'

Ross thought about Mr Trevelyan, but only for a moment, before he handed over his credit card and two passports. He looked around to check if anyone in uniform was entering the terminal. Several cabin crew, but no sign of a policeman.

The clerk handed back their passports along with two first-class tickets. 'Thank you, Mr Hogan,' she said. 'Your flight has just begun boarding.'

'Thank you,' replied Ross, his Irish accent more pronounced. They both left the desk and quickly headed for Departures.

The officer at passport control only glanced at both passports before stamping them. 'You'd better hurry, Mr O'Reilly,' he said. 'Your flight will be departing in a few minutes' time.'

• • •

The Chief of Police's car came to a skidding halt outside the entrance to the airport. He jumped out of his car with Khalil a yard behind and ran into Departures. He went straight to the British Airways desk.

Slightly out of breath, the Chief asked, 'Have you booked two passengers on your flight to Heathrow during the last hour?'

'Several,' replied the booking clerk. 'Do you have a name?'

'O'Reilly,' said Hani Khalil, who had caught up with him.

'No one has booked in with that name,' she confirmed.

'Tall man, around forty, accompanied by a good-looking blonde in her early thirties,' said Khalil. 'The man has an Irish accent.'

'Ah yes, I do remember them. Mr and Mrs Hogan,' said the booking clerk, once again checking her computer. 'They only just made it.'

'That has to be them,' said the Chief.

'They were among the last passengers to book in,' said the clerk, 'first class.' She glanced up at the departure board. 'But the gate for that flight has already closed.'

'Get me air traffic control now,' barked the Chief.

• • •

Ross and Avril made it to the check-in desk a few minutes before the gate was closed. They were the last to enter the aircraft and were quickly taken to their places at the front.

Ross remained calm as he fastened his seat belt, while Avril's eyes never left the open door, and she didn't begin to relax until it was slammed shut.

A member of the cabin crew took them through the safety procedures on this particular aircraft, first in Arabic, then in French, then in English, which Avril thought would never come to an end.

At last, the stewardess returned to her seat at the front of the plane and fastened her seat belt as the cabin lights were dimmed.

Moments later, the four massive engines began to whirl, becoming faster and faster as they prepared to take off.

• • •

Suddenly, without warning, the engines began to slow down, before finally stopping.

'This is your captain speaking,' announced a voice from the flight deck. 'I'm sorry to inform you that there will be a slight delay,' he added without explanation.

A groan went up throughout the cabin when the captain

appeared and gave the purser an order to open the cabin door.

No sooner had he pulled it open than the Chief of Police and Khalil marched in.

'Do you have a Mr and Mrs Hogan on board?' he demanded.

The purser checked his manifest. 'No, sir,' he replied. 'However, they were no-shows, and as they didn't have any luggage on board, we were given clearance to take off.'

The Chief of Police sighed. He turned to Khalil and said, 'You underestimated Hogan.'

Khalil let out a string of invective, before he said, 'Then they must both still be somewhere in the airport.'

'I doubt it,' said the Chief, looking out of the cabin window to see an Air France plane gathering speed on the runway before taking off.

'Get them to turn back,' shouted Khalil.

'Only the Minister can authorize that,' said the Chief calmly, 'and if you want to wake him, be my guest.'

The plane disappeared into the clouds.

CHAPTER 7

'WE'RE DOING *WHAT*?' SAID AVRIL, as they left the terminal at Heathrow and walked out onto the pavement.

'Taking a coach to Victoria,' replied Ross.

'You must be joking,' she said. 'You pay six hundred dollars not to sleep with me, we fly back to London via Paris first class, and now you expect me to take a coach to Victoria? Have you run out of money?'

'Not quite,' said Ross.

'There has to be a simple explanation.'

'What I like about you,' said Ross, 'is how quickly you catch on.'

'And what I most like about you, Mr Hogan, is one can never be sure what to expect next.' Avril reluctantly chased after Ross as he followed the signs for coaches.

'We could still grab a taxi,' said Avril, as they passed the queue at the rank, but Ross ignored her as he strode past them, not stopping until he reached a coach that was being boarded by a long line of waiting passengers.

Just as they reached the end of the queue, a second bus appeared and parked behind the first.

Ross climbed onto the second bus as the queue continued to board the first.

'We get to Victoria quicker on the first one,' suggested Avril.

No sooner had Ross and Avril climbed aboard than the doors closed firmly shut and the coach moved off.

'Hi Danny,' said Ross to the driver, before he led his charge to the back, where two men Avril didn't recognize stood up and introduced themselves.

'Jack Hawksby,' said the Commander, 'and this is my colleague, William Warwick.'

'When you've been in my profession for as long as I have,' said Avril, as she shook hands with both of them, 'you know a policeman when you see one. So, am I about to be arrested, or released with a caution?'

'Neither,' said the Commander, 'but we were rather hoping you might consider joining our team.'

'That's a first,' said Avril. 'Do I have a choice?'

'Avril,' said Ross, 'we're on your side, but while Simon Hartley is still in prison and Khalil stands to make a fortune if the French land the arms deal, your life could be in danger even though you're back home.'

'So what can I do to help?' said Avril, sounding serious for the first time.

'Perhaps we could start by asking you a few questions,' said William as the coach moved onto the motorway.

'Of course,' said Avril.

William asked his first question. 'Were you in the Overseas Club on the night Paolo Conti was murdered?'

'I most certainly was,' Avril replied without hesitation. 'In fact, I was sitting next to Conti at the time.'

'And was it Simon Hartley who literally put the knife in?'

'No, Hartley was seated at the other end of the bar having a drink with Khalil.'

'Then who did kill Conti?'

Avril hesitated for some time before she said, 'Prince Ahmed bin Majid, the second son of the Minister of Defence.'

'And if the case were to come to court, would you be willing to confirm that, under oath?'

She hesitated even longer, before saying, 'Yes, I would.'

'Thank you,' said the Commander.

'It's the least I can do,' said Avril, looking directly at Ross.

'And would you be willing to sign a statement to that effect?' asked William as the coach left the motorway and joined the Hammersmith flyover.

'Yes,' she whispered, almost indiscernibly.

William opened his briefcase and extracted a single sheet of paper which he handed across to Avril.

As she read the document, her hand began to tremble. 'It's my death warrant,' she said, still shaking.

'We're not going to allow anything to happen to you,' said William calmly. 'In fact, until Hartley is released, and especially while the Prince is in London, we'll have a team of trained detectives watching you night and day, with Ross in charge of the whole operation.'

'Couldn't Ross just kill Ahmed when he's in London?' suggested Avril, without any suggestion of irony.

'I'd like nothing more,' said Ross, 'but I don't think the Foreign Office would approve, while there's the slightest chance of closing the arms deal and getting Simon Hartley home safely.'

'So what do you have planned for me now?' asked Avril.

'We'd like you to stay out of harm's way while the Saudi delegation is in London, as we think it's just possible Prince Ahmed might come looking for you.'

'That shouldn't be a problem,' said Avril, 'as I have absolutely no desire to see that man again.'

'It should only be for a couple of weeks, three at the most,' said the Hawk, 'then you can go back to work.'

'Nicely put, Commander, if I may say so,' said Avril, 'but that could change when I return to Riyadh, appear in court and name Ahmed as the murderer.'

'I think you'll find Hartley will have been released long before then,' said William, as he handed her a pen.

She read the statement a second time before finally signing it above the name, Jenny Prescott.

'So what next?' asked Avril, as the coach turned right and continued on down the Earl's Court Road, while it made its way towards Westminster.

'Once we reach Whitehall,' said William, 'we can drive you wherever you like. Is there somewhere safe you can stay?'

'With my mother in Putney until I can find somewhere to rent.'

William nodded. 'It might be wise, given the circumstances, if you were to avoid letting your mother know about our agreement.'

'That shouldn't prove too difficult,' said Avril. 'She doesn't even know what I do for a living, so I certainly won't be telling her I'm mixed up with the police, the Foreign Office and a rather dubious foreign Prince.'

'How have you explained what you were doing in Riyadh?' asked the Commander.

'I was working as a personal assistant for the director of an oil company.'

'So why are you coming home?' pressed William.

Avril didn't answer immediately. 'It became a little too personal, so when his wife found out, I got the sack.'

The three men laughed.

'However,' she continued, 'I think I might tell her I've met a rather dishy man from Dublin called Declan O'Reilly who's trying to close an oil deal in Saudi. Nothing will please an old-fashioned Irish Catholic mother like mine more than the thought I might marry a fellow countryman.'

The Commander smiled. 'I think you'll find Inspector Hogan has other plans.'

'Lucky girl,' said Avril, as they drove around Parliament Square and came to a halt outside the Foreign Office.

The four of them climbed off the coach to find a car parked on a double yellow line waiting for them. William opened the back door to allow Avril to get in, but not before she'd kissed Ross on both cheeks.

'Some lady that,' said the Commander as the car drove off. 'But for now, Ross, you'd better report to Mr Trevelyan while we make our way back to the Yard. However, once he's finished with you, report to my office.'

'But how can you be sure which side I'm on?' Ross asked the Hawk, trying to keep a straight face.

'Don't forget,' said the Hawk, 'I've met Mr Trevelyan and he's not your type.'

'See you later, sir,' said Ross, before he disappeared into the Foreign Office.

'Heaven help us if Ross were working for the other side,' said the Commander, as the two of them headed back to Scotland Yard.

• • •

At her country home in Bucklebury, Lady Hartley sat at her writing desk in the corner of the drawing room. She'd spent the morning replying to strangers' letters, most of which were messages of condolence following her husband's death. Several mentioned Simon's plight, with one saying, 'Your son is a murderer and deserves to be hanged. I hope he rots in hell.'

The last letter she considered was from her bank manager, enclosing a copy of her latest statement. The account was in credit for a few thousand pounds, because her husband never left her short, but a few thousand pounds was not enough to cover the expenses of a funeral and other monthly bills that her husband would normally have dealt with. He had once told her that the eleventh commandment would have been 'thou shalt not be overdrawn', and she suspected Moses would have agreed with him. However, neither Moses nor he were on hand now to advise her. She had never discussed these problems with her husband in the past as he had assured her that Simon had it under control. Her husband couldn't possibly have foreseen that their son would end up in a foreign jail, leaving her to deal with day to day problems until he was released, or—

Her thoughts were interrupted by the phone ringing. She put down the bank manager's letter and picked up the phone.

'Good morning, Lady Hartley,' said a voice she didn't recognize. 'My name is Bernard Anscombe, and I'm the British Ambassador in Riyadh.'

'How kind of you to call, Sir Bernard,' said Lady Hartley. She had her first question already prepared in case someone from the Foreign Office rang. 'Have you been able to visit my son?'

'I managed to see him a couple of days ago,' the Ambassador replied, 'and can report that he's bearing up well.'

'But he's been charged with murder,' she said, trying to

remain calm, 'and I can assure you, Ambassador, Simon wouldn't harm a fly.'

In the past when he'd had to call mothers whose sons had ended up in prison, Sir Bernard had been only too aware they were guilty of the crime they'd been charged with, and there was little he or anyone else could do to reassure them. However, on this occasion, he didn't doubt his fellow countryman was innocent. He nevertheless measured his words carefully. 'I have spoken to the Chief of Police and can assure you we have made our position clear.'

'The Saudis still hang people for murder,' the distraught mother reminded him.

'I feel confident it won't come to that, Lady Hartley,' was about as far as protocol allowed the seasoned diplomat to go.

'Is he even aware his father has died?' she said, desperation creeping back into her voice.

'I did tell him,' said the Ambassador, 'but he seemed to be more worried about how you are coping. He told me you should read your husband's will carefully and then take legal advice. Meanwhile, I won't rest until your son has been released. I'll be calling your daughter-in-law next, and be assured I will keep you both regularly informed of what's happening this end.'

'That's kind of you, Sir Bernard.'

She was still clinging onto the phone long after the Ambassador had rung off. She thought about his advice, put down the phone and began to search for the card of the QC who'd come to the funeral and had offered to waive his fee because he admired her husband so much. He had come over as far more impressive than her local solicitor. When she finally found the card, she picked up the phone and dialled his number.

'Mr Booth Watson's chambers,' announced a voice on the other end of the line.

'I need to speak to the head of chambers, please,' she said.

'May I ask who's calling?'

'Lady Hartley.'

'I'll put you straight through.'

• • •

'I have to admit,' said Trevelyan, after Ross had delivered his report for the second time that morning, 'you did well, even though you're not one of us.'

'Thank you, sir,' said Ross, 'for the backhanded compliment.'

Trevelyan ignored the riposte and asked, 'Where's Ms Dubois at the present time?'

'Jenny Prescott is staying with her mother in Putney.'

'Let's keep it that way,' said Trevelyan. 'Don't forget the Saudi Defence Minister and his son, Prince Ahmed, will be visiting London next month, and the last thing we need is a diplomatic incident.'

'Heaven forbid!' said Ross.

'As Chief Superintendent Warwick will be in charge of security during the Minister's visit, perhaps I could suggest you take a well-earned holiday.'

'How very kind of you, sir,' said Ross, not reminding him he'd just had a holiday and had no intention of taking another one – not while Prince Ahmed was in the country.

'You'll be pleased to hear, Hogan, that I have sent a glowing report to Commander Hawksby on the way you conducted yourself while you were in Riyadh. Mind you, your expenses have raised a few eyebrows.'

'Didn't want to risk three billion for the sake of a miserly few dollars, sir,' said Ross, delivering a well-prepared riposte.

'I hope you got value for money,' said Trevelyan, without any suggestion of irony, and before Ross could respond, he added, 'but should we fail to pull off the arms deal and it ends up going to the French, we may have to rely on Ms Dubois's sworn testimony as to what really happened in the club that night, if we're to make sure that the Saudis are left with no choice but to release Hartley.'

'I think she'd be even happier if Prince Ahmed were to end up in jail, where he belongs,' said Ross, not mentioning Avril's heartfelt suggestion that he should murder him.

'That's not going to happen,' said Trevelyan, 'at least not while there's the slightest chance we could still be awarded the arms contract.'

'What if the French were to get the contract and Hartley isn't released?'

'We may well be calling on your particular skills once again, Inspector,' admitted Trevelyan, 'but until then, just make sure she doesn't go anywhere near the Defence Minister's son while he's in England. We'll have quite enough on our hands with the well-organised protests that are certain to take place during the visit. Is that understood, Hogan?'

'Yes, sir,' said Ross, who wanted to add 'three bags full, sir', but somehow restrained himself.

• • •

Once Ross had left the Foreign Office, he crossed Whitehall and headed for Scotland Yard. Once he'd entered the building he ran up the stairs to the third floor and knocked on the Commander's door.

'Come,' said a voice.

'You were right,' said Ross as he entered the Hawk's office. 'Trevelyan's not my sort of man.'

'Well, we're going to have to rub along with him during the next few weeks,' said the Hawk, 'while Avril is still in danger.'

'Perhaps we should exchange Trevelyan for Hartley,' said Ross, as William walked in and joined them.

'Did you learn anything worthwhile from the ubiquitous mandarin?' he asked.

'Not a lot,' admitted Ross. 'I don't belong to the right clubs for him to confide in me. But what I can tell you is the Foreign Office have their knickers in a twist about the upcoming visit of the Saudi Minister of Defence and are particularly worried about any protests that might take place if Prince Ahmed shows his face while Hartley is still in jail.'

'And so they should be,' said the Hawk, 'as the protestors will be well prepared and certain to park themselves outside Number Ten, and, frankly, I can't blame them.'

'I've already briefed my team on what to expect,' said William, 'and of course we'll have the Territorial Support Group on standby in Whitehall Court, should it get out of control.'

'Let's hope that won't be necessary,' said the Hawk. 'And by the way, Ross, congratulations on a job well done. But perhaps you ought to go home now and let Alice and Jojo know you've returned safely – and take tomorrow off.' He paused. 'That's an order.'

Ross didn't need much encouragement and, once he'd completed his report, he left the two of them to discuss the implications of the Saudi visit and what could go wrong.

Once Ross had left the building, he headed to St James's

Park, where he caught a tube to Sloane Square, hoping to get home before Jojo had gone to bed.

• • •

'Can I come to the Rembrandt unveiling?' asked Jojo, who was sitting on the floor surrounded by angels.

'Please,' said Alice.

'Please,' repeated Jojo.

'Of course you can. In fact, I think you'll find Beth is going to ask you to do something rather special that evening.'

'Like what?' demanded Jojo.

'You have been chosen to present a bouquet of roses to the Countess of Wessex when she visits the museum to unveil the Rembrandt.'

Jojo began leaping up and down, only stopping when she heard the front door open. She ran out of the room and screamed with delight when she saw her father walking towards her. She leapt on him and said, 'Hi, Dad. Have you heard the news?'

'No, but I have a feeling you're about to tell me,' said Ross, as they walked into the front room together, where Ross got a welcome-home kiss and a second hug from Alice.

'I've been chosen to present the Countess with a bouquet when she visits the Fitzmolean to unveil the *Angel*.'

'Your angel?' said Ross, looking down to see the floor was covered in his daughter's drawings.

'No, silly,' said Jojo, 'Rembrandt's Angel. And I'll need a new dress.'

'Of course you will,' said Ross, 'and as I've got the day off tomorrow, we can go shopping together.'

'Thank you, Dad,' said Jojo, who bent down, selected an angel and gave it to her father.

113

'I'll frame it,' said Ross, 'and hang it in my office at Scotland Yard.'

'Not many angels there,' said Alice, as Jojo gathered up the rest of the drawings. 'Now, time for you to go to bed, young lady. It's way past your bedtime.'

'Will you promise to come and see me when I present the bouquet to the Countess?' she asked, looking up at her father.

'Of course I will,' said Ross, once again taking his daughter in his arms.

'And will you come and read to me once I'm in bed?'

Jojo grinned, before leaving the room, humming a tune neither of them recognized.

'So you weren't arrested after all,' said Alice once the door had closed.

'No, but it was a close-run thing,' admitted Ross.

'And the girl you told me about before you left?'

'Is safely back in London and staying with her mother. But as I'm in charge of her protection, I can only hope you haven't got a lot planned for me during the next couple of months.'

'Nothing of any real importance, but don't forget you've now promised your daughter you won't miss the unveiling of the Rembrandt.'

'Of course I won't,' said Ross, as Alice joined him on the sofa.

'And thank you for agreeing to help her choose a dress for the occasion. She couldn't hide how happy she is to have you back.' She paused. 'And so am I.'

'Me too,' admitted Ross, as he took Alice in his arms and began to kiss her at first gently, and then more passionately. He was unbuttoning Alice's blouse when a voice behind them said, 'You two are gross.'

• • •

The first thing Beth did when William returned home that night was to ask if Ross had got back in one piece.

'Two pieces,' said William, without explanation.

'I won't ask you where he was, or what he was up to,' said Beth, 'not least because I know you won't tell me.'

'All I can say,' said William, 'is that Ross solved one problem but created another – one that we may not be able to sort out for some time.'

'Not until Hartley is released from prison,' suggested Beth, 'and Prince Ahmed returns to Saudi, also in one piece.'

'How do you know . . .?' began William.

'I've often advised you to read *The Guardian* and not simply rely on the *Daily Mail* for your news.'

'What I can tell you,' said William, 'is there's a story in the *Daily Mail* about your friend Christina that I'm fairly confident you won't see in *The Guardian*.' William flicked over a few pages of the *Mail* before he began reading out loud: 'Nigel Dempster claims in his gossip column this morning that – following a whirlwind romance – Mr Wilbur T. Hackensack III has married Mrs Christina Faulkner. Christina, Dempster reminds his readers, is the ex-wife of the fraudster, Miles Faulkner, who will be released from Wormwood Scrubs next week, having served three years. The marriage took place in St Mary's chapel in Monte Carlo. No other guests were present. The happy couple are expected to honeymoon in Venice before returning to London on the Orient Express. *Forbes* magazine claims Hackensack is a billionaire and known in his hometown of Columbus, Ohio as the "Refuse Collector". When asked if his second wife had signed a prenup, the Refuse Collector replied, "When you find the right woman, you don't need to sign a prenup."'

'I do hope she'll be back in time for the unveiling of the Rembrandt,' said Beth.

'It might well be annulled by then,' suggested William.

'I don't think so.' Beth smiled to herself, confident that Christina had found the perfect partner this time.

CHAPTER 8

'Good afternoon, Lady Hartley. What a privilege to see you again,' gushed Booth Watson. 'If you have come to consult me regarding your son's case, I fear there may be little I can do – although I have no doubt of his innocence.'

'How kind of you to say so,' responded Lady Hartley, as Booth Watson ushered his potential client into a comfortable chair by the fire, before taking the seat opposite her. 'But that isn't the reason I needed to seek your advice,' she volunteered.

Booth Watson remained silent.

'I confess, Mr Booth Watson,' said Lady Hartley, 'I had no idea how much the funeral would cost and I fear I've run up a small overdraft, which my husband would not have approved of.'

'But your husband must have left you a small fortune, dear lady,' suggested Booth Watson, hoping he hadn't.

'Small is the correct word,' said Lady Hartley. 'A family

fortune that has been dwindling over the years, not least because my husband considered public service more important than earning a living. MPs, as you will know, Mr Booth Watson, are paid a pittance, and ministers not a lot better, and while my son is away . . .'

Booth Watson took his time pretending to consider the problem before he offered, 'Is it possible you are in possession of something you might be willing to part with to help alleviate the immediate problem?' he asked, knowing exactly what he wanted her to part with.

Lady Hartley hesitated for a moment, before she said in a hushed tone, 'There is a Constable painting that was left to me by my late husband, of the old mill in Bucklebury, but I have no idea what it's worth.'

'I have a client who just *might* be interested in the Constable,' said Booth Watson. 'And if you'd like me to enquire . . .' he added, not sounding too enthusiastic.

'That would be most kind of you, Mr Booth Watson.'

'It's the least I can do, remembering how supportive your husband was over so many years.'

'I need a little time to consider your offer,' she said. 'May I let you know once I decide?'

'But of course, dear lady, there's no hurry,' replied Booth Watson, confident that her son wasn't going to be released for some time. He rose from his place and accompanied his unwitting client to the door.

Lady Hartley left the QC's chambers with a smile on her face.

Once she'd departed, Booth Watson returned to his desk, and began to make detailed notes, which in the fullness of time he would share with Miles, but not before he'd confirmed the value of the Constable, and, equally important, the estimate for a Declaration of Independence, handwritten by Jefferson, were it to come up for auction.

• • •

Miles left Wormwood Scrubs at nine twenty-three the following morning, having signed all the release forms. The only thing in his possession was a copy of Monet's *Water Lilies*, painted and signed by Billy Mumford – with a sketch of Rembrandt's *Jacob Wrestling with the Angel* discreetly hidden beneath the Monet.

'Home, sir?' asked Collins, once he'd placed the painting in the back of the Rolls and returned to the driving seat.

'No,' replied Miles. 'I'll be joining Mr Booth Watson for breakfast at the Savoy.'

'Of course, sir,' said Collins.

As the car moved off, Faulkner didn't once look back. Not one of his habits.

It took Collins forty minutes to drive the boss from the Scrubs to the Savoy. When he drew up outside the hotel, a doorman quickly stepped forward, opened the back door, saluted and said, 'Good morning, Mr Faulkner,' as if he'd never been away.

Miles made his way into the hotel, delighted to find Mario on duty, standing behind his upright desk in the Grill Room. Some things never change, he thought. The maître d' accompanied him to his usual table, where he found Booth Watson was already waiting for him.

'So much to discuss,' said Booth Watson, as he shook hands with his client. 'So where would you like to start?'

'Have you briefed Lamont?' asked Miles, as he sat down.

'Yes,' said Booth Watson, 'and I've arranged for the

ex-Superintendent to come to my chambers this afternoon so you can brief him.'

'Did he seem interested? After all, it's been three years.'

'All I can tell you,' said Booth Watson, 'is that his financial predicament hasn't altered since you last saw him. Don't forget, he had to forfeit part of his pension after Warwick was responsible for his unscheduled departure from the force.'

'How can you be so sure he's short of money?' asked Miles, as a waiter poured him a cup of black coffee.

'Same shiny suit, same creased tie, same well-polished shoes, but down at heel, and his first question was "how much?"'

'Good,' said Miles, 'because I prefer to work with empty stomachs, and I won't be tossing him any scraps unless he delivers.'

'But what exactly will he be expected to deliver?' asked Booth Watson.

Miles took his time briefing his silk, and it quickly became clear to Booth Watson that his client hadn't been idle while he'd been away.

'I've already transferred one thousand pounds to Mumford's account,' said Booth Watson, 'so should I assume the *Angel* is ready to fly?'

'Yes, but not yet ready to join the heavenly host,' said Miles.

'But what's in it for you,' asked Booth Watson, 'if all those present will know within moments they are staring at a fake?'

'But that's the point, BW,' said Miles, 'because once everyone realizes it is a fake, Mrs Warwick will have to resign as director of the Fitzmolean, and I can assure you it won't be to take up a new post as director of Tate.'

'Will that finally be enough for you to move on?' asked Booth Watson, as Mario appeared by their side.

'Far from it,' said Miles. 'I have no intention of moving on until her husband suffers the same fate, and his dream of becoming the Commissioner of the Metropolitan Police turns out to be a nightmare.'

'Would you care to order breakfast, Mr Faulkner?' asked the maître d'.

'Yes, I'll have the full English, Mario,' said Miles, not looking at the menu.

• • •

Simon had been locked up for days – or was it weeks? – since last seeing Sir Bernard. He had no way of judging the passing of time. When the cell door finally opened once again, he looked up to see three prison guards staring down at him.

One of them stepped forward and yanked him off the thin, stinking mattress and dragged him out into the corridor, where he came face to face with the Governor.

'Good morning, Hartley,' he said. 'You'll be pleased to hear we're moving you to cell block A, which only houses murderers, so you should feel at home, among friends.'

'I'm not a murderer,' spat out Simon, 'and you know it.'

'However,' said the Governor, who wasn't in the habit of being interrupted, 'you might not be quite so pleased to learn you'll be sharing your cell with a professional killer,' he added as they led the prisoner up a spiral staircase to the ground floor, one guard in front of him, one behind. 'And by professional, I mean he does it for a living, and you might be surprised by how little he charges.'

Simon would have been sick, had there been anything left in his stomach.

'And something else I feel I ought to let you know before

I introduce you to Sean O'Driscoll. He does enjoy having a cell to himself, and as his last three cellmates have died in their sleep, it might not be wise to doze off.'

Hartley got the message.

'The last piece of information I feel I ought to share with you,' continued the Governor, 'is that O'Driscoll was an IRA group commander, and if there's one thing he hates even more than us lot, it's an Englishman, especially an upper-class one – what he calls a toff. So let's hope you can survive for another couple of months, because that's how long he's got before we execute him in the market square, and if you're still alive then, it could be you who ends up with a cell to yourself.'

Simon watched as one of the guards took his time unlocking three locks before slowly pulling open a heavy door. The other guard threw him inside, and he landed at the feet of a vast bull of a man, who stared down at his new cellmate as if he were his next meal.

'See you in a few weeks' time,' said the Governor, as the door closed, 'but then again, perhaps not.'

Simon looked up at his new cellmate and began to wish he was back in solitary.

CHAPTER 9

ON THE MORNING OF THE unveiling the chairman, board of directors and senior staff stood in a semicircle admiring the drawing for some time before anyone spoke.

'How lucky we are,' said Beth, 'to be able to add such a magnificent example of Rembrandt's work to our collection.'

'Only made possible,' said a recently appointed board member, 'because of the remarkable generosity of an anonymous benefactor.'

'We should raise a glass to them on the night of the unveiling,' suggested Sir Nicholas.

'Perhaps they'll turn up, unable to resist a peep,' volunteered the keeper of pictures.

'Only if they are a patron or a friend,' Beth reminded them, 'otherwise they wouldn't be on the guest list.'

Christina stared at Rembrandt's familiar signature and smiled. How lucky they were to have acquired the drawing as part of the gallery's collection. The provenance of coming from the Duke of Hamilton's estate would leave no one in any doubt it was the original.

'It surely would have amused Rembrandt to know,' suggested Beth, 'that we had to raise a million to buy one of his drawings.'

'Especially when you remember,' said the keeper of pictures, 'that Rembrandt died a bankrupt.'

'Any last-minute news from the palace?' asked Beth.

'Yes,' said Sir Nicholas. 'I had a call from them this morning. HRH's secretary has confirmed she will be attending the opening at 7 p.m., which means of course 6.59.'

'A Dutch master to be unveiled by an English royal,' commented the keeper.

'Right,' said Beth. 'As there's nothing more we can do, I'm off home to change, but we must all be back on parade before seven.'

'Yes, ma'am,' they all said in unison.

• • •

Alan Roberts was standing on the top step of the Fitzmolean patiently waiting. He had received a call earlier that morning, so was expecting them. A van drew up outside the museum and parked a few minutes before five.

Roberts watched as the back door opened and five men dressed in police uniforms jumped out, accompanied by two sniffer dogs, both spaniels.

Alan stepped forward and introduced himself to the sergeant in charge, before leading his little group up the wide staircase to the Rembrandt room on the first floor, where the stage was set for the unveiling later that evening.

On the far wall hung a red velvet curtain with a gold cord attached, waiting to be pulled by Her Royal Highness the Countess of Wessex.

'If you and your team could wait outside and make sure no one enters the gallery while we do our job,' the sergeant said to Alan, 'this shouldn't take too long.'

Alan left them to allow the sniffer dogs to go about their task.

Twelve minutes later, the sergeant reappeared and said, 'All clear, Alan. However, one small problem has arisen, that I feel sure you can help me with.'

'Of course,' said Alan, as he followed him back into the main gallery.

'Where does that corridor lead?' asked the sergeant, pointing to the far side of the room.

'To a fire escape, which is only used in an emergency.'

'And the three lavatories?'

'Are for the use of the general public.'

'Would it be possible, Alan, to lock the ladies' toilet and keep it locked in case HRH needs to use it? It's most unlikely, but just to be on the safe side.'

'Consider it done,' said Alan, who took out his keyring, selected the master key and locked the door. 'And I won't unlock it until the principal guest has left,' he said, with an air of authority.

'Thank you for your cooperation, Alan,' said the sergeant, 'and as our job is done, we'll be on our way.'

Alan led the search party back down the stairs and out onto the street.

'I hope the evening will be a great success,' said the sergeant, as his team climbed into the back of the van with the dogs still wagging their tails.

'How did it go?' asked the driver, when the sergeant joined him in the front.

'Couldn't have gone better – but then, as you predicted, if you look the part, no one questions you.'

'Is the ladies' toilet locked?' asked the former Superintendent, as he switched on the ignition and moved off to join the early evening traffic.

'The head of security will personally make sure it isn't opened again until the Countess has left,' replied the sergeant, as the van came to a halt at the lights. 'He couldn't have been more cooperative.'

'Time to call the boss,' said Lamont. He picked up the phone, and the next voice he heard was Miles Faulkner's.

'Is the ladies' loo locked?' was his only question.

'Yes, it is,' he replied, as the lights turned green. Lamont switched off the phone, turned left and disappeared out of sight.

• • •

'Is everything in place?' asked Booth Watson after Miles had put down the phone.

'Exactly as we planned,' said Miles.

Booth Watson poured himself a drink. 'And no one was suspicious?'

'When five uniformed policemen with sniffer dogs turn up on your doorstep, even the most vigilant security guards fall in line. Lamont even called Roberts in advance to warn him they were on their way.'

'So, when HRH pulls the cord this evening . . .'

• • •

126

'I can't make up my mind what to wear for the unveiling,' said Beth as William stepped out of the shower.

'What's the choice?' he asked as he pulled open his shirt drawer.

'I'm down to the Gucci blue dress with a white collar that I bought in Milan when we were on holiday, or the Armani classic grey suit that Christina gave me.'

'I've always liked the blue dress,' said William, as he buttoned up his shirt.

'But is it the right look for the director of a national gallery when accompanying a member of the royal family?'

'Then it has to be the grey suit,' he said as he pulled on his trousers.

'But don't you think it's a bit dull for such a special occasion?'

'If you say so,' said William as he selected a dark blue suit from the closet, while Beth stood in front of the mirror in her underwear, holding up both outfits.

'How about the red cashmere suit Christina gave you for your birthday?' suggested William.

'I wore it for the board meeting last month.'

'Of course you did,' said William. 'But then there's the yellow jumpsuit I've always liked.'

'Not suitable for royalty,' she announced.

William selected a red silk tie from the rack.

'I think I'll settle for the blue dress.'

'Good idea,' said William as he tied his tie.

'But on the other hand . . .'

'Well, I'm off,' said William, 'but I'll let you know how it went, as soon as I get back.'

'Very funny,' said Beth, as she checked her watch. 'Hell, is it already six o'clock?'

'The grey suit,' said William firmly. 'Not that it matters, because whatever you wear, you'll be the most beautiful woman in the room.'

Beth hung up her grey suit and put on the blue dress. 'Yes, I think you're right,' she said as she looked at herself in the mirror.

'My first choice,' William reminded her as he put on his jacket.

Beth turned around, straightened her husband's tie and said, 'Nice suit, Chief Superintendent.'

'Got it in an M&S sale,' said William. He opened the door for his wife and waited, as she took one last look at herself in the mirror.

•   •   •

The welcoming party, as it was described in the royal briefing notes, consisted of the chairman of the Fitzmolean, Sir Nicholas Fenwick; the museum's director, Dr Beth Warwick; and the chair of the fundraising committee, Mrs Christina Hackensack. They would meet the Countess of Wessex on the steps of the gallery when she arrived at 7 p.m.

Once they'd accompanied Her Royal Highness into the gallery, Beth would introduce the Countess to the greeting party, sometimes known as the line, which would be made up of board members, senior staff and leading benefactors.

After the Countess had been introduced to the line, she would spend a few minutes mingling with the guests before the time came for her to deliver her speech and unveil the Rembrandt drawing. Among the palace's 'dos and don'ts' were clear instructions that she wouldn't eat or drink anything at any time.

Two outriders followed by a shining limousine appeared outside the Fitzmolean at 6.59 p.m. and Her Royal Highness stepped out as the hour chimed. After she'd had a short chat with the welcoming party, Sir Nicholas led his royal guest into the gallery.

All went to plan, until she reached the end of the line, when Jojo stepped forward and curtsied (she had been practising for several days), before presenting the guest of honour with a bouquet of Countess of Wessex roses.

So far, everything was running smoothly. That was until the Countess asked Jojo, 'Is Beth your mother?'

'No, my mummy died,' Jojo said with an honesty only a child can display. 'But my dad is over there,' she added, pointing to the other side of the room. 'Would you like to meet him?'

'Of course, I would,' replied the Countess, as if it was all part of the master plan.

Jojo took her by her hand and guided the principal guest across the room with the chairman and director following a few yards behind in her wake. Ross and Alice, who had been admiring a Jan Steen, worked out what was happening just in time.

'This is my dad,' said Jojo. 'He's a Detective Inspector with the Metropolitan Police.'

'How nice to meet you, Detective Inspector,' said the Countess.

'It's nice to meet you, ma'am,' said Ross, who bowed.

But before Beth could move her royal guest on, Jojo said, 'And this is Alice. She used to be my schoolteacher and now she lives with us.'

Ross, who was rarely embarrassed, was lost for words.

'I saw you admiring the Jan Steen,' said the Countess,

getting them off the hook. 'He's always been a favourite of mine.'

'The storyteller of Dutch artists, ma'am,' replied Alice, trying to recover, as Ross grabbed his daughter's hand and didn't let go.

The Hawk couldn't stop laughing as Beth led the Countess away and began introducing her to other guests.

'What do you find so amusing, Jack?' asked William's father, as he joined the Commander.

'I never thought I'd live to see the day when Inspector Hogan would be rendered speechless.'

Sir Julian couldn't resist, 'Then perhaps it's time for you to retire, old fellow.'

'Perish the thought,' said the Hawk. 'What would I do all day? I don't have green fingers or play golf, and can't abide those police dramas on afternoon TV, and there are only a certain number of Test matches each year to while away my time. Nevertheless, I have to admit *tempus fugit*. How about you?'

'Lawyers never officially retire,' replied Julian. 'We go on kidding ourselves someone will require our considered opinions on some matter of vital importance, unaware the phone has stopped ringing. Why don't you join me at Lord's for the opening day of the second Test? We can watch Darren Gough try and level the series.'

'Something to look forward to,' said the Hawk, raising his glass. He looked across at Ross, who was chatting to William, while still keeping a firm grip on Jojo's hand.

'How did *they* get invited to the opening?' demanded Ross, glancing across at Faulkner and Booth Watson, who were standing in one corner sipping champagne.

'Try not to forget,' said William, 'Faulkner is considered

by some to be a patron of the arts, having donated a Rubens to the Fitz some years ago.'

'In exchange for a lesser sentence,' Ross reminded him with some feeling.

'Something else you two haven't told me about?' asked Alice.

'Christina's looking particularly radiant this evening,' said William, quickly changing the subject.

Alice looked across to see Christina and Wilbur chatting to the Countess. 'She clearly adores her new husband,' she said.

'And he's a marked improvement on the old one,' commented Ross, without looking in Faulkner's direction.

• • •

'Come across anyone who might assist my latest cause?' Miles asked Booth Watson, as they stood apart from the rest of the crowd.

'Possibly,' said Booth Watson. 'I think you'll find Ms Eleanor Bates might just prove ideal for what you have in mind.'

'What are her particular qualifications for the job?' asked Miles.

'None that I can think of,' admitted Booth Watson, 'except for the fact she detests your ex-wife as much as you do, and certainly doesn't want her to be the next chair of the Fitzmolean when Sir Nicholas retires.'

'In which case, she sounds like the ideal candidate.'

'Then I'd better introduce the two of you before we leave this evening,' said Booth Watson.

Miles glanced around the room. 'Which one is she?'

'The lady hovering near the Countess, hoping to be introduced,' said Booth Watson, 'but I don't think Dr Warwick
will oblige her.'

'An added bonus,' said Miles, as Beth led the Countess
up onto the stage, while ignoring Ms Bates.

'Don't forget to look surprised when you first see the
drawing,' said Booth Watson.

• • •

'My lords, ladies and gentlemen,' Sir Nicholas began, 'it's my
pleasure, as chairman of the Fitzmolean, to invite the
Countess of Wessex to unveil the gallery's latest acquisition,
Jacob Wrestling with the Angel, by Rembrandt.'

Warm applause greeted the Countess as she approached
the microphone. She glanced down at her notes.

'What a real pleasure it is to be with you all this evening.'
She paused, looked up and said, 'That's the opening line of
almost every speech I make, the only change being morning
for afternoon or evening,' she confessed, which brought
laughter and a ripple of applause. 'But I will let you into a
little secret,' she continued, abandoning her script. 'I first
visited the Fitzmolean as a child with my mother, and fell in
love with the Dutch school. An affair that has lasted for the
past twenty years. So it's wonderful that, thanks to the generosity of so many people, not least one particular donor who
wishes to remain anonymous, that the museum has been able
to obtain this important masterpiece, which has the rare
distinction of being signed by the master.'

The Countess had to pause as loud applause followed.

'I would also like to thank the gallery's director, Dr Beth
Warwick, whose reputation has grown over the years and

rightly goes far beyond these walls, ensuring that the Fitzmolean is now justly considered to be among the leading museums in the capital.'

'Not for much longer,' whispered Miles, who was standing at the back of the gathering; but only Booth Watson heard the comment.

'So, it gives me considerable pleasure to unveil . . .' Her hand edged towards a gold cord, but at the last minute she paused once again before saying, 'I do hope there's a Rembrandt behind there, because quite recently I was invited to Plymouth to unveil a statue of Sir Francis Drake only to find, when I pulled the cord, it was Sir Walter Raleigh staring down at me.'

Laughter broke out as she pulled the cord, followed by a tumultuous burst of applause when the guests saw the *Angel* for the first time.

Beth happily joined in the applause, but when she turned to take a closer look at the unique drawing, she immediately sensed something was missing. She took a second look and stopped applauding, but it wasn't until her gaze reached the bottom of the picture that she realized what that something was.

How could it be possible, was her first reaction, when only hours before she'd seen the original being hung by the keeper of pictures before she went home to change. She looked down at the keeper, who'd also stopped applauding and turned ashen grey. He was staring at Beth in disbelief, a puzzled look on his face.

The enthusiastic reception continued unabated until first one and then another of the guests began whispering among themselves, until finally the whispers became louder and louder as they all realized it was Rembrandt's signature that was missing and they were looking at a fake.

Beth became painfully aware that the guests were no longer staring at the drawing, but at her, as they waited for an explanation. She didn't have one. She glanced across at the Countess who had somehow managed to retain an air of professional dignity, even if she wasn't sure what she was expected to do next. A freelance photographer began snapping away, aware this might be one of those rare occasions when he would see his work on the front page of every national newspaper.

William's first reaction was to look across at Miles Faulkner, who greeted him with a warm smile followed by a mock salute. William couldn't hide his anger and began thumping the side of his leg with a clenched fist. He wanted to march across the room and arrest the damn man. Even though they both knew who the guilty party was, what offence could he charge him with? Suspicion wasn't proof.

The Countess remained rooted to the spot, while attempting to look composed.

Sir Nicholas made an instant decision. 'Perhaps I should accompany you back to your car, ma'am,' he said to the royal visitor as the freelance cameraman kept on flashing to capture the not-so-triumphant moment.

The guest of honour seemed quite willing to take the chairman's advice, and quickly followed Sir Nicholas across the crowded room and down the grand staircase, pursued by the pack of journalists who no longer had a cosy 'royal unveiling' piece to file, but a lead story that would remove any other headlines planned earlier that day.

William's eyes never left Miles. He was chatting to a board member, whose name he couldn't remember. Booth Watson looked on, the only three people in the room who were smiling.

When the Countess left the room, William quickly pursued the royal party as they made their way down the wide staircase.

Once they were out on the street, the Countess climbed into the back of her waiting car and was whisked away. The cameras didn't stop flashing until the car had turned the corner and they were out of sight.

William turned around and headed back inside to find the entrance hall full of puzzled chattering guests, who were making their way out of the museum. He stopped in his tracks when he saw Miles Faulkner standing at the foot of the staircase.

William clenched a fist, but didn't raise it.

'If I might be allowed to give you a word of advice, Chief Superintendent,' said Miles, 'I'd tell your wife to go and spend a penny.'

William turned around, ran back up the stairs and into the gallery to find Beth standing alone on the stage, her eyes still fixed on the *Angel*. She was loath to admit it was an outstanding copy, which would have fooled most onlookers.

'I think I know where the original is,' whispered William, as he joined his wife on the stage.

'On the other side of the world by now,' suggested his wife, barely audible.

'Or perhaps it's closer than we think.' William looked across the room to see Alan Roberts standing in the corridor, about to unlock the door to the ladies' toilet.

William jumped off the stage, ran across the gallery and reached the open door just as an elderly lady was about to go in. He barged in front of her and quickly went inside.

'What a rude man,' said the lady, as the door was slammed in her face.

The first thing William saw, sitting proudly atop the toilet, was Rembrandt's *Angel*, the master's signature clearly visible for all to see. He lifted the *Angel* carefully from her place, opened the door and stepped back out into the corridor. He was relieved to see that almost all the guests had departed, except for Christina, who was on the stage trying to comfort Beth.

Beth stared in disbelief as William walked up onto the stage clutching the drawing. 'Where was it?' she asked.

'In the ladies' loo,' he replied.

Without another word William and Christina replaced the copy with the original, while Beth watched in disbelief.

'How did you know where it was?' she asked quietly.

'The person who put it there told me,' said William, 'and if I can identify the forger, I'll have them both behind bars before the end of the week.'

'Why bother?' said Beth. 'He's achieved what he set out to do.'

'But the *Angel*'s now back in place,' said Christina, 'and as she never left the building, what harm has been done?'

'No more and no less than he intended,' said Beth quietly. 'A missing masterpiece that ended up in the loo. A member of the royal family unveiling a copy in front of the museum's most important guests – what more could he want? Faulkner was well aware the story would end up on the front page of every national paper in the morning, leaving me with no choice but to resign.'

BOOK 2

Revenge is a dish best served cold.

Old English proverb

CHAPTER 10

AVENGING ANGEL, FITZMOLEAN FAKE AND ANGEL'S WINGS CLIPPED were among the banner headlines on almost every front page the next morning, accompanied by a photograph of the Countess of Wessex pulling a cord. Double-page spreads, comment columns and leaders didn't hold back in suggesting heads should roll – and one head in particular.

Several touched on the news that the *Angel* had miraculously reappeared within an hour, and the *Sun* couldn't resist adding, *after spending that hour on the toilet.*

However, it was the *Evening Standard* that moved the story on with their first edition headline *Who? and Why?*

Commander Hawksby and Superintendent Warwick could have answered both those questions, but no editor would have considered printing their thoughts, well aware that a libel writ would have landed on their desks within hours.

'We don't have any proof,' admitted the Hawk, after a discussion had gone back and forth for over an hour.

'That won't stop me interviewing Faulkner under caution,' said William, 'in the hope he says something he later regrets.'

'Not a chance while his puppet master is standing by his side delivering a well-prepared script,' said the Hawk. 'But while you're at it, William, you may as well send Ross and Rebecca to the Fitzmolean to interview their head of security.' He looked down at his notes. 'Alan Roberts – I suspect he's no more than an innocent bystander, but he might have something worthwhile to contribute.'

'And follow that up with a visit to Wormwood Scrubs,' said William. 'I find it hard to believe that Faulkner and Billy Mumford, the most celebrated forger in the country, just happened to be in the same prison at the same time.'

'Then you and Inspector Adaja had better get moving,' instructed the Hawk, 'because you can be sure Faulkner will be waiting for you.'

William left the Hawk's office, feeling that Faulkner may as well have heard every word that had passed between them.

● ● ●

When William and Inspector Adaja arrived at Booth Watson's chambers in Middle Temple half an hour later, they were not surprised to be kept waiting. Ironically, Booth Watson played into William's hands, because during the fifteen-minute wait, Jackie called to let William know that a thousand pounds had recently been deposited in Billy Mumford's account.

When a secretary eventually showed them into the senior silk's office, they found Booth Watson sitting behind his desk, with his client in a chair beside him, looking smug.

'Let me make it clear from the outset, Chief Superintendent,' Booth Watson began, 'no one was more surprised than my client to discover the Rembrandt was a fake, but he'll be only too happy to help with your enquiry. As you will know, my client has been a model citizen since his release, even attending classes on becoming a reformed character.' He somehow kept a straight face.

'Then perhaps you can explain, Mr Booth Watson,' said William, 'why your client transferred one thousand pounds to the personal account of a Billy Mumford, a convicted forger, while you were both in the same prison.'

'I bought a copy of Monet's *Water Lilies* from Mumford the day before I was released – a painting I purchased with the Governor's approval,' said Faulkner, delivering a well-prepared response. 'I paid no more than the going rate and, of course, it was signed by Billy, as he had no desire to mislead anyone. Should you wish to see the painting, Chief Superintendent, you are most welcome to visit my home in Chelsea, where it hangs above the fireplace in the drawing room.'

'But did your client also purchase a copy of Rembrandt's *Angel* at the same time?' asked Inspector Adaja. 'As one thousand seems a little excessive for a fake.'

'Certainly not,' said Faulkner. 'In fact, I was as surprised as you were, Chief Superintendent, when the Countess unveiled the drawing to see it hadn't been signed, showing it had to be a copy. However, I was delighted to hear how quickly the original was returned to its rightful place as the centrepiece of the exhibition.' He paused, looked directly at William and said, 'But not before the penny had dropped!'

Paul was beginning to wonder if he would have to step in and stop William thumping the damn man.

'I am, as you will know, Chief Superintendent,' said Miles, 'a patron of the Fitzmolean, and if you felt there was anything I could do to help your wife's cause, don't hesitate to call on me, as I consider it most unfair that some of the more scur-rilous members of the gutter press are calling for her resignation,' he added, making no attempt to dampen the flames.

'I think she'll somehow manage to survive without your help,' said William.

'Let's hope so,' replied Faulkner, 'but, sadly, I can't see her making it onto the shortlist for director of Tate. But I could be wrong.'

'Let me remind you, Mr Faulkner,' said William, ignoring the comment, 'that you are currently on probation, and the CPS can, at our request, send you back to prison to complete your four-year sentence while we continue to carry out our enquiries.'

'You can, indeed, Chief Superintendent,' came back Booth Watson, 'but only if you can show that my client was in any way involved in the temporary removal of Rembrandt's *Angel*. I have a feeling, if you were foolish enough to go down that road, it would only put your wife back on the front pages for all the wrong reasons, shortly before she appears in front of the board of the Fitzmolean to explain how this embarrassing situation could have possibly arisen in the first place.'

William wondered how Booth Watson could know that Beth had agreed to face the board, as a date hadn't even been fixed.

'And the last thing I would want,' continued Booth Watson, 'is for the press to speculate that you might have unjustly sent my client back to prison while your judgement was influenced by your wife having to consider her position as director of the Fitzmolean.'

'Are you threatening me, Mr Booth Watson?' said William, taking a step forward. 'Because if you are—'

'I am doing no more than defending my client's rights and making sure he has his say in the court of public opinion,' said Booth Watson, 'as you seem determined to deprive him of those rights, dare I suggest, for personal reasons. So, if you're not going to arrest my client, Chief Superintendent, can I advise you to leave, and only return when you have some proof, not just idle speculation.'

Before William could respond, Booth Watson rose from behind his desk, walked across the room, opened the door and waited for them to depart.

The two police officers left with nothing.

'How many years do you think I'd get,' asked William, as he and Paul walked down the stairs, 'if I were to murder both men and claim excessive provocation?'

'Ten at most. Both might be considered excessive,' said Paul, as they climbed back into the waiting squad car. 'But if you could settle for just Faulkner . . . That's assuming your father would be representing you, I've no doubt he could get you a couple of years off for good behaviour.'

'I'd settle for that,' said William, as they drove out of Middle Temple and made their way back to Scotland Yard.

• • •

Detective Inspector Hogan and Detective Sergeant Pankhurst were met on the top step of the Fitzmolean by Alan Roberts, the head of security. He checked their warrant cards carefully.

'I feel a complete ass,' Alan admitted as he accompanied them into the Fitz. 'I offered to resign immediately, but Dr Warwick said I wasn't the one to blame, but if I wasn't, who the hell was?'

Ross didn't comment.

'Can you believe I was waiting for them when they arrived, accompanied them upstairs to the gallery, even kept out of their way while they made the switch, and then agreed to their suggestion that I should lock the ladies' loo until the Countess had left the premises. You should arrest me for being asleep on the job.'

'Don't be too hard on yourself,' said Rebecca. 'You were dealing with a bunch of pros who knew exactly what they were doing.'

Alan shook his head, clearly not convinced. 'They even called my office in advance and made an appointment, which is why I was waiting for them on the top step.'

When they reached the Rembrandt room, Ross could only just see the *Angel*, as the masterpiece was surrounded by a vast crowd, with a large group waiting to take their place.

'Were you able to trace that call?' asked Ross.

'Not until after your boss found the *Angel* sitting on the toilet.'

'And where was the call made from?' pressed Rebecca.

'A public phone booth in the Hilton Hotel, Park Lane.'

'One of the busiest hotels in London,' said Ross, noting that once again Faulkner had covered his tracks. 'Did the caller have an accent by any chance?'

'A slight Scottish burr, which is always more pronounced on the phone than face-to-face,' said Alan.

Rebecca wrote down: *Lamont?*

'Walk me slowly through everything that happened from the moment they arrived.'

'A police van pulled up outside the museum just before five,' said Alan, still unable to hide his frustration. 'A sergeant got out of the front while four other officers and two sniffer dogs piled out of the back.'

'Did the sergeant produce a warrant card?' Rebecca asked.

'Yes,' said Alan, 'but as I'd seen several over the years, I confess I didn't give it more than a cursory glance.'

'Because, like the van and the uniforms, it was probably the real thing.' Ross looked back towards the entrance of the gallery. 'And while they were in the Rembrandt room, purportedly carrying out an inspection, you were asked to wait outside.'

'Worse than that,' admitted Alan. 'The sergeant asked me to make sure no one disturbed them while they were carrying out their search.'

'No more than standard procedure if they had been carrying out a real inspection,' said Rebecca, 'which we do regularly for the Queen or the Prince of Wales, but not for the Countess. They were simply playing it by the book.'

'And I should have looked at the last page of that book,' said Alan, 'because twelve minutes later, they came back out and gave me the all-clear.'

Ross didn't speak, while Rebecca continued writing.

'That's when the sergeant asked me if I would lock the ladies' toilet and keep it locked until after the Countess had left, in case she needed to use it. An order I obeyed without a second thought,' Alan spat out.

Ross produced a photograph from an inside pocket, and asked Alan, 'Was this man among the five who carried out the inspection?'

Alan studied an image of Lamont for some time, before he said, 'No, none of the men were as old as that.'

'But he could have been the driver,' suggested Rebecca, glancing across at Ross.

Alan looked hopeful for the first time. 'Does that mean you know who committed the crime?'

'Suspecting and having proof, Alan, as you well know, are not the same thing,' said Ross. 'And even if we did have irrefutable proof, the CPS would still have to come up with a charge that would stand up in court.'

'How about theft of a million-pound masterpiece?' suggested Alan.

'The legal definition of theft,' said Rebecca, 'is dishonestly appropriating property belonging to another with the intention of permanently depriving the other of it. And as the drawing never actually left the building, it wasn't exactly appropriated – nor have the Fitzmolean been deprived of it.'

'But what I can't work out,' said Alan, sounding genuinely bemused, 'is if they never had any intention of stealing the drawing, what were they hoping to achieve?'

Ross avoided a question he wasn't willing to answer with a question of his own, 'Do you know if Dr Warwick is in her office?'

'Not at the moment,' replied Alan. 'It's her lunch break. As I told you, Inspector, I offered her my resignation in the hope it would help, but she rejected it out of hand.'

'It wasn't your resignation he was after,' said Ross, and he left the gallery before the head of security could ask who he meant by *he*.

· · ·

'Where to next?' asked Danny when the two of them climbed back into the car.

'Wormwood Scrubs,' said Ross, as he pulled the door closed.

'We didn't learn a lot from that,' said Rebecca as Danny drove onto Brompton Road.

'Except that Alan Roberts wasn't in any way involved, which didn't come as a surprise, whereas I have no doubt Billy Mumford was. But proving it might not be quite that easy, so don't be surprised if after the interview I say *he saw us coming*, because one thing's for sure, Faulkner will have seen him long before us.'

The phone in the armrest began to ring. Ross grabbed it. 'Hogan,' he said.

'We got nowhere with Faulkner,' William said, unable to hide his frustration. 'And you?'

'Didn't find out a great deal we didn't already know,' admitted Ross.

'Then Mumford is still our best bet,' said William, before adding, 'pull his toenails out,' he paused. 'Slowly!'

'Don't tempt me,' said Ross. 'But I will remind him that he's due out on parole in about a month, and if he's still hoping . . .'

'Let me know how you get on,' said William.

'Will do boss,' replied Ross as the car drew up outside the Scrubs.

The gate had opened even before Ross was able to produce his warrant card, and as they drove into the outer yard, a figure came striding towards them, whom Ross recognized immediately.

'I haven't warned Mumford you're coming,' said the Governor, after he'd been introduced to Rebecca.

'He'll recognize me immediately,' said Ross, 'but I'm still hoping to take him by surprise.'

The Governor nodded, turned, and led the two police officers across the barren yard towards Block B.

When the prisoner's door was opened, Mumford didn't appear at all surprised to see them, and indeed had a ready reply to the Inspector's first question.

'Without a word of a lie, guv, I admit it was me what drew the *Angel*, but I can promise you,' he said, 'the last time I saw her, she was sitting on an easel in the arts and crafts room. I had always promised to give it to the Governor as a farewell present when I left, but then some bugger must have pinched it and run off with her.' He paused, smiled and said, 'But then, you have to remember, Inspector, we are in a prison.'

'Then perhaps you can explain why Miles Faulkner, a fellow prisoner, transferred one thousand pounds to your bank account in Little Hampton shortly before he was released?' demanded Ross.

'I sold him a copy of Monet's *Water Lilies*, didn't I?' said Mumford. 'With the Governor's approval, of course.'

Rebecca continued to write down his words, although there wasn't any doubt he and Faulkner were singing from the same hymn sheet, which had certainly been composed by Booth Watson.

'He wrote to tell me the picture was hanging in his front room, even sent me a photo.'

It was becoming clear to Ross that every line had been rehearsed, probably in the prison library, only days before Faulkner was released.

'If you don't believe me, guv,' said Mumford, as he opened the small drawer in his bedside table, 'I'm happy for you to read the letter Mr Faulkner sent me, as well as show you the photograph of the Monet.'

He handed the envelope over. Ross studied the familiar hand and the photo for some time before passing them both to Rebecca.

Mumford was still smiling. 'It's not as good as the Murillo I did that ended up in the Prado, which was what got me banged up in the first place.'

Ross would, as William had suggested, have liked to extract Mumford's toenails slowly, one by one, but he suspected Rebecca wouldn't approve.

Both Chief Superintendent Warwick and Inspector Hogan returned to the Yard empty-handed.

• • •

'Have you forgotten, Mumford,' said Booth Watson, 'that I told you never to call me under any circumstances?'

'But Inspector Hogan visited me in prison this morning and asked some awkward questions,' insisted Mumford.

'I warned you he would, and gave you the answers.'

'I know, but he threatened to . . .'

'Sticks and stones,' said Booth Watson.

'But I had to admit it was my drawing.'

'Proving nothing,' said Booth Watson. 'They don't have a shred of evidence that would stand up in court, otherwise he would have arrested you.'

'I'm meant to be getting out of here in a month's time, Mr Booth Watson,' Mumford reminded him.

'And you still will,' responded Booth Watson, 'as long as you can keep your mouth shut.'

'Not a word, I promise you,' said Mumford. 'I'm a great admirer of Mr Faulkner.'

'And if it should ever cross your mind to turn Queen's evidence,' said Booth Watson, 'you ought to be aware that Mr Faulkner considers the death penalty shouldn't have been abolished for sheep stealing.'

'Got the message,' stammered Mumford.

'And one more message before you go,' said Booth Watson, 'and I mean go – don't call this number again unless you want a visit from someone a lot more unpleasant than Inspector Hogan. Think about it.'

Mumford thought about it.

• • •

The full team met later that afternoon in the Hawk's office. Once William and Ross had delivered their reports, the Commander knew he'd been left with a difficult choice. 'My personal responsibility is the allocation of time and resources – neither of them infinite – for any particular project, so I have to decide if pursuing Faulkner is the best use of our time, and whether we should be concentrating on more important issues.'

'Like what?' said Ross jumping in.

'Like being responsible for the Saudis when they land on our shores in just over three weeks' time, while our masters attempt to close a deal worth billions. Should anything go wrong there, the consequences will be far more lasting than trying to put Faulkner behind bars for another twelve months. It doesn't help that we have almost no proof he was involved in any crime in the first place, or even if it *was* a crime. Meanwhile, Simon Hartley is languishing in a foreign jail for a murder he didn't commit, while Inspector Hogan is meant to be protecting the one witness who could be responsible for saving his life.'

Ross frowned. 'So Faulkner gets away with it yet again?'

'Not for much longer, I suspect,' said the Hawk, 'because the more Faulkner believes he's invincible, the bigger risks he will take, until he finally takes one risk too many. What we have to decide, at this moment in time, is what our first priority should be: Faulkner and a drawing that is already back in place, or Hartley, who is still in jail, and a Saudi contract that would guarantee thousands of jobs for our fellow countrymen.'

'I reluctantly agree with you,' said William, taking them all by surprise, 'though after all my wife has been through because of that man, it isn't always easy to see the bigger picture.'

'Understandably,' said the Hawk, 'and—'

'I don't agree,' said Ross, butting in. 'I know it could be said that I'm also personally involved, but don't expect me to be pleased that we're letting Faulkner off the hook.'

'Not for too long, I suspect,' came back the Hawk. 'Paul, what do you think, as you're not someone who's personally involved?'

'True,' said Paul, 'although I sympathize with what Dr Warwick is going through, I also want to see Simon Hartley released as soon as possible. However, we need to play our part in helping secure the arms contract ahead of the French – and keeping Avril Dubois safe, while allowing her to get on with her job.'

The rest of the team burst out laughing, which helped to get things into perspective.

'One thing remains constant,' said Ross, once the laughter had died down, 'Faulkner is clearly still bent on revenge and there are no prizes for guessing who will be his next target,' he said, looking across the table. 'We'll have to try and stay one step ahead of Faulkner if he's not to succeed once again, while we try to do six other jobs at the same time.'

'Agreed,' said the Hawk. 'But for now, let's spend our energy preparing for the Saudi visit. With that in mind, Chief Superintendent Warwick will continue to take overall charge of the operation, while Ross will watch the Black Prince's every move from the moment the official party lands at Northolt to the moment they climb back on their plane twenty-four hours later, before going on to Paris.'

'Paul, you will protect the Saudi Minister of Defence, while Jackie will be responsible for the safety of the rest of the official delegation. Rebecca, you'll continue keeping an eye on Avril Dubois during the day, and Ross will remain in charge of the night shifts. No time to waste,' he added, as the team began to gather up their files and prepare to leave. 'William, perhaps you could stay behind for a moment?'

The Hawk didn't speak again until the door had closed. 'If I could do anything to help Beth in her present plight,' he said, 'believe me I wouldn't hesitate, but . . .'

'I know,' said William, 'and I accept it's impossible to do anything while our hands are tied behind our backs, so we'll just have to be patient and wait for Faulkner to make his first mistake.'

'Which may take a little more time,' said the Hawk. 'And you'll also have to keep an eye on Ross, who doesn't consider patience is a virtue.'

'Agreed,' said William. 'But if you'll excuse me, sir, I ought to be going home. Beth will soon be facing a committee meeting that may well decide her fate.'

'Surely they will have the common sense to . . .'

'Have you ever known a committee that was overburdened with common sense?' asked William.

Finally a question the Hawk didn't seem to have an answer for.

CHAPTER 11

BETH WAS WEARING THE SAME suit, the same shoes and carrying the same handbag as she had on the day of her interview three years before as director of the Fitzmolean.

The chairman of the board, Sir Nicholas Fenwick, had made it clear before he asked Beth to attend the meeting and answer a few questions, that she had his whole-hearted support and considered the interview to be no more than a formality before she returned to her desk and got on with the job. The last thing he wanted, he confided in her, was to be looking for a new director just before he retired.

'However,' he warned her, 'a couple of members of the board' – Beth knew exactly who they were – 'have called for a full inquiry as to how it was possible for the *Angel* to have been removed from the gallery only to end up perched on the lid of a toilet in the ladies' loo during a royal visit.'

Beth had told the chairman she felt he'd been left with no choice but to instigate a full inquiry and was happy to answer any questions the board might throw at her.

153

Sir Nicholas asked her to remain outside in the corridor until she was called. 'We shouldn't keep you for more than a few minutes,' he'd assured her before he disappeared back into the boardroom.

Beth was surprised by how long they kept her waiting, and began to speculate on what they could possibly be discussing behind closed doors. She and William had endlessly gone over the questions she was likely to be asked and the answers she should give, and although the Rembrandt drawing had been safely back in place for over a week, the press interest had not diminished, only confirmed by the dozen journalists who were waiting downstairs in the lobby like jackals to hear the outcome of the meeting. The chairman had already told them to expect a short statement and hinted they should anticipate the board's unanimous support for their outstanding director. Not what they wanted to hear.

While she waited, Beth thought about her last three years in office when, as the arts correspondent of *The Times* had suggested, the gallery's reputation had gone from strength to strength under her leadership. But she recalled Dr Henry Kissinger's words, *reputations can take years to build, only to be shattered in a moment.* Was she facing that moment?

Beth knew she was by nature a glass half-empty person, while her husband was a glass half-full individual. William could not have been more supportive, although she gathered that his efforts to bring Faulkner to justice weren't exactly going smoothly, bearing in mind he was facing his own problems which he continually downplayed. But Beth knew it wasn't quite that simple, and his chances of succeeding the Hawk as Commander in a year's time had suffered a setback from which it wouldn't be easy to recover. 'No smoke without fire' was an easy flag to hoist up the flagpole of ambition by those colleagues who had their own agendas. His team's loyalty was never in any doubt, and Ross – a one hundred per cent glass-full person – let anyone know who cared to listen that this was nothing more than a vendetta against a first-class director who was simply doing her job. A points victory for Faulkner, but not a knockout.

But Beth accepted her fate was still in the balance, however much William had tried to persuade her otherwise.

Beth had already withdrawn her name from the shortlist to be the next director of Tate. As her father continually reminded her, loyalty is a two-way street.

The boardroom door opened.

'Would you be kind enough to join us, Dr Warwick?' asked the company secretary, not displaying his usual relaxed demeanour. She couldn't help thinking he hadn't called her Dr Warwick for years.

Beth followed him into the boardroom to find the members sitting in a semicircle around a single upright chair. She took her place, feeling a little like the young prince in Yeames's iconic painting, *And When Did You Last See Your Father?* Christina greeted her with a warm smile.

'Thank you for joining us, Dr Warwick,' said the chairman. 'We would like to ask you a few questions concerning the removal of Rembrandt's *Angel*, and its most fortuitous recovery so quickly afterwards. One or two members of the board felt it was nothing less than our statutory duty to try and establish what exactly happened that evening, so that we can prevent a similar incident taking place in the future. As you will know,' continued the chairman, 'we've already interviewed Alan Roberts, the museum's head of security. The board have concluded that he carried out the correct procedure in the circumstances and had no way of knowing that

155

the people carrying out the inspection earlier in the day were not police officers.'

'As director, I fully endorse that judgement,' said Beth, feeling on safe ground, 'and also consider it right that the board are taking this matter seriously, as there are questions that still need to be answered.'

'That's most helpful, Dr Warwick,' said Sir Nicholas. 'So I'll start by asking you where you were when the switch took place.'

'I had gone home to change in preparation for the unveiling.'

'So you weren't even in the building when the switch occurred?'

'That's correct, Chairman. When I returned, Alan Roberts told me about the police inspection that had taken place during my absence, which I assumed was standard practice whenever a member of the royal family makes an official visit.'

'So, like me, when the drawing was unveiled you had no reason to believe anything unusual was about to take place,' said the chairman, lobbing up another slow ball.

'No,' said Beth. 'The preparations for the unveiling had gone smoothly. In fact, I even checked the cord was working before I went home.'

'And I presume,' said the chairman, 'at that time the *Angel* with Rembrandt's signature was still in place.'

'She most certainly was,' said Beth. 'In fact, I spent a few moments admiring the drawing before closing the curtain.'

'Thank you, Dr Warwick. Now I will hand over to my colleagues, who I know have some questions.'

A board member seated at one end of the semicircle immediately raised a hand.

'Ms Bates,' said the chairman.

Beth wasn't surprised that Ms Bates wanted to ask the

first question. They had crossed swords several times in the past, and she had made no secret of wanting to succeed Sir Nicholas as chairman of the board when he retired in the autumn, which was one of the reasons Beth had allowed her name to go forward for director of Tate. And she hadn't been surprised when William told her he'd seen Miles Faulkner deep in conversation with Ms Bates only moments after the unveiling had taken place.

'Do you, by any chance, know who was responsible for the switch, Dr Warwick?' was her opening salvo.

'No, I do not, Ms Bates,' replied Beth firmly.

'It's just that it all conveniently took place while you were at home.'

'What are you implying, Ms Bates?' demanded the chairman.

'I wasn't implying anything, Sir Nicholas. However, I will reword my question, if you think it would help. Do you have your suspicions as to who it *might* have been?'

'No,' repeated Beth, not sounding quite so convincing.

'Despite the fact that your husband, Chief Superintendent Warwick, has been put in charge of the inquiry?'

'We avoid discussing work at home.'

'Perhaps, on this occasion, it might have been wise for you to do so, to quote one of your favourite expressions, given the circumstances.'

'I did what I thought was best at the time, Ms Bates. Unlike some, I have not been blessed with hindsight.' Beth immediately regretted her words. She could hear William saying, if you're provoked, remain calm, and whatever you do, don't rise. She had risen like a soufflé.

'Would you like to ask a question, Mr Davis?' said the chairman, wanting to move on, aware that Davis was a great admirer of Beth's.

'Thank you, chairman,' said Davis. 'Remembering that the drawing was back in place within an hour, and the gallery has been experiencing record numbers for the past week, can I ask if there have been any other repercussions since?'

'I do hope, Chairman,' interjected Ms Bates before Beth could reply, 'that Mr Davis isn't condoning theft, as long as it increases our footfall.'

'I didn't say that,' snapped Davis.

'Perhaps we should allow the director to answer the question,' suggested the chairman.

'I would be the first to admit,' responded Beth, 'that the unfortunate experience the Fitzmolean suffered on the night of the unveiling has not enhanced the gallery's reputation, even if it has increased its visitor numbers.'

'I couldn't agree more,' said Ms Bates, a little too loudly.

'However,' continued Beth, ignoring the comment, 'among the hundreds of messages I have received during the past few days, the vast majority have been supportive, and I feel sure the board will be interested to learn that among them was a charming letter from the Countess of Wessex, asking if I would be kind enough to show her children around the gallery in the near future.'

Ms Bates remained silent, while the chairman couldn't resist the suggestion of a smile.

Another hand rose.

'Lady Morland,' said the chairman, unsure which side of the argument the eccentric old lady would support.

'Allow me to ask you a question, if I may,' said Lady Morland sweetly, 'do you think the switch of our latest acquisition might have been prevented if you had not been the director?'

This even took the chairman by surprise. Beth considered the question for some time before she said, 'I'm not sure what you're getting at, Lady Morland.'

'I think you know exactly what I'm getting at, Dr Warwick, but allow me to put it another way: some journalists have been hinting that the whole incident was personal and would not have happened if you hadn't been the director.'

'The gutter press,' said Christina, coming to Beth's aid.

'Nevertheless,' continued Lady Morland, 'if you were to remain as director, do you consider there's a possibility that an incident like this might occur again?'

Beth could hear William saying, if you're in a hole, stop digging.

'I think it most unlikely,' said Beth, 'but I suppose it's just possible.' She could sense that the mood in the room was changing.

'Are there any more questions?' asked the chairman, hoping not.

'One last question, if I may, Sir Nicholas,' said the company secretary. 'I read in *The Guardian* that you've been shortlisted for the post of director of Tate. Is that correct?'

'It was at the time,' admitted Beth, 'but I have since withdrawn my name.'

'Voluntarily?'

'That was uncalled for, Ms Bates,' said the chairman – a sentiment that was accompanied by muffled hear, hears, which Christina took advantage of.

'Dr Warwick,' she said, 'can you remind the board how many more people have visited the gallery since you became director three years ago?'

'We've had around two hundred thousand extra visitors,' reported Beth, 'over half of whom were children.'

'Am I also right in thinking,' continued Christina before she could be interrupted, 'that those increased numbers have helped us make a small profit for the first time?'

'Greatly assisted by our conscientious finance director.'

'Who you appointed, if I remember correctly,' said Christina. 'And it was also on your watch that we raised enough money to secure Rembrandt's *Angel* and save it for the nation.'

'Made possible by a single generous donation of a quarter of a million pounds from an anonymous donor,' interrupted Ms Bates.

Beth wondered for the first time if Ms Bates knew who the anonymous donor was. She had always assumed it must be Wilbur Hackensack. She looked directly at Christina, whose head was bowed.

'If there are no more questions,' said the chairman, fearing the exchange between the two women was becoming a little too acrimonious, 'perhaps I can ask our director to step outside for a moment, as I feel confident we can deal with this matter expeditiously.'

'Thank you, Chairman,' said Beth before she rose, left the room and returned to her seat in the dock.

In truth, Beth would have preferred to be a fly on the boardroom wall so she could listen to the exchanges taking place – exchanges that took another forty minutes before the door finally opened and the chairman reappeared with a large smile on his face.

'I know you'll be pleased to hear, Beth, that the board have given you a vote of confidence and wish you to continue as our director.'

'Was it unanimous?' asked Beth.

The chairman hesitated for a moment before he said, 'I have to admit there were a couple of abstentions.'

'Only two?' pressed Beth.

'Well . . .'

'So, what was the final vote?' asked Beth.

The chairman didn't reply immediately, as if he were searching for the appropriate words.

'It will be recorded in the minutes for all to see, Chairman,' Beth reminded him, 'so I'm bound to find out eventually.'

'The board voted four to three in your favour with three abstentions.'

'But there were only nine board members present at the meeting,' Beth reminded him.

'True,' said the chairman a little uneasily, 'but when the tally was three all, and I couldn't budge any of the three abstainers, I used my casting vote in your favour.'

'For which I will be eternally grateful, Nicholas, but four–three with you delivering the casting vote can hardly be described as overwhelming.'

'But this will all blow over in a few days, Beth. Meanwhile, you can get on with what you do best – running the Fitz.'

'It's kind of you to say so, Nicholas, but we both know that's not realistic in the long term. The gallery has to be managed by someone whose authority is never in doubt. You don't need a wounded director whose decisions the board could question and, therefore, might have to resign at a moment's notice.' Beth tried not to show any emotion as she said, 'No, the wisest course of action for me to take as director – and you know it – is to resign so that you can move on with someone fresh at the helm.'

CHAPTER 12

ONE THING THE GOVERNOR OF 'Ulaysha Prison hadn't taken into consideration after he'd moved Simon Hartley into his new cell was that he had built his career on reading people – and Sean O'Driscoll made a particularly interesting case study, uneducated but no fool, and in different circumstances . . .

After three weeks in solitary, Simon accepted that he needed Sean to be on his side if he had any chance of beating the system, let alone the Governor who held most of the cards in his hand.

It had taken Simon twenty-four hours to work out O'Driscoll's strengths. He was amoral, ruthless and, as he had less than a couple of months to live, feared nobody. It took Simon a little longer to identify his one weakness: Sean had a wife and three children back in the Emerald Isle. His oldest son, Patrick, had written to tell his father he wanted to be a teacher, but his mother couldn't afford to send him to Trinity College, Dublin, on a cleaner's salary while she had two other children to support, however many hours she was willing to work.

By the end of their second week together, Simon had convinced his 'new best friend' that providence had thrown the two of them together. Providence consisted of Simon writing a letter to an old Harvard friend, now a professor at Trinity, to see if there was any way he could help young Patrick.

'What do you want in return?' Sean asked after Simon's old friend wrote back confirming a place had been found for his son at Trinity.

'Help to get me out of here,' said Simon, without guile.

'There's only one way out of this shithole,' said Sean, accompanied by several expletives, 'and that's in a coffin. I know, because that's the way I'll be leaving in twenty-three days' time after the bastards have hanged me in the market square, but at least then you'll have the cell to yourself.'

Sean had just given him the one piece of information he needed to plan his escape, but he still needed Sean's help.

Whenever one of the guards slid open the little shutter in the door to check up on the two prisoners, they were surprised to find them chatting away as if they were old friends – an observation they reported to the Governor, who wasn't pleased by the news.

After another fortnight, the Governor had no choice but to grant prisoner A6175 a second meeting with the British Ambassador. He couldn't hold up Sir Bernard Anscombe's persistent demands indefinitely, however much Khalil paid him.

By the time the meeting took place, Simon was well prepared, as he realized he wouldn't have a moment to waste.

He was accompanied from his cell by two officers who took him to a room at the other end of the prison that bore no resemblance to the life Simon led a block away. Neither man was fooled.

The first thing the Ambassador noticed when his countryman entered the dimly lit room was that, although Hartley's beard had grown, it was neatly trimmed. At first, Sir Bernard was relieved to find that Simon appeared to be surviving, despite the telltale signs of lack of sleep not helped by a prison diet. The poor man looked exhausted.

'I have spoken to your mother and your wife,' he said, even before he'd sat down, recalling that their last meeting had been cut short without warning.

'How are my family bearing up?' asked Simon.

'As well as can be expected given the circumstances,' Sir Bernard replied, 'but neither of them could disguise how anxious they are about your present situation. However, I think I was able to convince them both that it will only be a matter of time before you are released. The good news is that, with the Defence Minister's plan to visit London and Paris going ahead the week after next, the authorities are expecting you to be deported within days of the arms deal being signed.'

Simon wasn't convinced, but didn't offer an opinion.

'I suspect the Chief of Police hasn't yet decided which horse to back,' continued the Ambassador, 'as he knows only too well that Prince Ahmed is the guilty party.'

'But while he's receiving handouts from Khalil . . .' began Simon.

'That will all change when the King gets to hear what his young nephew has been up to.'

'But who will have the courage to tell the King?' asked Simon.

After a diplomatic silence, the Ambassador said, 'That's a question I'm not at liberty to answer.'

Simon recognized the uncommunicative expression on the diplomat's face and accepted it was pointless to press him.

'But, in return,' said the Ambassador, 'you'll be expected to remain silent about Prince Ahmed's involvement in Conti's death.'

'And if I don't agree?'

'I'll have to retire and you'll be found guilty of Conti's murder and hanged by the neck until you're dead. But,' the Ambassador assured Simon, 'I will attend the ceremony on the government's behalf, before reporting back to my masters.' He paused. 'That's what we in the Foreign Office call gallows humour.'

Simon managed a laugh. 'And Avril Dubois, will she also be safe once the arms deal has been signed?'

'Yes, but not before, and the police are still protecting her night and day.' He paused, 'On a personal note,' commented the Ambassador, 'you look a little better than you did when I last saw you.'

'Only thanks to my cellmate,' said Simon, 'who gets double rations and more time out of his cell than any other prisoner.'

'How come?'

'His days are numbered, so no one wants to cross him, including the Governor.'

'But doesn't that put you at risk?' asked Sir Bernard, sounding anxious. 'After all, he has nothing to lose.'

'I can assure you, Ambassador, my life will be in far more danger after he's executed, when I'll be joined by another murderer, who I suspect this time won't speak English.'

Before Simon could say anything more, a guard entered the room grabbed him by the arm and said, 'Time's up!'

'Then let's hope you'll be back in England before then,'

said the Ambassador, as his countryman was dragged out of the room.

'Let's hope so,' said Simon, 'as my cellmate only has a few more weeks to live.'

•   •   •

'Order, order!' declared the Speaker. 'Questions to the Foreign Secretary. Question number one, Mr Peter Bottomley.'

The member for Bucklebury rose from the opposition back benches and said, 'Thank you, Madam Speaker. May I ask the Foreign Secretary if any progress has been made on securing the release of my constituent, Mr Simon Hartley, who remains incarcerated in a Saudi Arabian jail?'

The Rt Hon. Robin Cook MP rose from his place on the government's front bench, placed a thick file on the dispatch box, opened it and began to read an answer that had been prepared for him by Mr Trevelyan.

'I can tell the Honourable Member that I have been in touch with my opposite number in Riyadh, and he assures me due process is being carried out, while further investigations take place.'

'Playing for time!' shouted a Tory backbencher.

'Flimflam!' offered another, before Mr Bottomley rose again to ask his supplementary question.

'The Foreign Secretary's reply, Madam Speaker, can hardly be described as encouraging, remembering how long my constituent has been languishing in prison, and that he still hasn't appeared in court to enter a plea to the charge made against him. And should the Foreign Secretary be interested to know what that plea might be, I can tell him, it's Not Guilty!'

Hear, hear! echoed around the chamber, and Robin Cook looked uneasy as he glanced down at his brief.

'I would like to know, Madam Speaker, why we will be entertaining diplomats from the Saudi Arabian government in ten days' time as honoured guests, when one of our country-men continues to be falsely imprisoned on that government's authority. Is it just possible, Madam Speaker,' continued Bottomley before the Foreign Secretary could reply, 'that the government is more interested in securing a lucrative arms deal than in pressing for the release of an innocent man?'

'Shame!' came from several members on the government benches, but Bottomley ploughed on. 'And if that is the case, Madam Speaker, I am bound to ask if this is just another example of how much his much vaunted "ethical foreign policy" seems to have evaporated into thin air within days of the Right Honourable Gentleman taking office.'

Hear, hear! came from all sections of the House when Mr Bottomley sat down. The Foreign Secretary resumed his place at the dispatch box. This time Mr Cook left the thick file unopened and pronounced, 'I sympathize with the Honourable Gentleman . . .'

'A fat lot of good that will do,' came back a cry from someone on the opposition benches, which was greeted with even louder cries of, 'Hear, hear!' and not just from his own side.

'Let me assure the Honourable Member,' continued Cook once the House had settled, 'that my department is doing everything in its power to speed up the process, and I will of course keep the Honourable Member informed of any progress.'

'Don't hold your breath,' shouted another backbencher as the leader of the opposition rose from his place on the front bench and placed his hands on the dispatch box.

'Mr William Hague,' said the Speaker.

'Madam Speaker, I'm bound to ask if we now live in a country where our opinions carry no weight beyond our own shores, as it's clear my Honourable Friend's constituent is being denied legal rights that by any standards are taken for granted in a law-abiding country. Perhaps the time has come for the Foreign Secretary to call for the Saudi Ambassador and explain to him the meaning of the words "habeas corpus".'

The Foreign Secretary returned to the dispatch box, drowned out by 'Hear, hear' now emanating from all sides of the House. Had he looked up at the press gallery, Cook would have seen pens furiously scratching across paper as journalists began to realize this was a story that could run and run.

'I can assure the Right Honourable Gentleman,' began Cook, 'that Her Majesty's government has made our position abundantly clear when it comes to their treatment of Mr Hartley. But following these exchanges on the floor of the House, I have no doubt the Saudi Arabian Ambassador will have been made well aware of our colleagues' strong feelings on the subject.' Robin Cook looked up to see the Saudi Ambassador peering down at him from the Distinguished Strangers' Gallery, not that he showed any sign of remorse.

The Foreign Secretary sat down, clearly embarrassed, and was relieved when the Speaker moved on. 'Question number two,' she declared, 'Mr Jack Ashley.'

Mr Trevelyan, who was seated on the benches behind the Speaker's Chair, reserved for civil servants representing the minister taking questions, was penning a note for his master to let him know that Lady Hartley had been present for the exchange and was now leaving the Strangers' Gallery.

• • •

When Lady Hartley arrived back in Bucklebury, dejected and weary, the first thing she did was take a card from her purse and dial the phone number below the name.

'I'm sorry to bother you, Mr Booth Watson,' she said, once she'd been put through, 'but there still seems to be no sign of my son being released,' she tried to remain calm, 'while the bills continue to come in.'

'I'm sorry to hear that,' said Booth Watson, who was absolutely delighted.

'So, I've made up my mind,' she announced. She took a deep breath, before she added, 'Please tell your client that I am ready to sell my Constable, and if he wishes to visit my home and consider any of the other watercolours left to me by my late husband, it can't be soon enough.'

'I'll get in touch with my client immediately.'

Booth Watson was as good as his word, because no sooner had he put down the phone than he picked it back up and dialled Miles's number.

•　•　•

They agreed to meet outside the Cabinet War Rooms at two o'clock. Booth Watson arrived a few minutes before Big Ben chimed twice. Miles came strolling down Birdcage Walk some fifteen minutes later.

The two men began a routine they had regularly carried out over the years when they didn't want to be overheard, except by squirrels, ducks and the occasional pigeon. They crossed the road, entered St James's Park and continued to walk beside the lake, passing tourists, who rarely spoke English.

'So what was so urgent it couldn't wait?' said Miles.

'A call from an elderly widow who has bills to pay and, while her son is locked up in prison, has no immediate source of income so is unable to do so. However, she has inherited a Constable.'

'Half the art world will also be aware if that's the case,' said Miles, 'including Sotheby's and Christie's.'

'Possibly,' said Booth Watson, 'but then again, possibly not.'

Miles walked for a few more yards before he said, 'I'm still listening.'

'The Constable is nothing more than a sprat,' said Booth Watson.

'So what's the mackerel?' asked Miles.

'A unique example of the Declaration of Independence, known as the Fair Copy, the value of which she might not be aware.'

'Why should that be of any interest to me?' asked Miles, as a duck waddled up to him and opened its mouth, but was not rewarded. Miles didn't deal in breadcrumbs, the only currency acceptable among the residents of St James's Park.

'A printed copy of the Declaration, published in Philadelphia by Benjamin Franklin around the same time, of which there are several still in circulation, recently fetched over a million dollars at auction,' said Booth Watson, 'and although I only saw this particular version for a few moments, I can assure you it was not a printed copy, but handwritten.'

'By whom?' asked Miles.

'None other than Thomas Jefferson.'

Miles stopped in his tracks. 'How can that be possible?' he said.

'It seems that Jefferson often visited London around that time. He was a friend of an MP called David Hartley, which would explain why it's still in the family.'

'Then you can be sure one of the family will be well aware of its value.'

'Possibly, but what I can tell you is that Lady Hartley only mentioned the Constable as being of any real value,' said Booth Watson, which caused Miles to stop once again.

'So the Right Honourable Lord Hartley, the former Home Secretary, has to be the deceased, and no doubt you discovered this after one of your funeral visits.'

Booth Watson ignored the slight and simply said, 'While the cat's away.'

'The cat being Simon Hartley,' said Miles, 'Lord Hartley's only son, who is locked up in a Saudi jail for a crime he didn't commit.'

'How can you possibly know he's innocent?'

'If you were to read the *Financial Times* and *Private Eye* instead of the *Daily Telegraph*, BW, you'd be far better informed. For weeks the papers have been full of speculation as to who the real culprit is – a young Saudi Prince seems the leading candidate. However, as the Saudi delegation is about to land on our shores, I suspect it won't be too long before Simon Hartley is released, and I suspect that may mean his mother will no longer need to sell the Constable or Jefferson's Declaration.'

'You're right in theory,' said Booth Watson. 'But as the dear lady approached me and not her family solicitor to solve the problem, we're still in with a chance. Her Ladyship also made it clear when I last spoke to her that she would be happy for you to visit Hartley Hall so you could view the Constable at your earliest convenience.'

'Whereas what we really want to get our hands on is the Fair Copy of the Declaration,' said Miles.

Neither man spoke for some time as they continued to

stroll along the narrow path that circled the lake and made their way back towards the War Rooms.

'Make it Tuesday or Wednesday of next week,' said Miles, 'so we don't look as if we're in a hurry, and that will still be a few days before the Saudis turn up.'

'I'll call Lady Hartley this afternoon and fix a time,' said Booth Watson, as Miles stopped to stare at the recently constructed London Eye that dominated the landscape, before turning back to look at Buckingham Palace.

'I can't believe,' said Miles, 'that Her Majesty ever thought she'd be confronted with something quite that vulgar whenever she looked out of her bedroom window.'

A swan raised its imperious head, as if in agreement.

CHAPTER 13

BOOTH WATSON ROSE EARLIER THAN usual that morning, as he needed to be in Cadogan Square by eight o'clock. He felt sure Miles would have had breakfast long before then, read the papers, opened his mail and be waiting for him . . . impatiently.

Although he'd left his flat in Middle Temple in good time, and the taxi dropped him off in Cadogan Square with nine minutes to spare, he could see Miles sitting in the back of his car reading the *Financial Times*. He paid the fare and asked the cabbie for a receipt.

'I've been doing some research,' Miles said, not bothering with a 'good morning' as Booth Watson joined him in the back of the car. 'The acknowledged authority on Jefferson is a Professor Saul Rosenberg, whose book *Monticello* confirms that the third president did write a Fair Copy of the Declaration of Independence including two extra clauses – one concerning the emancipation of slaves, while the other spelt out the details of America's relationship with King George III once it became an independent nation.'

'And if the Hartleys are in possession of the original hand-written Fair Copy . . .'

'It is, to quote Rosenberg, priceless.'

'I wonder if Lady Hartley knows that,' said Booth Watson.

'If she does, it will have been a wasted trip,' replied Miles, as Collins drove out onto the M4. 'Still, I'm bound to admit, if it is the missing Fair Copy, and we can get our hands on it, it will be a double bonus for you.'

'A double bonus,' repeated Booth Watson suspiciously.

'Yes. Thanks to your "no comeback" clause in my divorce settlement, I've finally got Christina off my back.'

'Eleven B, little c,' said Booth Watson, sounding rather pleased with himself, 'which states that should Christina marry again, you will automatically be released from all your present financial obligations, which have happily been passed on to one Wilbur T. Hackensack III.'

'Let's hope he got her to sign a prenup,' said Miles.

'Not according to the *Mail* he didn't,' said Booth Watson.

'Then he's about to find out that Christina will come up with expenses that would make a politician blush.'

'Perhaps she's keeping him happy,' mused Booth Watson, 'and he doesn't care. And I can tell you someone else who doesn't care, because she's also got in on the act.'

'Who?' demanded Miles, turning to face his legal adviser.

'None other than Mrs Beth Warwick, who I'm told will be returning as director of the Fitzmolean if Christina becomes chair, making your little coup with Rembrandt's *Angel* some-what short-lived. However, you'll be pleased to hear I've come up with a strategy that should kill two birds with one stone.'

Miles listened carefully as Booth Watson outlined his plan.

'I think you're going to have to pay another visit to Ms Bates,' was Miles's immediate response. 'It's already in my diary,' said

Booth Watson as they passed Bucklebury parish church, before turning left and proceeding down a long drive to see Hartley Hall looming up in front of them. Collins brought the car to a halt outside the handsome Elizabethan mansion.

Miles was the first to get out of the car, and the front door was opened even before he'd reached it. Lady Hartley's first mistake.

She greeted both her guests with a warm smile, before saying, 'How kind of you to take the trouble to come all this way, Mr Faulkner.'

'It's not a trouble, Lady Hartley, but a pleasure,' declared Miles with the sincerity of a canvassing politician.

'Please come in,' she said. 'I've made you both a cup of tea.'

'How kind of you,' said Miles as he followed her into the house. 'Of course, I've been following your son's disgraceful treatment at the hands of the Saudis with considerable interest. Not least because I was educated at the same alma mater as your late husband.'

Lady Hartley seemed to relax when she heard this news and led her guests into the drawing room.

'Mr Booth Watson, my distinguished advocate,' continued Miles, 'has briefed me on your present situation, and I wanted you to know that if there is anything I can do to help, I am at your service.'

'How considerate of you,' said Lady Hartley. 'And if only Simon were here . . .'

'But sadly, he is not, so we must try to do what he would have considered to be in your best interests,' said Booth Watson, as Miles's eyes settled on Constable's *The Old Mill at Bucklebury* that was hanging above the mantelpiece. He had to admit it appeared to be a fine example of the master's work.

'Of course, I will be sad to have to part with the Hartley Constable,' said her ladyship as she sat down, 'as it's been in our family for seven generations, but as my dear mother used to say, needs must when the devil is driving, and I think that particular devil is about to enter our gates.'

'And should you decide you would reluctantly have to part with the painting,' said Miles, 'I wondered if you had a price in mind?'

'The vicar told me that a Constable had recently changed hands at auction for five hundred thousand pounds,' she replied, 'so he felt that would be a reasonable price.'

'If you were to sell the picture on the open market, Lady Hartley, I think you will find the auction houses add twenty-five per cent to the hammer price, while a dealer would expect an even larger share, so I suspect four hundred thousand is in fact a more realistic price.'

'And the rest of the collection?' asked Lady Hartley, looking hopeful.

Miles's trained eye swept slowly around the room. A decent enough William Russell Flint of two ladies sitting by a swimming pool, a Brabazon Brabazon of Marrakesh, and a Bernard Dunstan of Hartley Hall. But nothing that would cause an auctioneer to delay proceedings for any length of time.

'I have to admit, Lady Hartley, it's a fine collection, but I am not an art dealer, just an enthusiastic collector whose walls are already full, so my only interest would be in the Constable.'

'Then I fear, Mr Faulkner, you've had a wasted journey, because I couldn't let the Constable go for less than five hundred thousand pounds.'

Booth Watson came in bang on cue, 'When I last visited you, Lady Hartley, I spotted a copy' – he emphasized the word 'copy' – 'of the Declaration of Independence hanging in your husband's study.'

'That's correct,' said Lady Hartley, after a moment's consideration. 'Something else that has been passed down from generation to generation, but I confess it's nothing more than a family heirloom of little value.'

Words that sang in Miles's ear.

'But . . . if you'd like to see it?'

'May as well while we're here,' said Miles, trying to look less than enthusiastic.

Lady Hartley rose from her chair, led them back out of the room and along the corridor to her husband's study.

While Booth Watson continued to chat to Lady Hartley about her husband's distinguished career, Miles took a closer look at the framed Declaration that was hanging on the wall in the late Lord Hartley's study. One glance and he was fairly certain it wasn't a printed copy, but handwritten, but written by whom? A scribe, a secretary, or might it possibly be Jefferson himself? He stared at the signature and wondered if it could be genuine. There was only going to be one way of finding out, and that would mean taking a punt.

'How interesting,' said Miles, 'and although I have no idea of its value, I would be happy to take it off your hands. In fact, if you felt able to part with both the Constable and the Declaration, I would be willing to pay the five hundred thousand you need, to solve your financial difficulties. I hope your husband would approve.'

'He would have been overwhelmed by your generosity, Mr Faulkner,' said Lady Hartley. She hesitated, before adding, 'Please allow me to return that generosity in kind.' She walked across to her husband's desk, pulled open the bottom drawer and extracted a number of handwritten letters, which she handed over to Miles. 'These letters were written by Thomas Jefferson to his friend David Hartley MP over two hundred years ago and I should like you to have them.'

'How kind of you.' Miles passed the letters over to Booth Watson, as if he were a lady-in-waiting receiving a bunch of flowers from a member of the Royal Family. Booth Watson checked Thomas Jefferson's signature on the bottom of each of the letters, while Miles stood by Lord Hartley's desk and said, 'May I?' He then took out his cheque book.

'Of course,' said Lady Hartley, who glanced at a framed photograph of her late husband being knighted by the Queen. Miles took a seat at Lord Hartley's desk, before he wrote out a cheque for £500,000, signed it and handed it over to a willing seller.

'You are a knight in shining armour,' Lady Hartley said as she studied the cheque, her hand trembling. Not an image Booth Watson had ever considered. Without another word, she led her two guests back into the drawing room and poured them a second cup of tea.

'I'll draw up a contract as soon as I return to my chambers,' said Booth Watson.

'Thank you,' said Lady Hartley.

'May I ask my driver to put both works in the back of the car?' Miles enquired as Lady Hartley handed him the cup.

'Of course,' said Lady Hartley, while offering Booth Watson a digestive biscuit.

After Collins had lifted the Constable off the wall, Lady Hartley looked up at the blank space in front of her, sighed and said, 'I shall miss it.'

'Of course you will, dear lady,' said Miles, 'and if you want to change your mind . . .'

'No, no,' she replied, while quickly placing the cheque in her handbag.

Miles glanced at his watch. 'I do hope you'll forgive me, Lady Hartley, but I ought to be getting back to London, before I change my mind.'

Lady Hartley laughed nervously as she got up and led her guests out of the room and along the corridor to the front door.

'Mr Booth Watson, you could not have done more,' she said as she opened the front door. 'You must be sure to send me your account.'

'Certainly not,' protested Booth Watson. 'I have only played a minor part in assisting your cause, which is no more than a repayment for my debt to your late husband for all the good advice he gave me over so many years.'

'How kind of you to say so,' said Lady Hartley as Collins placed the Declaration and the Constable in the boot of the car before returning to his place behind the wheel.

Lady Hartley remained standing by the front door, waving farewell, and didn't move until the Rolls was out of sight. She then went back into the house, closed the door, and returned to her husband's study.

She paused for a moment to look at the faded square on the wall where the Declaration had hung for the past two hundred years. She finally turned around to be greeted with her husband receiving his knighthood from the Queen.

'Do you think, John,' she said, staring down at the framed photo of her husband, 'I should have told the kind gentlemen why our version of the Declaration of Independence wasn't mine to sell?'

'And while you're at it, Sybil,' came back a voice ringing in her ears, 'perhaps you should also have told him the truth about the Constable.'

Lady Hartley felt ashamed, but the feeling didn't last for long.

• • •

'I think we should be making a move,' said Alice, glancing towards Ross. 'We promised the babysitter we'd be back before eleven.'

'And we'd better check that the twins haven't burnt down the house in our absence,' said Beth. 'Or worse, had a rave party.'

Christina laughed. 'When did they become so grown up?'

'Overnight! But, thank you for another fantastic evening,' said Beth, giving her friend and her new husband both a warm hug. 'You're such generous hosts.'

'I'm an American,' replied Wilbur. 'It's the way we've always treated the English – except during the War of Independence.'

Wilbur went to fetch their coats while Ross, Alice and William followed him. Beth hung back.

'Well?' she asked conspiratorially. 'Are you really going to stand for chair of the Fitzmolean?'

Christina left her friend in suspense for a few moments before saying, 'I submitted my name yesterday – and if I do become chair, my first executive decision will be to reappoint you as the director of the Fitz – that is, if you'd be willing to come back?'

'Of course I would,' said Beth without hesitation.

'Thank heavens for that,' said Christina. 'As I couldn't hope to do the job without you.'

'And so say all of us,' said Wilbur as they joined them in the hall.

'Another executive decision made in my absence,' said William, as he helped his wife on with her coat.

• • •

Artemisia and Peter sat at home on the bedroom floor studying several leaflets.

'The protest march will take place in Whitehall on the day the Saudi Minister of Defence visits London for talks with the Prime Minister,' said Artemisia.

Peter only had to read a couple of pages of the *Rallying Call* before he proclaimed, 'You're right, we shouldn't be making deals with countries that don't even give women the vote.'

'And Mum certainly wouldn't have been allowed to run a national gallery,' said Artemisia.

'They don't have a national gallery to manage,' said Peter, after turning the page of another leaflet. 'Just offices where women are expected to be secretaries and cleaners, and they can't even drive to work on their eight-lane highways as they're not permitted to have a driving licence.'

'And more important, Simon Hartley is still in prison for a murder he didn't commit, and worse,' continued Artemisia, turning a page of one of the leaflets, 'Prince Ahmed, a member of the Royal Family, is the one who should be locked up.'

'I'm not sure Dad will be happy if we . . .' said Peter, 'and Mum's got enough problems of her own at the moment.'

'There's no reason for them to find out,' said Artemisia, placing a finger over her lips as the front door opened.

'Quick,' said Artemisia. 'We have to be in bed, before one of them comes upstairs.'

Peter bolted.

• • •

Faulkner was on time for a change, and after the briefest of greetings, took the seat on the other side of Booth Watson's desk.

'Given the circumstances,' said Booth Watson, 'I considered it prescient to draw up a contract of ownership, so there could be no misunderstanding at a later date.'

Miles had to agree with his lawyer's judgement, when he realized just how much Jefferson's Fair Copy of the Declaration might be worth.

'Once the document had been notarized,' continued Booth Watson, 'I paid a second visit to Lady Hartley at her home in Bucklebury. She happily signed all three copies of the agreement – one of which she retained. Incidentally, she couldn't stop singing your praises, even though it might well turn out to be her Nunc Dimittis when she discovers what she's let go of for a mere bagatelle, which is precisely why I wanted to make sure everything was legal and above board. The last thing we need is a vexatious litigant pursuing you at some time in the future.'

'What's there to dispute?' asked Miles. 'It was a deal agreed by both parties and signed in good faith with a QC present.'

'It was indeed,' said Booth Watson, 'but unfortunately a complication has arisen.'

'What kind of complication?' demanded Miles.

'It concerns the letters Jefferson wrote to Hartley over the years, and one in particular.'

'But she gave them to me as a gift,' said Miles, not wanting to admit he hadn't read them.

'Five of them are of little interest, other than to historians of that period.'

'But clearly that doesn't apply to the sixth.'

'I'm afraid not,' said Booth Watson, 'because should you

decide to sell the Declaration, that particular letter will cause you an insurmountable problem to which I can find no obvious solution.' Booth Watson opened the file on his desk, extracted the uncompromising letter and handed it across to his client. It didn't take more than one reading for Miles to work out what the insurmountable problem was.

He read the letter a second time.

> *Hôtel de Langeac*
> *Paris*
> *August 11th, 1787*

Dear Mr Hartley,

I hope you will grant me your permission to impose upon your time by allowing me to send you my Fair Copy of the Declaration of Independence, which I earlier delivered to Congress for their consideration. You will see that it includes the two clauses you and I discussed in London, namely the abolition of slavery and our future relationship with King George III once we become an independent nation. Copies were made by my friend and colleague Benjamin Franklin and distributed among interested parties. Much to my dismay, when members of Congress divided, both clauses were rejected. However, I would not want you to think I had not taken to heart your wise and sound counsel and tried to convince my fellow congressmen of the merit of your judgement.

Once you have had a proper chance to peruse the Fair Copy at your leisure, perhaps you would be kind enough, in the fullness of time, to return it to me. I thought you would want to know that it is my intention to bequeath this memento to the Nation in order that future generations of Americans might fully appreciate

*what the founding fathers were trying to achieve, and
not least the role you played. I look forward to hearing
from you at some time in the future, and be assured of
my sincere esteem and respect.*

I remain, your most obedient and humble servant,

Thomas Jefferson

'Then why didn't he return the Declaration to his "old friend"?'
asked Miles.

'Your guess is as good as anybody's,' replied Booth Watson.
'Although I suspect the answer to that question has been lost
in the mists of time. Once Congress had approved the wording
of a final document that didn't include the two added clauses
in the Fair Copy, it might no longer have been considered
of any importance . . . who knows? Certainly Lady Hartley
can't have read this letter – if she had, she would have known
she didn't have the authority to part with the Declaration. I
presume her understanding is based solely on stories told to
her by her late husband.'

Miles nodded but didn't interrupt while Booth Watson was
still in full flow.

'However, one thing's for certain,' continued the QC, 'any
half-decent contracts lawyer, after reading Jefferson's letter
to Hartley, would rightly claim ownership on behalf of the
Jefferson estate, possibly even the US government, and I for
one wouldn't be willing to defend such a weak case, knowing
I'd be laughed out of court.'

'So what do you advise?'

'I believe you have no choice but to return Jefferson's Fair
Copy of the Declaration to the American Embassy in London,
for which I feel sure you will receive the grateful thanks of
their Ambassador on behalf of the American government.'

'But don't forget I parted with five hundred thousand for something it now turns out didn't even belong to her.'

'All is not lost,' said Booth Watson, 'as I suspect the other five letters Jefferson wrote would fetch a substantial sum were they to come under the hammer in New York, and don't forget you still have the Constable, so you shouldn't be out of pocket.'

'But it will be nothing compared to the price a Fair Copy of the Declaration would fetch – handwritten by Thomas Jefferson. Can you imagine how much that would make if it came on the open market?'

'That's anyone's guess,' responded Booth Watson. 'Although, as the US government would be certain to be among the bidders, along with a dozen or more of the world's leading collectors who'd like to get their hands on such a unique piece of history, I would have to suggest several million. However, the question is now academic, as Jefferson's letter to Hartley has left you with no alternative but to return the Declaration to its rightful owner.'

'I can think of one alternative,' said Miles.

'Namely,' said Booth Watson, an eyebrow raising.

Miles took a lighter out of his pocket, flicked it open, and watched as the flame flickered. He then held up Jefferson's compromising letter and paused for a moment, before setting it alight.

Booth Watson sat on the other side of his desk, his mouth open, though no words came out. He couldn't believe what he was witnessing. Over the years, he'd known his client to be involved in some outrageous behaviour, but nothing on this scale. Not for the first time he wondered if this was a step too far, and he would finally have to sever their relationship.

When the flame was just about to burn Miles's thumb and

forefinger, he finally let go, allowing a tiny corner of the damning letter to join the rest of the ashes in its unworthy grave.

CHAPTER 14

WILLIAM HAD LEFT THE HOUSE that morning before anyone else was awake, aware this was one day he couldn't afford to be late for work.

'Good morning, Danny,' he said as he climbed into the back of the waiting car.

'Good morning, sir,' Danny replied, switching on the ignition and joining the early morning traffic.

William sat back and tried to anticipate what could possibly go wrong. Best-case scenario, he would get home this evening with all the principals involved safely in bed and asleep. Worst-case scenario . . .

Beth was next up and was preparing breakfast when the twins walked into the kitchen, which took her by surprise as they were on holiday and she'd assumed they would want to lie in.

'What have you got planned for today?' she asked innocently.

'Visiting friends,' said Artemisia, delivering the line she and Peter had agreed on.

'Anyone I know?' enquired Beth.

'Don't think so,' replied Artemisia, not wanting to go into any detail. 'What about you, Mum?'

'I'm having lunch with Christina, when we'll be trying to work out what questions the board will ask her if she stands for chair of the Fitz,' her mother replied.

'She's bound to get it,' said Peter, determined to keep his mother off the subject of what they actually had planned.

'I wouldn't be so sure of that,' replied his mother, without explanation. 'I'll see you both for supper, but don't expect your father to join us, as he's unlikely to be back before you've gone to bed.'

We'll be seeing him long before we've gone to bed, thought Artemisia.

• • •

Danny drove into Northolt just as Beth finished washing the dishes and the twins were going over the details of their plan for the last time.

William was pleased to find that the rest of the team were already in place, carrying out their different responsibilities in preparation for a royal visit. They were well acquainted with the protocol whenever the Queen or the Prince of Wales returned home following an overseas visit – they would escort them back to Windsor Castle, Buckingham Palace or Clarence House to be greeted by cheers from onlookers – but this was a foreign royal who would be visiting Windsor Castle and Number 10 Downing Street, when jeers were more likely than cheers from the public.

The next person to appear on the runway was the Defence Secretary, followed shortly by the Foreign Secretary, the

Cabinet Secretary, the Permanent Secretary and Mr Trevelyan, the Permanent Secretary's Permanent Secretary. The ministers formed a line to greet their foreign guests, while behind them hovered Chief Superintendent Warwick, Detective Inspector Paul Adaja and several armed officers.

Parked in a separate line and facing the opposite direction were seven police outriders from the Met's special escort group, six chauffeur-driven Jaguars and three luxury coaches.

They all looked up as a private 747 descended through the clouds and landed on a runway used only by foreign heads of state and visiting royalty. The Chancellor of the Exchequer had recommended during Cabinet that – as three billion was at stake – Prince Majid bin Talal Al Saud, the King's cousin, should on this occasion be afforded the same privileges as a visiting head of state. The Prime Minister had agreed.

Once the plane taxied to a halt and the steps had been wheeled into place, the aircraft door was finally opened. The first person to emerge was the Saudi Minister of Defence. As his entourage came down the steps, all dressed in identical white thawbs and keffiyehs, William wondered which one of them was the Minister's son.

Standing on the balcony behind them, binoculars trained on the arriving party, Ross picked out the Black Prince immediately, and never let him out of his sight as he was accompanied to a waiting limousine.

The Foreign Secretary stepped forward, bowed, shook hands and welcomed His Royal Highness to Britain on behalf of Her Majesty's government.

The Prince went down the line and shook hands with the greeting party before they all took their allocated places in the cavalcade of waiting limousines. On a signal no one other than a seasoned professional would have spotted, the special escort group set off. Their responsibility was to make sure the convoy didn't stop moving until they arrived at Farnborough forty minutes later, where another greeting party was already waiting.

William, who was in the car bringing up the rear, picked up the phone in his armrest as the well-ordered convoy made its way out of Northolt onto the main road. He listened carefully.

'There are only a few protestors at Farnborough and almost none at Windsor,' reported Jackie. 'Not least because they wouldn't be able to get anywhere near our visitors. However, that doesn't apply this end – a large crowd's already gathering in Trafalgar Square, who I'm told plan to march down Whitehall and greet the Saudi delegation before they meet the Prime Minister. There is also a helicopter already hovering above Whitehall.

'The march organizers have assured me,' continued Jackie, 'that it will be a peaceful demonstration. However, that won't stop the usual bunch of thugs, who will turn up for any protest simply to cause trouble.' Jackie paused. 'Don't you sometimes wish, sir, we had the authority to ban marches like these?'

'No,' said William. 'On balance I still prefer democracy to dictatorship.'

He ended the call as the convoy continued its journey down the outside lane of the motorway. It always amused William that the sight of police outriders, lights flashing, sirens blaring, ensured that anyone on the outside lane slipped into the middle lane and quickly fell below the speed limit.

• • •

Peter and Artemisia crept out of the house a few minutes after ten and caught the number 14 bus to Piccadilly, climbed upstairs and took a seat near the back. They were so nervous that hardly a word passed between them.

When the bus came to a halt at the top of Piccadilly Circus, they got off and joined a large group of protestors who were carrying banners and chanting as they made their way towards Trafalgar Square.

With each step they took, Artemisia became more and more exhilarated by the thought of taking part in a demonstration that would surely leave both governments in no doubt how people felt about the treatment of Simon Hartley.

As she turned the corner at the bottom of Haymarket, her heart leapt when she saw what must have been a hundred thousand people gathered to add their voices to the cause. She stood on the fringe of the vast crowd and listened to speeches by Tony Benn, Tariq Ali and Dennis Skinner, whose words were regularly interrupted by prolonged cheers.

● ● ●

The long black convoy of nine vehicles drove into Farnborough thirty-nine minutes later and came to a halt on the perimeter of the runway.

As the visiting party made their way onto the parade ground, Company Sergeant Major Fletcher sprang to attention, and, in a voice that frightened away any stray pigeons that had dared to waddle onto his parade ground, bellowed, 'Present arms!'

A platoon of Grenadier Guards in full dress uniform carried out the order.

The royal prince and his party were escorted to a small

stand that wouldn't have looked out of place at Royal Ascot, but had only been erected the day before.

No sooner had the visiting party sat down than they had to stand up again while the band of the Royal Marines played two national anthems – 'God Save the Queen' followed by 'God Save the King' – as a squadron of Tornados came out of the clouds and flew above them in a V formation, with the white and green colours of Saudi Arabia evaporating behind them.

There then followed two hours of parading the vast array of equipment that three billion pounds would acquire, should the Saudis decide to sign the British contract. William kept his eyes firmly fixed on the royal party as others watched the display.

When the demonstration finally came to an end, William had no way of knowing if the visiting Minister of Defence had been impressed. However, he couldn't believe the French would possibly equal the sheer range of sophisticated battle equipment that had been on display, including Challenger 2 tanks and Tornados.

Ross continued to keep a close eye on Prince Ahmed, who he noticed yawning from time to time and making no attempt to hide the fact he was bored. Khalil had already advised the French to put a woman next to him, preferably a young woman. The French got the message.

After the Marines had presented arms a second time, William continued to shadow the Saudi Defence Minister as he was accompanied back to his car by the Foreign Secretary who, along with a select group, would join the Queen for lunch at Windsor Castle.

They left Farnborough a few minutes late but arrived on time at Windsor, where a private secretary escorted them to the audience room. Her Majesty was waiting to greet the King's cousin. One of them bowed.

William remained in his car, munching a cheese sandwich, as he waited for the Foreign Secretary to reappear with the Saudi Minister by his side.

• • •

Peter and Artemisia took their place at the back of a long line as Tony Benn and Tariq Ali led the boisterous crowd out of Trafalgar Square. As they moved along Whitehall, carrying banners high in the air, they continued to chant *Free Hartley* and *Arrest the Black Prince*, while the police lined the pavements on both sides of the government buildings.

The slow march came to a halt when they reached Downing Street, where they crammed themselves together five deep like a football crowd.

Some of the organizers were handing out banners, while others offered eggs to eager onlookers. Peter held up a banner while Artemisia took a couple of eggs. Her heart was thumping, as she waited for the Saudi delegation to appear.

• • •

The extended convoy left the grounds of Windsor Castle at 2.59 p.m. and headed for the motorway. When they arrived in Whitehall at 3.58 p.m., they were greeted with screams of derision as the protestors surged forward, determined to make their presence felt. The police cordon only just managed to hold them back.

Peter held his banner high in the air just as Artemisia hurled her first egg, which landed in the middle of the road, unnoticed. She quickly pushed her way to the front of the crowd and took aim a second time, delighted to see her egg land on the windscreen of the third car, causing it to slow down before it turned into Downing Street.

She leapt up in triumph, but before she landed, two policemen's arms encircled her, just as her father's car swept by. They quickly bundled her away to a side street, where she was thrown into a waiting van along with half a dozen other protestors. She sat back, out of breath but proud to have played her part.

Peter watched as his father's car disappeared into Downing Street, the vast iron gates slamming closed behind him. He dropped his banner and ran into the side street where his sister had been taken, only to see the police van being driven away. His heart hammering, Peter kept on running, heading for the Embankment in search of a red telephone box.

'Scotland Yard,' said a voice.

• • •

The Prime Minister was standing by the front door waiting to greet his guest when the Saudi Prince's car pulled up outside Number 10 Downing Street.

If Prince Majid was surprised by the size of the press corps herded behind barriers on the far side of the road, or by the crowds of protestors they had driven past as they turned into Downing Street, he didn't show it. But as he got out of the car, he was clearly disturbed by the journalists shouting questions that had nothing to do with the purpose of his visit. William suspected no one shouted at His Royal Highness when he was in Riyadh, and if he was ever asked a question, he would be given prior notice – in writing.

'When are you going to release Simon Hartley?' screamed the *Daily Mirror.*

'Has anyone told you who the real murderer is?' demanded *The Observer*.

'Does your country believe in justice and a fair trial?' hollered the *Express*.

'Do you know why your son is known as the Black Prince?' – the BBC.

After an unusually short photocall on the steps of Number 10, the Prime Minister hurriedly whisked his guest inside.

William assumed the Number 10 press secretary had warned the Saudi Minister's opposite number what to expect, and told him that the Prime Minister had to face such an onslaught every day, even though the hacks knew he wouldn't consider answering any of their questions.

When Prince Majid emerged from Number 10 an hour later, he quickly climbed into the back of his waiting car, which immediately sped off. When the gates at the end of Downing Street opened, having ignored the cries of the press corps, he was greeted once again with the screams of protestors, who made the journalists look restrained and polite.

William followed the Prince's cavalcade as it made its short journey from Whitehall to the Saudi Embassy in Charles Street, where the visiting party was greeted by a smaller but equally vociferous group who screamed *Free Hartley*, *Arrest the Black Prince*, and *Go home murderers*, as the government's guests disappeared inside their embassy.

• • •

Ross looked around before he picked up the phone and dialled a number he hadn't called for some time. When the phone was answered, he said, 'Please put me through to Superintendent Wainwright.' He hoped he was still the station commander.

'Who shall I say is calling?'

'Detective Inspector Ross Hogan.'

Ross waited to be reconnected with an officer he'd walked the beat with in Lambeth when they'd first passed out of Hendon Police College as probationer constables.

'If it's you on the line, Ross, it can only mean trouble,' were Wainwright's first words, 'because leopards don't change their spots, particularly Irish leopards.'

'Especially when it comes to protecting one of their cubs.'

'Let me guess,' said Wainwright. 'Artemisia Warwick, the daughter of your boss.'

'I'm her godfather,' said Ross.

'A nice kid,' said Wainwright. 'Spent most of her time taking care of one Robert Hartley.'

'The elder son of Simon Hartley?'

'I'm afraid so,' replied Wainwright. 'I decided not to clap them both in irons, but I will be sending them home with a slap on the wrist. What I didn't tell them is that, given half a chance, I would happily have joined them on the other side of the barricades.'

'Me too,' admitted Ross. 'Let's just hope Arte gets home before her father does.'

'I only wish I could say the same for young Hartley,' said Wainwright, 'who had every right to protest his father's innocence.'

'Agreed,' said Ross.

'Will you be telling her father?' asked Wainwright.

'I don't always tell the Chief Super everything,' admitted Ross, 'especially when he doesn't need to know.'

'If you did,' said Wainwright, 'you'd have been locked up years ago.'

• • •

Artemisia saw him crouched in a corner on the floor. He was about her age, maybe a year or two older, sitting with his head down, arms tucked around his legs, quietly sobbing.

She sat down beside him. 'They don't lock you up in England for throwing eggs at policemen,' she said gently.

'My father's locked up in one of their prisons for a crime he didn't commit.'

'You're Simon Hartley's son?' said Artemisia, unable to hide her surprise.

'Yes . . . Robert,' he mumbled incoherently.

'Artemisia, but my friends call me Arte,' she replied. 'I'm so sorry about what's happening to your father.'

'You know about my father?'

'It's one of the reasons I was at the protest,' admitted Artemisia. She looked up to see an officer talking animatedly on the phone. 'You want to hear the bad news?' she said, hoping to cheer him up. 'My father is in charge of the Saudi Minister's protection.'

'I could kill him,' said Robert.

'My father or the Saudi Minister?' asked Artemisia, as she placed an arm around his shoulder.

'The Minister,' said Robert, 'though I must admit, I may have thrown an egg at your father.'

'Me too,' said Artemisia, laughing. 'Do you think we'll have to spend the night in jail?'

'Let's hope so,' said Robert. 'It's the least I can do for my father,' he added as the officer put the phone down, walked across and smiled at the two of them.

'Right, you two, shove off.'

'But I want to be charged,' said Robert, 'and put in prison.'

'It won't help your father,' said the officer quietly, 'and believe it or not, we're all on his side.'

'Will you be telling my father?' asked Artemisia.

'That's way above my pay grade,' said Wainwright, 'so why don't you go home? By the way, both your fathers would be proud of you.'

Robert burst into tears.

Artemisia took his hand and led him quietly out of the police station.

CHAPTER 15

WILLIAM TICKED OFF THE LAST of the dinner party guests as they left the Saudi Embassy. He checked his watch: just after eleven. Most of the protestors had also departed – nothing like a cold night and PC Rain to assist the police with their job. William decided to go home and find out if he still had a wife and children.

He was just about to tap Danny on the shoulder when a young man, no longer in a keffiyeh and thawb but wearing a casual sports jacket and an open-neck shirt, came out of the rear of the embassy. William recognized him immediately.

'Time for some old-fashioned foot slogging,' said William, who quickly jumped out of the car, making sure he didn't lose sight of the Black Prince as he made his way along Curzon Street, past his favourite bookshop and on towards Park Lane.

Prince Ahmed kept a steady pace and never once looked back.

William wondered where he could be going at this time of night, unaccompanied by his usual hangers-on.

When the Prince reached Park Lane, he turned right and headed in the direction of Marble Arch, but had only covered another hundred yards before he reached the entrance to a hotel where the head porter bowed low and said, 'Good evening your Royal Highness.'

William kept his distance and hung back before entering the Dorchester a few moments later, as if he were a guest. He remained out of sight as the manager escorted the Prince to the nearest lift.

William walked slowly across the lobby, his eyes fixed on the indicator above the lift that showed Ahmed was heading for the ninth floor. When the night manager returned a few minutes later, William was standing in the corridor waiting for him.

'Can I help you, sir?' he asked.

'I'm responsible for the Prince's security,' said William, producing his warrant card. 'It would be helpful for my team if we knew if His Royal Highness has retired for the night or has plans to go out again. I want to make sure he gets the best protection possible while he's a guest of the British government.'

The manager looked suitably impressed. 'All I can tell you, Chief Superintendent, is that His Royal Highness is expecting a guest in about twenty minutes' time, and has no plans to go out that I'm aware of.'

'Thank you,' said William. 'That's most helpful. And I feel sure we can rely on your discretion.'

The night manager nodded before returning to the reception desk.

William was puzzled by who could possibly be visiting Prince Ahmed at that time of night. He assumed it had to be a young lady who charged by the hour. He hoped it wasn't one in particular, because if it was, he would have no way of protecting her.

He allowed a policeman's curiosity to get the better of him, walked back across the lobby and remained secreted behind a pillar in the far corner that gave him a clear view of the revolving door, as well as the bank of lifts to his left. He didn't have to wait long.

When he saw who it was entering the hotel, he assumed it had to be a coincidence, but then policemen don't believe in coincidences. He remained behind the pillar as the night manager greeted the guest and accompanied him across the lobby to a waiting lift. When the doors slid closed, William walked across to see that the little arrow didn't stop until it reached the ninth floor.

If this had been Moscow or even Washington, the room would have been bugged, but it was London, so William could only hazard a guess as to what they might be discussing. He returned to his place behind the pillar and wondered how long he would have to wait.

• • •

As Miles made his way up to the ninth floor, he felt unusually nervous. Dealing with petty criminals and people who relied on his patronage was one thing, but having to handle a prince of the Royal Blood was quite another, especially as this particular Prince was not in need of financial succour. But then, perhaps he had something to offer that he needed more than money. He hoped that half the stories about the Black Prince were true.

When Miles stepped out of the lift on the ninth floor, he made his way across to an un-numbered door. He pressed the little pearl button and, moments later, it was opened by a man dressed in a light blue suit and open-neck shirt, who thrust out his hand and said, 'I'm Hani Khalil, His Royal Highness's senior consultant.'

Miles shook hands with a man he instantly disliked, but returned his insincere smile before being led into the presence of his master. Prince Ahmed was sitting in a large, comfortable chair as if it were a throne; he made no effort to welcome Miles. The two men stared at each other like a mongoose who's come across a snake, each waiting for the other to strike. Ahmed waved an imperious hand in the direction of the seat opposite him to let him know he could sit down. Khalil remained standing.

Miles sat on the edge of his seat and took a closer look at his would-be collaborator. He exuded arrogance, vanity and entitlement in equal measure – three weaknesses he always welcomed whenever he was trying to close a deal. Miles bowed low and said, 'How kind of you to spare the time to see me, Your Royal Highness,' playing his first card: flattery.

The Prince didn't respond; clearly this was no more than he expected from an infidel.

'His Royal Highness,' said Khalil, 'understands you have a proposition to put to him, Mr Faulkner, and as he is expecting another guest to join him in a few minutes' time, perhaps you could tell us the purpose of your visit.'

'Avril Dubois,' said Miles, who didn't have to wait for a reaction.

The Prince lurched forward in his chair, as if he was about to attack the mongoose, but the snake remained uncurled.

'I have it on good authority,' continued Miles, 'that when the trial comes to court, Ms Dubois will be returning to Riyadh as part of a British defence team, when she will produce irrefutable evidence that His Royal Highness might find extremely embarrassing.'

The Prince shifted uneasily in his chair, but still didn't comment.

'She wouldn't get past immigration control,' said Khalil.

'Which is exactly what the Foreign Office are anticipating,' said Miles, not missing a beat, 'and is why she will also be accompanied by foreign correspondents from *The Guardian*, *The Times* and the *New Statesman*. I have to warn you they have already written their copy, which will not read well.' Miles paused before he played his trump card. 'However, if you think it would be helpful, I can make sure she doesn't reach the airport.'

'And what would you expect in return?' came back Khalil.

'That Simon Hartley also doesn't make it to the airport.'

There was a short silence, during which time Khalil and the Prince exchanged glances.

'Why is Hartley so important to you?' demanded Khalil.

'For the same reason Avril is important to you,' said Miles. 'A great deal of money is at stake.'

Miles waited for a response, aware that all the information Booth Watson and ex-Superintendent Lamont had supplied had hit home.

'You have a deal, Mr Faulkner,' said the Prince, speaking for the first time. He rose from his place and shook hands with Miles as if they were old friends.

Miles bowed low once again before he said, 'It's been a pleasure doing business with you, Your Royal Highness.'

The Prince simply nodded to indicate that the meeting was over. Khalil accompanied his guest back to the lift, but this time, when he offered his hand, Miles didn't shake it.

'Now listen to me carefully, you little shit,' said Miles as he waited for the lift to appear. 'Should you fail to keep your end of the bargain, I would advise you not to return to your homeland, because if you do it won't be your wife and children waiting to greet you in the Arrivals hall.'

Khalil was still shaking when the lift doors opened. Miles stepped inside, pressed G, and continued to stare at Khalil as the doors slowly closed. Once he'd returned to the ground floor, he walked across the lobby and out of the hotel to his waiting car, with William following his every step.

As Faulkner climbed into his Rolls, William took out his mobile and dialled a number he didn't need to look up. It was some time before a voice came on the line and barked, 'Who's this?'

'Warwick, sir,' William replied. 'We have a problem.'

• • •

Chief Superintendent Warwick arrived back at his home just after three o'clock that morning. He closed the front door quietly, crept upstairs and slipped into bed, hoping not to wake Beth.

He lay awake for the next four hours with only one question on his mind.

He slipped out of bed just before seven, took a cold shower, brushed his teeth, dressed in the dark in yesterday's clothes and left the bedroom without turning on the light. He crept back downstairs, went into the kitchen, grabbed a bowl of cornflakes, and made himself a cup of tea and a slice of toast which he spread with marmalade. He ate and drank at the same time.

He'd left the house before anyone realized he'd even been home.

• • •

Once again, they all stood in line and watched as the Saudi Defence Minister and his son climbed on board the 747 and disappeared inside without once looking back or offering the traditional wave.

William, who was standing some way off from the main party, breathed a sigh of relief when the cabin door finally closed.

As the Foreign Secretary watched the plane slowly begin to taxi towards the runway, he remarked to Trevelyan, 'So now it's anyone's guess who will end up with the arms deal.'

'I can't pretend to be over-optimistic about our chances,' responded Trevelyan. 'The only time the damn man was polite was when he was with the Queen.'

The sound of the four jet engines roaring into life drowned out the Foreign Secretary's reply as the plane took off.

Once William had accompanied Robin Cook safely back to his office in Whitehall, Danny drove him on to Scotland Yard so he could brief the Commander on how the morning had gone.

Without a hitch, but last night . . .

• • •

William arrived at the Yard just after eleven to find the Commander already seated behind his desk. Within minutes, Ross, Paul, Rebecca and Jackie had joined them and taken their places around the conference table.

'What I can't work out,' said the Hawk, as he took his place at the top of the table, 'is why would Faulkner visit Ahmed in the middle of the night.'

'Ahmed must have something Faulkner wants,' suggested Ross.

'But what could those two possibly have in common?' said William.

'They'd both murder their grandmothers if there was something in it for them,' commented Jackie.

'I would guess,' said Rebecca, 'that an extra one hundred and fifty million pieces of silver is more than enough for Ahmed and Khalil to want to risk anything to ensure the French and not the British end up with the arms contract.'

'But Faulkner's never shown any interest in arms or oil in the past,' said the Hawk, almost talking to himself. 'It's not his world.'

They all fell silent until Rebecca said, 'It isn't their grandmothers they'd have to kill to make sure the French get the arms deal.'

'Only Avril Dubois,' said William. 'But that still doesn't explain what Faulkner's involvement is.'

'If Prince Ahmed arranged for Faulkner to have Avril killed,' said Ross, 'Ahmed would be off the hook and the one hundred and fifty million would be his.'

'But what would Faulkner expect in return?' said Paul. 'It has to be more than thirty pieces of silver to take such a huge risk. If he was implicated in Avril's murder, he would be spending the rest of his life in prison.'

Another long silence followed before the Hawk said, 'That's one mystery we won't solve sitting around this table, so we'll have to keep Faulkner under surveillance twenty-four-seven, because if he does plan to have Avril killed, he'll have to employ someone else to do his dirty work, and I need to know who, and even more important, when.'

CHAPTER 16

MILES TOOK HIS TIME FILLING in the form, especially when it came to *previous offences*.

After signing his name on the bottom line, he posted the application recorded delivery, but didn't receive a reply confirming his request had been granted for another five days.

He made a note in his diary.

• • •

Ross burst into William's office when he was on the phone. 'Faulkner's applied for a prison visit next Thursday,' he said.

'I'll call you back,' said William, before putting down the phone. He looked at Ross and all he asked was, 'Who?'

'Tulip. His eyes and ears when he was in the Scrubs.'

'Serving twelve years for the murder of a police witness during one of Faulkner's earlier trials, if I remember correctly.'

'The same,' said Ross.

'Then I want to know every word that passes between them, because it may be our only hope of finding out what the connection is between Miles Faulkner and Prince Ahmed.'

Ross nodded. 'I'll have the four best lip readers available on the balcony, picking up every word.'

'They'll need to be good, because those two will know they're up there.'

'They're the best,' said Ross, 'and Faulkner and Tulip may not be able to spot them,' he added without explanation.

'And Ross,' said William firmly, as he got up and turned to leave, 'for obvious reasons I don't want any of our team anywhere near the Scrubs next Thursday. So pick your contacts carefully, because one or two of the prison officers could well be on Faulkner's payroll.'

'I'll keep the information to the bare minimum and report back to you.'

William picked up the phone as the door closed, dialled a number and said, 'Sorry about that, sir, but I think we may have a breakthrough in the Faulkner case.'

· · ·

Miles was driven into the visitors' car park long before the appointed hour. He strolled across to the waiting room and filled in yet another form before he was handed a disc with the number three on it. He then exchanged a five-pound note for five canteen vouchers, took a seat and waited and waited. He finally gave up and began to read the *Prison News*.

'Numbers one to five,' said a prison officer just before three o'clock struck. Miles rose and, along with seven other visitors and one protesting baby, followed the officer out of the waiting room, across a yard and into the reception area. He handed over his mobile phone, wallet and leather belt, not needing to be told he could pick them back up after the visit.

The same officer led the eight visitors out of the reception area, across the barren weed-infested yard surrounded by a high wall that Miles had stared at for three years.

Miles shivered when he stepped back into the prison and was escorted down a long brick corridor to another waiting area. He joined a little queue at the mobile canteen, handed over his five coupons and in return received a cup of coffee, a ham sandwich, two bars of KitKat and a packet of cigarettes. He wasn't offered any change.

A buzzer sounded. Two officers appeared and led the first eight visitors into a large open room full of circular tables spread well apart from each other. There was a red chair on one side of each table for the prisoner and two blue chairs on the other for his visitors.

Miles looked around the room to see Tulip giving him a wave. He weaved his way through the tables and, when he reached the prisoner, placed all his purchases on his side of the table.

'Don't look up,' said Tulip as Miles took the seat opposite him. 'I've already spotted two lip readers on the balcony, and I assume there have to be more.'

'Then I'll act as the ventriloquist,' said Miles, 'and you can be my dummy. I'll make it clear what I want, while you talk gibberish.'

Tulip nodded. 'I read all about the *Angel* shutting herself in the toilet in the *Sun*,' he said. 'You must have enjoyed that. So what's next?'

'I need a removal man and quickly,' said Miles, his head bowed, his lips barely moving.

'I hope you like the *Water Lilies* that Billy Mumford painted for you,' said Tulip, after taking a sip of coffee.

'What's the going rate?'

'What do you expect him to paint next, the Virgin Mary?'

'No. A prostitute from Putney.'

'I think he's now charging around twenty thousand, possibly more. But he'll need a photo of the model.'

'Tell him to visit me at my office overlooking the river, when I'll hand over a photo and the cash.'

'I'll let him know,' said Tulip as he grabbed the ham sandwich and took a bite, before asking, 'When?'

'Sunday, three o'clock,' said Miles, his lips not moving. 'It's always the busiest time of day. But warn him I'm being followed, so only join me if I put my hands in my pockets.'

'I'll let him know,' said Tulip, before taking another bite of his sandwich.

'What are your chances of parole?' asked Miles, speaking normally now that he had completed his business.

'I've had my first interview,' said Tulip. 'Tried to convince them I was a reformed character and had turned over a new leaf.'

'When will you find out if they believe you?'

'Not for several months,' said Tulip. 'Nothing, as you know, moves quickly in prison.'

'Are you still working in the library?'

'Yep, it's still the easiest job in this place – and allows me to keep in touch with everything that's going on in the outside world.'

A buzzer sounded to warn visitors they only had another five minutes.

Miles looked around to see lovers kissing their partners and fathers hugging children. At the next table, a woman cradling a baby in her arms couldn't stop crying.

'Anything you need?' asked Miles.

'No,' said Tulip. 'Thanks to you, I'm well taken care of.' He leant back and drained his coffee.

The buzzer sounded a second time.

'See you next Sunday,' said Miles, who rose from his place and made his way quickly out of the room so that he would be among the first to be escorted back to reception. He didn't look back, but if he had, he would have seen Tulip devouring the second KitKat and placing the packet of cigarettes in his pocket before being escorted back to his cell.

Miles joined a group of visitors who were being accompanied to reception, where he collected his mobile phone and wallet and slipped on his belt.

Once he'd escaped – because that's how it felt – Miles returned to his car and was driven away by the only chauffeur in the car park.

• • •

The lip reader in chief, as she was known at the Scrubs, arrived at Scotland Yard just after Miles had reached his home in Chelsea.

Once Kimberley Young had introduced herself to the two police officers, William didn't waste any time before asking his first question: 'Did your team come up with anything we might find helpful?'

'Hard to tell,' admitted Kimberley, 'because they were clearly aware of our presence and played the double conversation trick to near perfection. While one of them delivered a well-prepared script, the visitor replied while his lips barely moved. So we have one side of a non sequitur conversation, while the other is a series of random words that I can only hope will mean something to you. However, even the most accomplished ventriloquist finds certain letters are almost impossible to pronounce without their lips moving.'

'Which ones?' asked William.

'B F M P R W all present their own problems. I challenge you to say, without moving your lips: Betty Wilson works at a beauty parlour in Peterborough and is married to a farm labourer from Richmond who smokes Benson and Hedges.'

Both of them had given up before they reached Peterborough.

Having proved her point, Kimberley handed over a second sheet of paper, with the few words her team had managed to pick up from Faulkner's conversation. *Removal, prostitute, Putney,* followed by *three, busiest,* plus *hands in my pockets, my office overlooking the river* and *see you next Sunday.*

They both studied the words for some time before William said, 'He must have been asking Tulip to recommend a hit man to remove Avril, and he wants to meet him at his office overlooking the river.'

'On Sunday at three o'clock,' added Ross.

'What makes you say that?' asked Kimberley.

'Because Faulkner doesn't have an appointment to see Tulip next Sunday,' said William.

'And in any case, Billy the Forger would never expect to be paid twenty thousand, even for a painting of the Virgin Mary,' said Ross.

'The river in question has to be the Thames, but our Marine Unit can't be expected to patrol the thirty-seven miles from one end to the other,' said William, 'even if we have got the time right.'

'They could be meeting on a barge, river boat, even a ferry,' suggested Ross.

'Unlikely,' said Kimberley. 'One of my team would have

picked up river boat, barge or ferry. R B B and F,' she reminded them.

'But,' said William, 'how did you pick up *see you next Sunday* when Faulkner could have delivered that sentence without having to move his lips?'

'Because at the time,' said Kimberley, 'I was sitting on the next table to Faulkner, clutching onto a baby while my deputy sat opposite me. Not something we'll be able to do twice,' admitted Kimberley. 'But you did tell me, Inspector, that it was top priority, as a young lady's life might be in danger.'

'Is in danger,' said William.

CHAPTER 17

BOOTH WATSON HAD LEARNT OVER the years that when-ever Miles used the word *urgent*, he meant yesterday, which was the reason he turned up outside 57 Cadogan Square within an hour of Miles summoning him, despite it being a Sunday. If there was anything else he'd learnt about his client, it was that it was a pointless exercise to try and second guess why he wanted to see him and it was wise to never appear surprised, whatever he came up with.

The reliable Collins answered the door. 'Good morning, sir,' he said before accompanying Booth Watson through to his master's study, when it became clear from the look on Miles's face that he was in a foul mood. He quickly found out why.

'I've had the Hartley's Constable valued by Christie's,' said Miles before Booth Watson could open his Gladstone bag and take out a yellow pad and fountain pen.

'How much did they estimate it would fetch?' asked Booth Watson as he sat down.

'Ten thousand pounds at most,' said Miles.

After recovering from the initial shock, Booth Watson said, 'So it clearly isn't a Constable.'

'School of,' said Miles. 'The Christie's expert is fairly certain it was painted by a Breck LaFave, one of Constable's more accomplished pupils, but a pupil nonetheless.'

'I wonder if Lady Hartley was aware of that when she sold you the picture,' said Booth Watson.

'A question I've asked myself several times, but I still can't make up my mind.'

'If she was,' suggested Booth Watson, 'she might also have known about the sixth letter, the one that—'

'You don't have to remind me,' said Miles. 'But even if she did, she's unlikely to be shouting it from the rooftops.'

'What makes you say that?' asked Booth Watson, pen moving briskly across the paper.

'Because if she knew about the letter, she also knew she had no right to sell the Declaration, but just needed the money quickly.'

'That doesn't apply to her son,' Booth Watson reminded him.

'But while he's holed up in a Saudi jail, he's unlikely to cause me any trouble.'

'For now, possibly,' said Booth Watson. 'However, *The Times* are suggesting that the Saudi delegation visit went well and are hinting that once the arms deal has been signed by either side, it won't be too long before Hartley is released. And if he sees his mother before the Declaration comes up for sale . . .'

'I can assure you, BW, that problem is being taken care of. So the sale will go ahead. In fact, I'm off to Newark, New Jersey, this evening,' said Miles, 'from where I will be driven to Princeton University to seek the advice of Dr Saul Rosenberg, the emeritus professor of American history, who's considered by his fellow academics to be the pre-eminent authority on the constitution.'

'That won't come cheap,' suggested Booth Watson.

'Wrong again, BW. Retired professors will happily supply you with all the information you require in exchange for a free lunch and a half-decent bottle of burgundy. Mind you, I did tell him I was crossing the earth in the hope he would sign my first edition of *Monticello*, his Pulitzer Prize-winning biography of Thomas Jefferson. And after I've seen him, I'll be going on to Christie's in New York.'

'And when will you be back?' asked Booth Watson.

'Not before a particular story hits the front pages,' replied Miles. 'Call me as soon as the news becomes public.'

'It would help if I knew what I was looking for,' said Booth Watson.

'You'll know when you see it.'

Booth Watson stopped writing. He had no idea what Miles was referring to, but he did know it would be pointless to ask him.

• • •

Ross was parked about a hundred yards from Faulkner's house in Cadogan Square – out of sight, but with a perfect view of his front door. He'd seen Booth Watson come and go, but since then, no one had left the mews house.

Rebecca was seated in a Pret A Manger, toying with a cold coffee while she looked out of the window. She couldn't see Faulkner's front door, but she couldn't miss anyone coming down the street towards her.

Paul was sitting on a motorbike on the corner of Sloane Street, ready to move the moment Faulkner's driver turned right or left. He could weave in and out of traffic and didn't need to break the speed limit – useful when cars in London only managed an average of eight miles per hour.

Jackie was sitting behind the wheel of a taxi at the other end of Cadogan Square, the *For Hire* sign never alight, as it was part of the Met's private pool.

William was seated behind his desk back at the Yard, a row of phones and a large map of London spread out in front of him. A winding river stretched from the top corner of the map to the bottom. One of the phones went straight through to the headquarters of the Marine Unit, who had every available boat out on patrol that afternoon, all looking for one man – a needle in a haystack, and this particular haystack was the Thames.

• • •

'Faulkner has just left his house,' said Paul over the radio. 'He's wearing a blue tracksuit and trainers and looks as if he's put on a few pounds, unless . . .'

'He's getting into the back of his car and they're heading towards you,' said Ross. 'Stay out of sight, Rebecca, because he's about to pass you.'

Rebecca turned her back on him as the Rolls swept by.

'Jackie?'

'Contact with the target,' she responded. 'I have eyeball – three for cover – waiting to see which way he turns when he reaches Sloane Street.'

Collins turned left, which took them all by surprise; the only water that way was the Serpentine. Jackie kept her distance, but never let them out of her sight. She could see Paul ahead of her, while a glance in her rear-view mirror showed that Ross was another couple of cars behind.

• • •

'We are being followed,' said Collins as he glanced in his wing mirror.

'Now there's a surprise,' said Miles, without looking back.

'A taxi that was parked at the other end of the street isn't far behind,' said Collins, 'and a man on a motorbike ahead of us has looked back once too often.'

'Not taking any chances, are they?' said Miles as Collins came to a halt at the lights at the top of Sloane Street.

When the lights turned green, Collins took his time before turning left onto the Brompton Road. Paul and Jackie remained in touch, but Ross got stuck behind a bus and didn't cross the lights in time.

'They are down to two – the taxi and the motorbike,' said Collins as he drew up outside the front door of Harrods.

A liveried doorman stepped forward and opened the back door of the Rolls. Faulkner got out and strolled into the store, while Collins drove off.

'Faulkner's disappeared into Harrods,' said Paul over the radio, 'which has at least half a dozen exits.'

'Don't lose him,' said Ross, who had just turned the corner, 'and I'll follow the Rolls in case he's picking him back up. Jackie, you cover the back entrance, as I don't think he plans on buying anything.'

Paul dumped his motorbike, ran into the store and saw Faulkner leaving luxury goods and entering the food hall. By the time he'd caught up with him, Faulkner was heading for a side door that led on to Hans Crescent.

'He'll be coming out of the east entrance of the building at any moment,' said Paul over the radio.

Jackie immediately took off and turned left into Hans Crescent, just as Faulkner stepped out onto the pavement.

She slipped into a residents' only spot and watched as Faulkner crossed the road and climbed onto the back of a motorbike. They sped off, the wrong way down a one-way street, leaving Jackie unable to turn around and follow him.

Paul watched as the motorbike turned left and disappeared out of sight. 'We've lost him,' he said in an exasperated voice.

'I got the number plate,' said Jackie, which William passed on to the Met's main control room.

The motorbike had covered less than a mile before it came to a halt at a bus stop. Miles got off and climbed onto the first approaching bus. He jumped aboard, not interested in where it was going. He got off at the next stop, crossed the road, hailed a taxi and told the cabbie 'County Hall'.

'All of you head for the Thames,' said William. 'Ross and Paul cover the South Bank side, Jackie and Rebecca the Westminster embankment. I know it's a long shot, but he hasn't left us with a lot of choice.'

• • •

The cab crossed Westminster Bridge and came to a halt outside County Hall. Miles got out and checked both ways before he handed the cabbie a five-pound note. He didn't wait for any change. He began to jog through the members' car park until he reached the South Bank, where he joined several other joggers out on their Sunday afternoon run.

When Miles saw the long queue waiting to board the 'London Eye', he slowed down and made his way to the front.

'I'm sorry, sir,' said the ticket collector, 'but you'll have to join the queue.'

Miles handed over his 'priority' ticket to the young man, who said, 'Sorry, sir.'

Faulkner looked around and, confident he had shaken off any pursuers, placed his hands in his pockets.

'Are you on your own, sir?' asked the attendant as an empty capsule appeared.

'No,' said a voice from behind him.

Miles looked around to see a man of average height, wearing an unmarked baseball cap, dark glasses, grey T-shirt, grey sweater, faded jeans and black trainers. You would have walked straight past him without giving him a second look, which was exactly what he would have wanted. He jumped into the empty capsule ahead of Miles.

• • •

'I'm driving along the Albert Embankment,' said Ross, 'and almost every building I pass is overlooking the Thames.'

'I'm on the other side,' came in Jackie, 'heading towards the City. No offices, but no shortage of people enjoying an afternoon by the river.'

'And you, Paul?' asked William.

'Someone stole my motorbike,' he said, causing Ross to stifle a laugh. 'I'm currently walking past the Saatchi Gallery. Crammed with tourists. But no sign of Faulkner.'

'Which is exactly why he chose a Sunday afternoon,' said William. 'How about you, Rebecca?'

'I'm just coming out of Westminster tube station,' she said, 'and will head towards the river.'

'All of you, keep looking,' said William, trying not to sound desperate.

• • •

'I like your office overlooking the river,' said the stranger, not introducing himself.

'It takes the wheel about thirty minutes to complete a full circle,' said Miles as he sat down beside him, 'so we can't afford to waste any time.'

'How did you manage to get an empty capsule all to yourself?' asked the stranger.

'I had to buy all twenty-five tickets to make sure no one else could join us,' Miles explained as they set off on their upward journey.

The stranger looked out over the skyline. 'So, who's the mark?'

'A common prostitute called Avril Dubois,' said Miles. 'She works at the Down and Out Club, so shouldn't be too difficult to find.'

'But she'll have a dozen protection officers watching her every move,' said the stranger, taking Miles by surprise.

'What makes you say that?'

'Don't insult my intelligence, Mr Faulkner,' said the stranger. 'When Tulip told me the mark would be a prostitute, I realized the last thing she would be was common. You only have to read the tabloids to discover Ms Dubois will be the principal witness for the defence in the Simon Hartley trial – so the one thing you can be sure of is she'll be well protected,' he paused, 'night and day.'

'Does that mean you're no longer willing to do the job?' Miles asked, as the wheel reached its peak of 135 metres above the Thames.

'No,' said the stranger, 'but it's going to cost you double.'

'But we agreed on twenty thousand,' said Miles.

'That was before I realized the mark was Avril Dubois.'

'I only have twenty thousand on me,' said Miles, tapping his waist.

'Then I'll have to take your watch,' said the stranger, as he glanced across the river to see a traffic jam building up on the far side of the Thames.

'But it's a Rolex Daytona,' protested Miles, 'and cost me over forty thousand.'

'I'll be lucky to get twenty thousand for it on the second-hand market,' said the stranger. 'Take it or leave it.'

Miles considered the alternative as the capsule began its descent. Finding someone else to take his place at such short notice had to be weighed against how much he had to gain if he could keep Hartley out of the way long enough for Christie's to auction Jefferson's Declaration. He took off the Rolex and reluctantly handed it to the stranger.

'And the other twenty thousand,' said the stranger as he strapped on his new watch, 'in cash.'

Miles lifted his tracksuit top, unfastened a thick money belt and placed it on the seat beside the stranger, who slipped it around his waist and fastened the strap without bothering to check the contents. They were both well aware that if his client had short-changed him, the job wouldn't get done.

'When will you carry out your side of the bargain?' asked Miles, as the capsule continued on its downward journey.

'It won't be for at least a week,' said the stranger casually. 'I'll need to visit the Down and Out Club several times to become familiar with her routine and see just how many protection officers are involved before I can make a move.'

'How will you let me know when the job is done?'

'You'll know,' said the stranger.

• • •

After Ross had crossed Tower Bridge, he swung left and slowed down when he reached the Tower of London. He wondered if the meeting could be taking place in the Jewel Room – but surely even Faulkner wouldn't have the gall to risk that a second time. He accelerated as he headed on towards Upper Thames Street and the Victoria Embankment, hoping the others were enjoying more success.

Paul was walking beside the river, ignoring the buskers, conjurers and street entertainers that littered the South Bank on a sunny afternoon, while his eyes never stopped roaming. But not once did he see anyone resembling Faulkner.

Jackie was driving so slowly on the other side of the river that impatient motorists held up behind her were beginning to make their presence felt, with more than the occasional blast on their horns. She ignored them as she continued her search for Faulkner, but to no avail.

Rebecca was leaning over Westminster Bridge, double check-ing the boats passing below her. But it was when she looked up that her eyes settled on the London Eye. She shouted, 'In my office overlooking the river.'

She immediately contacted Chief Superintendent Warwick on her radio and told him what had been staring them in the face. William ordered the rest of the team to head for the Eye, sharpish, hoping it wouldn't be too late.

• • •

'Just remember one thing, Mr Faulkner,' said the stranger as the wheel completed its circle. 'I don't work for the same client twice, so don't bother to contact me again.'

Before Miles could reply, the man had jumped off the moving wheel and disappeared into the crowd, lost within moments.

Miles stepped off more cautiously and began walking in the opposite direction. When he reached Westminster Bridge, he waited for the light to turn red before he crossed the road.

'Clocked him,' said Rebecca over the radio, just as Faulkner reached the other side.

'Where is he?' asked William.

'Outside St Thomas's Hospital, getting into the back of his car. But he can't be going home, because he's travelling in the opposite direction.'

'I can see the Rolls,' said Jackie, coming on the line. 'They're driving across Westminster Bridge and are heading west.'

'Don't lose him,' said William, 'and keep your line open while I call the Commander.'

• • •

William picked up the phone.

'Did you find out who the contract killer is?' was the Hawk's first question.

'No, sir,' replied William. 'We think Faulkner's office overlooking the river was the London Eye, but we didn't spot him until after he'd got off.'

'So the killer could be on the other side of the world by now,' said the Hawk.

'I don't think it's the killer who's heading for the other side of the world,' said William.

'Evidence.'

'Faulkner's car is heading west down the Cromwell Road, so my bet is that he's on his way to the airport.'

'So he'll be out of the country when the killer strikes,' said the Hawk.

'Establishing an alibi,' said William, 'which must all be part of his plan.'

'Then the deal must have been struck,' said the Hawk, 'so we'll have to double our surveillance team. And tell Ross, while Faulkner's away, to make sure he doesn't let Ms Dubois out of his sight.'

• • •

'The woman in the taxi is following us once again,' said Collins as he emerged from the underpass.

'Good,' said Miles. 'Then she'll see me getting onto the plane.'

'When should I expect you back, sir?' asked Collins.

'That's not being decided by me,' said Miles. 'But I'll let you know.'

Faulkner got out of the car and joined a slipstream of passengers making their way into the airport.

He only stopped to look up at the departure board: Newark New Jersey flashed up on the screen, Gate 23. Estimated take-off time 17.12.

Miles checked his watch. It wasn't there.

• • •

'Faulkner's boarding a British Airways plane for Newark New Jersey,' said Jackie as she watched him disappear up the steps and inside the aircraft.

'Don't leave until you've seen it take off,' said William, 'and even then, double-check the passenger list.'

Jackie's eyes never left the aircraft.

• • •

Miles took his seat in first class, pleased that everything, so far, had gone to plan, even if he would have to buy a new watch. He took a copy of Rosenberg's *Monticello* out of his briefcase, turned to the index and checked the letter D. Sixteen references for him to consider.

He switched on the reading light above his head, settled back and began to turn the pages, confident that by the time they landed in the States, he would know the right questions to ask Professor Rosenberg.

During the flight, his mind occasionally returned to his meeting with the stranger on the London Eye. Miles felt confident he would keep his side of the bargain, and more importantly, that Simon Hartley wouldn't be around for much longer to cause him any trouble.

He fell asleep with the book in his lap.

• • •

When Jackie reported that the plane had taken off with Faulkner on board, William only had one question: why was he flying to Newark and not New York?

He didn't come up with an answer. However, he knew someone who just might have one. He placed a call through to an old friend in Washington.

CHAPTER 18

MILES WAS AMONG THE FIRST off the plane. When he emerged in the Arrivals hall, he searched among the names being held up on boards by different drivers, pleased to see FAULKNER was among them.

'Good morning, sir,' said his driver when Miles pointed at the card and said, 'That's me.'

'Are you the gentleman I'm taking to Princeton and then on to New York?'

'That's right,' said Miles. 'How long will it take to get to Princeton?'

'About an hour, sir,' said the driver as he guided his passenger towards the short-term car park.

• • •

'Are you sure this is the right address?' asked Miles, when the car finally drew up outside a small, isolated cottage on the outskirts of Princeton. He'd seen bigger garages in London.

'This is the address they gave me,' said the driver.

'Then you'd better wait,' said Miles. 'This shouldn't take too long.'

Miles got out of the car, opened the little wicket gate, walked up a short weed-infested path to the house and knocked on the door. He waited so long he began to wonder if anyone was at home, even though he'd made an appointment. He banged louder a second time, and the door was opened almost immediately.

'Sorry, sorry,' said an unshaven elderly gentleman. He was dressed in an open-neck plaid shirt and baggy corduroy trousers held up by a pair of red braces, while wearing two different-coloured slippers. But there the appearance of age ended, as the sharp penetrating eyes, lined forehead and silver-grey hair suggested this wasn't a man to be trifled with.

'Good morning, sir,' said Miles.

'Good morning, young man,' said Rosenberg. 'Welcome to my humble abode.'

Miles couldn't remember when he'd last been called *young man*.

He followed the professor into the house and along a dark corridor that displayed several academic citations and lifetime awards, illustrating a long and distinguished career. The professor led his guest into a room that didn't appear to have any walls, just books stacked from floor to ceiling, while others were randomly scattered all over the place, with a few – very few – in neat piles. The old man didn't seem to notice as he took a circuitous route to the only two chairs in the room, which stood in front of a fireplace with ashes waiting to be cleared. He collapsed into one of the chairs, which was already occupied by a large, furry ginger cat who clearly knew her place.

'Forgive the mess,' he said. 'It's never been the same since

Maud died, and I'm afraid the cleaner only comes once a week.'

When Miles sat down in the other chair, a cloud of dust rose to greet him.

'May I say from the outset, Mr Faulkner, how flattered I am that you took the trouble to cross the Atlantic to see me.'

'I've wanted to meet you for some time,' said Miles, who had only recently heard of Saul Rosenberg.

'So do tell me, how can I assist you?'

'Perhaps I should begin, sir, by asking you to sign my first edition of your prize-winning book, *Monticello*, which is among my most treasured possessions and which I have read several times over the years.'

'I'd be delighted to do so,' said the old man.

Miles bent down, took a book out of his bag that he'd purchased recently, of which he'd only read one particular chapter on the plane. He passed it across to the professor and Rosenberg took his time turning to the title page of a volume that didn't look as if it had been read several times. He squiggled his signature, adding the date before passing it back to his guest.

'Thank you,' said Miles, 'I'll treasure it. In return, may I present you with a small memento, written by one of our greatest statesmen, whose alma mater I had the honour of attending.' Miles handed over a black, gold-leafed, leather-bound volume.

'Churchill's *My Early Life*,' said the professor, handling the book with great care. 'I have a copy, of course,' he added, looking around the room, 'but not a first edition, and certainly not signed. I'm most grateful.'

'It's an inadequate gift to thank you for the pleasure you have given me over so many years.'

The professor didn't comment, other than to say, 'But how can I possibly return such munificence?'

'I wondered,' ventured Miles, setting about his purpose, 'if I might be allowed to ask you one or two questions about your life's work?'

'Yes, of course. Do you have any particular period in mind?'

'Thomas Jefferson and the Declaration of Independence – as you're considered the leading authority in the field.'

'I'm flattered, and will do my best to press a tired old brain back into action.'

'I was fascinated to discover when reading *Monticello* that you were in no doubt that, in 1776, Jefferson must have written a Fair Copy of the Declaration for Congress to consider before they took the final vote on their future as an independent nation.'

'Absolutely no doubt,' repeated the professor. 'After all, it's been well documented over the years. Indeed, I have proof at hand – if you would be kind enough to turn to page 171 of *Monticello*, you will find the facsimile of a letter written by Jefferson to Benjamin Franklin in early May 1776, stating unequivocally that, as his clauses had been rejected, he intended to send his Fair Copy to a friend in England to show him that at least he tried and request it should be returned to him in the fullness of time. That individual has never been identified, and search as I might for any clue to his name or whereabouts in other letters, journals or any relevant documents of the period, I have been unable to unearth who Jefferson was referring to when he wrote to "a friend in England". I have collated a shortlist of seven possible candidates,' mused the professor, 'but it's not a historian's responsibility to hazard a guess.'

Miles could have told him which of the seven it was, but

had no intention of enlightening the old man. He satisfied himself with, 'Do you consider it possible that the Fair Copy could still be out there somewhere?'

'I suppose it could be languishing in some French chateau or holed up in an English country house, as both Jefferson and Franklin spent many years in London and Paris, making several friends on both sides of the Channel.'

'You pointed out in your book, sir, that Jefferson's Fair Copy included an important clause on his strongly held views on slavery. You even went so far as to suggest that, had Congress included this clause, the Civil War might have been avoided,' said Miles, trying to prove he'd read the book and not just one chapter.

'The privilege of hindsight is the historian's most reliable source,' said the professor. 'However, it's well known that Congress did debate at great length how the new government should deal with the problem of slavery, not least because Jefferson had several slaves himself at the time and, after the death of his wife, lived with a black woman who bore him six children, only four of whom survived. But that didn't stop the great man drafting the clause you refer to, because he felt slavery was an anathema and should be abolished. Sadly, Congress ignored his advice.' The professor leant back, closed his eyes and raised his hands until the tips of his fingers touched as if in prayer. 'Let us pray my memory does not fail me.

'*The King has waged cruel war against human nature itself, violating its more sacred rights of life and liberty in the persons of a distant people who never offended him, captivating and carrying them into slavery in another hemisphere, or to incur miserable death in their transportation thither, this piratical warfare, the opprobrium of infidel powers, is the warfare of the Christian King of Great Britain, determined to keep open a market where men should be bought and sold, he has prostituted his negative for suppressing every legislative attempt to prohibit or restrain this execrable commerce.'*

Professor Rosenberg opened his eyes, lowered his hands and began stroking the cat, who rewarded him with loud purrs.

'That was worth the trip alone, sir,' said Miles. 'But can I ask, if the Fair Copy were to be found after all these years, would you be able to authenticate it?'

'I'm only surprised you need to ask that question,' remonstrated Rosenberg, as if addressing an idle student who hadn't been paying attention. 'Especially as you say you've read my book several times.'

Miles couldn't remember being admonished in that way since leaving school, but he didn't reply in kind, as he still had several questions he needed answering.

'And what else is remarkable about that letter?' asked the professor, still not convinced his guest had even read his book.

Faulkner got as near to feeling embarrassed as he was capable of.

'You will, of course, remember,' said the professor, 'that it's the only occasion, to my knowledge, when Jefferson misspelt Franklin's name, with a "y" and not an "i" – a mistake, as far as I'm aware, he never made again. But then, as you will find if you turn the page, and read on, Franklin, curmudgeonly old character that he was, severely reprimanded his friend for making the mistake.'

Miles felt equally chastised but was determined to plough on. 'Dare I ask, sir, if the Fair Copy were to be unearthed, how much do you think it would fetch on the open market?'

The scowl returned to the professor's lips, while the lines on his forehead became even more pronounced. 'I fear, Mr

Faulkner, I'm not best qualified to answer that particular question as I'm a historian, not an economist. However, I think one can safely say it's quite simply priceless. Not least because if it were to come on the market, the government would, in my opinion, be left with no choice but to outbid any rivals for what is, quite literally, a unique piece of American history.'

Miles tried to hide his excitement before saying, 'One final question, sir, before I leave, as I have already taken up too much of your time.'

He looked across to see that the old man had dozed off and was quietly snoring. Miles got up from his chair, crept out of the room and quietly closed the door behind him.

The old man opened his eyes and waited until he heard the front door close before he began to stroke the cat.

'You know, Martha,' he said, 'I don't trust that man.'

The cat arched its back.

• • •

Miles climbed into the back of the car, well satisfied with his meeting. After all, Rosenberg had made it clear that he would recognize the Fair Copy when he saw it, and his seal of approval would be more than enough to convince any sceptics, which could only add millions to its value.

Miles would have happily paid Rosenberg a hundred thousand dollars to authenticate the document, but as the professor pointed out, he was a historian not an economist, so a copy of Winston Churchill's memoirs had proved to be more than enough.

CHAPTER 19

SURVEILLANCE WORK IS AMONG THE most demanding
– while at the same time the most boring – any police officer
has to carry out. The problem is quite simple. You have to
be alert for several hours on end and then ready to move at
a moment's notice, and should you take a couple of minutes
off to make a phone call, grab a bite, take a pee, you can be
sure that will be the moment the predator strikes. You will
then spend the rest of your life remembering, and being
remembered for, what happened when you blinked.

Ross had often thought that protecting the President of
the United States must be among the most exciting and
demanding jobs on earth. A lifetime of specialized training
and dedication in preparation for something that might never
happen. The detail on duty in Dallas on the morning John
Kennedy was assassinated had the rest of their lives to
consider if they'd done everything possible to prevent his
death. One of the officers on duty that day committed suicide,
two resigned, and three had taken early retirement.

After a month of no income flowing in and bills mounting up, Avril left her mother's house in Putney, found a small flat in Pimlico and went back to work. Ross begged her not to take the risk, but she didn't listen.

He and his small surveillance team, led by Paul and Rebecca, assisted by a group of young detectives, remained vigilant and thorough. They didn't have to be reminded that a young woman's life was at stake.

The daily routine began at midday, when Avril woke, having returned home around three, sometimes four in the morning. Normal people's lunch was her breakfast, but not before enjoying a long warm bubble bath to wash away the night before. This was followed by a twenty-minute jog, with a police officer not far behind, another twenty minutes on the weights and a final twenty under the tanning machine, so that she never looked pale.

During the afternoon, Avril went shopping at her local Waitrose and Boots, and if she needed a new outfit, she took a trip to Carnaby Street or the King's Road. Price didn't seem to matter, but then she had chosen a profession that only dealt in cash payments, so she never received any brown envelopes from the taxman and never had to claim unemployment benefits.

The day job – night job – began around six, when she would prepare for the evening shift. A warm shower, not a bath. Make-up and dressing would take at least an hour, if she hoped to lure a rich client.

At eight o'clock a taxi would pick her up from her flat and take her to the Down and Out Club in Soho where she had her own table. Avril sipped only orange juice while she waited for an insect to land in her web. Some left after a few minutes, after they'd discovered she wasn't in their price range, while others lasted the course and went home with empty wallets, as cheques and credit cards were not acceptable to either side.

Ross always covered the night shift, when he knew Avril would be at her most vulnerable and any predator might strike.

Having been warned of the possible danger, Avril was every bit as alert as Ross and his team, and if she was in any doubt about a punter, he was dismissed out of hand, however much he offered her.

Ross had begged her to go into hiding while Faulkner was away, even offered her a safe house, but she was adamant.

'If he's that good, he'll find me,' said Avril, 'and if you're that good, it won't matter. In any case, a girl's got to earn a living, and don't forget, like footballers and ballet dancers, we have our sell-by date.'

The customers who approached her ranged from young men, who were often shy and nervous, to rowdy drunks who wanted ten minutes in the backyard and were summarily dismissed, to middle-aged businessmen who were usually well-dressed, polite, and looking for what Avril described as a 'girlfriend experience'. They were her favourite customers, because they never caused any trouble and often became regulars. In fact, to Ross's surprise, problems were rare – the occasional drunk who became aggressive, an angry punter who found he couldn't afford her, and the vain men who assumed they wouldn't have to pay – but they were few and far between, and one look at Ross and they were off.

Nine days after Faulkner had boarded a plane for Newark, New Jersey, the Hawk warned Ross that he couldn't justify the expense for much longer. Then it happened.

• • •

Ross sat bolt upright when Avril came out of the Down and Out Club. He switched on the ignition, while Rebecca's eyes never left their mark. Avril was accompanied by a client who was hailing a cab – a client who definitely fell into the middle-aged businessman category. Smart, well-tailored double-breasted suit, blue shirt, silk tie, even a rolled umbrella.

A taxi pulled up. The man opened the back door of the cab, put up his umbrella to protect Avril from the rain and then waited for her to climb in. Definitely after the 'girlfriend experience' thought Rebecca – probably divorced and lonely.

Ross palmed the gear lever into first and eased his car out to join the late evening traffic, while never letting the taxi out of his sight. Fifteen minutes later, the cabbie drew up outside the Colony Hotel in Mayfair. Ross slipped in behind a parked car on a single yellow line and waited.

Avril climbed out of the taxi, while the mark paid the fare. When he joined her, they linked arms and strolled into the hotel together, chatting amiably.

Ross sat back and tuned into Classic FM as he and Rebecca settled in for yet another version of Beethoven's 4th. Avril sometimes reappeared within the hour, after what she described as 'a quickie'. Ross preferred this group, as it allowed him the chance to get home in time to catch up with Alice and hear about her day.

That's when he spotted him: a man entering the hotel on his own, trying to look inconspicuous. Ross immediately recognized him but couldn't remember where from. He'd arrested so many people over the years . . . But he wasn't willing to take any chances.

'Wait here,' he said to Rebecca, then leapt out of the car, ran into the hotel and spotted the man standing at the reception desk. Ross kept his distance.

Just as the man turned around, a young lady approached him.

'Can I have your autograph?' she asked excitedly.

'Yes, of course,' said the man, giving her a warm smile. 'Who should I dedicate it to?'

'Suzie. Can I have a selfie with you?'

The man placed an arm around Suzie's shoulder and smiled, while her friend took a couple of shots.

Ross slipped away, left the hotel and walked quickly back to the car.

'False alarm?' asked Rebecca as he got back in.

'Lightbulb moment,' admitted Ross. 'He's Alice's favourite chef, has his own programme on the telly, but I still can't remember his name.'

'Good thing you didn't arrest him,' said Rebecca.

• • •

'What do you do?' asked Avril as they got out of the lift and began walking down the corridor.

'Nothing that glamorous, I'm afraid,' her client replied, as he unlocked the door to his room and stood aside. 'I'm a car salesman.' He placed his umbrella by the door. 'But I do have the BMW franchise for Coventry, which allows me the occasional luxury.'

'Married or divorced?' she asked.

'Married, but she's back in Coventry while I'm up here attending the motor show at Earl's Court tomorrow. You should see the latest BMW Sports coupé. The bodywork . . .'

'Perhaps that's not the only bodywork you'll want to see,' Avril teased, as she slipped off his jacket and let it drop onto the floor. 'Nice watch,' she remarked as he took her in his arms and began to kiss her.

'Money in advance,' she said, breaking away.

'Sorry,' he said, 'of course.' He picked his jacket up off the floor, took out his wallet, extracted five crisp twenties and handed them to her.

Avril took the cash and deftly slipped it in her bag while glancing at his wallet to see that there was a lot more where that came from, and wondered how many extras she could offer him.

'Why don't you get undressed while I freshen up?'

He began to unbutton his shirt. 'But please leave your bra and knickers on,' he said shyly before she disappeared into the bathroom.

Once Avril had closed the door, she took a mobile out of her bag and dialled Ross's number.

'Room seventy-six, seventh floor. I like this one. I think he could be an all-nighter, so why don't you both go home?' said Avril, even though she knew it was a risk Ross wouldn't consider. 'Good night, lover,' she said to a man she'd never slept with.

Avril slipped off her dress and looked at herself in the mirror. Not bad for thirty-four, going on twenty-nine. She took a tissue out of her bag and slowly removed her lipstick. All-nighters never liked lipstick. She then unscrewed the top of a small bottle of Chanel No. 5 and put a dab behind each ear. She finally pulled up her stockings and, after one more look in the mirror, convinced herself she was ready for the car salesman from Coventry.

As she opened the door, she put on her sweet girlfriend smile, only to find the punter had put his jacket back on and had even picked up his umbrella.

'Changed your mind, honey?' she said, sounding disappointed.

'No,' he replied, as he touched a tiny button on the handle of the umbrella. It didn't open up, but a long thin blade with a serrated edge shot out of the tip. Avril froze.

The stranger lunged forward, and with one single movement, thrust the blade between her second and third rib, a hit worthy of an Olympic swordsman.

Avril let out a piercing scream as she fell back and hit the floor with a thud. He let go of the umbrella, quickly grabbed a pillow from the bed, knelt down and held it firmly over her mouth. She tried to put up a fight, but within moments her head fell back and she lay motionless on the floor.

The stranger checked her pulse to make sure she was dead. Satisfied, he spent the next few minutes removing any suggestion that he'd ever been in the room. Once he'd double-checked everything, he walked slowly across to the door, opened it and looked up and down the corridor. No one was in sight.

He switched off the light, stepped out into the corridor, pulled the door closed, and headed for the staircase.

• • •

'A quickie,' said Ross, when he saw the light on the seventh floor go out. 'She'll be disappointed, but at least it means we can have an early night for a change.'

Ross's eyes never left the front of the hotel as he waited for Avril to reappear, so that he and Rebecca could drive her home. He was just about to call William and tell him that the back up team could stand down when the man in a three-piece suit strolled out of the hotel.

'Gloves,' said Ross.

Rebecca turned to face him. 'What's the problem?'

'He's wearing gloves,' said Ross, his voice on edge, 'and where's the umbrella?'

'He's probably left it in his room.'

'That's the problem – it was *his* room, not Avril's. *She* should be going home, not a man wearing gloves without his umbrella.' Ross had already unfastened his seat belt and was getting out of the car when he said, 'Follow him, Rebecca, but remember he'll be looking out for you, so keep your distance.'

Rebecca got out of the car and slipped into the shadows, while the suspect lengthened his stride as he made his way towards Hyde Park Corner. He looked back, but she just kept on walking.

'Red alert,' shouted Ross over the radio as he began running towards the hotel.

William responded immediately.

'We need AC1 and AC2 *now*,' said Ross. 'Rebecca is following the suspect and will keep you briefed.'

Ross pushed his way through the revolving doors of the hotel, causing the man in front of him to arrive in the lobby far more quickly than he'd anticipated.

Ross dashed past him towards the lifts and jumped into one just as its doors were closing, joining three other guests. He jabbed the seventh-floor button, and prayed the other three had a higher calling. But the lift stopped on the fourth floor, where two of them got out. He pressed the close button, but the lift continued on at its own pace, stopping again at the sixth to allow the only other guest to depart.

When the doors finally opened on the seventh floor, Ross leapt out and began running down the corridor, past room 70, 72, 74, coming to a halt outside 76. He banged on the door with a fist, while pressing the bell with his other hand, but there was no response.

He stood back and charged at the door, but unlike in films, it remained resolutely closed. He was about to try a second time when the lift door opened and out stepped a waiter, pushing a drinks trolley.

Ross grabbed the trolley from the startled waiter.

'Sir,' he protested.

'Police,' shouted Ross, as he propelled the trolley towards the closed door with the same result, except that several bottles ended up on the floor.

Ross pulled the trolley back a second time when the waiter quickly joined him. Together they hurled the trolley towards the door, which loosened its hinges, but was still only half open. Ross pushed his way through the gap to find Avril lying on the floor in a pool of blood, a sword sticking out of her chest, a blood-soaked pillow by her side. He fell on his knees and took her in his arms.

The waiter fainted.

• • •

'Where are you?' asked William.

'Walking along the north side of Piccadilly,' replied Rebecca. 'The suspect is about forty yards ahead of me and keeps looking back.'

'That's because he suspects someone might be following him. AC1 and 2 are already on their way and should be with you in minutes. Just make sure you don't lose sight of him.'

'Where are you, AC1?' said William, flicking a switch.

'Rounding Hyde Park Corner, sir. Can't risk turning on my siren as it would alert him, but we should still be there in a couple of minutes.'

'AC2?' snapped William.

'Just passing St James's Church, heading west along Piccadilly. ETA three minutes. Also no siren or lights.'

'Rebecca?'

'He's just passing the Athenaeum Hotel but I think he's spotted me.'

'Hardly surprising,' said William. 'He'll assume someone's out there. Remember, he'll be a master at losing them, and the darkness is in his favour, but keep going.'

'AC1,' said a voice. 'I can see Sergeant Pankhurst but haven't identified the suspect yet.'

'Forty yards ahead of me, thirty, thirty-five, smart double-breasted suit, walking quickly,' said Rebecca.

'Got him,' said AC1 as the suspect disappeared underground.

'He's gone into Green Park tube station,' said Rebecca. 'Do I follow him?'

'No,' said William, 'he'll have shed you before you reach the bottom step. Cross the road and keep out of sight, because it's still a fifty-fifty chance he'll come back out on the other side in a couple of minutes' time.' He paused to think, then said, 'Paul?'

'Sir,' came Paul Adaja's immediate reply.

'Green Park is on the Victoria, Piccadilly and Jubilee lines. Call the control director and ask him to shut down all trains going in either direction and to keep the passenger doors closed until I give the all-clear.'

'On it, sir.'

William moved on. 'Jackie, I need every officer on duty in the Piccadilly area to get themselves over to Green Park sharpish.'

'I've got seven of them already on their way, sir,' came the quick response.

'You were right, sir,' said Rebecca, as she watched a familiar figure emerge from the station. 'The suspect has just come out of Green Park on the south side and is heading towards the nearest bus stop. He keeps looking across the road.'

'He wants to make sure he's shaken you off. But looking for you,' said William, 'gives you a slight advantage, but only slight. He'll take the first available bus and get off at the next stop – when we have to be waiting for him, otherwise we'll never see him again.' He flicked a switch. 'AC1, where are you?'

'On the wrong side of the road, sir, heading east – and because of the barrier, I can't turn back until I reach the lights by the Ritz, so I've lost a couple of minutes.'

'AC2?'

'I'm just passing Fortnum's, sir,' came back the reply. 'I can see three double-decker buses ahead of me, should reach Green Park in about a minute, no more.'

'He's getting on the number nine bus,' interrupted Rebecca, 'and going upstairs.'

'Join him,' ordered William, 'but stay on the lower deck.' 'Jackie?'

'The number nine is on its way to Kensington,' she replied, 'and will be heading towards Hyde Park Corner.'

'I'm on the bus, and it's now on the move,' said Rebecca. 'He's still on the top deck. What next?'

'Tell the driver to take the underpass.' William flicked a switch. 'AC1?'

'We've made a U-turn, sir, and we can see AC2 just ahead of us.'

'That's no surprise,' said AC2. 'While I can see the number nine ahead of me, sir. They are just entering the underpass. I'll be with them in sixty seconds.'

'Paul, give the traffic controller at Green Park the all-clear and thank him. Jackie, block the far end of the underpass now – *now*,' he repeated. 'Rebecca?'

'I'm standing next to the driver. He's moving slowly through the underpass.'

'Tell him to stop.'

'While we're still in the tunnel, sir?'

'Yes,' said William. 'Now.'

The driver began to slow down, as Rebecca looked back to see the first of the squad cars speeding towards them. She immediately accepted that the suspect would have also spotted them.

The bus came to a halt in the middle of the tunnel.

'Open the door,' Rebecca shouted at the driver as she began to run up the stairs. When she reached the top step, she saw the suspect advancing towards her, his arm around the neck of a young girl.

'If you don't get out of my way,' he shouted, 'I'll break her neck.'

Rebecca didn't doubt it, and took a pace back, horrified to see a teenager getting up from the seat behind him and walking towards them. He touched the man on the shoulder and said, 'That's my sister, mister, and if you don't . . .'

The man half turned and with his other arm swept the boy aside, while never letting go of his sister. The boy stumbled backwards onto the ground. The man looked around to see Rebecca charging towards him. He was about to take a swing at her when the first of the officers appeared at the top of the steps.

Rebecca hurled herself headlong at the man, causing him to topple backwards and let go of the girl, by which time the first officer was on top of him. The second held him down, while a third handcuffed him. Moments later, two of them yanked him back up and led him off the bus to loud applause.

'Thank you,' said Rebecca.

'Who are you thanking?' asked William over the radio.

'The real hero,' said Rebecca, 'the young lad who saved his sister.'

This caused a second round of applause, while one of the women officers knelt down beside the two kids to check if they were all right. They were the centre of attention – all smiles.

William was back on the radio. 'Paul?'

'The underground is back to normal, sir.'

'Jackie?'

'The tunnel is back open,' Jackie replied, 'and I can see AC2 heading towards me at speed with the prisoner on board, no doubt on their way to the nearest police station.'

'And AC1?'

'We never needed them in the first place,' quipped a voice.

AC1 maintained radio silence.

'Rebecca?' asked William.

'The bus is back on the move,' she confirmed. 'The two kids are shaking hands with everyone on board and having their photographs taken, I've thanked the driver and the passengers.'

'And Ross?' said William.

'They are putting Avril's body in an ambulance,' said a faltering voice, 'and I'll be accompanying her to the nearest hospital.' There was a long pause before Ross added, 'If I'd done my job properly, she'd still be alive.'

BOOK 3

'For now they kill me with a living death.'

Richard III, William Shakespeare

CHAPTER 20

MILES CALLED HIS LAWYER, WHO was fast asleep when the phone rang.

Booth Watson knew exactly who it would be on the other end of the line at that time of night. He now also knew what it was his client had anticipated would be dominating the news headlines while he was on the other side of the Atlantic.

Booth Watson had left his copy of the *London Evening Standard* on the table by the phone. He picked it up and once again glanced at the front page as he answered the phone.

PROSTITUTE MURDERED
IN WEST END HOTEL
MAN ARRESTED

Booth Watson had read the story twice before he worked out the connection between Miles and the death of a London hooker. It wasn't until he'd turned the page that he realized

Avril Dubois, aka Jenny Prescott, was the woman who was rumoured to be the defence's key witness in the Simon Hartley trial. You didn't have to read between the lines to realize that not only would her evidence have proved Hartley was innocent, but that she would have also named the guilty party.

It had taken Booth Watson a little longer to work out what Miles would expect in return for making sure Ms Dubois never got as far as the airport.

He waited for his instructions, assuming he would be representing the man who had been arrested.

Booth Watson began to wonder, for a moment, just how much longer he could go on representing a man who had no moral compass, and considered the murder of a young woman and the theft of a national treasure were no more than an inconvenience if the financial reward was big enough.

'I've just left Christie's,' said Miles, 'and I think you'll find my five hundred thousand pounds has been well invested, and you'll be well rewarded for attending Lord Hartley's funeral.'

The moment of doubt had passed.

• • •

The team sat in silence around the Commander's desk, as they read the headline in the first edition of the *Evening Standard*. Long before the morning papers had hit the streets, their crime correspondent had worked out the Saudi connection, guaranteeing that while Simon Hartley was still languishing in jail, the story would run and run.

Ross continued to stare at a photo of Avril that dominated the front page, before saying, 'I have no choice but to resign.'

'That would be the easy way out,' said the Commander,

'because if you were to resign, you'll be leaving the rest of us to pick up the pieces.'

'You won't need to, I'd take the law into my own hands,' said Ross. This created a different silence which the Commander broke, as if he hadn't heard the threat.

'Let's start by trying to piece together the few facts we have at our disposal,' said the Commander. 'We think Faulkner met the accused on the London Eye some time on the afternoon of Sunday the sixth. However, other than a blurred CCTV image of a man wearing a baseball cap and dark glasses, what else do we have to go on?'

'The accused, Kevin Scott, is being represented by none other than Mr Booth Watson QC, which one might feel is more than a coincidence.'

'He'd happily represent the devil,' said Ross. 'But not until his fee had been agreed.'

'Has Scott said anything that might incriminate him?' asked the Hawk, once again ignoring him.

'After six hours of interrogation,' said William, 'all we have for our troubles is one of his three names, along with four addresses.'

'We're clearly dealing with a pro,' said the Hawk.

'Where was Booth Watson's principal client when the murder took place?'

'He's still holed up in his hotel suite in New York,' said William, after checking an email that had just been placed in front of him from his friend, Special Agent James Buchanan in Washington. 'During the time he's been in the States, he's visited a Professor Rosenberg in Princeton, New Jersey, and attended at least two meetings with the chairman of Christie's auction house in New York.'

'So what's the connection between those two?' said the Hawk. 'Is it possible Faulkner was doing no more than establishing an alibi, to show he couldn't have had anything to do with Avril's murder, as he was on the other side of the Atlantic at the time? But do we have anything other than Booth Watson to link the two men?'

'Two damning pieces of evidence,' said Paul, opening a thick file. 'Four fifty-pound notes and a Rolex watch.'

'Why are they of any importance?' pressed the Commander.

'If you draw a suspiciously large sum in cash from your account,' said Paul, 'under the 1995 Proceeds of Crime Act, your bank has to report the withdrawal to the National Crime Agency. These four notes,' said Paul, holding them up, 'have been traced back to the cash Faulkner withdrew from his bank in Mayfair.'

'Fingerprints?' said the Hawk.

'No such luck,' said Jackie.

'Then the CPS won't find that's enough to open an inquiry,' said the Hawk. 'What about the watch?'

'It's a Rolex Daytona valued at around forty thousand,' said William.

'But Scott will claim he purchased it legally – he probably even has a receipt to prove it.'

'Then it can only have come from a pawnbroker,' said William, 'because inscribed on the back are the words: *Happy Birthday, Love Christina.*'

'There are a lot of Christinas in the world,' said the Hawk, 'so it will be important to get a statement from his ex-wife confirming she gave it to him as a birthday present.'

'I've already fixed an appointment to see her this afternoon,' said William.

'But how did Scott get his hands on the watch anyway?' asked the Hawk.

'That was another question he failed to answer, sir,' said

Paul, 'but you can be sure he'll have come up with an explanation long before he enters the witness box.'

'We still need a smoking gun,' said the Hawk, 'if we're to convince the CPS to go ahead with a prosecution and not dismiss our findings as coincidence.'

'I think I may have found a connection between Faulkner, Rosenberg and Christie's,' said Rebecca. 'One that Booth Watson won't be able to dismiss as a coincidence.'

Rebecca had the team's undivided attention.

'Rosenberg is the leading authority on the American constitution,' Rebecca reported, 'and Christie's are selling a copy of the Declaration of Independence on Faulkner's behalf.'

She handed copies of a Christie's catalogue to her colleagues before she continued. 'If you turn to page 49, you'll find Lot 91 is the Lot concerned – the sale of a copy of the Declaration written by Thomas Jefferson, known as the Fair Copy.'

They all followed her instructions.

'But what I want you to look at is not the Lot, but the provenance, because you'll find their description of the most recent owner of the Declaration is a "Titled Lady" – a quaint expression auction houses use when they wish to show the property has been in the possession of an aristocratic family for several generations.'

'This is leading somewhere, Sergeant Pankhurst,' said the Hawk.

'It most certainly is, sir,' said Rebecca, 'because I think I can prove who the "Titled Lady" is. Christie's are also selling, along with the Declaration, five letters written by Jefferson to an MP called David Hartley. So I think it's possible that the lady in question could be—'

'Lady Hartley,' said William, catching up with her.

'And if I'm right,' said Rebecca, 'it might explain why Faulkner held a meeting with Prince Ahmed at the Dorchester and what the Prince would be expected to do in return for Ms Dubois not being able to appear at Hartley's trial.'

'As Faulkner's involved, anything is possible,' said the Hawk. 'William, call your friend, Special Agent Buchanan, in Washington, and bring him up to date. And while you're at it, make an appointment to see Lady Hartley. She may have the keys that will unlock several doors.'

'I'll take Ross with me,' said William, 'A little Irish charm—'

'You can count me out,' said Ross firmly, his gaze returning to the photo on the front of the *Evening Standard*, 'because nothing will change the fact that Avril would still be alive if I'd done my job properly. You'll have my resignation on your desk by the morning.'

'Why don't you take a few days off, Ross, and think it over?' said the Hawk in a conciliatory voice that the rest of the team rarely experienced. Ross didn't respond. 'I just want to be sure you don't do something you'll later regret.'

'I'll regret Avril's death for the rest of my life,' said Ross, his voice flat and uncompromising, 'and there's nothing you can do to change that.'

Ross got up from his place, turned his back on them and left the room without another word.

William feared they might never see him again. Ross's life was always black or white, he didn't deal in shades of grey.

When Ross had slammed the door behind him, the Commander said, 'William, perhaps you'd better have a word with Alice, as I suspect she's the one person who might drum some common sense into the man.'

• • •

When Ross arrived home, Alice was waiting for him, having already had a call from William. There were no newspapers to be seen, the television had been turned off, and the phone taken off its hook. She cooked him his favourite meal, Irish stew. He ate in silence and didn't raise the subject.

Alice lay awake all through the night, and when he finally told her what he had planned, all she said was, 'Whatever you decide, I'll support you.' He fell asleep.

The following morning, Ross wrote a resignation letter to the Commander. The narrative didn't flow easily, but after a third attempt, he somehow put some words together. He opened the top drawer of Alice's desk but couldn't find a stamp. How unlike Alice to run out of stamps.

He left the envelope on the hall stand before joining Alice and Jojo for breakfast. Jojo was telling her father about a boy who wouldn't stop pulling her pigtails, but he wasn't listening.

'Time to clean your teeth,' said Alice, as she began to clear up.

Jojo left the table, and when she came back downstairs, she took the letter off the hall stand, slipped it into her satchel, ran out of the front door and didn't stop running until she reached a litter bin.

It didn't take a trained detective for Ross to work out what his daughter had been up to, because when she returned to the house, Jojo avoided him and quickly disappeared upstairs.

Ross returned to his study and made a fourth attempt to write the letter, but it wasn't any easier. He sealed the envelope, and this time left it on his desk. In the afternoon, he walked to the local post office and bought a second-class stamp.

In the evening, Alice and Jojo took him out for supper at his favourite Italian restaurant, when he was told in great detail about the boy who kept pulling her pigtails. He grinned at his daughter and realized just how lucky he was and didn't bother to tell her the little boy was in love with her.

Alice woke in the middle of the night to find Ross in tears. She held him in her arms and was taken by surprise when he finally spoke.

'I sometimes forget,' said Ross, 'how lucky I am to have such a remarkable woman in my life.'

'Two remarkable women,' Alice reminded him.

Ross laughed for the first time in days.

He sat up, turned on the light and said, 'I should have done this a long time ago.'

'Turn off the light you silly man! It's three in the morning,' said Alice, covering her eyes.

'Shush, woman – I'm finding it hard enough to ask you to marry me.'

'So romantic!' said Alice, as she took him back in her arms.

'What's your answer?'

'Where's the ring?'

'I'll get it in the morning.'

'So romantic,' repeated Alice, grinning.

Ross got out of bed, fell on one knee and said, 'Alice, I adore you and I want to spend the rest of my life with you. Please say you'll be my wife.'

'On one condition,' Alice replied.

• • •

The following morning, Ross went back to his study before Alice awoke. He picked up the letter on his desk and tore it into little pieces.

He didn't attempt to write a fifth one.

• • •

When Sean O'Driscoll returned to his cell after his shift in the kitchen, the first thing he said to Simon was, 'I've picked up some information on the prison grapevine you'll want to know about.'

Simon's heart began to beat more rapidly, as he had a feeling that what he was about to hear wouldn't be good news.

'Some tart from London called Avril, who used to work in one of the local clubs, has been murdered, and for some reason the Governor's pleased about it.'

Simon stared at him. 'He's pleased,' he said quietly, 'because her death means that Prince Ahmed is off the hook – and I'm back on it.'

'I could kill the Governor if you wanted me to,' he said matter-of-factly.

'It wouldn't make a blind bit of difference,' said Simon, unsure if his cell mate was serious, 'because now nothing will stop the French being awarded the arms contract, and Prince Ahmed getting his extra five per cent.'

'How can I help?' said O'Driscoll. 'Once I'm out of the way, you'll be next on their shopping list, because one thing's for sure: they won't want your trial to come to court.'

'Then you'll somehow have to get me out of here before the trial can take place.'

'I'd do anything I can to help,' said O'Driscoll, as he sat down on the bunk next to his friend, 'but as I've already warned you, there's only one way out of this shithole, and that's in a coffin.'

'Then that's exactly how I'll have to leave,' said Simon, 'but it's me you're going to have to kill, not the Governor.'

CHAPTER 21

MILES WAS OBLIVIOUS TO WHAT was taking place in two kingdoms on the other side of the world as his car pulled up outside Christie's on Rockefeller Plaza. When he entered the front door, he found a secretary was waiting for him. He was ushered straight up to the managing director's office.

Miles didn't waste any time on small talk. Once he'd shook hands and sat down he said, 'Bring me up to date.'

'I don't think it's an exaggeration, Mr Faulkner,' said Chris Davidge, the managing director of Christie's, 'to say that when Jefferson's Fair Copy of the Declaration of Independence comes under the hammer, it will be one of the most sought-after items in the auction house's long history.'

Miles allowed himself a smile.

'I will be chairing a press conference later today in a room that would normally hold around two hundred,' continued Davidge, 'but we've already received over three hundred requests from the world's media to attend.'

'The Fair Copy,' chipped in the public relations director,

'will go on display at midday today, and I can report that a queue began forming on the street outside in the early hours of the morning, which hasn't happened since Vincent van Gogh's *Irises* came under the hammer in 1987.'

'Have you been able to put an estimate on how much the Declaration might fetch?' said Miles, moving on to his only real interest in the unique item.

'That's anyone's guess,' said Davidge. 'However, we do know that a printed copy of the Declaration, published in Philadelphia by Benjamin Franklin, which was owned by John Adams, the second President, and left to his son John Quincy Adams, the sixth President, fetched $4.3 million dollars when it came up for auction last year. All I can tell you is our principal auctioneer plans to open the bidding at five million.'

'Have you had any interest from what one might describe as serious bidders?' asked Miles.

'A not unknown commodities trader called Bunker Hunt,' said Davidge.

'And only this morning,' added the PR director, 'Donald Trump phoned to let me know he's already selected the place where it will hang in Trump Tower. I can also tell you, in confidence, I had a call from the chairman of the Smithsonian, to advise me that he will be bidding on behalf of the government. So if you were to press me on an estimate, I would have to say fifty million wouldn't surprise me, and it's certainly the figure I've been hinting at whenever a journalist enquires.'

Miles didn't need to make a note.

'Have you come up against any problems?' asked Miles, fairly sure he knew what the answer would be.

'One or two journalists have been sniffing around asking about a letter Jefferson might have written at the time, which would show that the Fair Copy legally belonged to its author and, following Jefferson's death, the American people.'

'Pigs would have a better chance of sniffing around for truffles in Central Park than journalists finding a letter that doesn't exist,' said Miles, 'so you can stop worrying about that.'

'Let's hope that's the case,' replied Davidge, 'because if such a letter were to surface, and Professor Rosenberg verified it as having been written by the former President, we would be left with no choice but to withdraw the Fair Copy from the sale and hand it over to the government.'

'Even Saul Rosenberg can't verify something that doesn't exist,' said Miles, leaving no further room for discussion. 'So, what other items will be coming up in the sale?' he said, wanting to change the subject.

'Several pieces of historic memorabilia from around the period of American Independence, as well as the Jefferson letters you were able to supply from your own remarkable collection.'

'It will allow me to give even more money to charity,' said Miles, with an ingratiating smile that didn't fool either of them.

'How many reserved seats will you require on the day of the auction?' asked Davidge. 'I only ask because it's already oversubscribed.'

'Just a couple for my lawyer, Mr Booth Watson, and myself,' said Miles. 'In the front row.'

'Of course,' said Davidge. 'Would you also like to join me at the press conference later today?'

'No,' said Miles firmly, well aware that if he did attend, the jackals would only have one question on their lips, one that he wouldn't want to answer. 'No, I have a meeting with my lawyer, who has just flown in from London.'

· · ·

Miles wasn't surprised to find Booth Watson waiting for him in the bar of the Park Plaza like a dutiful lapdog. If he'd had a tail, it would have started wagging the moment he entered the room.

'Any news from London?' Miles asked, after ordering a whisky mac.

'Scott has been charged,' replied Booth Watson, 'but you can be assured, they'll not find anything that links him to you. And I know you'll want to know that the Fitzmolean board will be meeting to elect their new chairman tomorrow evening.'

Miles nodded. 'And Ms Bates is well prepared to play her role?'

'She's word perfect,' Booth Watson assured him.

'If Ms Bates is elected as chair,' said Miles, 'I might even get my Rubens back, once you've explained to her, BW, what "on permanent loan" actually means. But on to more important news. Davidge is predicting that when the Declaration comes under the hammer, it could fetch as much as fifty million.'

'Not a bad return remembering you only paid half a million for it in the first place,' said Booth Watson.

'As well as a Constable that wasn't a Constable,' Miles reminded him.

'Did anyone raise the subject of the missing letter?' asked Booth Watson, moving on.

'In passing,' said Miles, 'but more important, Rosenberg has confirmed the Fair Copy is unquestionably authentic, and when they asked him about the letter, all he said was he hasn't come across anything to show such a letter ever existed.'

'So you've crossed that hurdle,' said Booth Watson.

'That man's honesty will surely get the better of him one day,' replied Miles.

'Which I can safely predict, Miles, will never be a problem for you.'

'Try not to forget which side you're on, BW,' said Miles.

• • •

Miles checked his new watch. 'I have to make a call,' he said, 'but I'll be back in a few minutes.' Once he was safely back in his room, Miles sat down and dialled the number slowly. He had to wait for some time before the call was answered.

'Who is this?' asked a suspicious-sounding voice.

'Miles Faulkner. As I'm sure you know, we've kept our side of the bargain. But I can't see any sign that you've kept yours.'

'That hasn't proved quite as easy as I'd originally thought,' said Khalil.

'Then you'd better listen carefully to my next question Mr Khalil,' said Miles. He paused for a moment before he asked, 'When is your next birthday?'

'In a couple of months' time,' said Khalil. 'Why do you ask?'

'Because if Simon Hartley makes it back to England, you won't be opening any presents this year.' Miles hung up and went back down to join Booth Watson at the bar.

• • •

William dialled his number just after lunch, assuming Special Agent Buchanan would be at his desk by then.

'I know exactly why you're calling,' said an unmistakable transatlantic voice, when he picked up the phone. 'And the answer is yes.'

'Yes?' repeated William.

'Yes, Miles Faulkner is still in the States, and yes, we have been keeping a close eye on him.'

'And?' asked William.

'I'm sure you know that a rare copy of the Declaration of Independence, handwritten by Thomas Jefferson in 1776 and known as the Fair Copy, is coming up for auction at Christie's next week.'

'Yes, I did know, and I am well aware that Faulkner is the seller. Any more clues?' asked William, pen poised.

'The Declaration is going on sale along with five letters written by the former President,' said James as he flicked through the catalogue, 'all sent to a Member of Parliament called David Hartley.'

'I will be seeing Lady Hartley tomorrow,' said William.

'Who's she?' asked James.

'The titled lady mentioned in the catalogue.'

'So where does she fit in?'

'It's a long story, James, but what I can tell you is you've supplied several missing pieces of the jigsaw.'

'I'm lost,' said James.

'So were we until I called you,' admitted William, who spent the next twenty minutes filling in the gaps of the jigsaw, telling his old FBI friend the connection between Miles Faulkner, Lady Hartley and her son, now locked up in a Saudi jail.

'But how did Faulkner ever get his hands on the Fair Copy of the Declaration in the first place?' asked James.

'I don't know the answer to that question,' admitted William, 'but I expect I will by this time tomorrow.'

• • •

Hani Khalil arrived outside the front gate of 'Ulaysha Prison lugging a heavy suitcase. One tap on the door and it was immediately unlocked by the officer of the watch. Khalil followed him into the reception area as if he were a guest at an hotel and wanted to book a room. He placed a hundred-dollar bill on the counter.

Without a word passing between them, the officer of the watch pocketed the money before leading the visitor out of reception and across a yard, where the searchlights had been switched off.

Once they reached the other side with the help of a pen torch, the officer unlocked a door that led into the administrative block. Once inside, the officer accompanied his after-hours guest along a dimly lit corridor, only stopping when he reached the door at the far end. He knocked once, opened it, and stood aside to allow Mr Khalil to enter the Governor's office.

'Good morning,' said the Governor, which was only just accurate as it was three minutes past midnight, an hour chosen by the Governor to ensure that no one other than the three of them was aware the meeting had ever taken place.

Once the door had been closed, Khalil heaved his heavy suitcase up onto the Governor's desk, unzipped it and lifted the lid to reveal row upon row of freshly minted hundred-dollar bills in neat cellophane packets, that filled every inch of space available.

The Governor continued to stare at the bribe, like a parched man in a desert who had finally come across an oasis. He was in the desert, but happily staring at his pension plan.

The Governor rose from his place, lowered the lid and zipped the case back up. He shook hands with his visitor to seal a deal that wouldn't require any paperwork.

Khalil left the office to find the only other person involved in the subterfuge waiting for him in the corridor. He followed him back to reception, where, having not checked in, he didn't check out. The officer of the watch unlocked the front gate and Khalil slipped him another hundred-dollar bill, as if he were tipping a doorman. The officer returned to his post and switched the searchlights back on.

Khalil stepped out of the prison into the cold night air to find his chauffeur waiting for him.

As he was driven home, Khalil thought about what had taken place during the past sixteen minutes. A decision that had caused him to empty his bank account, in preference to digging his own grave.

The empty bank account would be temporary once the French had been awarded the arms contract. But death is permanent.

He would call Mr Faulkner in the morning.

CHAPTER 22

'I SHOULD HAVE WORN MY pink dress,' said Christina.

'No way,' said Wilbur as they drew up outside the Fitzmolean. 'Your dark blue Armani suit is just perfect for the occasion. Makes you look every bit a board chair.'

'What do I say if they ask me if I will be happy to remain on the board and serve under Ms Bates, should I fail to be elected?'

'You must be magnanimous and tell the board you'll be happy to remain on the committee, as you consider the Fitzmolean bigger than any individual, but it's not relevant,' said Wilbur, 'as I've no doubt you're going to win.'

'I'm not so sure,' said Christina. 'Only one thing's certain, it's going to be a close-run thing. Three of the board, including the chair, have already told me I can count on their votes, but I know at least three others who still haven't made up their minds, and I'm sure Ms Bates is being briefed by Booth Watson.'

'I'd rather have Sir Nicholas on my side than Miles Faulkner,' said Wilbur. 'All you'll need is a couple of the undecideds to back you and you'll be home and dry.'

'Do I show them the letter?' she asked.

'Only if the question arises,' said Wilbur. 'And even then, you'll have to gauge the feeling of the meeting before you make that decision.'

'It should be you, not me, who's standing for chair,' said Christina.

'Certainly not, my darling. They couldn't get anyone better for the job.' Wilbur leant across and gave his wife a gentle kiss. 'Better get going. Can't afford to be late.'

When Christina got out of the car, her legs felt so weak she wondered if she'd make it up the steps to the front door, let alone to the boardroom. She somehow managed to push her way through the revolving door and get as far as the lift.

She stepped out onto the first floor and headed for the boardroom, to see the chairman walking towards her. The selection committee were clearly waiting for her.

'I'll do everything I can to assist,' whispered Nicholas.

Christina followed him into the boardroom and took her place in the only empty chair at the top of the table. Several board members smiled, but just as many didn't.

'Welcome, Christina,' said the chair once he'd taken his seat at the other end of the table. 'I'll begin by running through the procedure I intend to adopt while conducting this inter-view. I will start by asking the first couple of questions, and my colleagues will then follow up with any supplementaries.' Sir Nicholas checked his notes before he began. 'Having played a leading role in the Fitzmolean's success over so many years, I wonder if there are changes you would make as chair that you feel might benefit the museum in the future?'

'Let me begin by thanking you, Chairman, for your un-wavering support during those years, and say how difficult it will be for anyone to fill your shoes.'

No one could have missed Ms Bates's eyes rolling like a toy dog in the back of a moving car.

'But to answer your question, Sir Nicholas,' said Christina, 'as you know, I have always been a passionate advocate of free entry to the main gallery. However, I do feel that when we mount a special exhibition at some considerable cost, we should perhaps consider charging a one-off entry fee. Our current Rembrandt exhibition, for example, has attracted over three hundred thousand visitors, and if we had levied a five-pound ticket charge, we could have raised well in excess of a million pounds, which would not only have covered our costs but shown us a modest profit.'

'Would students and old-age pensioners also be expected to contribute?' asked the chair.

'Absolutely not,' said Christina. 'They, along with any chil-dren accompanying their parents, would be exempt.'

'Certainly worthy of serious consideration,' said the chair, 'and while we're on that subject, what is your view on the government's new tax incentive scheme?'

'I welcome it,' said Christina without hesitation. 'It's another opportunity for us to raise some extra, much-needed revenue, which we should take advantage of. I would also suggest that we replicate what the Americans call "see-through guilt boxes", where visitors who can afford to pay are encouraged to contribute a fiver, possibly more. The Victoria and Albert are raising an extra million a year this way, and I feel we should be following their example.'

'Thank you, Christina. I shall now—'

Ms Bates immediately raised her hand, leaving the chair

with little choice but to select her. 'How can the board be confident of your loyalty to the Fitzmolean while you remain a close friend of Beth Warwick, our former director, who left in – to say the least – unfortunate circumstances?'

'Beth is one of my closest friends, and always will be, but both of us are first and foremost loyal supporters of the Fitzmolean. As chair, I would always put the museum first, as Beth did when she resigned. However, I can tell the board that she deeply regrets no longer being our director.'

'How convenient,' said Ms Bates. 'Does that mean if you became chair, you would ask her to return as director?'

'Most certainly I would,' said Christina without hesitation. 'I don't always agree with Beth, but I've never doubted that she always had the best interests of the museum at heart.'

'Have you discussed the possibility with her?'

'Yes, I have,' admitted Christina. Another question she was well prepared for.

'And what was her response?'

'She could not have been more positive about the whole idea, and even wrote me a letter to confirm her position.' One sentence too many, she could hear Wilbur saying.

'Do you have that letter with you, by any chance?' asked Ms Bates.

Christina hesitated for a moment before she said, 'Yes, I do.'

'And would you allow the committee to see it?'

Christina opened her bag and took out an envelope, which she sent on a relay down one side of the table to the chair.

Sir Nicholas opened the envelope, extracted the letter and read it. A few moments later, all he said was, 'I am able to confirm that should Christina become our next chair, Dr

Warwick would be willing to return as director, but only if that was met with the approval of the board.'

'How considerate of her,' said Ms Bates, 'but may I ask, Sir Nicholas, as you are the only member of the board who has read the letter, if Dr Warwick would be willing to make the same commitment should someone else be appointed as chair?'

Sir Nicholas looked embarrassed, and before he could respond, Christina said, 'It's a very personal letter, Ms Bates, and I think the chair has answered your specific question.'

'But not the one you seem unwilling to answer?' came back Ms Bates. 'So I am bound to ask—'

'Don't you think, Ms Bates,' interjected the chair, 'that it might be time for someone else to ask a question?'

'I didn't realize you were putting a limit on how many questions one could ask, Sir Nicholas, before we consider the only important decision the board will make, possibly for the next ten years – namely who should be our next chair?'

'I will allow you one more question, Ms Bates,' said Sir Nicholas, sounding exasperated, 'but then we must move on.'

'Mrs Hackensack,' said Ms Bates. 'As chair of the fund-raising committee, do you know the name of the extremely generous benefactor who donated the two hundred and fifty thousand that made it possible for the Fitzmolean to acquire Rembrandt's *Jacob Wrestling with the Angel*?'

This was the one question Christina had been dreading, even though she'd given it some considerable thought. But Wilbur had warned her, that if she was asked, there was no way she could do anything other than tell the truth.

'Yes, I think I do,' she said truthfully.

'Then allow me to ask which of your husbands it was who so generously made that donation.'

Christina knew she'd been trapped, but she had no choice but to say, 'The donation did not come from my husband.'

'Your ex-husband, perhaps?'

'Possibly,' admitted Christina.

'Do you think Mr Faulkner would have been quite so generous had he thought you might be our next chair?'

'You do not have to answer that question, Christina,' said Sir Nicholas.

'Why not?' demanded Ms Bates.

'Lady Morland,' said the chair, ignoring the interruption. 'Can I ask you, Mrs Hackensack, if your present husband supports your ambition to succeed Sir Nicholas as chair?'

'One hundred per cent,' said Christina. 'Not only did he drive me here this evening, but he's now sitting in the car outside, waiting to find out how I've got on. "Could have done better", I shall tell him!'

A little laughter broke out, which helped Christina to relax, but not for long.

'I think there's time for a couple more questions,' said the chair, looking around the table.

One of the waverers raised a hand, and the chair nodded.

'You were on the premises when Rembrandt's *Angel* was switched right in front of our eyes, so I wondered if you had any theories as to how that happened, or who was responsible for such an inexplicable and very embarrassing sequence of events?'

Christina could once again hear Wilbur whispering in her ear: *whatever you do, don't even hint that you know only too well who orchestrated the whole performance, because if you do, and you're not willing to name him, the waverers will no longer be wavering.*

'Like you, Mrs Amhurst, it remains a mystery to me.'

'Despite the fact your close friend, Dr Warwick, warned us that if she were to continue as director, it might well happen again, rather indicating *she* did know who it was?'

'Let me assure you, Mrs Amhurst, that if I am fortunate enough to be appointed chair of this great institution, I will not make decisions based on speculation, but on advice from experts I respect, backed up with facts. Otherwise, we will all end up as victims, continually looking over our shoulders, frightened of making any serious decisions in case some malevolent outside force disapproves.'

Hear, hear! erupted from one side of the table.

'Thank you, Christina,' said the chair, 'for handling such a plethora of demanding questions so graciously, while at the same time displaying the resolution required to be a good chair.'

Smiles and blank looks greeted the chair's closing remarks in equal measure.

'Thank you, Sir Nicholas,' said Christina. 'Allow me to say before I leave, whatever the board decides, serving the Fitzmolean has been a privilege I will always treasure.'

One of the waverers managed a smile as Christina got up and left the room.

'The board will now go into closed session,' said Sir Nicholas, 'but first I would suggest we take a short break before returning to decide who will be the next chair of the Fitzmolean.'

• • •

When the phone rang later that evening, Christina continued to read her magazine as if it wasn't ringing.

'That's the third time you haven't answered it,' said Wilbur, looking up from his copy of the *New York Times*. 'But you'll have to eventually, as Sir Nicholas is a persistent sort of guy at the best of times.'

'But this could be the worst of times,' said Christina as she put down her magazine, got up, and walked slowly across the room in the hope it would stop ringing before she reached it.

But as Wilbur had predicted, the caller was persistent.

She reluctantly picked the phone up but didn't speak.

'Are you there, Christina?' said a voice she recognized.

'Yes, I am, Chairman,' Christina replied.

'No longer,' said Sir Nicholas.

'Why not?'

'I'm no longer the chairman and, according to the minutes, at 6.34 this evening, you were elected to take my place. I was calling to congratulate you.'

Christina dropped the phone, but quickly picked it back up again. 'By how many votes?'

'One,' said Sir Nicholas.

'Your casting vote?' asked Christina.

This time it was Nicholas's turn to hesitate. 'Yes,' he admitted, 'but I have some good news. Ms Bates and Mrs Amhurst have both resigned from the board, so that's two of your problems in the out-tray. So I do hope you're not, like Beth, going to change your mind at the last minute.'

'No way,' said Christina. 'I agree with Sir Winston Churchill – one vote is more than enough.'

'That's a relief,' said Sir Nicholas, accompanied by a long sigh. 'We ought to get together, as soon as it's convenient, so I can arrange an orderly changeover. But for now, I'll leave you and Wilbur to celebrate, and I'll call you again in the morning. Many congratulations. I couldn't be more pleased,' he added, before putting down the phone.

'I'm the new chair,' announced Christina, jumping up and down as if she'd just been appointed head girl.

'I'm well aware of that,' said Wilbur, putting down his paper before giving his wife a round of applause.

'You knew all the time?' said Christina, staring at her husband in disbelief.

'Yes,' admitted Wilbur, 'but I confess I enjoyed watching you suffer.'

Christina picked the phone back up and began dialling. 'Don't you want to know who I'm calling?' she asked.

'I know exactly who you're calling,' said Wilbur, 'and I can tell you, she's standing by the phone waiting.'

Christina turned back to face him. 'Don't tell me she already knows, as well.'

'No, she doesn't,' said Wilbur, 'but then I thought, if you were going to have to suffer, so should she.'

'Are you the new chair?' asked a voice on the other end of the line.

'Sure am,' said Christina, 'and the first thing I want to know, Dr Warwick is, are you willing to come back as the museum's director?'

'Of course I am,' said Beth, 'and while I've got you on the phone I have several ideas I need to discuss with you before the next board meeting, not least . . .'

CHAPTER 23

'WHAT ARE WE HOPING TO achieve?' asked Ross as Danny drove out of the Yard onto Victoria Street.

'I'm not quite sure myself,' admitted William, 'but if the "Titled Lady" referred to in the Christie's catalogue is Lady Hartley, we're going to have to tread carefully, remembering she's recently lost her husband, and her only son is locked up in a Saudi jail charged with a murder he didn't commit.'

'And the real mystery,' said Ross, 'is how did she ever come into contact with Miles Faulkner?'

'I think it's more likely she crossed paths with Booth Watson, remembering – after all – her husband was the Home Secretary. We'll have to be especially careful, as it's possible the wily old lawyer even represents her.'

'What makes you think that?' asked Ross.

'Rebecca,' said William. 'A force to be reckoned with. Sergeant Pankhurst visited Bucklebury yesterday afternoon and had a word with the vicar, amongst others, who told her he met Booth Watson at the wake.'

'Help!' said Ross. 'That means everything we say could be reported back to Booth Watson within minutes of us leaving.'

'And to Faulkner seconds later, and remembering that, I've prepared a list of questions we need answers to, and have divided them between us.'

'Of course you have,' said Ross, as William handed him a long list of questions, which he began to study.

'We're sorry to impose on you at this particular time, Lady Hartley, but . . .'

By the time they reached Bucklebury a couple of hours later, they were confident they had their good cop/good cop routine in place. They just hoped Her Ladyship would be willing to play her part.

While Danny parked the car in the drive outside Hartley Hall, William rapped once on an ancient oak door and took a pace back. A few moments later, the door was answered by a frail old lady, who didn't seem surprised to find two policemen standing on her doorstep.

'Do come in, Chief Superintendent,' she said after William had shown her his warrant card. 'I've been expecting you for some time.' This took both of them by surprise, as it wasn't on their list of possible responses.

Lady Hartley didn't speak again until she had accompanied them into the drawing room. Once they were settled, she said, 'You have to understand, I wouldn't have done it if I hadn't been desperate.'

'Done what?' enquired Ross, coming off script.

'Sold the Constable painting of the old mill at Bucklebury for five hundred thousand pounds to that kind gentleman,' said Lady Hartley, looking up at the faded rectangle on the wall above her, where the painting had hung for over two hundred years.

'But that's not a crime,' suggested William, as he took the seat opposite her.

'It is when you know it wasn't by the master,' said Lady Hartley. 'Even though it was painted by Breck LaFave, one of Constable's most accomplished pupils, it can't be worth more than a few thousand pounds at most.'

'I think it might be wise to consult a lawyer before you say anything else, Lady Hartley,' said William, a suggestion he had never made in the past when someone was in the middle of a confession. To his surprise Ross nodded, closed his notebook and put his pen back in his pocket, as William had also abandoned the script.

'No, I can't do that,' said Lady Hartley firmly. 'I haven't had a good night's sleep since I deceived the poor man, so I have to get it off my chest.'

'The poor man,' said William, repeating her words.

'Mr Booth Watson,' said Lady Hartley, 'a distinguished QC, who was a friend of my late husband.'

'Do you know Mr Booth Watson well?' ventured William. Back on script.

'No. I have to admit I'd never come across him before he attended my husband's funeral . . . But, even worse,' continued Lady Hartley, 'I sold Mr Faulkner something that wasn't mine to sell.'

This time William did remain silent, as he suspected she was about to reveal something of real importance.

'He seemed genuinely interested in Jefferson's Declaration of Independence, which never belonged to the family in the first place. If truth be told, we should have returned the Fair Copy to its rightful owner years ago. However, I did throw in the six letters Jefferson wrote to David Hartley, MP, my late husband's distinguished ancestor.'

'Six?' repeated William.

'Yes. They were all dated and signed by the former president.'

'But there are only five on offer in Christie's catalogue,' Ross said hoping to elicit a response.

'So he's decided to sell the letters?' said Lady Hartley, clearly surprised. 'Well, who can blame him, when I cheated him out of half a million.' She paused for a moment before she added, 'But that's strange, because I can assure you there were six letters.'

'Do you have any idea,' asked William, 'why he would have kept the sixth letter?'

Lady Hartley didn't reply for some time, before she said, 'I suppose it might have been the one in which Jefferson asked Mr Hartley to return the Fair Copy to him in the fullness of time.'

'I have to tell you Lady Hartley,' said William, 'that Mr Faulkner has offered up for auction at Christie's in New York, not only the five letters but Jefferson's Fair Copy of the Declaration.'

The old lady looked humbled, but didn't speak.

'I don't suppose your late husband kept a copy of that particular letter, by any chance?' threw in Ross.

'Why should he bother to, Inspector, when he knew all six of them off by heart?'

This statement rendered them both speechless.

'I'm not sure I understand, Lady Hartley,' William eventually managed.

'It's quite simple really. He didn't need to make a copy of any of them, because he kept the words in his head.'

'But why would he do that?' asked William, genuinely puzzled.

'It's a long-held Hartley tradition,' she explained, 'passed down from generation to generation, that the firstborn must be able to recite the Declaration of Independence off by heart before their twelfth birthday; if they could do so they would receive a hundred guineas. Quite an incentive, I think you'll agree.'

'As well as all six letters?' pressed William.

'Which my husband would recite at midday on the fourth of July every year.'

'And did your son carry on with this tradition?' asked Ross.

'Yes, along with my grandson, Robert, who was word-perfect long before his twelfth birthday, and deserved every penny of his hundred guineas so I couldn't pretend I wasn't aware what was in that letter,' said Lady Hartley. 'Frankly, I have been dreading the day Mr Faulkner returned and quite rightly demanded his five hundred thousand pounds back.'

'I don't think you need worry about that any longer, Lady Hartley,' said William. 'We think it's quite likely the kind gentleman in question has already destroyed that letter, because, with it out of the way, he's convinced he'll make a fortune by selling the Declaration.'

'But that would be dishonest,' said Lady Hartley, sounding genuinely shocked.

'It would indeed,' said William.

Lady Hartley remained silent for a moment, before she said, 'Before I offer you a cup of tea, Chief Superintendent, can I ask you if you're going to arrest me?'

'Not today, Lady Hartley,' said William, 'but you could play an important role in helping us arrest the "kind gentleman".'

● ● ●

'Not a woman to be underestimated,' said William as he climbed into the car and looked back at the old lady who was waving at them.

'To think we've been trying to get the better of Faulkner for the past twenty years,' said Ross, 'and she managed it after one meeting.'

'And even more important,' said William, 'she finally confirmed the reason Faulkner visited Prince Ahmed at the Dorchester in the middle of the night. It doesn't take a great leap of imagination to work out what Faulkner would have expected in return for removing the one witness who could not only bring down Prince Ahmed but also stop him making a vast fortune without lifting a finger.'

'So it will be greed that gets both of them in the end,' said Ross with some feeling.

'The most common vice for explaining most crimes,' said William, 'but the first thing I'll have to do when we get back to the Yard is phone the Foreign Office and warn Trevelyan that Simon Hartley's life is in danger, so he can brief our man in Riyadh.'

'Sir Bernard Anscombe,' said Ross.

'As you already know the Ambassador, perhaps you should return to Saudi, see Hartley and get him to repeat the wording of the all-important letter that Faulkner has clearly destroyed?'

'I can't go back to Riyadh,' said Ross.

'Why not?'

'Khalil would work out within minutes why I'd returned. Don't forget, he thinks I'm Declan O'Reilly, the Irish Minister of Marine and Natural Resources. However, Faulkner is presumably unaware that there's another person who knows the wording of that letter of by heart.'

'Simon's son, Robert,' said William, 'who Lady Hartley said could recite the Declaration and the six letters long before his twelfth birthday.'

'For which he was well paid,' said Ross.

'The Hartley heritage,' they both repeated in unison.

'So my next problem,' said William, 'is how to get in touch with young Robert Hartley before Faulkner realizes that he's just as much of a threat as his father.'

'That's something you can leave to me.'

'But how can you possibly have come across Robert Hartley?' asked William as they joined the motorway and headed back towards London.

'Don't ask,' said Ross.

• • •

Prisoner number 147296 stood in front of the Governor at 'Ulaysha Prison, his arms and legs bound in shackles.

'I need you to do a job for me,' said the Governor, as if he was asking him to make him a cup of tea. 'However, I can assure you, your reward won't be in heaven.' He opened the top drawer of his desk and removed ten cellophane packets, each containing a thousand dollars – far more than the usual payment when the Governor needed to call on O'Driscoll's particular skills. However, this job was likely to end in a judicial inquiry with witness statements, even if they wouldn't be able to interview the suspect, as he would have been summarily executed long before an inquiry could take place.

The Governor wasn't the only person who'd worked that out.

'If you expect me to kill Hartley,' said the prisoner calmly, 'I won't do it for less than a hundred thousand.'

The Governor hadn't anticipated how much Simon Hartley had taught a willing pupil during the past two months. He was about to tell him to get lost when he remembered that, as his execution was set for Sunday afternoon, O'Driscoll would only be around for a few more days, so he was confident he would be able to retrieve most of the money.

But O'Driscoll hadn't finished bargaining.

'And I'm not interested in cash,' he said. 'The full amount must be transferred to my wife's account in Dublin before I'll lift a finger, and even then, I'll need to hear her voice on the other end of the line confirming she's received the money.'

'You don't trust me?' said the Governor, attempting to look surprised.

'Frankly, Governor, your word isn't worth a riyal, let alone a hundred thousand dollars, but I'll leave the choice to you.'

'You're not the only available candidate for the job,' the Governor reminded him.

'But I'm the only one,' said O'Driscoll, 'who won't be around when they want to interview the suspect.'

The Governor knew when he'd run out of options.

CHAPTER 24

ROSS WAS TORN AS HE wrestled with the moral implications, even before he began to consider the risk factor.

He realized if he went ahead with his plan, he would be breaking the law, which he accepted was an even greater offence if you're a law officer, and if he was caught he could end up with a long prison sentence. But if he didn't go ahead, Faulkner would once again get away with it, and heaven knows what else he had up his sleeve for encores.

Ross also accepted that his chances of pulling off the coup had to be less than fifty-fifty, not least because he couldn't discuss his idea with anyone, even Alice. She would have told him in no uncertain terms her views on the morality of the whole idea, and she certainly wouldn't have given his chances of getting away with it as any better than ten per cent – though he wasn't in any doubt she would have understood why he felt he had to do it.

William would have disapproved on principle and made his position clear from the outset, but as Faulkner had been responsible for Avril's death, he would have understood why Ross had decided he had to travel down that particular road.

The Hawk wouldn't have been at all surprised by Ross's strongly held beliefs. He would still have been left with no choice but to accept his resignation with regret, although he might have admitted, when looking in the shaving mirror, 'If I were twenty years younger, I might well have done the same thing myself.'

Ross's noncommittal comments over supper the evening after his visit to Lady Hartley had caused Alice to ask, 'What aren't you telling me?'

'I've got a problem at work,' he admitted, which had the virtue of being half true.

What he didn't tell her was he'd made up his mind to go ahead with his particular brand of risk-taking and if, as a result, he had to resign – or even worse – so be it.

• • •

Ross waited until William turned up for work before he rang Artemisia on her mobile. His goddaughter picked up the phone almost immediately.

'Have you by any chance kept in touch with Robert Hartley?' he asked, hoping the question sounded casual.

Artemisia didn't answer immediately. 'Are you asking me as a policeman, my godfather or a friend?' she eventually asked.

'All three,' said Ross.

'He's my boyfriend,' admitted Artemisia. 'In fact, I thought it might be him on the line, because hardly a day goes by when we don't talk to each other. But why do you ask?'

'He could help me with something I'm working on,' said Ross.

'Will it help his father?' asked Artemisia. 'Because that's all I care about.'

'I feel confident his father would approve – but that's about as far as I can go at the moment.'

'That doesn't answer my question,' said Artemisia, sounding so much older than her years.

'Because I *can't* answer your question,' admitted Ross. 'However, what I can tell you is it won't do Robert any harm and, in the long term, his family will be grateful.'

'In which case, I'll do anything I can to help.'

'You can't ask me how,' said Ross, 'but I know that Robert can recite the contents of a letter written by Thomas Jefferson in 1787 to one of his ancestors.'

'Robert can recite the entire Declaration of Independence, including the two clauses Congress rejected,' replied Artemisia. 'I know, because I've heard him do it.'

'One letter will be more than enough for what I have in mind,' said Ross.

• • •

Ross slipped out of the office early that afternoon without letting anyone know where he was going.

After a short journey on the tube, he spent a couple of productive hours in the Old Kent Road, searching for what he would require if he hoped to fool the aficionados and collectors alike. He strolled up and down a mile-long market that could supply almost anything a cash customer might need, from a sepia photo of Edward VII at Balmoral to a campaign medal from Mafeking. Ross visited several stalls, none of them interested in the twenty-first century.

He came away with half a dozen sheets of heavy letter

paper, three envelopes, two quill pens and a bottle of black ink, all of which you could have purchased in the same market over two hundred years ago.

• • •

Ross took the following day off. He told Alice he might be home late, as if that was something unusual. He also let William know he wouldn't be coming in to work that day, which only made him wonder what Ross was up to. He didn't ask.

Ross left the house that morning before Alice had stirred, looked in on Jojo just before he departed and plonked a kiss on her forehead.

He jumped on a bus to King's Cross from where he caught a train to Little Hampton in Yorkshire. He used the three-hour journey, one change, to go over his plan again and again.

He had been in touch with the Governor of Wormwood Scrubs and the North Yorkshire constabulary earlier in the week. No more than a routine enquiry, he'd assured them, but he came away with some useful intel. Billy Mumford had been released from prison a few weeks ago and had returned to his home in Little Hampton. Most mornings, he could be found at the Dog and Duck, the local constable told him, while he spent every Tuesday and Thursday evening at a dog track in Pontefract, where he could be relied on to part with his money. Whenever he ran out of cash – a regular occurrence – he got drunk and, after recovering from the hangover, knocked up another masterpiece, which he sold to a dealer in Doncaster. They never put his work on display, but still seemed to have a regular flow of willing customers who wanted to impress their friends.

Mumford was about to have a visit from another willing customer.

If he said 'no way Chief Inspector', then Ross would be back at home in time for tea with Jojo. If Mumford showed any interest in the idea, he'd be lucky to make it for supper with Alice.

Ross was the only person who got off the train at Little Hampton. He handed in his ticket at the barrier and made his way into a village that would have been lucky to get a passing mention in any guidebook. One pub (free house), one church (Norman) and a stream that even an over-zealous councillor might have been pushed to describe as a river.

Ross sat down on a bench opposite the church and admired the eleventh-century tower while he waited for Mumford to appear. When he saw him strolling across the green, he looked the other way. Once Mumford had entered the Dog and Duck, Ross only waited a few minutes – time for him to buy a pint – before he joined him.

A bell tinkled above the door as Ross entered the pub. A few locals who were sitting at the bar gave the intruder a fleeting glance before returning to their ale. 'A southerner,' one of them remarked, as if there could be no greater insult for a man to bear. Ross looked around the room to see that one table was occupied by a familiar figure studying the back page of the *Yorkshire Post*.

Mumford looked up and immediately recognized him. His hands began to tremble as the policeman walked towards him.

'You can't have travelled all this way, Mr Hogan, just because I failed to turn up for one of my probation meetings,' he protested as Ross took the seat opposite him.

Ross couldn't have asked for a better opening.

'I'm afraid so. It's just been one too many,' he threw in, hoping he was on the right track.

'I swear it's only been the once, guv,' said Mumford, unable to hide the desperation in his voice.

'Not according to your probation officer,' said Ross, pushing his luck. 'I'm sorry, Billy, but I've got my orders. I've been told to arrest you and take you back to the Scrubs so you can complete your sentence – unless of course I think there's a possibility you might reform your ways, which seems most unlikely.'

'I don't want to go back to prison, Mr Hogan,' said Billy as Ross took an arrest warrant out of an inside pocket, a document Mumford immediately recognized. He turned white.

'I'm sure you don't, Billy, but unfortunately I've got my orders.'

'Is there nothing I can do, Mr Hogan, to convince you that it will never happen again?' pleaded Billy.

Ross remained silent for some time, before reverting to prison lingo: 'You scratch my back, Billy, and I might just consider scratching yours.'

'I don't have any spare cash at the moment, Mr Hogan, but if you'd like a painting, I could knock you up a Picasso, a Monet, even a Rubens – mind you, that would take some time.'

Ross pretended to be considering the proposition, before he let him know what he really wanted, 'There is something, Billy, that you just might be able to help me with.'

'Anything, Inspector, anything – just name it.'

Ross placed his briefcase on the table, opened it, and took out a copy of Rosenberg's prize-winning volume, *Monticello*, before turning to a well-thumbed page. 'If I wanted you to produce a letter as if it had been written by this man,' he said, pointing at the page, 'could you do it?'

Billy studied the handwriting for some time before he said, 'That shouldn't be a problem, Mr Hogan.'

'What about the signature?' said Ross.

Mumford took a second look. 'Not exactly Leonardo da Vinci, is it?'

'And how long would it take you?' asked Ross, moving on.

'A couple of days.'

'I need it by midday on Tuesday, no later.' Ross's hand dipped back into the briefcase. 'Let's make the challenge a little more interesting,' he said, producing a sheet of paper with the words Robert Hartley had recited to Artemisia. 'This is a copy of the letter I want reproduced as if it had been written by Thomas Jefferson.' He paused. 'Word for word.'

Mumford only had to read the script once before he said, 'Consider it done, Mr Hogan.'

Ross finally produced, like a conjuror from a hat, the necessary props to complete the forgery, including two quill pens and a bottle of black ink. 'I want the letter written on this paper, and the envelope addressed to the Rt Hon. David Hartley MP, Hartley Hall, Bucklebury, England,' said Ross, handing over the spoils of his trip to the Old Kent Road.

'I can see you've given this a lot of thought, Mr Hogan,' said Mumford, sounding suspicious for the first time, 'so I have to ask, what's in it for me?'

Ross took the only remaining document out of his briefcase, held it up long enough for Billy to see it was an arrest warrant with his name printed in capital letters on the dotted line. He began to tear it up before Billy had the chance to see it hadn't been countersigned by a local magistrate.

'Thank you, Mr Hogan,' said Billy, sounding genuinely

relieved as he watched the little pieces drop like confetti back into the briefcase. Only one thing remained in the briefcase which Billy couldn't take his eyes off: a pair of handcuffs.

'There are conditions I'll expect you to keep to if you don't want to go back inside,' said Ross, 'so listen carefully.'

The look of apprehension reappeared on Billy's face.

'I'll be back next Tuesday at twelve o'clock with another warrant, and if the letter isn't up to scratch, your feet won't touch the ground until you're safely back in your old cell at Wormwood Scrubs.'

'I can promise you, Mr Hogan, you'll get your letter, and even Mr Jefferson will think he wrote it.'

'And one more thing, Billy, before I leave,' said Ross. 'If you're stupid enough to get in touch with Mr Booth Watson, the deal is off, and I'll personally deliver you to the Scrubs on the same day. And let me also warn you that should it cross your mind to scarper, I've instructed the local police to keep an eye on you twenty-four-seven, and when they catch up with you – and you can be sure they will – it won't be twelve months you'll be looking at.' Billy began to tremble again. 'Think about it,' said Ross as he closed his briefcase, and delivered his parting words, 'See you midday on Tuesday, Billy. Make sure you're on time.'

'I'll be here waiting for you, Mr Hogan. You can rely on me.'

'Let's hope so, for your sake,' said Ross as he got up and left the pub without another word.

As he began to walk back to the station, Ross checked his watch. With a bit of luck, he'd be home in time for tea with Jojo.

CHAPTER 25

PRINCE MAJID BIN TALAL AL Saud checked his watch. This was one meeting he wasn't going to be late for.

When he left his office on the forty-third floor, a lift that could only be occupied by one person whisked him to the ground floor without stopping. He stepped out and headed for the entrance where another door was being held open for him. He then strode out of the building to find his chauffeur standing by the car. He didn't open the back door until the Minister was three paces away, as the intense, humid heat could turn the car into an oven in a matter of seconds.

As the car drove off, the Minister of Defence glanced out of the window and once again marvelled how much the skyline had changed in his lifetime. He had been born in a tent in a hot and freezing desert, and five decades later he was being driven along a six-lane highway in an air-conditioned car at seventy miles an hour through the most modern city on earth.

During the next twenty minutes, the Defence Minister considered a dozen scenarios for why the King would want to see him. Eleven of them were unfavourable. He stared at the phone in the armrest, but despite his fingers twitching, he left it in its place untouched.

He'd received a call from the King's private secretary the previous evening, asking him to attend a meeting with His Majesty at 10 a.m. the following morning. He hadn't slept. The King only requested an audience if you were about to be promoted or sacked, and Prince Majid was sure of one thing – he wasn't about to be promoted.

But why? Could the stories about his son possibly be true? Because he'd dismissed them as tittle-tattle, was he about to lose his job?

At last, the palace gates came into sight, and he knew it would not be too much longer before he discovered his fate. The gates began to open slowly when the car was still a hundred yards away from the entrance. Two uniformed guards sprang to attention and saluted as the ministerial car swept by and continued along a drive that led up to the largest palace in the world.

Al Yamamah Palace made Buckingham Palace look like a semi-detached and the gardens of Versailles like an allotment. A vast marble building that housed one monarch, nine hundred and eighty-nine servants and four wives. The gardens stretched as far as the eye could see and the boundaries were surrounded by a thousand pines imported from Norway. A lake larger than the Serpentine contained four hundred Japanese carp that had to be fed twice a day.

Behind the trees, well out of sight, were four helicopter pads and a runway for the King's three private jets. His Majesty didn't visit airports.

When the limousine finally came to a halt outside the entrance, a tall, elegant man in a long white thawb stepped forward and opened the rear door. His only job.

Prince Majid got out of his car to see the King's private secretary was waiting on the top step, but he turned his back on the Minister of Defence even before they could greet each other. Without a word passing between them, he led the Minister slowly down a long, wide, thickly carpeted corridor past full-length portraits of former rulers – some of whom had never lived in a palace – and on towards a state-room he'd only entered once before. When he was still a few paces away, the two vast doors that led into the throne room opened like a trap door.

The Minister entered and walked slowly along the red carpet towards the King. When he reached the throne, he looked up at his monarch, bowed low and said, 'Good morning Your Majesty.'

He received no salutation in reply, nor was there any suggestion that he might sit on one of the many comfortable cushions surrounding the throne.

'Does the name Simon Hartley mean anything to you?' asked the King.

'He's the British representative for the arms deal, Your Majesty.'

'And where is he at the moment?' the King asked.

The Minister of Defence hesitated.

'You clearly know where he is, and it is your son who is responsible for him being there.'

Prince Majid didn't suggest otherwise.

'And Avril Dubois?'

The Minister bowed his head. He had read about her death in the newspapers, but couldn't accept that his son was in any way involved. All Khalil had told him was Hartley was responsible for the hooker's death.

'I am willing to believe,' said the King, 'that a father's love for his child is the reason you have overlooked some of your son's minor indiscretions. But causing the death of an innocent man while having another man jailed for the offence – and all for the sake of another five per cent – is unacceptable by any standards.'

So the rumours *were* true, thought the Minister, and no one had had the courage to tell him . . . except the King.

'Your son will be stripped of any position he currently holds and will be punished according to Sharia law, while the Englishman will be released from prison without delay. Do I make myself clear?'

'Yes, Your Majesty,' mumbled the Minister, his head still bowed.

'I will allow you one week to sort out the problem, and should you fail to do so, you will also be relieved of your duties.'

The King didn't need to say another word, because it was clear the meeting was over.

The private secretary bowed, took a few paces backwards and left the Minister standing there.

Prince Majid forgot to bow, turned and chased after the private secretary. He only caught up with him by the time he'd reached the entrance to the palace. The Minister kept on walking down the steps and disappeared into the back of his car. When he looked up, the private secretary was nowhere to be seen and the palace doors had already been shut behind him.

During the journey back into the city, the Minister considered his options and came to the conclusion that he didn't have any, if he hoped to survive. A career ruined by the black sheep of the family – although he accepted he had not been a good shepherd.

When his limousine finally came to a halt outside his office, he leapt out of the car and hurried into the building before the chauffeur had time to open the back door. He took the lonely elevator up to the forty-third floor, and went straight to his office.

He'd begun dialling even before he'd sat down at his desk.

The Chief of Police had never before received a personal call from the Minister of Defence. Usually from a secretary, and on rare occasions his deputy, but never the Minister himself. He even wondered if it was really him on the end of the line.

'What can I do for you, Minister?' asked the Chief of Police, standing to attention behind his desk.

• • •

O'Driscoll sat up as the key turned in the first lock.

'I think the money must have been transferred,' he said.

The key turned in the second lock.

'Then I must be a dead man,' replied Simon, smiling. 'But remember, when you're negotiating with the Governor, you have nothing to lose.'

'You've taught me well,' said Sean, as the heavy door was pulled open. 'I only wish we'd met thirty years ago.'

'O'Driscoll,' said a prison officer, standing in the doorway, 'the Governor wants to see you. Now!'

Sean winked at his cellmate before he stepped out into the corridor and followed the armed guard on the long walk to the Governor's office. A sharp knock on the door before he was allowed to enter, where he found the Governor seated behind his desk.

The guard closed the door and waited outside. The moment the Governor saw O'Driscoll, he began to dial. When a voice came on the line, he handed the phone across to the prisoner.

'You've got one minute,' he said, 'no more.'

O'Driscoll grabbed the phone. 'Is that you, Molly?' he asked.

'Yes, my darling,' said a familiar voice that came crackling down the line.

'Did you get the money I sent you?'

'Yes, but I couldn't believe it, Sean. A hundred thousand dollars has been deposited in my account. But then you always said you'd make a fortune if you went to Saudi.'

He couldn't get the words out to express his feelings.

'When will they be releasing you?' she asked. 'The kids can't wait to see you, especially Patrick.'

'It won't be long now,' he said, but what he didn't tell her was it would be in a coffin.

The Governor pressed down the receiver, and the line went dead.

'I think you'll agree I've kept my part of the bargain,' said the Governor. 'Now I expect you to keep yours.'

'Consider it done,' said O'Driscoll, bringing his fingers together as if he was clutching someone's throat. 'But you'll need the coffin to have left the prison, before the doctor comes on duty at eight o'clock tomorrow morning.'

'However,' said the Governor. 'There's been a slight change of plan.' His turn to take O'Driscoll by surprise. He opened the top drawer of his desk and this time produced two small white pills, which he placed on the table in front of him. 'Cyanide,' he explained. 'Just drop them in a glass of water and he'll die within moments. If you were able to get a suicide note with a written confession, that would be a bonus. If you do, I'd send your wife another hundred thousand.' Not that he had any intention of doing so.

'Fifty thousand in advance,' said O'Driscoll, 'in cash, if you want a suicide note as well as a written confession.'

The Governor hesitated before he opened the top drawer of his desk and handed over the fifty cellophane packets, confident he would be able to retrieve every last cent long before Hartley's body had been buried.

It was only after O'Driscoll was being escorted back to his cell, his pockets stuffed with notes, that the Governor began to wonder why he wanted cash.

• • •

Tony Blair sat alone in his study at Number 10, waiting for a call that had been booked for three o'clock. She was never late.

The phone rang at one minute to three.

Blair picked up the phone after one ring and said, 'Good afternoon, Your Majesty,' aware there could only be one person on the other end of the line.

'Good afternoon, Prime Minister,' said the Queen. 'I have, as you suggested, had a word with King Fahd, and he assured me he will resolve the matter we discussed earlier.'

'I am most grateful, ma'am.'

'And I think we might still be in with a chance of the contract, after he told me he wanted to buy one of my thoroughbreds – a negotiation that took considerably longer. You should be hearing from Riyadh soon. Good day, Prime Minister.'

The line went dead, and moments later his private secretary came into the room.

'How did it go?' he asked.

'That woman's an Exocet,' said the Prime Minister. 'I think she might have just blown the French out of the water – and Hartley will be on his way home by the end of the week.' He paused, looked up at his private secretary, and said, 'If only the British people knew the half.'

CHAPTER 26

THE BRITISH AMBASSADOR WAS DELIGHTED to receive a coded cable to let him know that, because of the King's intervention, Simon Hartley would be released in the next few days. He performed a Highland reel.

He then pressed the little button under his desk and looked up, expecting his secretary to join him. She didn't.

He pressed the button for a second time, but still no response. He left his finger on the button a little longer the third time, and when she didn't appear he began to wonder if there was a problem.

Sir Bernard got up from behind his desk, walked across the room, and opened the door that led to Sally's domain. He stood in the doorway and stared at a woman who rarely showed any emotion. Sally was sitting at her desk, head in hands, weeping.

He quickly joined her and placed an arm around her shoulder, something he'd never done before. She didn't say a word, just looked up and handed him a letter.

Dear Ambasador,

I'm sorry to burden you with this letter, but I've just been told by the Governor about the tragic death of Avril Dubois. There seem to be no lengths Khalil will not go to in order to ensure the French are awarded the arms contract, and he gets his extra five per cent.

So now I must be realistic about my own future and accept that while Avril can no longer give evidence to show that it was not me who was responsible for Paolo Conti's death but Prince Ahmed, I have no hope of being found not guilty, and therefore at best will have to spend the rest of my life in this hellhole, although it seems more likely I will suffer the same fate as my cellmate Sean O'Driscoll. Not something I'm willing to endure. With this in mind, I hope you will understand why I have decided to take my own life as, to quote Shakespeare's Richard II: 'For now they kill me with a living death.' I confess it's the coward's way out, but still preferable to any other alternative.

I wonder if I might call on you to do me a kindness by telling my beloved wife, Heather, and our two daughters that my final thoughts were of them, and I can only hope they will understand why I have made this decision, and find it in their hearts to forgive me.

I remain, yours sincerely,
Simon Hartley

A smile appeared on the Ambassador's face.

'No need for tears,' he said after he'd read the letter a second time. Sir Bernard handed the letter back to her with the words, 'See if you can spot the three mistakes.'

Sally read the letter once again, smiled, wiped away the tears and said, 'Four.'

Sir Bernard began to read the message for a third time. 'His wife is called Hannah, not Heather, he has two sons, but no daughters, and he misspelt "Ambassador", so what else have I missed?'

'Shakespeare's quote is from Richard III, not Richard II.'

The Ambassador bowed low and said, '*Chapeau*. I'll have to call London and advise them. Wheels within wheels,' he explained. 'But we'll have to move quickly, before the Governor works out the significance of the words "I remain".'

• • •

The Ambassador's limousine, flags at half-mast on the bumpers, came to a halt outside the prison ten minutes before the appointed hour. The Foreign Office were not in the habit of being late or early for any occasion but were always on time. Ten minutes to ten was the appropriate time to attend a funeral. Sir Bernard got out of the car and stood behind a hearse, leaving his secretary sitting in the back of the car, head bowed, quietly weeping.

The Ambassador was dressed for the occasion. A dark double-breasted suit, a black tie, and a black armband on his left sleeve. He stood alone beside the waiting hearse, as the sole representative of the British government.

Without warning, the vast wooden gates blocking the bleak edifice swung slowly open to reveal six prison guards marching towards him, carrying a coffin on their shoulders. The Governor, head bowed, walked a few paces behind. The solemn cortège came to a halt at the back of the hearse. They lowered the coffin slowly from their shoulders, before easing it into the back of the waiting limousine. Having completed their task, the six men turned and marched back into the prison at a slightly faster pace.

The Governor tentatively approached the Ambassador and held out his hand. Sir Bernard would have avoided returning the compliment with this loathsome individual, but he needed to keep up the pretence for a couple more hours.

'I cannot express how sad we all are,' said the Governor, 'that Hartley felt it necessary to take his own life.'

'I agree,' replied the Ambassador, 'especially as a court order granting his release had just been sanctioned, and he would have been a free man within days.'

'If only I'd known earlier,' said the Governor, 'I feel sure I could have prevented the tragedy.'

Sir Bernard wondered when the Governor would find out the truth. He walked slowly back to his car, while his secretary slipped out of the other side and made her way across to the hearse. She was carrying a wreath of red roses, which she placed on top of the coffin.

Once the rear door had been closed behind her, she pulled a Swiss penknife out of her bulky handbag. Like the good Girl Guide she had once been, Sally extracted a sharp knife and began to scrape away at the join between the lid of the coffin and its base. When a small gap appeared, she replaced the knife with a screwdriver, which she wedged into the gap and, with all the strength she possessed, slowly levered up the lid until there was a large enough space to allow some oxygen to flow in through the gap. When Sally heard heavy breathing, she wanted to let out a yelp of delight, but satisfied herself with looking out of the back window.

'What I'm at pains to understand,' said the Ambassador,

playing for time, 'is how it was possible for my countryman to get hold of the poison in the first place.'

'That puzzled me too,' said the Governor. 'I feel guilty about the fact I wasn't on duty last night, but I will be setting up an inquiry to find out who was responsible, and you can be assured when I find out who it was they will be suitably punished.'

The Ambassador glanced towards the hearse, to receive a nod from his secretary. He immediately got into the back of his car, avoiding having to shake hands with the man a second time. He was putting on his seat belt when the hearse set off at a funereal pace. But once they had turned the corner, they accelerated, to become the fastest hearse in history. They began to overtake startled drivers and bemused onlookers – but then they had a deadline to keep to.

The Governor waited until they were out of sight before he made his way back into the prison. He'd already decided that the inquiry would show he had been at home last night and had immediately sacked the officer on duty. However, he would add that he felt he'd been left with no choice but to resign, without mentioning the one hundred and fifty thousand dollars that were still locked in his desk, or that he only had one more year to serve before retiring.

But he still had one last duty to carry out that would ensure none of the blame could be laid at his door. As he passed reception on the way back to his office, he barked at a passing prison guard, 'Fetch O'Driscoll and bring him to my office immediately.'

The guard scuttled off.

The Governor had already prepared a statement for O'Driscoll to sign that would show he was in no way involved. He would promise O'Driscoll that if he signed the confession, another fifty thousand and the money would be transferred to his wife's account in Dublin immediately. Not that O'Driscoll would live long enough to find out one way or the other.

• • •

'Did you check the flight was on time?' asked the Ambassador as his driver continued to pursue the hearse down the outside lane.

'Yes, sir. I've already briefed the officer in charge of flight control to let him know we're on our way.'

'And Sally?' asked the Ambassador.

'She's clinging onto the coffin handles for dear life. The wreath has gone AWOL, but I can see the coffin lid is slightly raised.'

Sir Bernard let out a sigh of relief, but knew he wouldn't relax until the plane had taken off.

• • •

There was a sharp knock on the Governor's door and a senior prison officer charged in unannounced.

'You'd better come quickly, sir,' was all he said before rushing back out.

The Governor knew from the expression on the officer's face that it had to be a riot or a suspicious death. He quickly left his office, ran after him, and didn't stop running until he reached Block A, where he noticed all the doors were locked, except one.

He entered O'Driscoll's cell to see the prison doctor leaning over his patient.

The doctor answered the Governor's question before he could ask it. 'He's been dead for about an hour.'

'Cause of death?' stammered the Governor.

'Poisoning,' said the doctor. 'The bitter smell of almond rather suggests cyanide. However, I'll know much more after I've carried out a full analysis, I'll have a report on your desk later today.' He paused while he looked up at the Governor. 'What I can't understand is how it was possible for O'Driscoll to get hold of cyanide, when there is none in my pharmacy.'

The Governor wasn't taking in the doctor's words, as his mind was already at the airport.

• • •

The limousine shot off the motorway and headed for a gate reserved for VIPs and special assignments. The Ambassador's cortège fell neatly into both categories. As the hearse approached the entrance, it once again slowed back down to a funereal pace, not wishing to attract any unnecessary attention. It proceeded slowly into the airport and drove across the tarmac to a waiting plane on the far side of the runway.

Hani Khalil stared down at the two cars from the observation deck on the fourth floor. He watched as the hearse came to a halt at the back of an aircraft, which had its cargo door lowered in preparation for the sad occasion. He even wore a black armband on the left sleeve of his suit.

Six coffin-bearers, who carried out this exercise fairly regularly, stepped forward as the driver opened the back door of the hearse, to find Sally, head bowed, weeping. They assumed she had to be the widow accompanying her dead husband.

The six men eased the coffin out of its resting place and in one well-practised movement lifted it up onto their shoulders. They then slow-marched in step towards the open door. They proceeded with dignity up the wide ramp and disappeared into the hold, closely followed by the Ambassador and Sally, who continued to play their role in the fiction.

Khalil was unable to see what was going on inside the hold, but only had to wait a few moments before the six coffin-bearers reappeared and made their way back into the airport, at the same slow respectful pace, having completed their task.

Khalil's eyes never left the gaping hole as he waited for the Ambassador to reappear. When he eventually did, the Lebanese agent was surprised to see that Sir Bernard Anscombe was accompanied by a man in a British Airways uniform. Khalil assumed he must have been waiting for them on board.

Sally did not join them, but quickly returned to the car. Khalil was puzzled why she'd even gone into the hold in the first place, but he was now concentrating on the tall thin man, who had an unkempt beard and whose jacket was a little too large and hung on him like a coathanger. The Ambassador accompanied him to the steps of the plane, where the two men shook hands. Both Sir Bernard and Khalil watched him as he climbed the steps and disappeared inside the aircraft.

Once the cabin door had closed, the Ambassador walked back to his car, where he joined his secretary. She opened her bulky handbag, and Sir Bernard stared down at the fifty thousand dollars in cash that she had removed from the coffin.

'My bonus?' asked Sally hopefully.

'No such luck, Sally,' said the Ambassador smiling. 'Simon explained that the money belongs to Sean's wife, so I want you to deposit the cash in the Embassy account and ask them to transfer the full amount to a Mrs Sean O'Driscoll at the Bank of Ireland in Dublin. I'll have to call her later today, and try and put a gloss on it, but it won't be easy.'

The Ambassador sat back and watched as the plane left its stand and began to taxi towards the far runway, before taking its place in a long queue waiting for take-off.

Khalil was surprised that the Ambassador's car remained by the runway. What was he waiting for?

Then, just as British Airways flight 017 reached the head of the queue and was waiting for the tower to allow take-off, another car came speeding through the VIP gate, lights flashing, siren blaring, and didn't slow down as it headed towards the waiting aircraft.

The Governor had already called ahead to warn air traffic control that an escaped prisoner was on board and to order them to instruct the pilot to return to his stand and await further instructions. He jumped out of his car, assuming his orders would have been obeyed without question and the plane would return to its stand.

He watched in disbelief as the aircraft continued to move, first slowly and then more quickly as it accelerated along the runway, before finally taking off.

He stared up at the plane as it rose in the sky, unable to understand why his clear orders had been ignored. Who would have the nerve to countermand them?

Khalil also watched the plane take off, and two things puzzled him. Why had the Governor turned up at the last minute, only to watch the plane as it disappeared above the clouds? But, even more puzzling, who was the man dressed in a British Airways uniform that didn't fit?

The Ambassador's car didn't move until he'd seen the plane disappear, when he relaxed for the first time. He picked up the phone in his armrest and dialled the Foreign Office in London.

'He's on his way.'

'God save the Queen,' said Trevelyan.

'God save the King,' said the Ambassador.

CHAPTER 27

HANI KHALIL LOOKED UP FROM behind his desk when the Chief of Police and his deputy came barging into his office without an appointment.

'Good afternoon, Chief,' said Khalil. 'To what do I owe this pleasure?'

'It is indeed a pleasure,' said the Chief, 'to finally place you under arrest.'

'On what charge?' asked Khalil calmly.

'Bribing a public official.'

'Anyone in particular?' asked Khalil, trying to make light of it.

'The Governor of 'Ulaysha Prison.'

'Can't say I've ever come across the man,' responded Khalil, testing the water.

'You had a meeting with him in his office on Tuesday, just after midnight.'

'You have proof, of course,' said Khalil, now more cautious.

'A signed confession,' said the Chief, 'admitting that you

offered him three hundred thousand dollars in cash to have Mr Simon Hartley killed.'

'Hearsay at best,' said Khalil, now on the defensive, 'and in any case, as you well know, Mr Hartley is very much alive – and, I'm told, on his way back home.'

'But what isn't hearsay,' replied the Chief, 'is that last Monday you withdrew three hundred thousand dollars from your personal account, one hundred and fifty thousand of which has ended up in a bank account in Dublin in the name of Mrs Sean O'Driscoll.'

'Not a name I'm familiar with,' said Khalil.

'That much I believe,' said the Chief, 'but – unfortunately for you – the Governor has handed over the remaining one hundred and fifty thousand. He's agreed to take early retirement and will be appearing as a government witness in exchange for no charges being brought against him.'

Khalil shifted uneasily in his seat, and this time didn't come up with an immediate response.

'If I had to guess,' said the Chief, 'I suspect you're looking at ten years in 'Ulaysha Prison where, I can assure you, you won't be getting ten per cent of anything.' He paused, 'Unless of course . . .'

'Unless of course?' repeated Khalil, now clinging onto a lifeline.

'You're finally willing to tell the truth about who did kill Paolo Conti at the Overseas Club, because it certainly wasn't Simon Hartley, as the barman and the security guard on duty that night have already testified.' He paused to let the information sink in. 'They've both confirmed in a written statement that it was in fact Prince Ahmed bin Majid who stabbed Conti, and not Mr Simon Hartley, who they both say was *your* guest at the club that night, despite the fact you claimed at the time you didn't know him.'

'But if I were to do that,' said Khalil, 'I would be signing my own death warrant.'

'Not if your friend Prince Ahmed is in prison, while you're safely back at home in Lebanon.'

Khalil took his time considering the percentages in this particular deal, and decided the odds weren't fifty-fifty. 'If I were to agree to make a statement confirming it was Ahmed who killed Conti, will you guarantee that I can leave the country without being charged?'

'I'll give you twenty-four hours,' said the Chief, 'no more. If you're still around after that, I will arrest you.'

• • •

When the aircraft door opened, Simon stepped off the plane to be greeted with the wonderful sight of a London drizzle. He walked unsteadily down the steps, surprised not to be hounded by baying journalists or the flashing bulbs of photographers desperate for a picture – all part of the agreement struck between the new Saudi Defence Minister and the British Ambassador.

A solitary figure was waiting for him at the bottom of the steps. Simon had met Mr Trevelyan during his Westminster briefings before leaving for Saudi and had at one time wondered if they'd ever meet again.

'Welcome home, Mr Hartley,' said the Foreign Secretary's private secretary.

'Thank you,' said Simon, 'and I must also thank you for the role you played in getting me home safely.'

'Don't thank me,' said Trevelyan. 'It was a far higher

authority who oiled those particular wheels. But before you join your wife and family, there is one more thing I need to brief you on.'

Simon had thought nothing would surprise him, after what he'd been put through in Riyadh, but he was wrong.

• • •

When Khalil finally agreed to the inevitable, the Chief of Police took a prepared statement out of his briefcase and placed it on the desk in front of the witness.

Khalil read the damning words, and for a moment seemed to hesitate, until the Chief reminded him, 'Ten years in 'Ulaysha, or the chance to go home and be with your wife and family. Your choice, of course.'

The Chief picked up the pen on Khalil's desk and handed it to him. After another moment of hesitation, Khalil signed on the dotted line.

The policeman waited for the ink to dry before he slipped the confession back into his briefcase and checked his watch. 'Twenty-four hours,' he reminded him before he and his deputy departed as quickly as they had come.

'Where next?' asked the Chief's driver as the two police officers jumped into the back of their waiting car.

'The Overseas Club,' replied the Chief, 'where we will still have to get statements from the barman and the security guard who were on duty that night, which shouldn't prove too difficult, now we have a written confession from Khalil.'

'And after that?' asked his deputy.

'We arrest Prince Ahmed bin Majid.'

• • •

Hannah had been waiting in Arrivals for over an hour. When she saw her husband for the first time, she ran towards him, threw her arms around him – or what was left of him – and clung on, still finding it hard to believe he'd arrived home safely.

Simon placed an arm around her shoulders as she led him unsteadily towards the car park. So many questions she wanted to ask, and now a lifetime to ask them. She lowered him gently into the car and put on his seat belt before taking her place behind the wheel.

As they drove out onto the road, Simon watched as the rain stopped and the sun began to rise on a blissful English autumn morning. Simon had forgotten how he'd taken for granted the simple pleasures of life he feared he might never experience again: church spires gleaming in the sunlight, birds tweeting merrily on high, patrons of local pubs spilling out onto the pavement, clutching onto pints of warm beer, children playing football on the village green and a bobby on his bicycle doing the afternoon rounds.

When the Old Vicarage came into sight, Simon finally believed it wasn't a dream. His eyes filled with tears when he saw his two sons standing on the doorstep waiting for him.

He jumped out of the car and began running towards them, but his legs gave way and he collapsed onto the ground. Robert ran to his side, scooped his father up and became his crutch as he helped him into the house.

Hannah closed the door on the past.

• • •

The Speaker rose from her chair in the Commons and called for order, before inviting the Foreign Secretary to make a statement on behalf of the government.

Robin Cook took his place at the dispatch box, opened his red ministerial folder and said, 'With your permission, Madam Speaker, I will make a statement concerning the negotiations the government has been conducting with Saudi Arabia for a long-term arms contract.'

The House fell silent.

'I am delighted to announce,' continued the Foreign Secretary, 'that Sir Bernard Anscombe, our Ambassador in Riyadh, this morning signed a comprehensive agreement on behalf of Her Majesty's government for a three-billion-pound arms contract with Saudi Arabia.'

Hear, hear! echoed from the government benches, but they were far from universal.

'Full details of which will be available to members in the order office immediately following the conclusion of this statement.'

The House listened intently as the Foreign Secretary took them slowly through the details of the agreement, ending with the words, 'This contract, Madam Speaker, will cement a long-term relationship with the Middle East, making possible the immediate employment of some three thousand support staff on the ground and a further twenty thousand in factories up and down the country.'

The hear, hears were a little louder this time.

The Foreign Secretary turned to the last page of his statement. 'I know the whole House will want to congratulate Mr Simon Hartley, who has quite recently returned to this country, on the role he played in securing this historic contract.' Mr Trevelyan had drawn a line through the words *and not always in the easiest of circumstances.*

Hear, hears emanated from around the house, having finally found something they could all agree on.

'Madam Speaker, I commend this statement to the House.'

After the background noise had subsided, the Speaker rose again and called for the shadow frontbench spokesman to respond.

William Hague entered the fray. He gripped the dispatch box and, looking directly at the government benches said, 'While congratulating the Foreign Secretary on this historic agreement, may I remind the House that it was Margaret Thatcher who opened these negotiations . . .'

Cheers and jeers in equal measure emanated from both sides of the chamber.

CHAPTER 28

DURING THE NEXT FEW DAYS, Ross had assumed the Hawk would summon him to his office at a moment's notice to tell him he'd had a call from an outraged QC who was demanding an explanation as to why one of the Met's senior officers had been attempting to bribe one of his clients while he was out on parole. Ross accepted if this were to happen, it would be him and not Mumford who would be looking at an arrest warrant, and this time it would already have been signed by a local magistrate. But the summons hadn't come.

As soon as he sat down at his desk on Monday morning, Ross gave the local police at Little Hampton a call to check that Billy had reported – on time – for his weekly probation meeting. He had, the desk sergeant confirmed, which gave Ross some confidence that Mumford was keeping to his side of the bargain. It didn't stop him lying awake at night.

The next morning, he left the flat before Alice and Jojo had woken, closed the front door quietly, climbed into his car and headed for the Great North Road. This time Ross had decided – once the exchange had taken place – that he would be travelling on to Bucklebury and then Heathrow. He wouldn't have a moment to spare if he still hoped to be on time for his flight.

When he drove into Little Hampton three hours later, he was already running a few minutes late, so didn't waste any time admiring the Norman tower. He parked his car outside the pub, grabbed his briefcase, and immediately went into the Dog and Duck.

When he entered the pub, it was as if time had stood still. At the bar were the same locals sipping the same ale, who this time didn't even bother to give him a second look. Ross only had to glance around the snug to see Billy was sitting at his usual table, but this time there was no sign of the *Yorkshire Post* – just the copy of *Monticello* and a large brown envelope, accompanied by a smug smile on his face.

Ross took the seat opposite his unaware accomplice, who wasted no time in passing over the envelope, the smile remaining in place.

Ross could feel his heart beating as he pulled open the flap and slowly extracted a single sheet of paper and a small faded cream envelope addressed in black handwriting to the Rt Hon. David Hartley MP, Hartley Hall, Bucklebury, England.

He turned to page 171 of Rosenberg's *Monticello* before he began to study the letter. After making a comparison between Jefferson's script and Mumford's forgery, he had to admit he couldn't tell the difference between them. Billy had earned his reputation as a master forger.

Ross placed the envelope, the letter and his copy of *Monticello* back in the briefcase before he extracted another arrest warrant, which also hadn't been countersigned by a local magistrate. But before Billy could take a closer look, he once again tore it to shreds, dropping the little pieces back in his briefcase.

'Now listen and listen carefully,' said Ross, as he stood up and peered down at his accomplice, 'if you don't want to go back to the Scrubs, this meeting never took place. Don't even think about contacting Booth Watson or sharing our little secret with anyone else, because if you do—'

'It wouldn't even cross my mind, Mr Hogan,' said Billy. 'Not a word, I promise, to anyone.'

Ross closed his briefcase and said, 'Let's hope we never meet again.'

'The feeling's mutual, Mr Hogan,' said Mumford.

Ross quickly left the pub and got back into his car, ready to set off on the second part of the triangle.

Before he turned on the ignition, Ross couldn't resist opening the briefcase once again and taking another look at the letter. Nothing had changed, except that he was running late. He switched on the engine, and quickly made his way out of the village. As the miles ticked over on the journey back along the motorway, Ross began to think about just how much he would tell Lady Hartley and, equally importantly, how much he would leave unsaid. No more than necessary, he decided, and rehearsed his script several times before he arrived outside the gates that led up to Hartley Hall.

The beautiful Elizabethan mansion looked far more welcoming than a rundown pub in Little Hampton, and the warm greeting he received from Lady Hartley couldn't have been in greater contrast to the monosyllabic grunt he'd got from the landlord of the Dog and Duck.

Ross had heard on the news that Simon Hartley was back in England and even wondered if he might be staying with his mother. It was a relief to discover he wasn't.

Once he had settled in the drawing room – he admired the watercolours, particularly the Russell Flint – and been offered a welcome cup of tea and a shortbread biscuit, he ventured, 'You may be wondering why I asked to see you again, Lady Hartley.'

'I assumed it must have something to do with the auction that's being held in New York tomorrow and the missing letter I foolishly gave to . . .' She paused mid-sentence.

'You're quite right,' said Ross, not wasting a moment. He opened his briefcase, took out the large brown envelope and extracted Mumford's copy of the letter, which he handed over to her.

The old lady's hands began to tremble as she read it. 'How clever of you, Inspector,' said Lady Hartley. 'I had assumed he'd destroyed it,' once again not mentioning Faulkner by name, 'and that I would never see the letter again.'

'Are you absolutely sure that is the letter you gave him, Lady Hartley?' asked Ross.

'It has to be,' said Lady Hartley. 'I remember my husband repeating it word for word. But may I ask you a question?'

'Of course,' said Ross.

'Does this mean . . .?'

'Let's hope so,' Ross replied, before she could complete the sentence.

'Then we ought to be opening a bottle of champagne to celebrate,' said Lady Hartley, 'whereas all I can offer you is another cup of tea.' She picked up the teapot.

'That's very kind of you,' said Ross, slipping the letter back into its large brown envelope, 'but sadly I must leave you if I'm to get to Heathrow in time to catch the last flight to New York this evening.'

'Then I won't hold you up any longer,' said Lady Hartley,

rising from her place, and without another word, she accompanied her guest back to the front door.

'Thank you once again,' said Ross as he stepped out onto the drive. 'And congratulations on your son's release – I know you must be relieved.'

'More than I can say,' said Lady Hartley. 'But can I ask you one more thing before you leave, Inspector?'

Ross stopped in his tracks. He waited for a question he'd been anticipating but had hoped she wouldn't ask.

'Does that mean Mr Faulkner will be expecting me to return his money, because I fear . . .'

'No. I can promise you, Lady Hartley, you won't be hearing from Mr Faulkner again,' said Ross, as he climbed into his car. She couldn't hide her relief as she watched him drive away.

Ross waved to her as he drove out of the grounds and back onto the main road. An innocent bystander, he thought, who was about to play a major role on the world stage without even realizing it.

Once he was back on the motorway, Ross pressed a number on his mobile, aware that his co-conspirator would be on the other end sitting at his desk, anxiously waiting for the call.

A voice answered after one ring and said, 'James Buchanan.'

'I have the letter you require,' said Ross, 'and with a fair wind, I should be landing at JFK at around ten tomorrow morning.'

'I'll be there to meet you when you get off the plane,' said James, 'and by then I should have everything in place. Have a good flight.' Not a man who wasted words or gave anything away that might be overheard.

Ross switched off his phone. When he wasn't looking out for airport signs revealing the number of miles to go, he was continually checking the clock on his dashboard that was ticking over far too quickly. It was going to be tight, even though he continued to ignore the speed limit while he was on the motorway. Once he joined the slip road leading to the airport, he ignored several amber lights, forgetting he was an ordinary citizen and not a policeman on official duty.

On arrival at Terminal Three, he dumped his car in the short-term car park, jumped out and began running, now checking his watch every few seconds.

As he charged into the airport, he looked up at the departure board to see Gate 19 flicking over to be replaced by the words Gate Closed. He accelerated out of the blocks like an Olympic sprinter, and began to follow the signs to Gate 19, relieved he was only carrying a briefcase, which contained his passport, ticket, mobile phone, car keys and the large brown envelope. But by the time he arrived at the check-in desk, he looked out of the window only to see the aircraft steps being wheeled away.

'I'm so sorry, Mr Hogan,' said the lady after checking his ticket, 'but as you can see your flight is about to take off.'

'Are there any other planes going to New York tonight?' he asked desperately, between breaths.

'Only Concorde,' she replied. 'But I can book you on to our first flight in the morning.'

'That will be too late,' Ross said without explanation, as he wondered what a flight on Concorde would do to his bank balance. 'Are there any seats available on Concorde?' he asked, painfully aware he'd been left with no choice.

'Let me check,' said the attendant as she began tapping away on her computer. Moments later, a smile appeared on her face. 'Yes, I can still get you on that flight, but you will have to hurry.'

'Thank you,' said Ross, who set off again, and this time

managed to reach the Concorde desk with a few minutes to spare. He handed over his credit card, relieved when moments later he saw the word APPROVED appear on the little screen.

He quickly made his way to the departure gate, still out of breath. Once on board, he settled into his seat and phoned James Buchanan just before the plane took off. 'Slight change of plan!' he announced.

• • •

Ross woke to find a flight attendant standing by his side. 'Mr Hogan?'

'Yes,' said Ross, stifling a yawn as he looked up at him.

'Once we land, we've been allocated an airport apron and my supervisor has asked me to make sure you're the first passenger off the plane.'

'Thank you,' replied Ross, and then frowned. 'I had a bad dream.'

'I'm sorry to hear that, sir.'

'Could you please open the compartment above me and tell me what you see?'

The flight attendant carried out the passenger's request, and said, 'A black leather briefcase with the initials RH etched in gold.'

'It wasn't there in my dream.'

'I'll come and get you, sir, once we've been cleared to disembark,' said the senior flight attendant, none the wiser.

'This is your captain speaking,' said a voice from the flight desk. 'We will be starting our descent shortly and the good news is that we're a few minutes ahead of schedule.'

Only Ross knew why.

• • •

Special Agent Buchanan thanked the director of air traffic control for his assistance. A triple-A request from the FBI usually meant the arrival of a head of state or a criminal on the 'most wanted' list. He hadn't asked which.

James left him and made his way across to Gate 41, the nearest exit to the highway, although he accepted not even his boss could control the bumper-to-bumper traffic into Manhattan – a monster with a mind of its own.

'BA017 has just landed,' said James over the radio to his number two back at HQ. 'Make sure the operations team are waiting for me in the briefing room by the time I get back, and ask Professor Rosenberg if he would be kind enough to join me in my office, as I need to ask him to make a sacrifice for his country.'

He made a second call to the director to bring him up to date as he watched Concorde turn off the runway and begin to taxi towards him.

The director told his special assistant, 'I have spoken to the President and assured him the letter is on its way.'

• • •

When the seat belt light went off, Ross was the first out of the blocks. He quickly opened the locker above him, grabbed his briefcase, and clung on to it as if it were full of precious gems. One uncut diamond.

'Follow me,' said the authoritative voice of the chief steward – a command Ross was happy to obey, stopping only when he reached the front of the cabin to observe several inquisitive eyes staring up at him, wondering who he was.

When the door was finally heaved open, Ross jogged down

the steps and almost fell into the arms of Special Agent Buchanan. Without a word passing between them, Ross opened his briefcase, took out the large brown envelope and handed the baton on to the next relay runner in the team.

James extracted the letter but didn't comment until he'd finished reading it – a second time.

'I'm convinced,' he said with a shrug of the shoulder, 'but I'm not the person who can offer an authoritative opinion. But if Rosenberg isn't willing to stamp his imprimatur, I may have to stand my team down.' He slid the letter back into the envelope, opened the back door of the car and asked, 'Do you want to join us at the auction?'

'Can't risk it,' said Ross. 'There will be two people sitting in the front row who, if they spot me, just might work out why I'm there.'

James simply replied, 'On behalf of a grateful nation, thank you, Inspector.' He then shook Ross by the hand as if he was an American general awarding him a medal. 'That sounded a bit pompous, didn't it?' James added. 'But I meant it.'

'Will I see you at my wedding?' asked Ross as James climbed into the car.

'Wouldn't miss it. I can't wait to meet the woman who's willing to marry you.'

Ross left him to join the other passengers as they made their way into the airport.

Once he'd gone through passport control followed by customs – nothing to declare other than a half-empty briefcase – he headed straight for the BA counter to book the next flight back home.

• • •

'Out on Concorde and back on economy on the same day,' said the booking clerk, unable to hide her surprise. 'That's a first for me.'

'Me too,' admitted Ross without explanation.

The booking clerk began tapping away, looked up and asked, 'Are you Mr Ross Hogan, by any chance?'

'Sure am.'

'Then you're already booked to fly back on the Concorde.'

'Can't afford it, I'm afraid,' said Ross.

'Yes, you can,' said the booking clerk, 'because you won't be paying.'

'How come?' asked Ross, genuinely puzzled.

'Your flight has already been paid for by the government – the FBI no less,' she said, giving him a warm smile, 'so you're either being deported, or you're very important.'

'Neither,' admitted Ross, as he looked up to the heavens and thanked James.

'And for your bonus point,' added the clerk, 'your inward flight has been refunded, so clearly you're not a fugitive.'

'Is there somewhere I can get a cup of coffee and a sandwich before we take off?' asked Ross.

'You're welcome to have a complimentary meal in the Concorde lounge, and I can recommend the sole meunière, with a bottle of Chablis to wash it down.'

Ross took her advice and joined a group of passengers in the Concorde lounge who he'd never travelled with before, and doubted he would ever again.

•   •   •

The front doorbell rang. Although he'd been home for only a few days, Simon wasn't altogether surprised to find Hani

Khalil standing on the doorstep. It had to happen sooner or later. Better sooner.

'You look fantastic, Simon, given what they put you through,' were Khalil's opening words.

Don't you mean what you put me through, Simon wanted to say, but not while he still needed to pick up some inside information, even if it came from such an unreliable source.

'I thought you'd want to know the latest news concerning our contract,' said Khalil, emphasizing the word 'our'.

Simon reluctantly stood aside to allow Khalil to come in. He took him through to the drawing room, where he plonked himself down in the most comfortable chair, as if it was his own home. Simon took the seat opposite him, while making no suggestion of offering him a drink.

'You wouldn't believe how much I had to cough up to get you out of that hellhole,' said Khalil. 'But then it was the least I could do for an old friend.'

You're right, I wouldn't believe it, thought Simon, but let him go on talking.

'But I always knew it would work out for the best, because you're the type of guy who always keeps his side of a bargain. Which is why I wanted you as my partner in the first place.'

'How much do I owe you?' asked Simon, somehow controlling his temper.

'It cost me three hundred thousand dollars to ensure you got away safely, but let's settle on a couple of hundred for old times' sake.' Simon wondered if the man even listened to his own words. 'Of course, you'll appreciate there were a lot of people who had to be paid off,' continued Khalil. 'Not least the Governor and several of his officers who were on duty that day, not to mention countless airport officials.'

Simon could only admire the man's nerve and his ability

to deliver lie after lie, while a look of sincerity never left his face. Time to throw in a few questions of my own, thought Simon.

'I presume we've lost the arms contract to the French?'

'No, no,' insisted Khalil. 'Thanks to my efforts, the British secured the contract as your Foreign Secretary announced in the Commons this afternoon.' Something Simon was well aware of, but he hadn't finished with Khalil yet.

'I wouldn't have thought that possible,' said Simon trying to sound surprised.

'I confess it took me some time to convince the new Defence Minister that they should back you rather than the French. Mind you, the final contract can't be signed until you've confirmed my ten per cent.'

'Only ten per cent,' said Simon.

'That is what we agreed,' said Khalil, 'but as you well know Simon, once I've given my word . . .'

Simon did know, but couldn't resist, 'I thought the French—'

'Were definitely in with a chance,' said Khalil, 'until I was able to persuade the new Defence Minister that the British equipment was far superior to anything the French had to offer.'

'True enough,' said Simon, playing along.

'I think I can honestly say, with hand on heart, that I've earned my meagre commission.'

And I think I can honestly say, with hand on heart, you won't be getting it, Simon was about to tell him, when his wife entered the room, a wicker basket filled with roses cradled under one arm.

'How very kind of you to take the trouble to visit my husband, Mr Khalil,' Hannah said, taking Simon by surprise.

'What beautiful roses, Mrs Hartley,' responded Khalil. 'In full bloom, just like you, if I may say so.'

'How sweet of you,' said Hannah, 'and I'd love to show you around my garden, if you have time.'

'I can think of nothing that would give me greater pleasure, Mrs Hartley.'

'Hannah, please,' she said as she led him out of the room, with a dumbstruck Simon following in her wake.

When they reached the front door, Hannah opened it and stood aside to allow her guest to step out onto the path while she remained on the doorstep. 'My grandfather used to tell me when I was a little girl,' said Hannah, 'that the English language was so exquisite, every word should be treasured.'

'I couldn't agree more,' said Khalil.

'Then I can only hope he'll forgive me when I tell you to fuck off, Mr Khalil, because you won't be getting a penny.'

Hannah slammed the door in his face and couldn't resist a smile.

Simon stared at her in disbelief and said, 'It's possible, my darling, that you've just lost the British government three billion pounds.'

'Worth every penny,' said Hannah as she walked into the kitchen, selected a vase and began to arrange the roses.

CHAPTER 29

THE AUCTION HOUSE WAS PACKED, with almost every seat taken, by the time Miles Faulkner walked onto the stage, like a Shakespearean actor on the opening night.

He made his way slowly down the centre aisle, enjoying the whispered conversations when heads turned to look in his direction as he and Booth Watson took the two remaining seats in the front row.

Miles opened his catalogue to check the next lot: Number 88 – perfect timing. Three more lots to come under the hammer before Lot 91 would be offered to the public, although only a handful of people in the room could afford to join in the bidding. He looked around the packed auditorium, his eyes settling on Michael Bloomberg, who'd just announced he was running for mayor, seated four rows back on the centre aisle, studying the catalogue.

'Lot Eighty-Nine, a walking stick owned by Alexander Hamilton. I have an opening bid of ten thousand dollars.'

Miles's eyes continued to scan the room, stopping only

when he spotted two empty seats six rows back, on the other side of the aisle. He could only wonder who would make such a late appearance for the sold out show. Moments later, his unasked question was answered when the late arrival made an entrance worthy of Augustus Caesar, lacking only a drum roll and a trumpet fanfare.

'Sold! For twenty thousand dollars,' said the auctioneer, but the audience were no longer interested in Hamilton's walking stick now that Donald Trump had entered the room and was walking slowly down the aisle to a buzz of heightened conversation. He stopped several times to shake outstretched hands, and didn't sit down until he was confident everyone was looking at him.

'Lot Ninety,' said the auctioneer, trying to recapture the audience's attention as Trump and Melania took the only two unoccupied seats in the room. 'A quill pen owned by John Adams, the second president, with which it is thought he signed the Declaration of Independence.'

The crowd went on talking as the quill pen held little interest for most of them, and there was almost a sigh of relief when the hammer finally came down at $25,000 and the auctioneer announced Lot 91. Suddenly, for a surreal moment, the room fell silent, and the ringmaster was finally back in charge.

'A unique copy of the Declaration of Independence,' declared the auctioneer in a stage whisper, 'penned by Thomas Jefferson, and known by scholars as the Fair Copy.' He allowed himself a dramatic pause as he looked down at the framed lot that two porters were placing on an easel in front of him.

'Before I begin the bidding, I should point out that this item has been verified by Saul Rosenberg, the emeritus professor of American history at Princeton University, who is universally acknowledged as the leading authority in the country on the constitution, having been awarded the Medal of Honour by Congress for his service to education.' A thousand eyes looked up when the auctioneer announced, 'I have an opening bid for the Declaration of five million dollars.'

Six, seven, eight, nine and ten followed in quick succession. But even Miles was taken by surprise when an unmistakable voice cried, 'Twenty million,' and everyone turned to look in Trump's direction, as he raised a clenched fist in the air, accompanied by his trademark smile.

A moment later, a more refined hand was raised by one of the Christie's phone reps, who was standing behind a long table on the left side of the room, along with several of her colleagues, all with telephones pressed against ears, waiting to find out if their anonymous client wished to join the circus.

'I have a bid of twenty-two million,' said the auctioneer, looking towards the bank of phones.

Miles wondered who it might be on the other end of the line, aware that phone bidders considered their anonymity paramount, and even the auctioneer would be unaware who the Christie's rep was representing. Miles had a feeling it might be George Soros, who had recently sold the pound short and made a killing and, when he was asked by *Time* magazine if he would be bidding for the Fair Copy, had been unusually reticent.

'Twenty-five million,' said Trump, like a heavyweight boxer going for the knockout.

But the phone bidder wasn't quite so easily floored, and the rep raised her hand once again.

'Twenty-seven million,' the auctioneer announced.

'Thirty million,' declared Bloomberg, before Trump could land the next blow.

The bated breaths were replaced by gasps.

331

'I have thirty-three million,' said the auctioneer, nodding in the direction of the telephone bidder.

'Thirty-five,' said Trump and Bloomberg at the same time, and the auctioneer would have been left with an embarrassing choice had he not been rescued by the unannounced arrival of a team of FBI agents wearing their familiar blue jackets who swarmed uninvited into the gallery, quickly taking up positions on both sides of the room, which created a different kind of eerie silence.

The agents were followed by two men: one a well-dressed man who Miles didn't recognize, while the other he would never forget.

The tall, smartly dressed man approached the rostrum and had a quiet word with the auctioneer, before showing him his official writ. The auctioneer studied the document for some time before standing down and allowing the officer to take his place on the podium. The FBI agent didn't pick up the hammer, but he did tap the microphone a couple of times before he spoke.

'My name is James Buchanan,' he said, 'and I'm a special assistant to the Director of the FBI. I apologize for interrupting this auction and can only hope that when you have heard what I have to say, you will welcome the news.'

Miles, Trump and Bloomberg all sat on the edge of their seats, waiting to decide which way they would jump.

'Many of you will have heard the rumour that Jefferson wrote a letter that accompanied the Fair Copy and was believed to have been lost in the tide of times. I know you will all be delighted to learn that the missing letter has finally come to light.'

Miles turned to Booth Watson and whispered, 'Risen from the ashes, more like. Who's kidding who?'

Booth Watson placed a finger to his lips and murmured, 'Let's hear what Buchanan has to say before we decide what our next move should be.'

'With your permission,' said James, 'I will now read that letter to you.'

If he had dropped a pin, it would have sounded like a volcano erupting.

Hôtel de Langeac
Paris
August 11th, 1787

Dear Mr Hartley,

I hope you will grant me your permission to impose upon your time by allowing me to send you my Fair Copy of the Declaration of Independence, which I earlier delivered to Congress for their consideration. You will see that it includes the two clauses you and I discussed in London, namely the abolition of slavery and our future relationship with King George III once we become an independent nation. Copies were made by my friend and colleague Benjamin Franklyn and distributed among interested parties. Much to my dismay, when members of Congress divided, both clauses were rejected. However, I would not want you to think I hadn't taken to heart your wise and sound counsel and tried to convince my fellow congressmen of the merit of your judgement.

Once you have had a proper chance to peruse the Fair Copy at your leisure, perhaps you would be kind enough, in the fullness of time, to return it to me. I thought you would want to know that it is my intention to bequeath this memento to the Nation in order that

*future generations of Americans might fully appreciate
what the founding fathers were trying to achieve, and
not least the role you played. I look forward to hearing
from you at some time in the future, and be assured of
my sincere esteem and respect.*

I remain, your most obedient and humble servant,
Thomas Jefferson

The audience rose as one, some clapping, others cheering, with only two exceptions, who remained seated in the front row, speechless.

James didn't step down from the rostrum, and it wasn't until silence had been restored that he spoke again. 'There may be those among us,' he said, staring down at Miles and Booth Watson, 'who for personal reasons may wish to throw doubt on the validity of this document.' He held up the letter for all to see.

'With that in mind,' added James, 'I have asked Professor Rosenberg to offer his considered opinion on the credibility of the letter.'

Rosenberg couldn't hide from the glare of the spotlight. The diminutive, shabbily dressed figure rose slowly from his place near the back of the room to give a lecture to the most attentive group of students he'd ever come across.

'Ladies and gentlemen,' he began in a quiet but authoritative voice, 'I have studied the letter most carefully, and have been able to compare it with several others I have seen over the years. The script leaves me in no doubt it is in keeping with that period, the text certainly resembles Jefferson's distinct style and, perhaps equally important, the paper on which the letter was written, examples of which I've seen when I was a young doctoral student, almost certainly come from a batch used by Jefferson at that time. But for those for whom "almost certainly" will never be enough, what finally convinced me,' continued Rosenberg, 'is that the Fair Copy was previously owned by a Lady Hartley, who sold it to its present owner a few weeks ago. She has also confirmed it was the letter that had been, along with five other letters, part of her family archives for over two hundred years.'

Several people turned and stared at Miles as if he was a criminal on the run.

'Lady Hartley,' continued Rosenberg, 'is the wife of the late Lord Hartley, a direct descendant of the Right Honourable David Hartley MP, a distinguished member of the British Parliament and a supporter of American Independence. He was also a friend of both Thomas Jefferson and Benjamin Franklin, and there is a considerable amount of correspondence conducted between the three of them at the time that is in the public domain. This was the compelling reason why I was finally convinced the letter is authentic, and therefore can say without fear or favour that the Fair Copy belongs to the American people.'

A third cheer went up that was the loudest of all, and the acclamation continued for several minutes, even though the professor had sat down and once again disappeared from sight.

Miles leant across to Booth Watson and whispered, 'You and I both know Rosenberg is well aware it's a copy – the question is: how can we possibly prove it?'

CHAPTER 30

BILLY ROSE EARLY THAT MORNING – early by his standards, but then he had a busy day ahead of him. He needed to study the form before he set off for Pontefract.

Once he was dressed, he went downstairs, picked the *Yorkshire Post* off the mat and strolled into the kitchen. He filled the kettle and made himself a cup of tea before he turned to the sports pages. An hour later, he'd selected three dead certs to make up for last week's surprising losses: Lucky Jim in the six o'clock, 4–1; Dog's Dinner in the seven fifteen, 10–1; and Artic Circle in the seven forty-five, 3–1.

He decided to place fifty pounds on each race and another fifty on an accumulator. If all three won, he would make a killing. Just one win and he'd break even. He checked his watch: not yet time to go to the pub for lunch, so he turned the paper over to see if there was anything going on in the world he ought to know about. When he saw the headline, he broke out into a cold sweat.

MULTIMILLION-DOLLAR AUCTION STOPPED BY
DISCOVERY OF MISSING JEFFERSON LETTER

He read the article first quickly, and then very slowly, aware he would have to make a decision. Did he keep his mouth shut and hope Mr Faulkner wouldn't find out he had been responsible for losing him at least thirty-five million? Or should he let him know he'd written the letter, not Jefferson? If he went down that route, he'd be back in the Scrubs by nightfall.

Billy began walking around the kitchen and changed his mind several times during the next hour, but after considering the odds one more time, he selected the favourite for the Jefferson letter stakes, rather than the police horse ridden by Ross Hogan.

After all, one per cent of thirty-five million would keep him in clover for the rest of his life, even if he did have to spend a few more years in prison before he could hope to enjoy a happy retirement.

He knew he'd seen the name of the hotel buried somewhere in the story, so he began to read the article for a third time, only stopping when he reached the words, *he is currently staying at the Park Plaza*. With the help of directory enquiries, he eventually found the number and asked the international operator to put him through.

'Park Plaza Hotel, how may I help you?'

'I'd like to speak to Mr Booth Watson,' said Mumford, still trembling.

'You do realize it's four o'clock in the morning in New York,' the receptionist said.

Billy hadn't realized but decided it couldn't wait. 'I do, but it's an emergency.'

'And who shall I say is calling, sir?'

'Billy Mumford.'

Billy could hear the phone ringing in the background, but it was some time before a voice eventually came back on the line. It wasn't Mr Booth Watson, but the receptionist.

'I'm sorry, sir, but Mr Booth Watson is not available.'

'Did you tell him it was an emergency?' asked Billy.

'Yes, I did, sir.'

'Will you please try again?' said Billy.

'Mr Booth Watson made it clear,' said the receptionist, 'if you were to call again, I was not under any circumstances to put you through.'

The line went dead.

'Well, he can't say I didn't try,' said Billy, who ignored the headline on the front page and returned to the sports pages so he could concentrate on what really mattered.

He put fifty pounds on State Secret to win the last race of the day. It came second.

• • •

Miles read the article in the *New York Times* a second time, studying every word of Jefferson's letter, and one in particular that Rosenberg clearly ignored, before he yelled out loud, 'Gotcha!' One thing was certain: he needed to tell Booth Watson immediately. He checked the clock on his bedside table – five to seven, and wondered if Booth Watson was awake. Not that he gave a damn. He jumped out of bed, put on a dressing gown, and ran out into the corridor.

He banged on his door, waking Booth Watson for a second time that morning. Booth Watson wasn't in any doubt who he would find standing outside in the corridor. He climbed out of bed, and was putting on a dressing gown when the banging began again, if anything even louder.

He walked slowly across the room, removed the chain from its hook, and had only just opened the door when Miles came barging in, a copy of the *New York Times* under his arm, and announced, 'They made one big mistake.'

Booth Watson closed the door, took a seat in a comfortable chair and waited to hear what was the one big mistake, while Miles began to march around the room.

'Let's begin,' said Miles, 'with the simple fact that we know Jefferson's so-called letter is a forgery.'

'But we can't tell anyone why we know,' Booth Watson reminded his client.

'Agreed,' said Miles, 'but there is someone who can.'

'Rosenberg?' said Booth Watson.

'No, I'm convinced the professor knows only too well the letter wasn't written by Thomas Jefferson but has abandoned scholarship for country. However, there's someone else who can prove it's a forgery and his word wouldn't be questioned.'

'Namely?'

'Simon Hartley,' said Miles, a note of triumph in his voice. 'When he sees the letter he'll know immediately it's a fake and will be left with no choice but to admit it.'

'Why?' demanded Booth Watson.

'You clearly haven't read the *New York Times* this morning, BW, because if you had,' said Miles, handing over his copy, 'you would have realized that Jefferson couldn't have written the letter that FBI guy read out at the auction.'

Booth Watson took his time reading the article in the *New York Times*, and although he didn't shout, 'Gotcha!', a smile appeared on his face. 'I'll call Special Agent Buchanan and demand a meeting with the bureau's lawyers this morning.'

'And if he doesn't agree?' said Miles.

'I'll call the *New York Times* and explain to the editor the difference between "y" and "i".'

• • •

Three men were seated on one side of the long oak table, representing the Americans. Two sat on the other side, on behalf of the British. In medieval times, the rivals would have sat on horses, carried lances, and worn helmets displaying feathers revealing their allegiances. In the twenty-first century, they sat in comfortable leather chairs, wore tailored suits, carried fountain pens and sported old school ties. They still faced each other, prepared to do battle, but in this case a battle of words.

One of them raised his visor and said, 'My name is Casper Shaw. I'm the senior partner of Shaw, Renwick and Kline. I am joined this morning by a partner, Andrew Renwick,' he glanced to his right, 'who specializes in litigation. We are also assisted by Special Agent Buchanan who represents our clients, the FBI.'

Not for much longer, thought Booth Watson, but kept his counsel.

Shaw looked across at his opponents and waited for them to raise their visors.

'My name is Booth Watson. I am a Queen's Counsel, and a bencher of Middle Temple. I'm accompanied today by my distinguished client, Mr Miles Faulkner, who I've had the privilege of representing for many years. Mr Faulkner is a leading businessman who is well known throughout the British Isles for his philanthropic work supporting many worthy causes, including the Fitzmolean Museum, to whom he has given several major works over the years, including a Rubens and a Rembrandt. Indeed more recently, he donated a quarter of a million pounds, making it possible for the museum to acquire *Jacob Wrestling with the Angel*, one of Rembrandt's most iconic works. May I open proceedings by saying how much we appreciate you agreeing to this *without prejudice* meeting at such short notice, but as we all know a great deal is at stake.'

'And not just money,' suggested Shaw, re-entering the fray, 'because on this occasion our firm has the privilege of representing the American government and its legitimate claim to the ownership of an historic document that clearly belonged to the third President of the United States. We are also in possession of a letter written by Thomas Jefferson that proves that the Fair Copy was his by right,' he paused before adding, 'beyond reasonable doubt, to quote a legal maxim your countryman will be well acquainted with.'

'Nevertheless,' came back Booth Watson, 'my client disputes your claim and asserts that the letter is a forgery. I must, therefore, inform you that we will be issuing a writ against your government for the amount of forty million dollars plus expenses in compensation.'

The expression on Special Agent Buchanan's face gave nothing away.

'We do not dispute the fact,' continued Booth Watson, 'that the paper on which the letter was written may well have been produced in the late eighteenth century, along with an envelope and a quill pen from that same period. But we maintain that the letter itself is a fiction – a forgery. Nothing more and nothing less, and perhaps, more important, we will supply evidence that even Professor Rosenberg will be unable to refute.'

'We will, of course, be happy to accept your writ on behalf of our client,' said Shaw, 'but should the matter come to court, we will defend the action vigorously with the complete confidence that a jury will find in our favour, not least because it will be twelve God-fearing American citizens who are asked to choose between the word of a three-times convicted criminal and the opinion of the nation's leading authority on the constitution.'

Booth Watson accepted the battle lines had been drawn, and the visors were back in place.

'We acknowledge without question that my client purchased the Declaration from Lady Hartley,' said Booth Watson. 'In fact, it is proof that Mr Faulkner is the legitimate owner of the Fair Copy. She also gave my client five letters that Thomas Jefferson wrote to her husband's distinguished ancestor, but these were a gift.'

'It may interest you to know,' interrupted Shaw, 'that earlier this morning I contacted our Ambassador in London, who confirmed that Lord Hartley, a distinguished member of Her Majesty's Privy Council, had made an appointment to see him for the sole purpose of returning the Declaration to the American people.'

'But unfortunately for you, that meeting never took place,' came back Booth Watson, 'so in the end it will be the facts that matter, and the fact is that Lady Hartley sold the Declaration to my client in good faith, proving there can be no dispute that Mr Faulkner is the lawful owner of said document.'

'But this letter,' said Shaw, holding it up once again, 'proves beyond question that Lady Hartley did not have the authority to sell your client the Fair Copy.'

Booth Watson took his time opening his Gladstone bag and rummaging around in it, before extracting three copies of *Monticello*, two of which he handed to Shaw and one to Buchanan. 'May I suggest you open the Pulitzer Prize-winning book at page 171, where you will find another letter written by Thomas Jefferson, the authenticity of which we accept without question.'

Shaw and Buchanan reluctantly turned to page 171.

'If you study the words of that particular letter carefully,' continued Booth Watson, 'you will find that Jefferson spells the name of Franklin not with an "i" but with a "y". This would only be of academic interest had Professor Rosenberg not stated unequivocally that this was the first time Jefferson wrote to Franklin, and the *only* occasion on which he misspelt Franklin's name; indeed, if you turn the page, you will discover that Benjamin Franklin later chastised his friend for the error, which I would suggest was why a man of his intelligence would never have made the same mistake again. And perhaps more damning,' said Booth Watson, 'if you read the other five letters that came up for auction yesterday, Jefferson spells the name Franklin with an "i" not a "y", rather proving that he had learnt his lesson.'

Shaw and Buchanan took their time checking both letters, but didn't offer an opinion.

'And, what's more,' continued Booth Watson, sounding even more confident, 'I couldn't help noticing that the distinguished professor is not present today.'

'No,' said Shaw. 'The professor returned to Princeton last night, unaware that you would be demanding to see us this morning.'

'So I'm bound to ask,' Booth Watson went on, 'from whom you obtained the letter.'

'From a member of the Hartley family is all I'm at liberty to say,' said Shaw.

343

'But that's not possible,' Miles blurted out.

'That's an interesting admission,' said Buchanan, 'which would rather lead one to believe—'

'I don't have to remind you,' said Booth Watson, gripping his client's arm, 'this is a "without prejudice" meeting, and nothing said in this room can be repeated in a court of law.'

'But if it were to end up in a court of law,' said Shaw, 'let me assure you Professor Rosenberg will confirm this letter is genuine.'

'Then it will be his word against mine,' said Faulkner.

'Let's hope so,' said Shaw.

Buchanan allowed himself a smile before he said, 'We accept without question that Mr Faulkner purchased a Fair Copy of the Declaration in good faith, and with that in mind, we are willing to reimburse your client the five hundred thousand he paid for the document, as well as any reasonable expenses he may have incurred in the process.'

'Dream on,' said Miles, unable to remain silent any longer. 'We will be demanding at least forty million, not to mention unreasonable expenses.'

'Then we will look forward to seeing you in court, Mr Faulkner,' replied Shaw.

'And not just me!' said Miles.

Booth Watson quickly rose from his place, grabbed his client and escorted him out of the room, before he could say anything else he would later regret.

Once the door had closed, James Buchanan turned to Shaw and said, 'We have a problem.'

• • •

Miles fastened his seat belt, but didn't answer Booth Watson's question until the plane had taken off, unwilling to voice an opinion while they were still on American soil.

'Did you notice, BW, that when I said "and not just me", Special Agent James Buchanan didn't look surprised,' said Miles.

'Yes, I did,' said Booth Watson, 'so you can be sure he'll be on the phone to his friend Chief Superintendent Warwick long before our plane has landed.'

'Which will give Warwick more than enough time to get in touch with Simon Hartley before we can.'

'I think you'll find Hartley is like Washington,' said Booth Watson. 'He cannot tell a lie, and will therefore admit it's a fake.'

'Then it's game, set and match,' said Miles.

'Until Hartley asks you what you've done with the original, because it can only be a matter of time before he works out that you must have destroyed it.'

Miles remained silent for some time before he said, 'Then we may have to cut him in on the deal.'

'Has it ever crossed your mind, Miles,' said Booth Watson, 'that Simon Hartley might be someone who can't be bribed?'

'Every man has his price,' said Faulkner.

• • •

Ross picked up the phone and wondered who could possibly be calling him in the middle of the night.

'We have a problem,' said a transatlantic voice Ross recognized immediately.

'Faulkner and Booth Watson are on their way back from the States,' continued Buchanan, 'and they have irrefutable proof that will leave Hartley with no choice but to confirm Jefferson's letter is a fake.'

'Proof?' asked Ross.

'Your man read page 171 of *Monticello*, but not page 172. Where he would have found out the difference between a "y" and an "i", a mistake Jefferson didn't make twice.'

'Mumford is a moron,' said Ross.

'Agreed, but it doesn't help. So you'll have to get to Hartley before Faulkner does, and try to convince him of the consequences. Because if he doesn't . . .'

'You call Trevelyan,' said Ross. 'And I'll call William.'

CHAPTER 31

MILES WOKE WHEN CONCORDE DRIFTED through a block of dense black clouds that seemed to have taken permanent residence above Heathrow. He leant across the aisle and said to his lawyer, 'We don't have a moment to waste, BW. As soon as we land, I'll ask Collins to drive us to Bucklebury in the hope we can get to Hartley before Warwick does.'

'I wouldn't bet on it,' said Booth Watson, but didn't add that he wished Miles had kept his mouth shut.

'Hartley won't be able to deny the letter is a fake,' said Miles, 'and once he does the FBI will have no choice but to settle.' He paused, looked across at his lawyer and said, 'For at least forty million.'

'Amen to that,' said Booth Watson, 'although it's possible Hartley may not fall in with your plans quite so conveniently.'

'Until I remind him that his mother sold me a fake Constable for half a million, because he won't want that to become public.'

'When he'll undoubtedly remind you that his mother gave

347

you six letters and not five,' said Booth Watson, which silenced Miles for a moment.

Booth Watson looked out of the cabin window when Miles asked him the one question he'd been dreading. 'Who do you think forged the Jefferson letter in the first place?'

'The FBI's dirty tricks department,' said Booth Watson, delivering a well-prepared response, now painfully aware why Billy Mumford had woken him in the middle of the night. 'With the whole exercise orchestrated by Special Agent Buchanan,' he added for good measure.

'I suppose that's right,' said Miles, as the wheels of the aircraft touched the ground and the plane's engines were thrust violently into reverse, before Concorde proceeded slowly towards its specially allocated gate on the far side of the airport.

Miles had unfastened his seat belt long before the warning sign had been switched off. He liked to be the last person to board a plane, and the first to disembark. He had left his seat and was already standing at the front of the line when the cabin door was pulled open.

'Not a moment to waste,' said Faulkner, before he'd even stepped onto the aircraft steps. Booth Watson tried to keep up with his client as he headed for customs at a speed he wasn't accustomed to. By the time Booth Watson reached the car, out of breath, Miles was sitting in the back impatiently waiting for him.

'Let's get moving,' Faulkner barked at Collins, even before his lawyer had closed the door.

'Home, sir?' asked Collins.

'No,' said Faulkner. 'Old Vicarage, Bucklebury.'

• • •

William and Trevelyan were speeding along the motorway just as Concorde touched down at Heathrow. They had spent the last couple of hours going over their script word for word, aware they might be facing one insurmountable problem, which Trevelyan had expressed with Foreign Office clarity. 'If Hartley is as honest as his father . . .'

When Danny drew up outside the Old Vicarage, it only took one knock on the front door before Mrs Hartley appeared. Once they had introduced themselves, Hannah led her two guests through to the library where Simon was seated at his desk. The recent removal of his beard made him appear pale and wan, though Trevelyan was pleased to see he'd put on a few pounds since he'd last seen him at the airport. Simon pushed himself up from his chair unsteadily, and welcomed them both before inviting them to join him around the fire.

Moments later, Mrs Hartley reappeared carrying a tray of coffee and biscuits, which she placed on the table between them.

'Thank you for agreeing to see us at such short notice,' said William as he sat down. 'We wouldn't have given you so little warning if it hadn't been urgent.'

Hartley's sharp eyes remained fixed on William, but he didn't express an opinion.

'Let me begin by asking you,' continued William, 'if you have come across someone called Miles Faulkner, or a lawyer by the name of Booth Watson.'

'Only what my dear mother has told me about them and what I've read in *The Guardian*. Their arts correspondent reported in detail what took place at the auction in New York a couple of days ago, which rather suggested neither of them could be trusted. Of course, I was delighted to discover the letter sent to my ancestor in 1787 was authenticated by no less a figure than Professor Rosenberg. I assume that means the Fair Copy of the Declaration will end up in the Library of Congress, as my late father always intended.'

William and Trevelyan exchanged glances.

'While Professor Rosenberg's opinion is greatly respected,' said William, 'there is only one person who can verify that the letter is authentic, and that, sir, is you.'

'And if you were able to,' added Trevelyan, 'the Fair Copy of the Declaration will undoubtedly end up in the Library of Congress as your father intended.'

'Then I'll need to see the letter,' said Hartley.

Trevelyan opened his briefcase and removed a single sheet of paper. He handed it across to Hartley before he said, 'This is, of course, a copy of the letter, which Special Agent Buchanan sent to the Foreign Office overnight. The original remains in New York in the safekeeping of the FBI.'

Simon took his time reading the letter while William and Trevelyan waited anxiously for his opinion. After a second reading, Simon handed the letter back to Trevelyan and said, 'I'm sorry to disappoint you, gentlemen, but this is not the letter Thomas Jefferson sent to David Hartley in 1787. In fact, it's a forgery – a damned good forgery, but nevertheless a forgery.'

'How can you be so certain?' asked William, fairly sure he knew what Hartley's response would be.

'In the letter I know and remember well, Franklin was spelled correctly with an "i" and not a "y",' said their host, with a finality that didn't brook discussion.

'So if you were subpoenaed to appear in court . . .' began William.

'I would be left with no choice but to tell the truth, Chief Superintendent.'

'And if we were to tell you, Mr Hartley,' said William, 'that it was Mr Faulkner who destroyed the original letter, with the sole purpose of making a fortune, without giving a damn about the reputation of your family, would that make any difference?'

Hartley's demeanour did not change. 'No, it would not,' he said firmly, 'despicable though that is.'

'Or that it was Faulkner who arranged to have Avril Dubois murdered, and then bribed the prison governor to make sure you suffered the same fate?'

'Something I already knew,' said Simon. 'However it doesn't alter anything, not least because I took advantage of the Governor's greed, and deducted one hundred and fifty thousand dollars for a better cause.'

'Do you not feel, Mr Hartley, that you could tell a white lie given the circumstances?' suggested Mr Trevelyan.

'There's no such thing as a white lie, Mr Trevelyan.'

William knew when he was beaten, even though Trevelyan battled on for a little longer, pointing out that Professor Rosenberg had managed to ignore the 'y'.

'While I sympathize with your cause, Mr Trevelyan, I must remind you that the truth doesn't come in different shades of convenience to suit the individual, or even the country, concerned.'

Eventually Trevelyan gave up, but not until his coffee had gone cold. He left, reflecting that the Foreign Office would have to advise Mr Shaw and Special Agent Buchanan to settle with Faulkner, as they could not hope to win should Hartley be called as a witness.

William also accepted that the CPS didn't have enough evidence to arrest Faulkner as an accessory in the murder of Avril Dubois, so there would be nothing to stop him appearing as a witness when the case came to court. They left the Old Vicarage empty-handed.

They had only covered a couple of miles on their way back to London when Danny interrupted their conversation, 'Straight ahead of you, sir.'

William looked up to see a Rolls-Royce heading towards them and, as they passed, he observed Faulkner and Booth Watson sitting in the back, deep in conversation.

• • •

The Rolls-Royce drew up outside the Old Vicarage a few minutes later.

Simon was checking the Stock Exchange prices in the *Financial Times* when he heard the front doorbell ring. He wondered if the Chief Superintendent and Mr Trevelyan had returned to make a further attempt to convince him he should change his mind.

His thoughts were interrupted when the door opened and Hannah reappeared. 'A Mr Faulkner and a Mr Booth Watson are asking to see you. Something to do with the family Constable.'

'Please show them in, my darling,' said Simon, 'and I'll need my cheque book.'

Simon pushed himself up as the two men entered the room. Once they had introduced themselves, he offered them both a seat, but not by the fire. Moments later, Hannah reappeared carrying a second tray of coffee and biscuits. She was trying to recall where she'd seen the older of the two men. She poured them both a cup of coffee before departing, and then she remembered.

'You will be aware, Mr Hartley,' said Booth Watson, 'that

your mother sold my client a painting, which she claimed was a Constable, for five hundred thousand pounds, but turned out to have been painted by one of his pupils.' Booth Watson chose his next words carefully. 'Of course, as you were abroad at the time, it's possible you were not aware of this.'

'My mother informed me as soon as I returned,' said Simon, picking up the cheque book Hannah had left on the tray, 'and I'm only too happy to repay the full amount,' he added, making out a cheque for £500,000. 'But, in return, I will expect you to return not only the painting, but also Jefferson's Fair Copy of the Declaration, which my father had intended to hand over to the American Ambassador. He sadly passed away before the meeting could take place, as I suspect you are both well aware.'

Faulkner smiled at Simon. 'Don't let's be too hasty, old chap,' he said. 'After all, we're both men of the world, and the last thing I'd want to do is embarrass your mother.'

'I can assure you, Mr Faulkner, it would take a lot more than that to embarrass my mother.'

'Nevertheless,' said Booth Watson, 'there is another matter we need to discuss.'

'And what might that be, Mr Booth Watson?'

Booth Watson bent down, unfastened his Gladstone bag and extracted a single sheet of paper, which he handed across to Simon.

'You will be aware that this letter, like the Constable, is a forgery,' said Booth Watson, 'but we need you to confirm that is the case.'

Faulkner offered him the same insincere smile, as he tore the proffered cheque in half.

Simon studied the forgery for a second time that morning,

but his thoughts were elsewhere. First with Avril Dubois, who would still be alive if it were not for this man, then with Hani Khalil and Prince Ahmed, whose only interest was another five per cent, and finally to a prison Governor who thought he'd poisoned him and got away with it. He glanced at the photo of his father on his desk and decided he would have agreed, on this rare occasion, that like Rosenberg had suggested it was acceptable to lie for your country.

He looked up at the two men seated in front of him. 'I know you'll both be pleased to hear,' said Simon, handing back the letter, 'that I can confirm this is indeed a copy of the letter that Thomas Jefferson wrote to David Hartley MP in 1787, which has been in the family archives for over two hundred years.'

'But if you look more carefully, Mr Hartley,' said Booth Watson, removing his glasses, 'you will see that Franklin's name is spelled with a "y" and not an "i", so perhaps you'd like to reconsider.'

'No, I wouldn't, thank you,' said Simon, 'because if it isn't the letter my mother gave to Mr Faulkner, he must still be in possession of the original, unless, of course, he's destroyed it?'

Neither man responded.

'And as you are a QC, Mr Booth Watson, I don't have to remind you, that it is your legal duty to disclose to the court should you become aware that your client was responsible for destroying material that is relevant to a case in which you are acting on his behalf.'

Booth Watson didn't need to be reminded that Hartley had studied law at university.

'Name your price,' said Faulkner, before Booth Watson could respond.

'Can one put a price on a young woman's life?' asked Simon.

'She was a common prostitute,' said Faulkner, 'and what's more, you know the letter is a fake.'

'Only three people can be sure of that,' said Simon, 'and all three of them are in this room. And I feel sure if you had any other way of proving this was a forgery, you wouldn't be here.' He paused for a moment before he rose from his place, picked up the two pieces of the cheque and said, 'I do hope you enjoy the Constable, Mr Faulkner, even though, like you, it's a fake.'

Booth Watson rose from his place and turned to leave without shaking hands with Hartley. He didn't need to be told that the jury had delivered their verdict. Faulkner remained in his seat, his insincere smile turning into a vicious glare as he uttered several obscenities that Simon wouldn't be repeating to his mother. Although he clenched his fist, he finally stood up and left the room.

When the door closed, Simon sat back down at his desk and once again looked at the photo of his father, who was smiling.

CHAPTER 32

'THEY DECIDED *WHAT*?' SAID ROSS, unable to believe what William had just said.

'The Crown Prosecution Service consider we have come up with more than enough evidence to convince a jury that Kevin Scott murdered Avril Dubois and we can, therefore, charge him.'

'However,' continued William before Ross could interrupt, 'they have also decided that the twenty-pound notes and the Rolex Daytona watch Scott was wearing when he was arrested, are insufficient proof that Faulkner was involved in the murder. *No smoking gun*, if I recall the director's exact words.'

'But the twenty-pound notes came from the same batch as Faulkner withdrew from his bank, and handed over to Scott when they were both on the London Eye.'

'The CPS went on to point out that we don't have any proof they were both on the Eye at the same time.'

'Booth Watson will be only too happy to remind any jury,' suggested the Hawk, 'there are millions of banknotes that change hands every day.'

'But on the back of the Rolex, in case you've forgotten,' came back Ross, 'are the words *Love Christina.*'

'Booth Watson will then point out,' said William, 'that there are a lot of Christinas in the world, and you can be sure that defence counsel will come up with a witness who will claim the watch was hers.'

'If only Christina would be willing . . .' began Ross.

'I agree,' said William, 'but Wilbur is convinced that if his wife's name appeared on the prosecution's witness list, you'd be condemning her to the same fate as Avril Dubois. And if Faulkner thought Christina's evidence would guarantee him ending up in prison for the rest of his life,' added the Hawk, 'Wilbur could have a point.'

The team sat there in despondent silence until Ross declared, 'I can think of a way of proving the watch belonged to Faulkner.'

'Legal and above board?' queried William, sounding sceptical.

'Not entirely,' admitted Ross, 'but it wouldn't leave a jury in any doubt who the watch belonged to.'

• • •

Miles picked up the phone on his desk and listened.

'Mr Faulkner?' said a voice.

'Who's asking?'

'Jake Burrows, sir. We were at the Scrubs together and . . .'

Miles was about to slam down the phone when Burrows added, 'I think I've got something that belongs to you.'

'Like what?' said Miles.

'A Rolex Daytona.'

'What makes you think it's mine?'

'It's got *Love Christina* inscribed on the back, and I

remember you wearing it when you worked in the library –
offered you ten thousand for it and you laughed at me.'

'How did you get hold of it?' asked Miles.

'A customer brought the piece into my shop a few days
ago, wanting to sell it. But you aren't the easiest person to
track down.'

'Describe him,' said Miles.

'Tall, thin, athletic build, wore dark glasses and a baseball
cap – but then a lot of my customers do, Mr Faulkner, if you
catch my drift.'

'How much did he want for it?' asked Faulkner, still probing.

'Ten thousand, but I didn't have that much in cash at the
time, so he settled for eight.'

'I'll give you six,' said Miles.

'But I paid eight for it, Mr Faulkner.'

'Stolen goods,' said Miles. 'One phone call and you'll be
back in the Scrubs.'

A long silence followed before Burrows said, 'You win, Mr
Faulkner. When can I expect you to pick it up?'

Miles hung up.

Burrows put the phone down and turned to face the man
standing by his side. 'Couldn't have gone better,' said Ross.
'Just remember to call me the moment Faulkner turns up.'

'Will do, Mr Hogan.'

'And I'll be taking any cash Faulkner gives you, as evidence.'

'Then what's in it for me, Mr Hogan?'

'I'm sure there'll come a time in the not-too-distant future,
Jake, when you'll be up in front of the beak and needing a
helping hand.'

Burrows couldn't disagree.

• • •

Burrows was just about to turn the sign on the front door from open to closed when a black cab pulled up outside the Roxy Cinema in the Commercial Road. The fare got out, his eyes darting in every direction, and although he couldn't spot anything suspicious, he didn't relax. He began to walk the last hundred yards, only stopping to look in a side window to check he wasn't being followed. He wasn't. He turned the corner and couldn't miss the three balls that hung above a sign declaring *Jake Burrows, Pawnbroker. Established 1983.*

He glanced inside the shop window to see an old lag he recognized seated behind the counter. He once again checked up and down the street. Still nothing. As he entered the shop, a bell rang above the door.

'Mr Faulkner,' said the pawnbroker, looking up. 'What a pleasant surprise.'

'Cut the crap,' said Miles. 'Where's my watch?'

'Locked up in my safe out the back,' said Burrows. 'Give me a moment and I'll go and fetch it.'

Burrows got up from the counter and disappeared behind a curtain. Miles looked out of the window to make sure another customer wasn't about to join him. If they had, he would have left without another word – not a risk worth taking.

He turned back. Still no sign of Burrows. Miles began to wonder what was taking him so long and was about to leave when he reappeared. He placed the timepiece on the counter.

'Quite magnificent,' said Burrows. Miles picked the watch up and checked the inscription on the back, before he strapped it onto his wrist. He took four pristine wrappers full of twenty-pound notes out of an inside pocket and placed them on the counter.

'But we agreed on six thousand not four, Mr Faulkner,' the pawnbroker reminded him.

'Like you,' said Faulkner, 'it was all the cash I could lay my hands on.'

Burrows stared at the money and then at Mr Faulkner before he picked the wrappers up and placed them under the counter.

Miles left the shop without bothering to say goodbye. He stepped out onto the pavement and closed the door behind him. He was hailing a cab when a voice behind him said, 'You're nicked, Faulkner, and this time you won't be able to claim the watch wasn't yours.'

Fair cop were not the words Faulkner expressed when Chief Inspector Hogan handcuffed him and led him away.

CHAPTER 33

'I WILL,' SAID ROSS.

The vicar turned to the bride and said, 'Will you, Alice, take Ross to be your husband. Will you love him, comfort him, honour and protect him and, forsaking all others, be faithful to him as long as you both shall live?'

'I will,' said Alice.

William stepped forward and handed the wedding ring to the vicar.

Alice smiled when Ross slipped the ring on her finger and repeated the wedding vows. Only the chief bridesmaid had a bigger grin on her face.

As the newly married couple walked back down the aisle together, they were greeted with smiles from both sides. Jojo, holding the train, followed them out into the churchyard, where a photographer was waiting.

He gathered the family together, along with the best man and the bridesmaids, before he took a series of snaps, while the rest of the guests made their way across to the Shamrock Hotel for the wedding lunch.

When the bride and groom appeared, everyone rose from their places and applauded Mr and Mrs Hogan as they made their way to the top table. Once the applause had died down, the guests remained standing while the vicar said Grace.

Only William ignored the smoked salmon as he turned the pages of his best man's speech once again – unnecessarily, as he knew the words off by heart. He looked up as his untouched plate of smoked salmon was whisked away, to see his father and the Hawk seated at the other end of the table, deep in conversation.

'So now the date of the trial has been fixed, Julian, should I assume you are confident of a guilty verdict and sending Faulkner back to jail?'

'Certainly not, Jack – one can never be certain of anything when Booth Watson is appearing for the defence.'

'I think even Booth Watson will find it difficult to convince a jury that the Rolex with Faulkner's ex-wife's signature etched on the back didn't belong to him, or that four cellophane packets each containing a thousand pounds didn't come from the same bank account as the ones found on Kevin Scott on the day Avril was murdered.'

'Booth Watson will remind the jury that Faulkner was in America at the time,' said Julian, 'and I confess it would have helped if Christina had been willing to give evidence confirming it was the Rolex Daytona she gave her ex-husband as a birthday present.'

'I think you'll find that it was Wilbur who talked her out of giving evidence,' said the Hawk, 'and who can blame him after what happened to Avril.'

'I'm only surprised Faulkner was granted bail,' said Sir Julian.

'Booth Watson, as we all know, can be very persuasive,' said the Hawk, as a waiter refilled his glass.

'However, Julian, on a more pleasant note, I can now tell you that next month William will be taking my place as the unit's new Commander.'

'Does that mean you'll be retiring?'

'No, I'm being kicked upstairs.'

'How far upstairs?' asked Julian.

'Assistant Commissioner in charge of public order and operational support,' announced the Hawk.

'Congratulations,' said Julian, 'but what does that actually mean?'

'I get all the toys: horses, dogs and helicopters, which will allow me to take charge of everything,' said the Hawk, 'from the Cup Final at Wembley to the Queen Mother's hundredth birthday celebrations.'

'William has a great deal to thank you for,' said Julian as he raised his glass.

'That's not a one-way street,' said the Hawk, also raising his glass as he looked across at his protégé, who was making a small emendation to his speech while his Irish stew went cold.

When William looked up from his speech, the babble of conversation in the room revealed how much everyone was enjoying themselves. He smiled at his wife, who was chatting to Wilbur.

'How's Christina working out as chair?' asked Wilbur. 'And don't flannel me.'

'Like a duck to water,' said Beth.

'Yet another English expression I've not come across before,' said Wilbur. 'Is my wife the duck or the water?'

'Christina is always so full of bright ideas that she wants done yesterday,' said Beth. 'My biggest problem is trying to keep up with her.'

'You're an ideal combination,' said Wilbur, 'madness and common sense.'

'On the madness front, has she mentioned the opportunity we have to purchase a Frans Hals for a million?'

'Regularly,' said Wilbur with a sigh.

'But if the Fitz *were* able to raise the full amount,' said Beth, 'the Earl of Banbury has agreed to part with the painting in lieu of death duties.'

'How appropriate,' said Wilbur, looking across at his wife. 'So how much is it going to cost me this time?'

'A quarter of a million would get the ball rolling,' said Beth.

'I only wish you'd spoken to me earlier,' said Wilbur, 'as I've already agreed to part with half a million. You know, Beth, I should have made a prenup with the Fitzmolean before I married Christina.'

'We are all most grateful,' said Beth, giving him a hug.

'And so am I,' admitted Wilbur, as he glanced across at his wife. 'Who would have thought Ohio Disposal would have helped build one of the great Dutch collections?' he said, as he smiled at William.

'Feeling nervous?' asked James, as William pushed the speech to one side.

'I'd rather address the Police Federation's annual conference than my father, Beth and the twins,' admitted William.

'I've just spotted my goddaughter,' said James, looking across the room, 'and, of course, Peter, but who's the young man holding Artemisia's hand under the table?'

'Robert Hartley.'

'Not . . .' began James.

'Yes, he's the son of Simon Hartley,' said William, 'and don't ask me how the two of them met, because I'm not supposed to know.'

'But you're going to tell me anyway,' said James, as he put down his knife and fork.

'In a prison cell,' admitted William. 'Both of them were arrested while taking part in a Saudi protest rally outside Number Ten. Young Hartley even threw an egg at me.'

'Did you have them clapped in irons?' asked James.

'They both would have been if Ross hadn't come to their rescue.'

'Join the club.'

William raised an eyebrow, but got no response. 'What's the latest on the Declaration?' he ventured.

'It's already hanging in the Library of Congress,' said James, 'and will be unveiled by President Clinton next month.'

'Without Faulkner or Booth Watson putting up a protest?' said William.

'We haven't heard a word out of either of them since Simon Hartley confirmed the Jefferson letter was the one that had been in their family archives for over two hundred years.'

'But Faulkner keeps telling anyone who will listen that the letter is a forgery,' said William.

'I know,' said James. 'And can you believe that Booth Watson is accusing the FBI's dirty tricks department of being responsible for the deception, even though I told him we could never be involved in such an outrageous activity?'

'It wouldn't be the first time,' suggested William.

'Nor the last. But not on this occasion,' said James, glancing across at Ross while wondering just how much William knew.

William looked back down to find his speech had disappeared. He wasn't in any doubt who the guilty party was. Someone who just happened to be chatting to Christina when his back was turned.

'So where are you two going on your honeymoon?' Christina asked.

'We're catching a plane to Dublin this evening,' said Ross, 'and will be staying at the Shelbourne Hotel where I once worked as a student.'

'You never cease to surprise me,' said Christina.

'Yes, I had a holiday job there as a bellboy. But I was sacked after only a couple of weeks.'

Christina smiled. 'Let me guess, one of the guests . . .'

'No,' said Ross. 'I was caught in a guest bedroom with a maid, and she wasn't making the bed.'

'And after Dublin,' said Christina, laughing, 'where else will you visit?'

'Limerick, Cork, ending up in Blarney.'

'Where I hear they'll be renaming the stone after you,' said Christina.

'Then we'll be flying back to London,' said Ross, ignoring the barb, 'by which time Faulkner should be safely locked up in the Scrubs with no chance of remission.'

'And when you're back,' asked Christina, 'are you also hoping to be promoted?'

'I'll be returning to the Yard as a Chief Inspector under my new Commander,' said Ross, looking across at his best man. 'William wants me to go undercover in the East End and find out who's taken over from the Richardsons.'

'That should keep you well occupied,' said Christina.

'And if that wasn't enough,' said Ross, lowering his voice, 'Alice is pregnant.'

'Congratulations,' said Christina, a little too loudly.

Ross's mother broke off from her conversation with Alice and asked, 'What are you congratulating Ross on?'

Christina was rescued by the tap of a spoon on a glass and

the words of the toastmaster, 'Ladies and gentlemen, pray silence for the best man.'

William rose nervously from his place, relieved to find Ross had returned his speech, even if the pages were no longer in the correct order.

'My lords, ladies and gentlemen,' began William, who paused, looked up and said, 'there are no lords and certainly no gentlemen present today, but several ladies and one in particular I wish to address. So let me start by telling you, Alice,' he said, turning to face the bride, 'that I don't know anyone more likely than your husband to drop a colleague in a hole – or anyone who would then do everything in his power to dig them back out and take the blame himself.'

The laughter that followed rather suggested there were several officers in the room who'd suffered from the same experience, while Ross looked rather pleased with himself.

'Ross has made so many appalling decisions over the years,' continued William, 'it came as a complete surprise that he was capable of making such a sensible one when it came to how to spend the rest of his life. However, I still can't understand how such a bright, beautiful woman could possibly have fallen for him – and then I remembered that Alice is a headmistress, and having to deal with errant children is simply part of the day job. Now she's on overtime. Truth is Alice,' said William looking directly at the bride, 'Ross has won life's lottery, while you have ended up with a losing ticket.'

The loud laughter and applause that followed allowed William to turn the page.

'Allow me to end,' said William, before realizing he had turned to the wrong page, but quickly replaced it, 'by saying how proud and honoured I was to be invited to be Ross's best man. I wasn't his first choice. In fact, six others turned the job down before he asked me. Unfortunately, the first three are on the "most wanted" list, the next two are on remand awaiting bail, and the sixth has yet to complete his sentence for daylight robbery. So, you ended up with a man' – William turned to face his closest friend – 'who admires you for your courage, integrity and possession of a moral compass that continues to guide us lesser mortals. The truth is, Ross, you're one in a million. And frankly, one is quite enough.'

William had to wait for the laughter to die down before he could continue.

'Allow me to try and end for a second time,' said William, but was stopped in mid-sentence when he looked up and saw three uniformed police officers entering the hall.

William immediately recognized the senior officer, who was heading towards the top table, but was taken by surprise when he spotted Miles Faulkner standing in the doorway, a huge grin plastered on his face. The senior officer only stopped when he reached Ross's side.

'My name is Derek Sinclair,' he said, 'and I am head of the anti-corruption unit.' Ross stared at a man he'd crossed swords with several times in the past. 'Inspector Hogan, I'm arresting you for attempting to pervert the course of justice by planting evidence on a defendant in the hope that it would influence the outcome of a murder trial in which you were the arresting officer.'

Beth immediately jumped up, put her arms around Alice and tried to comfort her, while Jojo wondered if this was something that always happened at weddings during the best man's speech.

'Don't say a word,' said an authoritative voice coming from behind them.

'Who are you, sir?' asked Sinclair, looking at an elderly gentleman who had appeared out of nowhere.

'Sir Julian Warwick QC and I will be representing the defendant.'

'That's your choice, of course,' said Sinclair scornfully, as two officers took hold of the prisoner.

'Is that really necessary,' interjected William, 'when the groom is about to leave on his honeymoon?'

'*Was* about to leave on his honeymoon, Chief Superintendent,' said Sinclair, 'and in any case I can't risk Hogan leaving the country only days before the trial.'

'You're a shit, Sinclair,' said William, standing between them, 'and don't forget I outrank you.'

'No one outranks an anti-corruption officer, Chief Superintendent, as I feel sure I don't have to remind you,' said Sinclair as he pushed the prisoner forward.

The best man followed the bridegroom as he was escorted across the dance floor by Sinclair. When they reached the door, Faulkner was waiting for him.

The two men faced each other like heavyweight boxers waiting for the bell to ring.

'Sorry to have interrupted your speech, Chief Superintendent Warwick,' he said, 'or is it Commander? But I just had to give Ross a wedding present, after all he's done for me in the past.'

William didn't flinch.

'Sadly, your friend will not be spending his honeymoon in Dublin, as originally planned, but in a prison cell bereft of his bride,' continued Faulkner, landing the first blow.

'Then let's just hope for your sake you don't both end up in the same prison,' said William, parrying.

'I can't wait to hear what you have in mind, Chief Superintendent,' provoked Faulkner.

'Life imprisonment,' suggested William.

'For buying a Rolex watch from an ex-con who was set up by your friend?' said Faulkner. 'I don't think so.'

William clenched his fist, looked his nemesis in the eye, but at the last moment somehow managed to restrain himself.

'In fact,' said Faulkner, the smug smile remaining in place, 'Mr Booth Watson assures me if your friend is the main prosecution witness, the case will never come to court, because as a convicted criminal he won't be able to lay a finger on me. So glad to hear your wife is pregnant,' he added, looking at Ross as he passed. 'If it's a girl you can call her Avril.'

Ross hurled his captors aside, leapt forward, raised a fist and with a single blow knocked Faulkner out.

'That's hardly going to help your cause,' suggested Sinclair, as his two officers grabbed Ross and handcuffed him.

'You may well be right, Superintendent,' said Ross, as he stared down at the prostrate body, 'but I can assure you it was worth it.'

HISTORICAL NOTE:
THE MISSING CLAUSES

Thomas Jefferson submitted two extra clauses to Congress to be part of the Declaration of Independence. Ultimately these were rejected by Congress. Historians have suggested that if the first clause concerning the abolition of slavery had been included, it might have prevented the American Civil War.

1st Clause: 'He has waged cruel war against human nature itself, violating it's most sacred rights of life & liberty in the persons of a distant people, who never offended him, captivating & carrying them into slavery in another hemisphere, or to incur miserable death in their transportation thither. This piratical warfare, the opprobrium of INFIDEL powers, is the warfare of the CHRISTIAN king of Great Britain. Determined to keep open a market where MEN should be bought & sold, he has prostituted his negative

371

for suppressing every legislative attempt to prohibit or to restrain this execrable commerce. And that this assemblage of horrors might want no fact of distinguished die, he is now exciting those very people to rise in arms among us, and to purchase that liberty of which he has deprived them by murdering the people upon whom he also obtruded them; thus paying off former crimes committed against the LIBERTIES of one people, with crimes which he urges them to commit against the LIVES of another.'

2nd Clause: 'A prince whose character is thus marked by every act which may define a tyrant, is unfit to be the ruler of a people who mean to be free. Future ages will scarcely believe that the hardiness of one man adventured, within the short compass of twelve years only, to build a foundation, so broad & undisguised for tyranny over a people fostered & fixed in principles of freedom.'

ACKNOWLEDGEMENTS

My thanks for their invaluable advice and research to:
Simon Bainbridge, Carol Burling, Jonathan Caplan KC,
Kate Elton, Billy Mumford, Mark Poltimore,
Alison Prince and Johnny Van Haeften.

Chief Superintendent John Sutherland (Ret.)
Detective Sergeant Michelle Raycroft (Ret.)

Special thanks to:
Willie Hartley Russell MVO DL

Dear Mr. Hartley

Hotel de Langeac Paris Aug 11. 1787

I hope you will grant me your permission to impose upon your time by allowing me to send you my Fair Copy of the Declaration of Independance which I earlier delivered to Congress for their consideration you will see that it includes the two clauses you and I discussed in London namely the abolition of slavery and our future relationship with king George III once we become an independent nation copies were made by my friend and colleague Benjamin Franklyn and distributed amongst interested parties much to my dismay when members of Congress divided both clauses were rejected however I would not want you to think I had not taken to heart your wise and sound counsel and tried to convince my fellow Congress men of the merit of your judgement once you have had a chance to peruse the Fair Copy at your leisure perhaps you would be kind enough in the fullness of time to return it to me I thought you would want to know that it is my intention to bequeath this memento to the nation in order that future generations of Americans might fully appreciate what the founding fathers were trying to achieve and not least the role you played I look forward to hearing from you at some time in the future and be assured of my sincere esteem & respect

I remain your most obedient and humble servant

Th Jefferson

An example, prepared by Billy Mumford, of what Benjamin Franklin's letter to David Hartley would have looked like.

The Rt. Hon. David Hartley the Younger.
Painted by George Romney, engraved by James Walker.

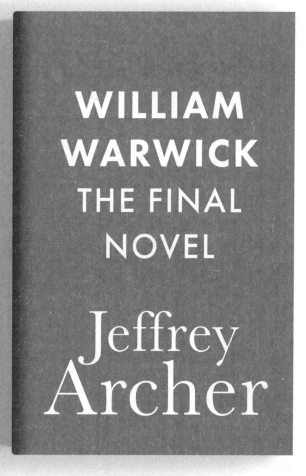